A STAR IS BORED ☆

A
STAR IS
BORED

☆　☆　☆　☆　☆　☆　☆

Byron
Lane

Henry Holt and Company
New York

Henry Holt and Company
Publishers since 1866
120 Broadway
New York, New York 10271
www.henryholt.com

Henry Holt® and 🏛® are registered trademarks of Macmillan
Publishing Group, LLC.

Library of Congress Cataloging-in-Publication Data

Names: Lane, Byron, 1978– author.
Title: A star is bored / Byron Lane.
Description: First edition. | New York : Henry Holt and Company, 2020.
Identifiers: LCCN 2019057802 (print) | LCCN 2019057803 (ebook) |
    ISBN 9781250266491 (hardcover) | ISBN 9781250266484 (ebook)
Classification: LCC PS3612.A54955 S73 2020 (print) |
    LCC PS3612.A54955 (ebook) | DDC 813/.6—dc23
LC record available at https://lccn.loc.gov/2019057802
LC ebook record available at https://lccn.loc.gov/2019057803

Our books may be purchased in bulk for promotional, educational, or
business use. Please contact your local bookseller or the
Macmillan Corporate and Premium Sales Department at (800)
221-7945, extension 5442, or by e-mail at MacmillanSpecialMarkets@
macmillan.com.

First Edition 2020

Designed by Donna Sinisgalli Noetzel

Printed in the United States of America

10   9   8   7   6   5   4   3   2   1

For Martha

"This is a work of fiction. Events, characters, and high crimes are products of the author's imagination or used in a fictitious manner. Any resemblance to reality is purely coincidental, including names, places, weapons, and sexual acts."

—*My attorney*[1]

"What? Where am I?"

—*Kathi Kannon*

1. But seriously, I repeat: This is a work of fiction. That you might speculate as to the identity of certain key characters does not alter the fact that all of the characters in the book, including incidental ones, their names, the dialogue, the locales, and all of the events recounted, are fictional products of the author's imagination and are not intended to describe or to identify real-life persons or events, nor should any such identification be inferred. Cameo appearances by certain named celebrities are also entirely fictional and are not intended to suggest or describe any association with real celebrities or events.

—*My publisher's attorney*

Part One

☆ ☆ ☆ ☆ ☆ ☆ ☆

ICARUS

1

☆

'm parked and panicked outside the estate of Hollywood royalty Kathi
Kannon, star of stage and screen and *People* magazine's Worst Dressed
list. The only barrier between us is her massive front gate, made of
wood and steel, elements at once both warm and hard, welcoming and
severe. The vertical beams of the gate are covered in art: an orange street
sign that says DUMP, a painting of Santa Claus smoking a cigarette, a banner announcing CLOTHING OPTIONAL BEYOND THIS POINT.

My car, like my life, is idling out here, a couple minutes early for this
job interview, the chance to be personal assistant to Kathi Kannon. My
windshield frames the scene in front of me: her gate, bordered by the
clear, cool landscape of Beverly Hills—blue sky above, bright greens
and hot pinks of sprawling bougainvillea on the left, aged branches of a
huge avocado tree on the right, and, along the bottom, the gold hood of
my used and tattered 2002 Nissan Sentra. *Mostly* gold, that is; the paint
is peeling off in some parts, exposing raw, rusted, pocked steel beneath.

I'm trying to chill out, wringing my hands, biting the inside of
my mouth—the familiar and faint taste of my blood always marks
occasions like this. When I'm nervous, when I'm insecure, when I

desperately want something, sometimes there's pain. I want to be inside this gate.

I'm thinking, *I don't belong here.*

I'm sweating and grossly unsure what's ahead for me. Through the beams of her gate, I see specks of an entire universe laid out in a curious mix of earth tones and neon. I can make out things shimmering and shining in her yard. It looks like a carnival. It looks like an acid trip. It looks like heaven.

I feel like I'm going to puke, sickened by the unfamiliar optimism that this may be exactly what I'm looking for—the beginning of something special for me. Her gate, an actual gateway to a better life.

I'm here for the opportunity of my lifetime, and I'm exhausted from having been up all night—not from partying or from insomnia or anxiety but working a job I hate; I'm a writer for local television news in Los Angeles. I've had the job seven years on the aptly named graveyard shift. I start at midnight and write, write, write news stories that go into some ungrateful server and through some disinterested wires and onto the emotionless teleprompter where the overpaid, contractually malnourished anchor reads the words I wrote with a smile on her face: *Your toothpaste causes cancer, a dozen orphans are dead in a fire, today is gonna be sunny!* We go off the air at seven A.M., and that's when I leave work every morning, depressed and bleary-eyed. I drive home to eat bland, stale cereal, then go to sleep as the rest of the world starts waking, living. Friends are impossible to service with this schedule. There's no line of lovers interested in me, a night crawler. My life feels like rot.

I'm desperate to change it all, and this meeting with Kathi Kannon is my foolhardy tug on a soggy wishbone. I've considered other career changes before, but none panned out, none made sense at the time, and none have been this exciting. Kathi Kannon, heroine of film, television, maybe my life: *Save me from my boring, worse than basic existence; I beg you, be my hope.*

I've loved Kathi since childhood, watching her as Priestess Talara, the leader of a future earth under attack by invaders in the epic film *Nova Quest*. Of course, I didn't know her real name back then, but I knew I loved her. I had almost every action figure in her franchise. *Almost*. I had the bad guy. I had multiple versions of the good guys. I had every robot, spaceship, castle. But I didn't have her, not for long, anyway. My sweet mother gave me the Priestess Talara action figure as an Easter gift—her royal silhouette replacing the boring chocolate bunny—but my dad wasted no time removing the priestess from my life. He thought female action figures were the reason I ran "like a girl," as he put it. One rainy day, after a game of soccer—a sport he forced me to play—where I was the only kid running around the mud puddles instead of through them, he yanked the priestess from my hands. I cried out, bawling, "No, don't take her from me!" I never saw her action figure again.

And now I'm outside her house. And not just hers but her family's. Kathi Kannon isn't famous only for film; she's famous for DNA. Her mother is *the* Gracie Gold, America's darling redhead sweetheart from countless Broadway hits and Hollywood films and TV shows and tabloid-magazine covers dating back to the fifties. Kathi's late father was also well known, a music executive courted and cajoled across Hollywood and New York before his recent death. I'll be entering not just Kathi's world but also that of Gracie; they live in separate houses in this same compound, the one that's now right in front of me, on the other side of this troublesome barrier.

Kathi's gate intercom call box is stretching toward me like an aggressive handshake, with its little silver button and the words engraved beside it: PRESS TO CALL. I'm about to push a button no doubt pushed previously by her rich and famous friends who, according to *Us Weekly*, visit her regularly—Johnny Depp, Candice Bergen, Matthew McConaughey. That button, silver and shiny and scorching hot from the summer sun. I'm thinking, *Pushing this button may burn me.*

I'm thinking, *This new job will be worth it.* I'm thinking, *This all might hurt a little.*

I always wondered how you get an opportunity like this. Turns out, a celebrity-assistant job only comes from one place: your enemy. The offer came spelled out in an email from Bruce, this guy I hate. I can't even say his name without an insipid inflection. *Bruce.* We accidentally met one night at a gay bar after he spilled an entire dry martini on me. I would never normally stay in touch with someone like him, but I keep running into him at the Rite Aid in my neighborhood—Rite Aid, that cruel vortex of people I would rather never see. I remember Bruce because he's hands-down handsome and uniquely annoying, overly obsessed with titles and social standing and the science of the fade of his buzz cut. And I suppose he remembers me because, although he can't seem to remember my name, he once said I look like Frodo, so I guess that counts as me making an impression.

"Hey, Frodo," he yelled as we bumped into each other a couple months ago near the pharmacy—him buying protein powder and me buying a neti pot.

"Please don't call me Frodo," I said. "I'm Charlie. Sorry."

"Apology accepted," Bruce said cheerfully, inexplicably giving me a thumbs-up. "I should be able to remember that. My ex ex-boyfriend had a dog named Charlie who got hit by a car and now has two legs and rides around in a little wheel thing with a diaper. It's cute."

The Rite Aid cashier piped up on the intercom, asking for help at the register. We're all drowning, apparently.

Bruce: I resent him, I abhor him, I friended him on Facebook. I like to see the lives I'm not living. Every time I read one of his posts, I literally groan, "UGH!" before I click LIKE. He works for Kathi's agent and was tasked with finding Kathi a new personal assistant. Bruce says Kathi's prior personal assistant was straight, hot, Peruvian, and her reps heard rumors the two maybe got a little *too* personal. So Bruce says they're looking for someone like me—a gay writer to help her keep her life together while specifically not having sex with her. Kathi's team also wants someone who will help her pen more novels. She isn't doing a lot of acting these days, and her books are apparently easy money. My job responsibilities would include: Encourage her to write, correct her punctuation, make her wear a bra. It took two seconds to consider my shit news job and then I told Bruce, "I want it!"

Outside Kathi's gate, at arm's length from her intercom, I roll down my Nissan's window and the old, bubbled, fraying tinting makes a horrible crackling sound as it goes down. I still have my journalism brain turned on, thinking in terms of news headlines, of what it will look like, the story of me making my way into Kathi Kannon's life.

The headline will read: LOSER GETS BIG BREAK.

The headline will read: MORON MEETS MOVIE STAR.

The headline will read: NERD'S DREAM COMES TRUE.

I close my eyes; I breathe deeply, sucking in that famous Beverly Hills air as I aggressively try to brush down my puffy hair, the bits on the sides that curl up, refusing to cooperate. My body often lets me down when I need it most.

I'm thinking, *Can I do this?*

My self-doubt is trying to ruin it. How hard can this job be? Sure, Kathi has some mental health issues she's openly discussed, but it's Hollywood—who doesn't? Sure, Kathi is a former drug addict, but I can manage that. I know I won't be an enabler, an assistant who drives their celebrity boss off the cliff. I know that cliff very well. I know nothing good comes from it. I know what self-destruction looks like. I have a long résumé of getting drunk and high and having unsafe sex a few too many times, a few too many close calls. My therapist calls it passive suicidal behavior and I figure she might be right. I've cut back on my drinking and smoking pot and casual fucking. If I'm going to kill myself, to end my crusty life, it will be *active* suicidal behavior.

Maybe if this job interview doesn't go well.

I'm not exactly suicidal-suicidal—I don't have a plan or anything—but suicide has always had a spot on my vision board. With my shitty news job and pathetic, lonely life, I admit I think of suicide like some people think of going back to college.

I reach my arm out of my trusty Nissan's window and press the call button on the intercom; it's hard to push and leaves a round indentation on my finger, like when I was a kid and squished my thumb down on the top of a pencil eraser. I've been in Kathi Kannon's orbit for only a few moments and, staring at my finger, I realize I'm already, deliciously, marked by her, when suddenly a voice from the intercom screams: "HURRY!" And then cuts out.

Was that her?

Confused, alarmed, I look around and shout back at the silver box, "WHAT?!"

Silence. I look around for answers, advice, but her trees, her gate, that smoking Santa Claus painting offer nothing but derision, mockery, jeering.

I turn back to the intercom. I'm listening for anything, any sign of what to do next, how to proceed. I'm ready to introduce myself. To sell myself. To humbly accept rescheduling if she tells me she forgot about this meeting.

I reach out, about to push the button again, but then—

I hear a little click.

Did I break something?

Then I see the gates to Kathi Kannon's estate parting, her world opening up to me, just like that, in a snap. Just like it's no big deal. Just like she doesn't even care if I could be a murderer, a stalker, a Mormon.

Did I break something? Did I break into something? Is something falling apart or snapping into place?

HURRY! I hear ringing in my ears.

I throw the Nissan into drive, gears catching and jolting, tires making a brief ripping sound as they catch the pavement, the car lurching forward toward the gates, which are opening slowly, slowly, slowly.

HURRY!

I inch and creep—start, stop, start, stop—through the gates until finally my side-view mirrors fit, and I speed onto the property toward some unknown emergency.

I'm thinking, *This is great.*

I'm thinking, *This is luck.*

I'm thinking, *This is crazy.*

2

☆

race up the driveway, passing a blur of Christmas lights (in daylight, in July!) glowing on trees that line the entrance. I pass a massive oak with an extravagant glistening crystal chandelier dangling from one of its heavy branches, a tennis court framed in thick artful vines, a three-car garage with all three doors open wide, no cars inside, just shelves and shelves and shelves filled with books and books and books. I can smell them, funky and old. I'm thinking, *All those poor books, exposed like this.* I'm thinking, *Kathi Kannon is a voracious reader. Or a hoarder.*

I park my Nissan next to a sign that reads, ANYONE CAUGHT SMOKING AND OPERATING A FORKLIFT WILL BE SENT HOME IMMEDIATELY. As I absorb the surroundings, sucking them into me like the clean air, I notice two pathways and wonder which leads to Gracie Gold and which to Kathi Kannon. One path is lined with stark gray cement and the other with weathered and rustic bricks, some of them painted bright red, some of them painted blue, green, pink. There's no question which path belongs to the colorful Kathi Kannon. I'm thinking, *Bruce should have given me all these details.*

I run up the splendid brick walkway, past a guesthouse with a sign out front that says, IN HELL FROM SEX, past a plastic porpoise inexplicably floating from fishing line tied to a tree branch, as if swimming up her hill. On the tree trunk is a 3-D hologram picture of a hand that flips the bird over and over as I hurry past.

I feel the hot Beverly Hills sun leave my back as I enter the shadow of her mansion, her front porch reaching out to me, consuming me. The home is L-shaped and made of old red bricks with a wraparound porch and red pottery-style tapered roof shingles. Plants and glass sculptures—birds, crystals, baby-doll heads—dangle from the wood beams.

I dash to her hulking front door and can practically smell the old solid wood used to make it—using a little knowledge I picked up as a contractor's son. The door is taller and wider than traditional doors, a throwback to the many years ago this house was likely built, a time way back when they made things custom, to fit this specific entryway, this singular portal to this one-of-a-kind habitat. Above the door is a phrase embellished like calligraphy, hieroglyphics, painted in lobs and fine strokes: KNOCK, KNOCK, KNOCKING ON HEAVEN'S DOOR. The brass door knocker is a ball sac. Beneath that, the door features a panel of stained glass featuring a weathered and saintly priest with a petite young altar boy kneeling before him, giving him a blowjob.

Through the glass, I see something, someone moving. I squint to make it out. A figure, a ghost, a shadow, getting bigger and bigger and bigger. Is that Kathi Kannon, movie star, the living action figure once ripped from my crying grasp? I take a step back. I look around frantically, like in movies before a dramatic explosion or abduction. Behind me, the earth gets quiet, birds flutter away, squirrels scatter across the tennis court, like they all know a storm is coming.

Knock, knock, knocking on heaven's door.

I'm thinking, *Here comes God.*

The air seems to thin out, to make way for her; the front door swings open, and like embers shooting up from a fire, she appears, her hair blown back by the door, an e-cigarette dangling from her mouth. Her eyes widen and her lips part and she says, "Hello, I'm Kathi Kannon from *Jaws 3*."

I hold my breath and stare at her, Kathi Kannon, Priestess Talara, real and living, barefoot and disheveled, dressed in a flowing black robe over a loose black T-shirt and tattered black leggings. She's wearing no makeup, no pomp or circumstance, no fucks to give. Her face is tired but alert, familiar and yet mysterious—she looks so much like the woman I remember from my childhood movies yet donning gravity and time like some kind of disguise, like some kind of mask that's taken up residence upon her, leaving her both an old beautiful acquaintance and a strange, fresh new one.

"You answer your own door?" I blurt, a mix of surprise and enchantment as my eyes adjust to her. Like they're suddenly seeing daylight.

"Yeah," she says. "We had a butler, but he died in the pantry a few years ago. Who are you?"

"I'm Charlie Besson. I'm a big fan."

"You don't look very big," she responds, intimidatingly sharp for being so tiny, five foot one, with all that life squeezed into that little frame. She grabs the door as if ready to slam it on me.

"I'm here for the personal-assistant job," I say.

"Not the colonic?" Kathi says, disappointed, yanking the e-cigarette from her lips and letting her hand flop to her side, her shoulders slumping, her other hand still holding the front door, letting it sway slightly closed then open then closed then open, as if she's considering.

Excitement drains from my limbs. A colonic? Ah, this is why I was granted such quick entry; she expected someone else. I'm not who she wants, of course.

"Sorry," I start, feeling the magnitude of the not completely unexpected moment—my unforgettable hero has forgotten we had an appointment. Cue my shame, horror, foolishness. Except I notice Kathi

Kannon beginning to smile. She stands up straight, pops the e-cigarette back in her mouth, lets go of her front door, allowing it to swing open.

"Acting," she says smugly, raising her eyebrows, proud of herself.

"Wow," I say, speechless, entranced.

"I'm just fucking with you," Kathi says dryly. "Come in." She turns casually and walks into the wonderland that is her home, motioning for me to follow. She moves with ease, her comfort and calm at odds with the commanding surroundings. We're in the definition of a "great room," with vaulted ceilings and a huge disco ball the size of an oven affixed high overhead. Sunlight from a skylight is hitting the little square mirrors of the ball and sending twisting and twirling bits of pinks and blues and purples all around. The far wall is covered in antique portraits of animals: Someone's beloved cat. An aristocrat's precious dog. A bird that looks suspiciously like Sean Penn.

Kathi turns back to me as I pass through the doorway. "Please wipe your feet," she says. "The floors are made of endangered trees."

I look down and wipe my feet on an absurdly tiny, vintage-looking Mickey Mouse rug resting on an ocean of caramel-colored hardwood flooring that stretches under us in all directions. This is not the kind of wood flooring I've ever seen before. These planks are not the kind from Lowe's or Home Depot. These look like huge, ancient, wide and thick rectangle-cut logs—no doubt from some haunting enchanted forest—which have supported this house and its various occupants over the years, through every earthquake, man-made and not. To my right is a massive roaring fireplace and, above the mantel, the mounted head of a huge hairy moose staring down at us. To my left is a piano covered in photos of Kathi Kannon's family and friends: Her flipping off a laughing Barbra Streisand. Her smoking with Bruce Willis. Her Lady-and-the-Tramp-ing a hot dog with Tom Hanks.

Kathi motions around us. "Here we are," she says, adding, "I think. There's no actual proof, existentially speaking."

Beyond the piano are a few stairs leading up to a dining area. A formal dinner table is another huge hunk of wood, spanning the wide length of the room, another piece of furniture that didn't come from West Elm. The walls are stucco, painted in faded hues of peach and blue with artistic minimurals here and there: stars, flowers, a guillotine. The accent lighting is neon pink and electric blue.

In the middle of the room, under the disco ball, directly in front of us, is a bright white Native American–style rug supporting a circle of nine old leather chairs. And that's where Kathi Kannon turns to face me again. She takes a seat, her legs folding unnaturally beneath her like a thousand-year-old yogi. She squints, taking me in as I sit across from her.

"How old are you?" Kathi asks.

"I think it's illegal to ask that," I say, regretfully but playfully.

"Well," Kathi says. "Brace yourself."

I smile. "Everyone says I look young. I'm twenty-nine," I say. "I guess it's my Louisiana genes. I'm from just outside of New Orleans."

"Interesting," she says coldly, in a tone that could be intrigue or disgust.

In the quiet that follows, I let my eyes dart this way and that, searching for something to keep the conversation going. It's not that there isn't something curious in the room to ask about, it's that there's too much, too many things requiring inquiry, so instead I turn to my arrival on this property, asking her, "Was that you who buzzed me in at the gate?"

"I don't know what happened," she says. "I just wanted the ringing to stop."

I clear my throat and instantly fear it's too loud. I swallow hard. I force an unnatural smile—I'm thinking, *How is it possible that I've forgotten how to smile?!* I try again to brush down the curl on the side of my head. I feel my body heating up, the warmth emerging unreservedly from my forehead, my back, my armpits, all traces of a cool countenance fleeing, oozing from my pores, from my very being.

Yet Kathi sits perfectly still, her body planted in the chair, her shoulders slightly hunched as if the idea of proper posture escapes her. She observes me without a real tell about how she's feeling about me, watches me like I'm a television.

She doesn't make another move, another comment; she doesn't budge. This is a woman who must be used to an awkward encounter, familiar with people who want something from her. Maybe she's used to waiting to be asked for things—a job, an autograph, an ovum. This is a woman with a lifetime of training in inconvenience, observation, assessing. This is a woman who, despite her stature and wit, fame and fortune, forceful and bold motions through life, doesn't seem to care who takes charge. Maybe she doesn't really give a shit whether I start talking next or she does, whether this conversation continues or not. Maybe the mystery of what will happen next is what is most amusing to her.

And so I blather. "These are cool chairs."

"Yeah, I like their attitudes," she replies, awakening from her easy-breezy trance. "I got them from a flea market in Paris and had them shipped over. I feel bad that they're made out of animal corpses, so I named them after Chinese emperors, and they all seem fine with it. You're sitting on Qin Shi Huang. How is he on your buttocks?"

"He's . . . nice."

She raises her eyebrows again, tilting her head slightly, as if to say, *What else?*

"Um. I'm very grateful for the opportunity to meet with you," I say.

"Me, too. For the opportunity to meet myself," she says quickly, like this is her tenth take of this scene. She sucks again on her electronic cigarette, then opens her mouth, letting the vapor float out; no blowing here, no exertion, this is not going to be hard work for her. The mist calmly dissipates like clouds in summer.

I'm in awe. Kathi Kannon seems brilliant but enigmatic. Pleasant, but her teeth are slightly clenched. There's a vibe—jesting but tangible—that she doesn't want to be doing this and doesn't want to be here and this whole day would be going a lot better if she was just in her bed taking a nap. I feel it as rejection, that familiar friend I've known since my earliest days in my lack of childhood playmates, my mother abandoning me with her tragic and early death, my father, who grew colder and colder the more I grew up and, to his horror, didn't grow out of my more effeminate qualities.

I struggle to keep it going, this new, semi-electrified life I started living back at Kathi Kannon's front gate and now want so badly to never end, as if I'm instantly important just by proximity to her. I decide to be bold; perhaps she's not used to people being frank and forward, perhaps that's what she's looking for.

"Miss Kannon," I say, trying to exhale away my encroaching stress-related neck pain. "I hear you're looking for someone who can help you with your writing, and I've been a writer for many years now, a journalist, so I'm trained to take down information and to be sure it is precise and accurate and grammatically correct. And I can do that for you, help you with your writing and whatnot, if you want."

She coughs, looks away, then back at me. "What?"

"I'm very responsible, I'm always on time, I'm hyper-organized, and no task is too big or too small."

I pause for her praise.

She says, almost with frustration, "I feel like I'm dreaming and if I could just wake up, I'd be thinner."

I continue, "I'm also good with things like organizing and maintaining a calendar. Do you have a scheduling system?"

"Yeah," she says, standing and reaching into her pocket, pulling out scraps of paper and reading them. "'Call Jessica Lange'—done," she says, tossing it onto the floor. "'Get erotic birthday cake for Russell Crowe'—done," she says, and again tosses it aside. She pulls another scrap and reads, "'Take birth control—'" then gasps, grabbing her stomach, "Oh my GOD!"

I grip the arms of the Chinese emperor chair and start to stand, to comfort her, to offer her peace, to counter my own confusion at how she can still be on the pill at fifty-six years old. Then she smiles.

"Acting," she says, sitting back down with a sigh, but one chair closer to me this time. I take it as a good sign and wonder what to do next. Another eternity passes in silence, and her face again cues me to keep going, get it over with, deliver this breech baby before we all die, her of monotony, me of inherent nothingness.

"You keep your calendar on scraps of paper?" I ask, like a stunned child who just accidentally saw Chuck E. Cheese take off his costume head, revealing an awful rat man.

Kathi collects the scraps of the calendar papers and stuffs them back in her robe like treasure, glancing at me as if to say, *Who doesn't?*

"Why do you want this job?" she asks.

"I hate my life," I say, regretting it instantly, feeling myself blush, my hand uncontrollably going to the curl on the side of my head. My unruly hair, an unhinged reminder that I was prepared for every question about my entire career history—college, experience, references—but I was not prepared for this simple one about my life.

Kathi lets out a *humph.* "I relate," she says, mostly to herself.

I count this as a tiny victory, so I press on, quick to turn the subject away from my neurotic problems and back to the measurable marks of this employment opportunity. "I was told you want to get serious with your life and career, that you need an assistant to help you be more professional. Do you want that?"

"I'll be honest, it doesn't sound like me. But when I'm bored, I'll say anything."

"Are you bored right now?" I ask.

Kathi apologetically nods, *yes.*

Despite my efforts, I can feel my body sinking with disappointment, failure.

She says, "But don't worry, it's not you, it's me. Or maybe it's us—it's too soon to tell. Maybe it's because we're not sitting on Emperor Yi." She nods to a leather chair across from us. We stare at it, as if he's about to talk. She looks at me. "Come on. I'll show you around."

Kathi Kannon stands, her legs unwinding beneath her. She turns and takes off to the right and I think I can hear the sound of her eye roll. I don't know if she's giving me a tour because she's warming to me or if she's apathetic and trying to pass the time as quickly as possible.

She motions to the room where we're standing. "This is the living room, as opposed to the dying room. I named it Mateo's room. That's Mateo the Moose up there." She points to the moose head above the fireplace. "I saw him in a hotel in Bulgaria and I just felt so bad for him and figured I'd try to give him a happy life. He's been here for so long. He once saw Jack Nicholson nude." She looks at me to gauge my reaction. Shock, of course. And fascination. She's pleased. Kathi turns to Mateo the Moose again. "My life's greatest mission is to find the back half of him and put it on the other side of the wall in the other room. Come see."

Kathi walks, and I follow, into the adjoining room, a bit deeper into her mansion, her world. The room is painted entirely red, like a womb, and is filled with boats—paintings, statuettes, drink coasters. Clusters of fragile model ships sit crammed, poised precariously, on the mantel above what I have now counted as the second raging fireplace. On the floor, there's an ocean of throw pillows large and small, patterned and solid colors, shapes like lips and flowers. I wonder why Kathi needs so many cushions—perhaps for when she has friends over for talking, reading, orgies.

In the corner is a bar, where Kathi Kannon, film icon, takes a glass from a shelf, grinds it into an ice bucket until the glass is full, and pours a Coke Zero on top, fizz and bubbles nearly spilling out in a close call that she doesn't even register. "Want one?" she asks.

I can't tell if she's being kind or if this is an order.

"Well, do you? I don't offer to serve people every day. This isn't Apple-tart."

"Applebee's?" I ask.

"Whatever the fuck," she says, taking a gulp of her soda like a kid drinking chocolate milk.

"No, thanks," I say. "I can't believe you make your own drinks."

"Who else is gonna do it? I have a few people on staff around here, but they're mostly just ambience. Sure you don't want one?" Kathi smirks, like she knows something. Like she's known all along what I want, one of many things she gleaned instantly upon meeting me, probably upon meeting anyone—she knows them. Maybe it's a natural, brilliant gift. Maybe it's because she's met so many people in her life, she can zero in on you like a laser. She's met every personality type, seen every quirk. And she's pegged me: Twitchy, uptight, wounded. And thirsty.

"Okay, sure," I say, "I'll take a Coke Zero." I'm thinking, *Why not— just another bit of texture to add to this weird experience.* I'm thinking, *I'll write about this in my suicide note after I leave, after she rejects me.*

"The most important part of the assistant job is . . ." Kathi starts, pausing to hand me my Coke Zero.

I chime in, "Keeping you organized, updating and backing up all of your phones and computers, helping you write every single day?"

"Keeping my e-cigarettes charged," Kathi says.

I say, "Right."

I say, "Got it."

I say, "That's the job."

She asks, "Have you ever had one?"

I ask, "A job?"

She says, "An e-cigarette." And as quickly as the question exits her mouth, the e-cigarette is headed toward me, Kathi Kannon holding it out to me, offering me a puff. I stare, hesitating a moment, a moment too long. She sighs and rolls her eyes, bringing the cigarette back to her, down to her shirt, wiping the mouthpiece off, and handing it to me again. "There," she says. "No more cooties."

I wince in shame. "Oh, no. It's not that. It's just, I don't smoke or do drugs or have fun," I blabber, betraying the reason for my hesitation, which was simply: I never smoked one of these. What if I make a fool of myself? What if I cough? What if I spit up on her?!

Kathi continues holding the e-cig toward me. "You can't turn me down. I taught Jamie Lee Curtis how to give a blowjob."

I nod as if to say, *It all makes sense now,* and I take the e-cigarette from her fingers. She watches me, a slightly devious smile in her eyes. I feel like the kid I always wanted to be—the kid getting initiated into the group of cool guys, the kid who's hip enough that he faces peer pressure, pressure to actually fit in versus the actual story of my life, the opposite of peer pressure, never pressured to fit in, always pressured to keep out.

I put the e-cigarette to my lips. I suck in. I imagine myself looking so, so cool. I nod and bob like I'm listening to reggae in my head; I imagine I look like the guy from *Grease,* until I start coughing uncontrollably.

The headline will read: LAME.

The headline will read: AMATEUR.

The headline will read: FAILURE.

"What's in this?" I ask.

"Water vapor and meth," she says.

My eyes widen.

"Just kidding," she says. "I haven't made meth in years."

"Acting?" I ask.

"Sure," she says with a shrug, taking back her e-cigarette. "I honestly don't know what's in it. But whatever it is, it has to be better than real cigarettes, right? Or drugs." She locks eyes with me when she says "drugs."

Drugs. She mentions them so casually and so quickly upon meeting me. I'm thinking of her story, her life as an addict since age thirteen, the topic or subtext of every interview and magazine article about her. I'm thinking of the promise I made to myself: I won't be an enabler, not of a drug habit, not of any bad habits. If I get this job, I promise myself, I'll protect her. *If.*

"You're a little odd," she says.

"Yes, ma'am. Thank you," I respond, like it's a reflex, a politeness reflex.

"Please don't call me ma'am."

"Sorry. It's my father's fault," I say, spitting out the word *father*. I'm thinking of my dad screaming at me as a kid: *ALWAYS SAY "THANK YOU"! ALWAYS SAY "YES, MA'AM"! ALWAYS SAY "NO, MA'AM"! YOU UNDERSTAND ME? MY ROOF, MY RULES!* His grating, gravelly, masculine voice is still screaming at me, in my head, all these years later, even while not under his roof, even while not under his rule, even while here, auditioning for a new role in Hollywood's royal court.

"Come on," Kathi says, marching onward, toward, yes, a third blazing fireplace.

I follow her through another living room to the backyard, which is like a showroom for folk art, with trees that have their trunks painted in different colors, mannequins fully dressed and posed in unspeakable acts with one another, and a flower bed in which the soil has been topped with glistening chunks of colorful broken glass—pale greens and blues. There's a trickling water fountain, flashing lights twinkling in random sequence along the roofline, and a fire pit emblazoned with the phrase BURN, FUCKER.

Little dollhouses line the side of a steep hill that borders her property, tiny lights are on inside tiny houses for what could very well be lucky, magical tiny people who get to live there, as if it's an entire universe in itself, a universe within a universe within a universe. She stops in front of the fountain at the center of the patio.

"I made this one night when I was bored. I smashed a bunch of plates and then had this idea to incorporate the broken pieces into cement as a fountain."

The water trickles, trickles, trickles.

"Oh. It's very interesting," I say.

"It leaks. We did something wrong and have to refill it constantly, but isn't that just a great metaphor for life."

"Like, life is garbage?" I ask, instantly exposed. I've let my guard down and perhaps spoken too much truth again, revealed too much about me. Kathi stares at me.

"No, like life is art," she says in a near huff, as if scolding someone who lacks understanding of basic language.

"Right, right," I say, blushing, sweating, back to being underdog.

Kathi turns slowly and starts to walk away. I follow. I can tell she's thinking hard—maybe about me. "My attorney told me there are a bunch of questions I'm not supposed to ask you, so I'd like to go ahead and get those out of the way," she says.

I cringe but manage, "Sure."

"Are you gay, married, impotent? Did your parents love you? When did you lose your virginity? Are you right-handed? Do you ever want to harm yourself or others? Do you have any fake limbs? Answer in any order you like."

To her back as we walk, I say, "Um, okay, well, I don't have any fake limbs."

"Are you at least open to having a fake limb?" she asks.

I hold my breath, then blurt, "Yes?"

"Onward," she says, moving purposefully now, e-cigarette back in her mouth, held in place by her teeth, breathing it like it's a ventilator keeping her alive. We walk across her patio to a gate with old brick steps up a hill leading to a little cottage-type structure. A giant pencil is poking out of the bushes. In the distance is a Native American teepee. A sculpture of a large black erect penis firmly resists falling over in the breeze.

"My mother," Kathi says, coughing out the word *mother,* pointing to the cottage, "had the pool house up there converted to an 'office,' which basically means she paid fifty thousand dollars to have a fax machine put next to a toilet."

"That must be a nice fax," I say.

"You have a very long neck," she says.

"Yes, ma'am—" I start, but then catch myself. "I mean, yeah, I do." I grab my neck like I'm choking. "With this thing, you know, I'm a god in some cultures."

"Me, too," Kathi says with her best Priestess Talara pose.

"What's your name again?" she asks.

I open my mouth but then she interrupts. "WAIT!" she says, facing me and grabbing my shoulders. I flinch, fearing she's about to do a headbutt.

"Don't tell me." She stares at me, thinking, struggling to recall it. "Okay. What's the first letter?"

I say, "C."

She blurts, "Cockring!"

"Uh, nope."

"Oh," she says, disappointed.

I wait for a second guess, and when none comes, I say, "I'm Charlie."

"Eek," Kathi says. "No. I'm sorry, I can't call you that," she explains. "You look more like a . . . Samuel. Or a Jimmy. How's that? Jimmy. Or . . . Cockring?"

"Between Cockring and Jimmy, I guess I'll take Jim—"

"Come on, Cockring," Kathi blurts.

She leads me up the hill, past the pool house, around a bend, passing twirling yard ornaments, statues of garden gnomes smoking weed, a fat Buddha with the face of that boy from *Mad* magazine. We walk past a pool surrounded by mountains and hills and trees and old Las Vegas-style neon signs that say DINOSAUR HOTEL and TOPLESS DANCERS. There's an old-fashioned Coke machine and lawn chairs with bright umbrellas. This job, should it become real for me, beats the hell out of my piece-of-shit cubicle in the newsroom with oppressive fluorescent lighting in the middle of the night. In the distance, I see a man who I assume to be a gardener. He looks like he's pretending to trim a small palm tree. He waves and I wave back like I belong there; I'm pretending, too.

Kathi leads me back into her home, into the red room with its fire and boats and floor pillows. She plops down on a cushion that looks like a Louis Vuitton toilet seat. I stand awkwardly nearby, considering my fate, wondering if I'm to be flushed.

Kathi grabs a TV remote and turns on a television behind me. *Gone with the Wind* is on, and Kathi turns up the volume. I'm not sure if we're still in the job interview or if I should sit beside her and watch. I look back and forth between her and the television.

"Do you have any other questions for me?" I shout over the sound of a screaming Southern belle.

"I don't know." Kathi sighs. She mutes the TV and looks at me. "I don't really care for this kind of thing. Hiring *employees*. I usually just pull people from wherever. I've never hired, like, a professional before. There's the other guy I met yesterday, but he's—I don't know. He likes sports. You like sports?"

"What's sports?"

Kathi smiles openly, naturally, for the first time, seemingly unguarded. Have I amused her?

I try to stay cool, but I'm thinking, *The other guy?* I try to hide the sting, the reminder that this job isn't mine yet, there are other candidates, that I'm competing—something that usually doesn't end well for me.

"Tell me about your award acceptance speech," she says.

"My—?"

"Everyone has one in their head. The speech you'll give if you win a big award. What's your speech like?"

"Uh, you first?"

Kathi Kannon hops up in an instant and approaches an imaginary podium and adjusts an imaginary microphone, into which she says, "They always size these things for someone taller. And thinner."

I look around, confused, unsure if she's talking to me or the imaginary cameras or the imaginary crowd. Maybe all three.

Like a switch is flipped, she suddenly starts crying. Her body heaving, the magnitude of the fantastic moment upon her just as real as the oxygen in the room, like a tonnage too heavy to bear. She clutches her heart, as if to find and hold a beat to prove that her body is still there. She turns, takes an imaginary award from an imaginary presenter, they exchange a real moment, whispers, a chuckle, she takes a breath. She reclaims her footing at the nonexistent podium. She looks right at me. She's locked onto me, onto her target, ready to launch. She's a goddess. I'm the audience, I'm the world, I'm a million viewers at home.

"My God," she says, sobbing into the imaginary mic. "This. Wow. Come on, words." I laugh quietly; she controls the room. She controls the world she just built around me in an easy instant. She's in my head, in my consciousness. How am I here with her?

She says, "This is the best moment of my life. Thank you."

As she steps away from the microphone, I applaud. She turns back to me and raises her eyebrows and picks at a piece of something stuck in her teeth, and the illusion is lost.

"Acting," she says.

My applause simmers awkwardly to a few little claps.

She says, "Now you do it."

"What? I'm not really prepared for that."

"Well, that's a good start," she says. "Start with that."

I awkwardly walk to the imaginary podium, to the place where she stood seconds ago. "Uhh," I say into her imaginary mic. "Is this thing on?"

Kathi rolls her eyes. "We'll work on it," she says, and sits back on the toilet cushion.

I feel our time is ending, so I step up. "Can I say something, in case I never see you again?" I say boldly, my face already turning red.

She stares at me, eyebrows raised.

"I just want to say I loved you in . . ." And I pause. This is the part Bruce *did* warn me about. "*Don't tell her about the action figures,*" he said. "*Don't tell her that you loved her space films,*" he said. "*Don't make a fool of yourself and act like a fan,*" he said.

With Kathi waiting for me to spit it out, I continue, "I loved you in . . ." *Don't do it.*

". . . *Mork and Mindy.*"

Kathi stares at me with the kind of comfort that only comes from a person used to being stared at. "Was I in that?" she asks, her expression not betraying whether she's joking or having actual memory failure.

"Yes! You were a guest star. It must have been one of your first acting jobs. It was one of the only shows my dad let me watch."

She stares at me intensely, like an old-timey actress staring at the silver-screen heartthrob who's going to break her heart. Her eyes narrow, squinting as if to put me in better focus. "You have a rich inner life I know nothing about."

"Thank you," I say, looking away briefly, avoiding the scrutiny, unsure how to respond, wondering if this is a moment calling for truth on my part—she can get to know me if she wants to, if she hires me—or a moment of uncertainty on her part, calling out the holes in my life and job history, which I know are technically vacant of the specific experience of being a celebrity assistant.

An awkward pause hangs in the air, and she's done. With a big exhale, she wiggles into a more comfortable position on her cushion and says, "Well, you seem groovy. Nice to meet you and all that."

"You, too," I manage, my body swaying slightly with insecurity and uncertainty.

Kathi turns back to her television, switches the sound back on, and I know I've lost her.

I put my half-nursed Coke Zero down on her bar.

I smile and turn and leave her, the Southern belle on TV screaming again about fire or food or God knows what.

And I leave that mansion, past the moose and the Chinese emperors.

And I leave that property, past the ball-sac door knocker and floating porpoise.

And I leave that fantasy, that other life, my limbs still fully intact, for now.

3

☆

My screen saver is fucking with me. It's cycling through exotic, peaceful, lush locations while I'm stuck at my dank desk, back at my news-writer job, stressed the hell out, not because of the workload but because it has been three days since I met Kathi Kannon and I've heard nothing.

I'm clutching my cell phone 24/7, in bathrooms, in movie theaters, in desperation, hoping to hear from her. What's taking her so long to decide? Maybe she has decided. Maybe I'm not good enough. Still, I want her to call. I want to hear that I'm rejected, feel my ear vibrate with the words. I want to feel the pain, my old friend.

My screen saver is showing me the Maldives and Bora Bora.

I'm seeing Fiji.

I'm seeing Tahiti.

I'm seeing Cape Town.

I know I'm deep in the muck of my misery when *he* comes to mind: *Bruce.* I pull out my cell phone, scroll to—ugh—his name, and smash the call button with such force I'm certain Siri feels assaulted.

"Go!" Bruce shouts. Or maybe "Yo." I don't know. I just can't with him.

"It's Charlie," I mumble, unsure if he already knows it's me, unsure if my name is even worthy of ever having been saved in his cell phone.

"Yeah, yeah," he says. "Frodo, right?"

"No," I correct him, listlessly, pointlessly. "Charlie. What's the latest on the Kathi Kannon job?"

"Dunno, bro," he says, chewing on something. "I heard your interview was fine, that it happened, you know?"

"That's it?" I ask. "It happened?"

"You have to wait. We're on her time now."

"Can you, like, ask her?"

"Ask Kathi? Are you fucking crazy? No. Not how it's done. These things—interacting with celebrities—these things are fucking serious. Surgical. Like, you know, don't spit on the queen and that kind of shit. And who else am I gonna ask, bro? Her maid? Kathi doesn't have an assistant to ask. That's the whole point of interviewing you people, right?"

"Right. Okay."

"If you don't get this job, maybe another will open up," Bruce says. "I hope to get promoted soon, and maybe you can apply for my job. Although, I'm an *executive* assistant, not to be confused with a *personal* assistant, of course. Executive is better. The *executive* assistant is like a mountain, like the sturdy mound that protects our boss from wind and invasion and guides him home in a storm. The *personal* assistant is like the valley. They collect the silt. Right?"

"Do you mean sediment?"

"What?" Bruce asks, putting another forkful of something in his mouth, in my ear.

"Don't you mean sediment instead of silt?" I ask. "I mean, silt requires flowing water, and sediment is actually critical to the environment and—"

"Huh?" Bruce asks, but I'm too dejected, too exhausted, to even say anything else. And the more he chews in my ear, the less hunger I have for answers, for continuing.

"Gotta jet!" he barks mercifully. "Have a blessed day!" he shouts, a toilet flushing in the background as he hangs up. What the fuck is he doing? God, I hate him.

I'm certain that I'm not going to get the job. This all feels like another in my life's long list of failures, just like my current employment. I'm a TV news writer because I'm not good enough to be a TV news reporter. I wanted to be seen in this life, to be one of the handsome guys on TV who tells everyone about the world, to be one of the people everyone else has to see the world through, to be a gatekeeper. Was my longing to be a TV newscaster rooted in vanity? Was it rooted in survival—a desperation to be validated, heard? *Look at me, the boy with acne, all grown up. Look at me, the fag bullied in the lunchroom, now pontificating about politics, traffic, weather.* Was it simple psychology? Was Hannibal Lecter right, we covet what we see? Did I simply covet the newscasters who had my asshole father's undivided attention every night at five, six, and ten?

My father: I picture him as if he's in front of me now, heavy and melted into his forest-green fake Microsuede recliner, the fabric on the arms dark and smashed where his thick, oily hands have gripped tightly, nightly, repeatedly, while raging at Tom Brokaw during stories about war and economics and environmentalism. My childhood memories are dog-eared not in photo albums but by news events that drew his ire.

"FUCK THEM!" he would yell about Democrats.

"FUCK THEM, TOO!" he would yell about Republicans.

"FUCK THEM ALL AND FUCK THEM TWICE AGAIN!" he would yell at the kicker—the last story in the newscast. Sometimes it was a waterskiing squirrel. Sometimes it was a dog that saved a family from a fire. Sometimes it was a kid who won a spelling bee. The networks all do it. They end on a positive story so you forget that you can't pay your mortgage, that tap water is poison, that your kids are brainwashed bisexuals.

"WHO FUCKING CARES ABOUT A SPELLING BEE? QUIT WASTING MY TAX DOLLARS!" he would shout at the TV, as if the news is tax-funded. His yelling, his own personal kicker each night. The bottom right corner of our living room TV screen was eternally clouded after bits of his spittle caked it during a particularly passionate night of news viewing. No one ever cared to clean it.

If ever something captured my father's imagination, caught his attention to the point of a near medical emergency, it was TV news. Everything else—eating dinner, commercials, me—were all simple distractions from what I suspect he really wanted each night in that recliner: to see the world but not be a part of it, to force his rule upon a kingdom behind glass, to watch with gross fascination a universe he couldn't really access. All those things he felt from watching TV, all that separation and frustration and longing to be seen, those are all the things I felt about him, sitting behind him, his only son, young and quiet and watching him profoundly interested in, well, not me. And it all got worse after Mom died. When it was finally just him and me, it felt like just him.

I could never get in front of my father, not in our living room and, years later, not from behind the coveted glass of his TV. I never made it as a TV news reporter. Maybe it was bad luck. Maybe I didn't have the talent or the right look. Maybe it was bad Louisiana genes, after all. The best I could muster was this middle-of-the-night news-writer job. And right here in the newsroom, reporters and anchors milling about, their very presence taunting my failure, I open the Notes app on my phone to compose a suicide note, but I'm too exhausted to finish.

I want to quit this job. To tell my boss to fuck off. I want to stand up and wave my arms and shout that I'm tired of these hours, these depressing news stories about corruption, death, and disease. I want to say I'm leaving for better things. I want to check out. Instead, I clock out.

I get in my trusty old Nissan, its frame bent and breaking but loved anew, appreciated just a little more after sharing in the Kathi Kannon experience with me. My Nissan, it was a witness to my close call, my almost moment into Kathi's world. I'm thinking, *Just get me home.*

My phone in hand—*Please call me, Kathi Kannon*—I'm feeling busted, feeling at one with the steering wheel, with the console, with the check-engine light, burned out because it was on so much, too weary from asking for help, too tired to keep going, too spent from being ignored. In this car, I have to actually hit potholes on purpose to rattle wires to make the radio work. You can't open the glove compartment without the whole thing coming off in your hand. The horn is dislodged, so when I honk, the speaker blares at me inside the car. I'm only ever honking at myself.

My shit car and my shit job match my shit apartment—three hundred square feet of warm darkness, the sunlight rebuked by my blackout curtains, no AC, my neighbor's relentless cigarette smoke wafting under the crack in the front door. I needed Kathi, I needed a change, I needed a course correction. Alas.

I sleep.

I wake.

What's Kathi Kannon doing right now?

When I was a kid, I would play a game called What's Madonna Doing Right Now? I would close my eyes and imagine at that very second where Madonna could be on earth and what she was doing. There was something special about imagining Madonna heating a Hot Pocket or using the bathroom.

What's Madonna doing right now? *What's Kathi Kannon doing right now?* I close my eyes. Is Kathi on the phone with Michelle Pfeiffer or Goldie Hawn? Is she making her bed? Is she putting on jewelry? Is

she in her bedroom? Her red room? Her living room with Mateo the
Moose? Is she watching TV? Is she planning her next book or her next
adventure around the world? Is she smoking e-cigarettes with her new
assistant, the one who must have stolen the job from me, who's better
than me, more charming, more clever, more apt—even if he does like
sports? Is she laughing and waxing about meeting me, the other guy—
groovy, unqualified, "a little odd"?

I spent hours of childhood lost in imagination, play, dance—any
and every fantasy that could one day get me on my father's television.
When I was thirteen, I choreographed an entire routine I fantasized
would be my audition for Ed McMahon's *Star Search*. I was dancing
to the 1961 song "Mother-in-Law" by Ernie K-Doe. (My dad only let
me listen to oldies, which were part of a collection of cassette tapes in
a plastic case shaped like a jukebox.) I wanted a costume with a pop
of flair, so I wore a black sweatshirt and black sweatpants and a pair of
my mother's pink socks. She had been dead a year by this point, but
her clothing was still in her dresser, everything like she left it except
for the few things I dared disturb, sometimes just to smell them, to
remember her.

In her pink socks, I was spinning in a circle, my arms free, my head
rushing, the song's simple melody imbuing me with drunk abandon as
I spun, spun, spun, and then came crashing down onto the floor with
a thud as part of my finale. Dad was instantly yelling.

"WHAT THE HELL IS ALL THAT BANGING AROUND UP
THERE? CHARLIE, GET DOWN HERE NOW!" He was screaming
for me from that recliner, with that crushed green material, I can still
smell it, a football game blaring on the TV—football, his other passion,
second only to TV news. Fear crept into me like a venom, but in my
dizzy euphoria I assured myself: *I can take care of him, don't worry.* I
was thinking, *I'll just appease him, apologize, and be back to my routine for Ed McMahon in a few seconds.* Funny, the times we feel brave.

Funny, the moments we think we're strong. I didn't even have hair in my armpits yet, but so earnest was I in my artful mission that I wasn't careful. Young courage—not always helpful.

Before going downstairs, I pulled the legs of my sweatpants as far down to my ankles as they would go to cover up the pink socks. I put on slippers to cover the rest. I was thinking, even then, that I needed to hide things from him, to protect myself from him.

I approached his recliner like the hand of the king approaches the throne, massaging the space closing in between us as if it were a living being. Finally before him, his gaze turning to me, I realized suddenly I was not an agent of a royal court but more like the jester, a clown, and the balls I was juggling scattered at my feet, rolling quickly away from me, away from him, smartly saving themselves.

Dad looked down at my socks as if they called out to him, as if bait on a fishing line, as if the hook were caught painfully deep in his gums. "YOU LIKE DRESSING IN GIRL CLOTHES?!" he screamed. He stood. He moved toward me.

Walking backward, I felt the socks, those pink terrors on my feet, moments ago sliding me across the floor in ecstasy, in another life, now sandpaper in my slippers.

"COME HERE!" Dad yelled, grabbing my *Star Search* wardrobe by the shoulder and lifting me slightly, bullying me to his bedroom. "UNDRESS!" he yelled. The same voice in my head that inspired my dancing had now turned on me, was now dark and cruel, and I obeyed it as it told me to obey him. I pulled off my sweatshirt, ashamed anew that I had no hair on my body, that I was nothing like the other kids at school who were growing their tufts of masculinity here and there.

When I stood shirtless before him, he yelled, "ALL OF IT!"

I pulled off my slippers and socks. I pulled off my sweatpants. I stood before him in my underwear, tattered, old, tarnished tighty-whities. He stared at me, the pores of his face so clear, and I knew he meant it. *All of it.* And I awkwardly slid down my underwear. They hooked on my right heel and I nearly toppled yanking them off. I couldn't look up at him.

"Go get a pair of your mother's panties," he said.

I turned away from him and toward Mom's dresser, the drawer where I borrowed her socks still open the slightest bit. I knew her underwear drawer was the bottom right; I knew where all her things were, my tears having dotted them like breadcrumbs in my secret visits to this dresser in the months after she passed. I chose a pair of her panties.

"PUT THEM ON," he said.

I slipped them onto my body, eager to hide my nakedness. I had to hold them up so they didn't fall off my thin frame.

"YOU LIKE THAT?" he yelled. "YOU LIKE DRESSING LIKE A GIRL?!"

I was utterly paralyzed.

A football game blaring.

And he left me there, crying.

He left me there, seeds of failure and disappointment and separateness not just planted inside me but blossoming, with roots stretching out, reaching deep.

And I never did make it onto *Star Search*. Another of my life's failures. Now my literal star search—for Kathi Kannon's employ—seems ended in flames, too.

I'm deep in expensive therapy about all this. Every session is a buffet of my childhood, my career, my suicide fantasies. My therapist is a petite woman, mostly a listener—rarely does she give me advice or conversation, preferring instead to stare at me, even after I ask a direct question, waiting for me to find the answer on my own. She has a habit of, occasionally and without impetus, quickly glancing down at her clothing, pulling her sweater closed, brushing flat the folds of her dress, clutching her collar, as if by some act of God one of her breasts or an edge of her nipple may be randomly, mysteriously exposed. Perhaps it's her clue, her signaling what she really wants most from me. She wants me to bare my vital organs, my breast, or what's beneath it, my heart. She's my Therapista, a warrior of my inner world.

Therapista says what you don't discuss is what you fear most.

Therapista says everything comes out eventually.

Therapista says everyone we meet is a teacher.

In our weekly sessions, I sometimes play her own trick on her, staring at her as if I'm confused or mute, waiting for her to elaborate. "What I mean," she says, "is that the slow driver in front of us is teaching us patience. The stressed-out waitress is teaching us the merits of inner peace. The broken heater is teaching us to find other ways to stay warm."

I don't mention to her that a broken heater can be deadly.

Therapista wants me to journal, to track my thoughts and feelings. "Get a little notepad," she says. "Or take notes in your phone. Just to get thoughts out of your head."

Hey, Siri, take a note. Are you there? Are you the one person listening?

Therapista says it's a friendly universe, that things happen for you, not to you, that if I don't get the Kathi Kannon job it's only because something even bigger and better is waiting for me.

Hey, Siri, are you getting all this crap?

I always nod and smile. Even when Therapista is wrong—the universe has failed me, Kathi Kannon has escaped me, and there is nothing that can replace her.

I'm dreaming I'm drowning in quicksand—except it's more like slowsand, and no one is around to help me. I'm clutching my phone in my dream as in real life, waiting for a call from Kathi Kannon, and it starts to vibrate, and I realize it's not just the dream. The wind-chime ringtone finally wakes me. I bolt up in bed: Is it her? Am I in? Did I get it? I reflexively hit the green button, only to accidentally answer a call from my father. I freeze, as if maybe not saying anything will make him go away.

"YOU GONNA ANSWER?!" he yells.

"Hello."

He lets out a sigh, a hot breath of air. "A CAT scan found FOUR polyps in my colon! I thought that you, OF ALL PEOPLE, would LOVE hearing about it."

Silence on the line. Both of us starkly quiet, suddenly serious, our chat quickly leading us onto thin ice, a tiny crack away from an entire conversation about how my father wrongly thinks being gay means I have an obsession with the workings of every human anus.

I'm thinking, *He's calling to tell me he's dying.*

I'm thinking, *He will die and I'll be officially, profoundly alone.*

I'm thinking, *Maybe I'm still dreaming.*

"Don't worry," Dad says. "I don't have COLON cancer."

"That's good," I breathe.

"But while they were doing the CAT scan, they found a tumor on my KIDNEY!" He drops the news like he's ordering a number three at McDonald's, and I'm not sure how to react.

"Wait. You have kidney cancer?"

"Yeah," Dad says. "Well, it's a kidney tumor. They have to cut it out and do tests and all that."

"Dad, I'm sorry. What can I do?" I ask out of habit, out of the politeness he bred deep in me. I regret it even before the words have escaped me.

What can I do?

Hey, Siri, how do I get out of this?

One moment I'm angling for a new life with Kathi Kannon, and the next I'm heading home to Louisiana to help my dad through kidney surgery. My life is actually going backward.

I meet Dad at his truck, parked at the curb outside baggage claim at New Orleans International. He looks me over, not a mystery in his eyes. "TUCK IN YOUR SHIRT! JESUS CHRIST!" he yells.

I shove a clump of my T-shirt into my waistband. I avoid his gaze, again, as usual. By this point in our lives he must know me best by the whites of my eyes. I get in his truck for the long ride to his house, the house I grew up in.

"I REMEMBER WHEN PEOPLE USED TO DRESS DECENT TO TRAVEL!" he shouts over the hot wind gushing in through the open windows—he says the AC burns too much gasoline.

Huge green metal signs on the highway chronicle our journey to my childhood home north of New Orleans. Those green metal signs, with white block letters, are announcing my fate: PERRIS: 200 MILES, and then 100, and then 50. Those signs, they jeer me toward my hometown, that little country speck-on-a-map with its cliché one traffic light. Those green metal signs, they're morbid taxpayer-funded mileage countdowns to my old house, to my dad's house, that rural home where I grew up so quickly, too quickly, me and him and, briefly, Mom, a dead woman I more and more realize I barely knew.

Dad moved us "to the country" to get away from the government, he says. He bought a gun. He unbanked. He buried gold in the backyard. His nightstand is a 370-pound fireproof safe full of bullets and silver and a tattered, dog-eared book about Freemasons. He sold us the idea of living in the country with talk of tree houses, canoeing, animals, and adventures on the five lush acres we would own, only to discover the land is crap. The pond in the back barely holds water, maybe mud, at best, in the winter, and in the summer, it's dry and cracked like the surface of Mars. The land is mostly red clay, so nothing grows. Chunks of the driveway wash away after a hard rain, our gravel and crimson clay trickling down the street like blood. The developer who put the subdivision together planted pine trees in straight rows for miles. He wasn't even trying. Nothing looks natural, nothing like the wild, real country we all imagined. I'm so, so far from Beverly Hills. My dad's neighborhood is called Jolly Pines Estates, though there are no "estates," and there's certainly nothing jolly about it. When I was a kid, I'd fool myself that living here was fun, then I downgraded it to interesting, then to harmless, at the very least. But now I look at all this, the pines and the red clay and my father, and all I see are lies.

"THE FUCKING GARBAGE MAN RAISED RATES AGAIN!" Dad yells as we pull into the driveway, past a pile of trash that will sit there until Dad or the trash man concedes.

My mind is racing, retreating into itself to cower from my father's random rages, longing to be anywhere but here in Perris. Over and over, I'm rewriting my awards speech, the one Kathi asked me about. If only my speech were better, maybe I'd be there, with her, in her employ, with a great excuse about why I can't be home helping my father through his medical moment, forcing him to inconvenience his neighbors or drinking buddies or church friends into helping him. *Kathi,* I should have told her, grabbing the imaginary microphone and screaming at the imaginary audience, *I'd like to thank my father for teaching me I don't matter!*

Therapista says change your thinking, change your life.

Therapista says emotional maturity is questioning our thoughts.

Therapista says hating others is hating yourself.

I hate it here, the house my father built, the home he never finished. The cobbler's kids had no shoes and the contractor's kids had no doorknobs, no paint, no carpet. The floors were (and still are) particleboard, strips of thin wood glued on top of one another that leave feet splintered and socks shredded, nothing like Kathi's smooth wood floors. My mom would complain about having to eat dinner while sitting on empty upside-down five-gallon paint buckets instead of chairs. My father would shout, "IF YOU DON'T LIKE IT, THERE'S THE DOOR!" He's not the kind of guy who could easily, mindfully handle criticism, or stress, or, finally, his own private nightmare when my mom did choose "the door." She told Dad she was leaving him, divorcing him, though she never had the chance to do it, never had the chance to be free, never had the chance to either regret it or revel in it. I was twelve when she died, just a week after announcing she wanted out but with no time to even file the paperwork. She collapsed at church, of all places. Her sweet, kind heart had a defect no one knew about, and her life, her suffering, was over in an instant. My father changed after that, becoming kinder, softer, rewriting their time together as something sweeter than it was. Over the following months, we moved on without her, and eventually Dad moved on, too, but backward, to become the same asshole he was before she died.

Therapista says how you are right now is how you will be forever.

My dead mother now lives in Dad's basement, all her stuff piled high in a corner, her clothes, her toiletries, her ashes. Everything was moved down there years after she died. It's not so much a shrine as it is an inconvenience. Dad uses the basement to store his construction-job tools and generally fix things—his relationship with my mother, the most perpetually broken and unfixable of them all. Across from a steamer trunk of her childhood memorabilia is a tractor engine, an ironing board that needs a new cover, a box of trampoline springs. Mom's boxes, marked DRESSES and TOILETRIES, are all in the way, but Dad won't part with them. He both hates them and treasures them. I feel the same way about her stuff. I like that everything is down there. It brings me comfort sometimes to see her hairbrush and flash to a happy memory—anything to disrupt the memory of her death, in the middle of offering the sign of peace, her collapsing, congregants screaming, me praying. And at the same time, I hate it that she's down in the basement, still trapped in this house she wanted so badly to flee.

I'm looking through a box labeled MOM JUNK, paying my respects in the basement, digging through and finding the old partially melted spatula she used to make me French toast on Saturday mornings. I find the scissors with the blue handles she used to trim my hair between barber visits. I find magazines with pages dog-eared for makeup or dresses she never had the chance to buy. I find her purse, the one she was carrying when she died. It's a peach-pink color, shiny and warped from age and the sad fate of being stuffed in some basement box. Inside the purse is her wallet, the cash gone—if there ever was any—but it's still full of change and balled-up cough-drop wrappers. There's her key chain—her house keys and car key still snugly on the metal spiral. Dangling from the spiral is a little fake-gold locket, oval shaped, about the size of a quarter. It was a gift I'd given her in second grade after my elementary school held a shopping fair. Every parent gave the school a bit of money for their kids to go shopping for Christmas presents for their family and friends. I hold the locket in my hand; it's cold and smaller than I remember. It has engraved swirling on the front, as if it's almost someone's name, and profound scratches on what was once a smooth back, before it was tarnished and scarred by the chaos of Mom's purse. A tiny clasp opens the locket—empty. There's no picture of me or lock of my hair. Maybe Mom didn't even know it opened. But she carried it with love. Inside that empty trinket, the metal shines and I see my reflection on both sides, a man nearly thirty years old, still missing his mom.

"JUNK!" Dad yells, startling me as he kicks a partially used box of bathroom tile at the entrance to the basement. He pauses when he sees me standing at Mom's shrine, my hands holding her old locket. Dad walks up to me and I shift in my shoes, the young coward still in me, still bracing to absorb whatever tantrum he may throw at me.

Clutching Mom's locket, I jam my fingernail under the spiral of the key ring. With each step Dad takes toward me, I spin the locket, spinning, spinning, spinning, until it's free of its binding. I slip it into my pocket as Dad approaches me, my fingertip throbbing under the nail.

Hey, Siri, I want to kill myself with this in my hand.

"I think about your mother every day," Dad says.

"I'm sure," I say, putting the rest of the key ring back in Mom's purse and the purse back in the box, burying it with magazines and kitchen utensils and feelings. I close the box tightly, my little effort to protect her from him. I put pieces of a tractor carburetor on top exactly as I found them.

Hey, Siri, I want out of this basement.

"I think if this kidney cancer kills me," Dad says, "the only good thing will be that I can be up there in heaven with her."

"I'm certain she would not want that," I say coldly, Dad not being one to catch the subtext. We're quiet for a moment, the house above us feeling so big, sounding so quietly loud. I wonder if Dad is happy he finally got the silence he demanded of me all those years. If, after I moved out, he finally reveled in not hearing my footsteps, not hearing my music, grateful that I'd never dance in that home again.

Kathi Kannon haunts this home I grew up in. The tiny plastic molds of her franchised co-stars still exist—sans her—in a toy box tucked deep in a closet in my old bedroom. They mean nothing to me. It's her I always treasured, taken from me years ago, gone at Dad's hands, and now feeling gone from me again, this time at my own hand, my own inadequacies. If only I had been more charming, more prepared to meet her, briefed on how to manage a celebrity. Ugh, *Bruce.*

I've considered telling Dad about my interview with Kathi Kannon, trying to share with him some of my unhappy life, but what's the point? I don't need lectures about careers and money and liberal Hollywood. But I do ask him: "Dad, remember that action figure I had? The lady from the movie *Nova Quest*? Priestess Talara?"

In that basement, all the moisture and memories stick to our skin, leave a taste in our mouths, our warm breath filling in the space left by our few moments of silence. I can't look at my father. I wonder if he heard me. I wonder if he's ignoring me. I wonder, if I did look at him, would he see my childhood face, remember my screaming when he took Priestess Talara away?

"Do you remember her?" I ask again, pressing gently. "In *Nova*

Quest she was played by that actress . . . I think her name was . . . Kathi Kannon?"

Dad says, "Who?"

Hey, Siri, I want to kill myself in Dad's hospital room.

Here I sit, cold, bored, staring at my father's weathered, sliced, and stitched body, and cursing Kathi Kannon for not hiring me, saving me from this. Cursing her for not picking me, cursing *Bruce* for giving me hope, cursing myself for accepting it. It has been eight days since I met her. *Hey, Siri, why can't I let it go?*

My dad survived surgery, of course. Therapista says it's normal to want a parent to die, because we know we'll have that pain eventually—no one lives forever—and sometimes we just want to get it over with. But like smallpox, he persists. He looks so sad in this bed, post-op, his gown askew, his tanned contractor's skin in stark contrast with the bleached white sheets, his hair unburdened of the hairspray he uses to vainly hide his balding. Whose shirt is untucked now?

I lean in toward his bruised body, hear his shallow breathing. "Mom didn't like you. You won't go to heaven with her," I whisper. I feel bold saying it audibly, a courage tempered by scars—I know what happens when I'm too comfortable around him. Sometimes I still feel those pink socks on my feet and my icy regret that I didn't just take the fucking socks off before I went downstairs. Sometimes I still feel angry that I wasn't more careful around his ire, more guarded against him breaking me. There are so many of those moments in my life where he muted me a little at a time. Just like those green metal signposts on the highway leading me home to Perris, I can look back at my life and see the moments building toward my complete cowardice. Two hundred miles, one hundred miles, fifty miles—there are so many childhood moments that are a countdown to my stunted adulthood. There was the episode where he made me wear Mom's underwear. There was the time he made me play tennis even though I had what we later learned was a hairline fracture in my wrist from tripping at school the day before; he didn't care. There was the time he made me sleep on the front porch because I lost my house key. There was the time he tore up all seven pages of a book report because I made one spelling error on page 5 and had to rewrite all of it; perfection, he wanted. And now I wish he was dead, and he's not. And now I wish I was back in L.A., and I'm not. And now I wish I was in a relationship—to have anyone significant in my life other than him—and I'm not.

I lean in again, and now louder I say, "I'm not afraid of you." I sit back and wonder if he can hear all this. If he'll wake and think it's a dream, that some angel spoke to him and his whole worldview will change.

I lean in once more, and even louder I say, "You ruined my life. All we had was each other and you fucked it up. You owe me an apolo—" but a nurse walks in.

I sit back in my chair, blood rushing to my face, blushing, busted.

"Hi, baby," she says, beelining to Dad's chart and clicking her ink pen to start making notes. "How's it going?"

Click, click, click.

She's New Orleans–sized—that is, stout, unkempt in a casual, easy, comforting way.

"He's alive," I say, a little more pert than I intended, than I feel.

"Thank you, Jesus," she says, with that familiar hint of Cajun French still slick on her tongue. She looks from one machine to the next, makes a note. She looks from Dad's wrist to his face, makes a note. She looks from the clock to her clipboard, makes a note. She looks at me, raises her eyebrows. "Any questions?"

I consider for a second. "Are you . . . having a good day?"

"Any questions about the patient?" she clarifies.

"Oh, uhh—"

Click, click, click.

She smiles. "Actually, I'm having a fine day. Thanks for asking. You?"

Some machine beeps. Some patient across the hall coughs. Some spell is cast upon me and I can't even manage a lie.

"Did I interrupt a little chat?" she asks.

"Maybe," I say, embarrassed.

"Don't worry. I interrupt little chats all the time, up and down these halls and left and right. The way I see it, some people are hard to talk to. Some people go through their whole lives unconscious, unaware of other people around them. Sometimes talking to someone when they're asleep is no different than talking to them when they're awake. So I always say, 'Have at 'em when you can.'"

Click, click, click. She tucks her pen in her jacket, nods, smiles, and slips out without another word, marching down halls full of other one-sided conversations, leaving me feeling less alone for the first time in years. I pull Mom's locket from my jeans and hold it in my hand. In the hospital light it looks so trashy, so grimy and bereft, like it belongs back in that basement with her other decaying possessions, forgotten and molding. But its empty encasement holds history. I can still see it dangling from her keys as she drove me to school, can see it twisting around her other keys when she unlocked the front door, her big smile when my childhood hands gave it to her all those Christmases ago. I'm holding this old locket like a rosary, like a magical bean.

I look up at a local newscast on the hospital TV strapped to the wall. It's hard to watch news because I know all the tricks. I know all the ins and outs of what's going on behind the scenes. I think about the hell of my job waiting for me back in Los Angeles—my newsroom, with clocks all over, the incessant tick, tick, tick. We, grunts of the news business, live and die by the second hand, twirling in its orbit and dictating our fate: how much time until we're on the air, how each second is accounted for, how each second is assigned to this story or that, how each second is allocated during commercials—for those seconds, the seconds of commercials, are the most important, for those seconds pay our bills. My livelihood depends on commercials for dentures, life insurance, erection medications.

It has been 691,200 . . . 691,201 . . . 691,202 seconds since I left Kathi Kannon's home.

Dad stirs a little in his bed. I consider trying to coax him awake, but I decide against it.

I'm uninterested in my usual time-wasters, but I turn to them anyway:

Facebook: I scroll through the list of my so-called friends, people I barely see because of my work schedule. I'm free while they're at work; I'm asleep when they're free. I resent them. It's less my friends list and more a cemetery of acquaintances. *Bruce,* ugh.

OkCupid: I stalk but never date. My OkCupid name is MardiGras-Guy, a stupid reference to being from New Orleans, which no doubt makes people think I'll show them my dick for trinkets—not totally inaccurate, I suppose, given my irresponsible sexual history. My dating profile isn't even finished. I have yet to fill in all the lame questions, take the stupid surveys. I just like to look around and see what I'm missing, or not. I'm not available for a relationship, anyway. My life revolves around sleeping. Some guy wants to take me out on a dinner date during the week—it will have to be at three P.M. No one wants that. I don't even want that. It was always much easier to go out on a Saturday night and meet some random guy at a bar and begin my so-called passive suicidal ritual: risky sex, wake up the next morning in a panic that I have HIV, rush to a doctor to get an emergency test. I'm thinking all of this seems way easier than a relationship. But I've never been in one. Not really. What's the point? I know what love looks like, and it's shit, it's lifeless, it's a cold urn in a basement in fucking Perris.

My father is slowly waking from surgery, and I know he's heavily medicated, because he smiles at me. I squeeze out a smile back. *ALWAYS BE*

POLITE! I hear him yelling in my head, the father who lives inside me, the villain of my inner world, and often my outer, despite my best efforts to unburden myself of his worldview.

"You just missed the nurse," I say as his eyes start to open.

"Of course I did," he says, surprisingly calm, present. "Healthcare in this country is shit. Democrats, you know?"

I keep my mouth shut.

"Did they get all the cancer? Did they take out my kidney?"

"They think they got all the cancer," I tell him. "And they didn't have to remove the whole kidney. You're expected to make a full recovery."

Dad's lips quiver. Not even all the manliness in the world can hide some emotions, especially when it comes to himself.

Some people go through their whole lives unconscious.

Even in these comically early stages of his healing, I'm plotting my escape again. It's a record on repeat. I'm once again dying to get out of this hospital and Louisiana, dying to get far away from my father. Sentimentality only travels so far.

776,214 . . . 776,215 . . . 776,216 seconds since Kathi Kannon.

Hey, Siri, maybe I'd prefer to kill myself back in Los Angeles after all.

I rub Mom's locket, feeling the engraving, feeling the scratches, rubbing it like it's Aladdin's lamp, carefully making just one wish.

4

☆

The text message wakes me from my morning's after-work nap.
I'm groggy and disoriented. The room is dark from my blackout
shades, noisy from my whooshing sound machine.

Ding!

My life's biggest and best moments all start as annoying interruptions to my sleep.

What time is it? Where am I? I grab my phone.

UNKNOWN NUMBER: Cockring?

I'm instantly blushing at maximum redness, my body reacting with
heat and a rush of blood to all parts far and wide. My eyes open. My
spine straightens. I stare at my phone. I'm not sure how to respond. Is it
her, is it her agent or manager? Is it a wrong number with just the right
message I need in this very instant? It has been eleven days—950,176
seconds—since I met her. *Hey, Siri, I've been clinging to life, hoping for
this moment, desperate for a do-over, for another opportunity to impress,
to be perfect.* I was giving her twelve days—1,036,800 seconds—before

I ended it, my desire to work for her, to improve my life, to continue my life. And now this?

It's a friendly universe.

Maybe Therapista is right.

I text back.

> ME: Who is this?
>
> UNKNOWN NUMBER: Do a lot of people call you Cockring?
>
> ME: . . .

I wonder how to respond, but there's no time. She's fast.

> UNKNOWN NUMBER: This is Kathi Kannon from the discount bin at Barnes & Noble.

Holy shit, I think, and eke out:

> ME: Hi.

Fucking boring loser.

> KATHI: I urgently need teeth splinter barfs.
>
> ME: . . .

I'm racking my brain. What's she talking about? Am I dreaming? Then I think, *Oh, wait.*

> ME: Toothpicks? You need toothpicks?

No response. I wait, but still nothing comes.

Panic! I hurl myself out of bed and whip open a blackout shade, the sunshine blinding me for a moment. I eventually see my body come into focus in the dirty mirror hanging on the back of my bathroom door. I'm a mess, my hair, my clothes—I'm still in the same outfit I wore yesterday, my depression lately manifesting itself in the pointlessness of washing either my body or my wardrobe.

I reread her message: *I urgently need?*

I roll around the options in my head. Maybe she's having a luncheon and, like, Steven Spielberg is asking for a toothpick. Or maybe she's got, like, Brad Pitt's kids over and they want to make some art project and she's humiliated that there are no supplies. Or maybe she just ate corn. Is this the final test for whether I'd make a good assistant: Do I understand her? Is she timing me? Can I drop everything for this?

I resent it.

And I accept it.

Therapista calls this *duality.*

My head is spinning, my inner world in turmoil.

Hey, Siri, I want this. I want to impress her. This time, I want to be perfect.

I rush to my car. I shoot her a text:

ME: On my way!

KATHI: Cackle Crumpet Cleaners

ME: . . .

KATHI: Hellscafoldspuntar

ME: I'm so confused what do you mean?!

KATHI: Horble twat

ME: Do you need more than toothpicks? I'm at the store.

KATHI: Bap

ME: What's Bap?!

KATHI: Gate code is 2625 spells COCK!

Cue sweating, heart beating, blushing.

I'm dashing.

I'm thinking, *Her gate code is COCK?!*

In Whole Foods on the way to her mansion, I'm buying every kind of toothpick—wood, plastic, assorted colors, mint-flavored, the kind with a point at one end and a flat rounded edge at the other.

I glide through the checkout line. I don't even linger long enough to get the change.

My Nissan Sentra is hitting every pothole in a race to the finish at her front gate, my radio utterly confused by all the rattling of wires. My keys are jingling in the ignition, aided by Mom's locket, which I hooked on to my key ring, neighboring my car key and house key, my efforts to add memories of Mom to my daily life. She's here with me in that little tattered old encasement, as I rush to meet my fate. I'm imagining the sports guy had this same test yesterday, and I want to beat his time.

I approach that magical address, 1245 Beverly Canyon Drive, the numbers stuck onto a common, unassuming mailbox, 1-2-4-5, as if the number 3, a digit fetishized in physics, space, time, religion, was just dropped, and all the other numbers onward throughout infinity are forced to shuffle forward, as if here at this address, the boring old order of common things is unneeded, unwelcomed. As if this place changes things.

That gate.

That keypad.

That *code!*

The front door, unlocked, unsafe.

No one is in the living room aside from Mateo the Moose, resting comfortably above the roaring fireplace, and little leather Emperor Xi and his friends, enjoying the dancing lights from the disco ball above. The animal portraits on the far wall stare at me, oddly encouraging. As I look at the painting that resembles Sean Penn, I'm thinking, *Hi, again!*

I hear something to the left.

I bolt past the dining table and into the kitchen. It's bright and feels surprisingly homey despite being huge. The stove is an industrial six-burner; there are two massive refrigerators covered in pictures and funny postcards; pots and pans are hanging over a marble-top island. The floors are a whole new expanse of wood planks painted lavender with tiny murals of dangerous plants in random spots, all labeled in yellow writing with their species and common name: *Toxicodendron Radicans (Poison Ivy); Oleander (Nerium Oleander); Papaver Somniferum (Opium Poppy)*.

A thin older woman is asleep in a breakfast nook. Asleep or dead. I walk up to her. "Hello?"

"Oh, hi, yeah," she says, jolting up, like she's been awake the whole time. She's cheerful but frail. "I'm Agnes! I have a brain tumor!"

"Hi," I say, still in a panic and not sure how to respond. "I'm Charlie."

"I'm the housekeeper and cook and whatnot," she says, flipping her hair back behind her shoulder.

"Nice to meet you. I'm the new assistant, I think."

"Oh, the guy from Louisiana, huh?!"

"Yeah," I say, looking away, a slight shadow of shame piled on top.

"No, no," Agnes says soothingly, kindly. "Be proud. Louisiana is a good thing. I'm from Louisiana. Shreveport. Kathi likes Louisiana people. Her ex-husband was from Louisiana. My whole Louisiana family works for Kathi. Worked for her for years and years—cooks, housekeepers, grass cutters. Yes, sir."

I can't help smiling ear to ear. Maybe my being a poor and unqualified, undeserving Louisiana boy has actually been an asset this whole time. Maybe this makes all of Perris somehow worth it. Is that another act of wizardry here at this estate, with fireplaces in the summer, birds chirping in the middle of this big city, electrified serenity in the thick of Hollywood—up is down, wrong is right, absurd is magical, Louisiana is cool? This place is transformative indeed. Is everything here just better?

This place changes things.

"Hiring someone, that must have been a tough decision for her," I say.

"Nah. Kathi was struggling with which one of you to pick and she eventually just was like, 'I guess the Louisiana one.'"

I'm thinking, *Well, whatever works.*

Agnes stands and starts to shuffle toward me. She's tall, with a body that looks like that of a former model, albeit somewhat bent and crooked here and there. She appears to be wearing disproportional designer clothes—plaid gray slacks that hang loosely from her hips and a colorful silky blouse made for a much smaller, shorter person— perhaps all hand-me-downs from Kathi. On her feet, no shoes, simply faded black socks that barely stabilize her on the shiny wood floors as she closes in on me, a stranger in her galaxy.

Agnes shakes my hand. "I'm eighty-three years young," she says. "I've worked for Kathi her whole life, since she was a little girl. I took her to all her school events and her first acting job and to the hospital seven times for overdoses."

My eyebrows raise and my mouth opens; words are slow to come, but eventually I say: "Glad to be part of the team."

"Not a big team. It's just you, me, and Benny," she says. "Benny is the handyman who doesn't seem very handy, if you ask me. It always looks like he's just pretending to work, but what do I know? Anyway, I think he lives in the shed because he has nowhere else to go."

"I think I saw him during my interview with Kathi."

"Did he look suspicious?" Agnes asks pointedly.

"Maybe," I say coyly.

"That's him."

"Kathi texted me she urgently needed toothpicks," I say, holding up the Whole Foods bag as proof. "Is she okay? Are her teeth okay? Is Brad Pitt here?"

"Who?" Agnes asks. "No, Kathi was just doing some baking." Agnes points to the counter. "She wanted to test if the cookies were done, but she got tired of waiting for your toothpicks and so I told her to just use a raw spaghetti noodle. They're cooling." She points to the calendar.

I look over to see a cookie sheet sitting on two pot holders. There's a dish towel on top of them and a Post-it note that reads, "Shhhh cookies sleeping."

My tension melts away; I feel both relief and rage.

Duality.

"Okay. I guess everything is all set," I say.

"What? What about the vet?" Agnes asks, cupping her hand around her ear, struggling to hear.

"No. I said, 'Guess everything is all set.'"

"I don't have any pets myself," she says. "Kathi had a bunch of dogs in the past, but they always got killed. Hit by cars or accidentally poisoned by stray pills. One of those damn dogs was sick in the head and had a seizure and died right in front of the hostess while me and Kathi and Miss Gracie were waiting for a table at La Scala."

Miss Gracie.

I swoon at the mention of Kathi's mother—Gracie Gold. I delight at her being mentioned so casually, in everyday conversation, in this, her daughter's home. I can't wait to meet *Miss* Gracie, to see the legend from which all this grew, this—Kathi's current life, and my budding new one. But first:

"Is Kathi here?" I ask.

"She's back in bed," Agnes says. "It was odd for her to be awake so early."

"It's eleven in the morning," I say, my adrenaline slowing down, my senses returning, the smell of the fresh-baked cookies finally reaching me.

"Is it?" Agnes asks, looking around for a clock, as if she has no idea where to find one, as if no one in this six-thousand-square-foot manor has ever had to worry about time, responsibility, accountability.

"Should I get anything else?" I ask.

Agnes shrugs.

"What should I do now?"

Agnes shrugs.

"Who's in charge?"

Agnes shrugs, staring at me. She's innocent, sweet, a brain tumor apparently behind her eyes, smiling, satisfied as her days are spent, literally spent—nearly gone—nodding off in the kitchen of Kathi Kannon, film icon.

And as Agnes turns away from me, turns back and looks up to Judge Judy on the television, I get it. I know who's in charge. Me. I am. I'm in charge. I'm responsible. I'm at the controls. I'm the adult in the room, in every room of this estate. And I know nothing.

Hey, Siri, I want to stake my claim in this home, in this life. I want to make this happen. I want to be an A-plus assistant like I was an A-plus student. Therapista says I'm a people pleaser, I'm an overachiever, I'm a perfectionist in an imperfect world. And I plan to put all those qualities to use immediately.

"Agnes, show me what needs to be done!"

Agnes can barely walk, barely stay awake, and barely show me the routine, the ins and outs of the job I've apparently won.

In the living room, she hands me a Barneys New York shopping bag full of bottles of prescription medications for Kathi's bipolar disorder. I pull out one of the bottles. The pills rattle around as I roll it to read the label. It's so strange to see a celebrity's name on a prescription bottle. It's odd, somehow reductive. Stars, they're just like us: menopausal, depressive, anxious. It reminds me of that out-of-place feeling I got as a kid when I saw my teacher carrying her purse in Walmart, as if that purse—these meds—made my teacher, make Kathi Kannon, somehow more real as people. As if before that, it's like they're not humans, just ideas, concepts.

My responsibilities include feed her, water her, medicate her.

"Every morning you'll go in her room," Agnes says, "wake her softly, greet her nicely with her pills for the day—make sure you get the pills right and don't kill her."

I stare at Agnes. The animal portraits behind me stare at Agnes. She's not joking.

She continues, "For breakfast, Kathi eats a bag of Weight Busters cereal. Dry. Also, bring in a glass of ice with a can of ice-cold Coke Zero. Pour the Coke Zero over the ice while you're in the room so that she hears it fizz and starts craving it, and that will help her wake up."

Agnes shows me the glasses in the bar, the same ones Kathi used to pour me a soda not long ago. "Kathi found these glasses in China. They're probably toxic but just the right size to hold one full can of soda with ice. Sometimes she'll wake up when you go in, and sometimes she'll want to sleep in. Make sure her electronic cigarettes are fully charged and stocked, and good luck." She shuffles away, nearly falling over twice as her slippery socks barely hold her wiry frame to the endangered floors. I'm thinking, *What else in this house is endangered?*

I sit in a Parisian chair and sift through the bag of meds, reading the instructions for each and sorting the daily pills into a pale-blue plastic pill dispenser with seven sections, one for each day of the week. I fill every section. Of course, these are not her assortment for the week, they're her assortment for the day; it's just that this massive number of pills won't fit into a single daily compartment.

Tap, tap, tap, as I put the day's pills in the various blocks. I'm working at an antique coffee table sculpted from a single piece of tree trunk, which sits in the middle of the circle of the leather-chair empire. There's a sculpture at the center of the table that looks like a hunk of driftwood adorned with the kind of garnish you put on a fancy Christmas present instead of a bow. Alas, maybe it's art. I'm just a kid from Louisiana, sitting in my first celebrity mansion, surrounded by more wealth than

I've ever known, more pills than I've ever seen, more uncertainty than I've ever felt.

Tap, tap, tap.

A short time later, per Agnes's instructions, I'm holding a tray with a cold, sweating can of Coke Zero, a full glass of ice, a gently crackling cellophane bag of Weight Busters cereal, and a container with a smattering of daily medications, all rattling as I walk down the hallway to wake a sleeping film giant.

I'm standing outside of her bedroom. The closed door is both disappointingly ordinary and utterly amazing—a lot like her. It's thick old wood, with history and survival in its grain. It has two long stained-glass windows—just shapes, no fellatio here, unlike the front door. It's dark in her bedroom. I can only imagine what it looks like from her point of view, the light out here flirting into her vision from my side of these stained-glass panes.

I knock gently on her door. Nothing. I turn the knob—an antique, wobbly, metal-and-glass door handle with an actual keyhole. I'm certain it's another antique throwback to a long-ago time—you can't get things like this anymore; everything here seems profoundly unique.

Light from the hallway jets into and across her room as I open the door. Things inside start to reveal themselves: a massive pile of clothes on the floor, an elliptical machine draped in evening gowns and a single dangling bra, a nightstand overwhelmed with books and papers and pill bottles and a lamp and a phone that's off the hook. A king-sized bed fit for a queen, *the* queen, *my* queen, my new boss, apparently, now reduced to a lump. She's a single woman and presumably alone in bed, but I'm not totally sure. She's under what appears to be a huge pile of quilts and blankets and throws knitted from the fur of some soft and exotic wild animal—like one of those creatures featured in *National Geographic,* previously living a life of horror, desperately avoiding predators, hungrily hunting for food, dying an early and violent death in a hot and miserable climate—now woven into a flat work of comfortable art adorning the body of an internationally celebrated millionaire.

The room is wall-to-wall blue shag carpet. Her bed looks as if it's made of pages of books, but they're just interwoven scraps of linen upon which pages of classic works of fiction have been printed: Shakespeare, Edgar Allan Poe, Kathi Kannon. E-cigarettes are charging in every power outlet, casting a pulsing, eerie red glow in the air.

"Good morrrrrrrrrrning," I softly speak-sing to her, my voice cracking, not used to this new cheery tone. She doesn't budge. Her body is so entombed in blankets, small and isolated like an island in the middle of a king-sized ocean, it's not possible to notice any movement, any breathing.

"Good morning," I say, louder and even cheerier, hoping she's not dead, which would end my life's rebirth, my new power position, my wresting of my dull life from the clutches of nothingness, before it even began.

"Hi," I say sweetly but more authoritatively. No movement. I swallow, my smile fades. "I brought you . . ." I say, looking down at the ice and soda and pills, ". . . breakfast."

I lean in, my eyes scanning this space where my childhood hero from TV and film has landed as a collection of actual living atoms and molecules.

"Are you dead?" I whisper kindly. (*ALWAYS BE POLITE!* I hear my father screaming in my head.) "Are you dead, ma'am—I mean, Kathi?" I look around for a clue, what to do next, but then I hear something.

"*Mmmmm,*" Kathi groans, and rolls onto her back. "What? Who?"

"I'm Charlie, your new assistant. I'm here. Obviously. I got your toothpicks. They're in the kitchen."

"My what?" she asks.

"And I have your breakfast here," I say, chipper, relieved, nervous, hoping I'm doing all of this correctly. I unsteadily balance the tray on one hand, and with the other I crack open the can of Coke Zero and pour its fizziness over ice. "It's a lovely day. Isn't it great to be alive?"

"I feel like I'm in a cocoon of quiet and not quiet," she says.

"Here's a soda and cereal and your favorite antipsychotic medications. Where do you want them?"

"Anally."

"Ha ha," I say. Literally the sound *ha* and then *ha*, the fakest enthusiasm I've ever heard, the faking of faking of real.

"Oh, my," she mutters, maybe thinking this has been a mistake, and by *this,* I mean me. "You must lighten up, Cockring." She checks out the goodies I'm carrying. "Just put all that stuff on the nightstand."

Beside her bed is not technically a nightstand but a weathered drop-front secretary desk, as if she's the kind of writer who can't bear to be far from her work, even while asleep. But there's no evidence of its intended use. It's covered in candy wrappers, books, jewelry, makeup, a huge lamp with a leather shade featuring cowboy patterns. I start to push the trash aside. I move a few half-full cans of Coke Zero to the back. I hang up her phone receiver.

"Thank you for the job," I say.

She says, "It's not a job, it's a lifestyle."

I continue to collect obvious garbage, a rock-solid half-eaten brownie, 7-Eleven receipts, a crusty spoon.

"What's happening?" she asks.

"I'm just making room for your . . . treats—"

"No, what's happening in the world?"

"It's a beautiful day outside. Life is glorious—"

She turns to me playfully, brushing wisps of hair out of her face, revealing evidence of the kind of night she must have had: thick mascara, glitter on her eyelids, a smudge of lipstick remaining on her lips. "Are any celebrities dead?"

I think for a moment.

She says, "I mean, I know there are dead celebrities in the universe at large, but are there any who are newly dead today?"

"Not that I know of," I say.

"I read yesterday that doctors removed a bird's feather from a boy's cheek. They have no idea how it got there."

I say, "Wow!"

She says, "Do you have any news like that?"

"Not immediately. But I'll get back to you."

"Am I still famous?"

"You're hanging in there."

Kathi chuckles, reaches for her soda, and takes a sip. "I was up all night. I kept getting emails from someone named Linda Kin. Who is that?" she asks, handing me her phone.

I look at her home screen, with 105,271 unread emails and 97 unread texts. My heart palpitates at the slow reveal of the scope of my new duties.

"Linda Kin. K-I-N?" I ask.

"Yeah."

Kathi's emails load and it becomes clear.

"Do you mean . . . LinkedIn?"

"Whoever she is, make her stop!"

I move the emails to her spam folder. She's trying to gift me a sense of humor; I'll try to gift her a sense of order.

"Want to do some writing today?" I ask. "Work on your next book? Do you want me to proofread anything, type anything up?"

"There's nothing to proofread. I haven't written anything. Yet! But we will, Cockring. Don't worry."

"Can I get you anything else?"

"No. Thank you, Cockring. I need to rest a little longer."

"Okay," I whisper, bowing only slightly, barely noticeable, as a servant leaves royalty. "Thank you again for the job."

"You mean the lifestyle," she whispers back, rolling farther away from me, deeper into her wrappings, sinking further into her memory foam and back into slumber.

"Yes, the lifestyle."

I put my hands in my pockets as I back out of her room, my right fingers rubbing my cell phone, my left fingers tracing my keys down to the key ring, to that familiar tiny, oval shape, down to my mother's locket. I'm thinking, *Hello, Mom*. I'm thinking, *Maybe you're really with me*. I'm thinking, *Did you make this happen for me?*

I gently close the door of Kathi Kannon's bedroom, the light retreating slowly from the lump of celebrity, the bed, the nightstand, the elliptical handlebars, the pile of gowns, the lonely bra.

The door clicks shut, and I exhale not just air but my very life force, breathing it out, shoving it from my body as if my heart is so full there's no room left to store anything in my lungs. My body heaves, my face turns red, not from the usual embarrassment or humiliation but, this time, from the physical need to refill my lungs. I left my physical form for a brief, heavenly second and now I'm forced back, that cruel twist of life, of living, that instinct to survive and even to thrive. I take a deep breath in and try to steady myself, my hero behind me, my future with her in front of me. I calm myself, surprised to feel on my face . . . that I'm smiling.

I'm thinking, *Thank you, Kathi Kannon. Thank you for my new life, my new lifestyle.*

5

⭐

My new office is a mansion. Oppressive lighting gives way to streams of sunshine from stained glass. Newsroom noise of police scanners is now silence, save for Beverly Hills birds chirping and squirrels chatting. *Hey, Siri, I want to relax, relish, enjoy this new me. I want to slow down, destress, and be my best, calm, less-suicidal self.* And so far, so good. The first week of my new lifestyle with Kathi Kannon is surprisingly simple. Being a celebrity assistant is glamorous, fancy, easy.

I sort Kathi's pills into a daily pill caddy.

Tap, tap, tap.

I bring Kathi her soda. I open it, pour it over ice.

Fizz, fizz.

I wield Weight Busters cereal, the small oat circles rolling around inside, the cellophane bag making that familiar sound in my hands.

Crackle.

And this becomes my little, luxurious life.

Tap, tap, tap. Fizz, fizz. Crackle.

I'm still feeling like an outsider, an observer, but no worries. I'm new. Feeling like an insider perhaps takes time. For now, I watch Agnes sleep in the dining nook all day. I wave to Benny pretending to do yard work. Kathi stays to herself, mostly in her bedroom, occasionally walking past me to the kitchen. I ask, "Can I get you anything?"

Smiling, she shakes her head *no*.

I get the sense I have to prove myself worthy of entry into the real inner workings of the world's kookiest country club. But I don't really know. I've never been a celebrity assistant before. I've never even *known* a celebrity assistant before. I don't know what this job is supposed to look like. I want to help, and so I do what I know how to do: follow directions.

Tap, tap, tap. Fizz, fizz. Crackle.

Monday, I get a text:

> KATHI: Nano-blap! Please find the nearest and dearest
> and dopest cobbler-arama. My fave-of-the-flave shoes
> have torn—rudely ripping themselves from my pointy
> loin at dinner of a fortnight ago—and the septic sight
> of my tepid tinkle toe gloriously appearing at the table
> nearly caused Frank Gehry to choke on his baby sheep
> dinner blox and think of all the lies people would say
> about me and him were he to die in my weeping moist
> embrace etc.

Translation: Get her shoes repaired, and I do.

Tap, tap, tap. Fizz, fizz. Crackle.

Tuesday, I get a new task. We're in her bedroom. She asks me to get her cell phone.

"Sure," I say. "Where is it?"

She looks up at me, sucks in a draw from her e-cigarette, and exhales, "In a toilet at Barneys."

And off I go to a luxury department store, to the lost and found, and up to a suspicious but handsome concierge who hands me a familiar cell phone. He says it was discovered not in a toilet but simply, mercifully, beside one. It's now wrapped in white tissue paper, tucked in a fancy black Barneys shopping bag as if it's a scarf or wallet. "My regards to Miss Kannon," he says.

Tap, tap, tap. Fizz, fizz. Crackle.

Wednesday, I get the plea for advice:

"Which porno should I send James Cameron for his birthday, Cockring? *Assablanca, Black Loads Matter,* or *Good Will Humping*?"

Tap, tap, tap. Fizz, fizz. Crackle.

Thursday is an adventure:

We're at an eye doctor's appointment so Kathi can get new glasses. She fills out the doctor's standard questionnaire and hands me the clipboard. "Will you give this to the receptionist, Cockring?" I take the form and read over what she wrote as I pass it to the front-desk clerk. We share a smile as she reads:

NAME: Marcia Gay Harden

ADDRESS: Hell

HEIGHT: Negative

WEIGHT: 600 pounds

REASON FOR VISIT: Sexual

Tap, tap, tap. Fizz, fizz. Crackle.

While Kathi sleeps the day away, I'm sitting in one of her Parisian chairs, her medications strewn about on the coffee table, waiting to be sorted and filed into the next day's pill container. I wonder about this place, a home that tabloids have lauded as being ground zero for legendary parties over the years. Did Madonna mingle here? Am I sitting where Anjelica Huston once sat, resting on the edge of the chair so she could lean in and hear some scandalous story being told by Warren Beatty? Which one of them left their drink on the coffee table too long, forever marking it with a circular stain that would give a curator a heart attack—a drink stain on this antique table! Alas, there is no curator here, just a sleeping celebrity, a dying kitchen helper, an unhandy handyman sleeping in the shed (allegedly), and me, a perfect stranger tasked with sorting the medication that keeps film icon Kathi Kannon alive and functioning, mostly. This could be the most important job I've ever had.

From Kathi Kannon's backyard, I call Jackie, my former news boss.

"What do you want?!" Jackie asks. This is how she always answers her phone. She's likely in the middle of managing live shots, keeping a newscast running, and has little time for me and details of my life.

I can hear my father screaming at me: *DON'T QUIT ONE JOB UNTIL YOU HAVE ANOTHER!* And in this rare case, I took his advice. When I got the job with Kathi, I put in for my two weeks' vacation at the TV station. Jackie balked at me taking all that time in one swoop, but she gets it, she relates to needing a break. She knows it'll be a nightmare to fill my shift whether it's one hour or ten days. I wanted to stay in her employ, to keep a two-week buffer in case the Kathi Kannon thing didn't work out, in case something went sideways. But now it's clear to me that I've got this, that I've got Kathi, that we have each other. I no longer need the deadweight of TV news. I can finally quit.

Holding the phone to my ear, I hear Jackie breathing and the bustle behind her, I hear her typing on her keyboard—never a moment's rest in a newsroom. I feel no sense of loss, no sense of missing out. I'm at a mansion, looking out at palm trees and dick sculptures. In my other ear, the free one, the one not assaulted by the phone and noise of the newsroom, I hear Kathi's world—birds, the garbage water fountain, the calm of the wealthy of Beverly Hills.

"I'm not coming back, Jackie," I say.

"Why not?"

"I'm starting a new life," I say, a swell of pride filling my chest, my eyes almost watering with tearful relief, finally being free, finally feeling ownership of my life. "I have a new job. I'm a personal assistant to Hollywood royalty. It's great and it's a fresh start for me and—"

"Yeah, right," she says. "In Los Angeles? Nothing stays fresh. See you back in a few weeks."

"No, no," I argue. "I'm done. I quit. I'm through working in the middle of the night, through working those depressing graveyard hours! I'm better than that! And I'll prove it!"

Silence on the line. I finally rendered her speechless! I look down at my phone. She hung up. But joke's on her. I won't be back.

Hey, Siri, quitting that job feels just as good as I'd always hoped.

My Kathi Kannon workday starts at ten-thirty A.M. and ends around six P.M. It's strange driving back to my apartment after my shift, during a time when I was previously in bed, weary and miserable from a life consisting of sleeping away prime hours of my youth. My keys jingle a bit more merrily—Mom's locket adding to the medley—as I drive past restaurants and cafés filled with people hanging out, having dinner and drinks with their friends. I pass by a mall bustling with people shopping and gawking. How much life did I waste working that overnight shift? Why did I stay so long? *WE ALL HAVE TO DO THINGS IN LIFE WE DON'T WANT TO DO!* Good old Dad, always in my mind with a cliché I don't want to hear.

Tap, tap, tap. Fizz, fizz. Crackle.

Friday, it's noon and Kathi Kannon's estate is quiet. Benny is outside pretending to water plants. Agnes is in the kitchen, sitting in her dining nook, staring out of the window, daydreaming of I-don't-know-what, maybe thinking, like I do sometimes, what would I do if this were my home? If I had these resources? If this were my life? What if I won the lottery? Would I live in a place like this? Yep. I'd take time to myself, sure. I'd travel and buy nice clothes, a new car (apologies to my trusty Nissan). I'd put some money away for loved ones. I'd try to invest in arts and theater. I'd have microdermabrasion on my acne scars, try to lose chunks off my love handles, get a trainer to beef up my biceps and thighs so eventually someone will love me. Sitting in that house, sure, I'd love this life to be mine, and isn't it now, a little?

Kathi is still in her bedroom, resting, from what I'm not sure. Maybe she has full nights, late mornings, secret parties she attends or hosts under moonlight. But there are no signs of a party here today, this morning, last night. No trash. Only sober sunlight and—*tap, tap, tap*—50 mg of this, 100 mg of that, 20 mg of these. The colors are beautiful: pale blues and peaches and reds. Do they purposefully design pills to look artful, inviting, delicious, bipolar beautiful?

After filling the pill containers, I pull out my laptop to kill time. I'm checking Facebook. I'm checking email. I'm checking OkCupid—just looking; I know no one wants me, not yet, anyway. I've only just begun my conversion to a cooler person, after all.

Another hour.

Another hour.

Another hour.

Am I allowed a lunch break? A break from what? I've hardly done anything.

Is this the primary job: waiting around while Kathi Kannon sleeps?

But then she emerges, and I jump to attention. She's dressed, electronic cigarette dangling from her mouth. She's texting and doesn't even look up at me. "I'm going out, Cockring."

"Somewhere fun?" I ask.

"*Vegas.*"

"You're driving to Vegas right now?"

"Not Vegas Vegas, just *Vegas.* I'll be back soon . . . ish."

"Is *Vegas* a restaurant?"

"It's nothing and everything," she says.

"Okay, have fun, I guess. Bye!" I shout as she exits the front door, leaving it wide open behind her. I close the door. I look around. This time of day, in my prior life, I'd be winding down, preparing for rest for the night shift. But this is the new me, trying to live a new life, seeing an unreal amount of sunshine and a change to my face—I'm looking rested, approaching happy.

Another hour.

What if she's gone the rest of the day? The week? The month? I'm now starving and feeling primal cravings for food. Is this the best job ever? Is this the worst job ever? Do I get a lunch break?

I wander into the kitchen. Agnes is asleep.

I wander to Kathi's empty bedroom. I make her bed. If Dad could see me now.

I think of the other me, the one who would stress and worry and simply not eat because—what if something happens?! But . . . *Hey, Siri, this is the new me.*

Fuck it.

I go to my Nissan.

I drive down Beverly Canyon to the shops of Beverly Hills.

I park at a rusty meter on a sleepy, shady street outside of Mickey Fine, the pharmacy where Michael Jackson got the medications that killed him. It's where Kathi has her meds filled and is one of the oldest institutions in Beverly Hills; it still has a greasy diner in the back.

I sit at the counter and order a cheeseburger and fries. I'm relishing the moment, teasing my vanity on a lovely afternoon, looking around and wondering what these other people at the diner would think if they knew they were one degree away from Kathi Kannon, that I am the degree, the key, the connection.

The waiter—a rugged man in a paper diner hat—fills my water glass as my phone vibrates in my pocket. I pluck it out and even the caller ID can't dampen my mood, even a conversation with Dad can't shake my good vibes, and I accept.

"Hi, Dad," I say, hoping he can hear the smile on my face. "How's the kidney?"

"Can you believe I'm not peeing blood?"

I nearly spit out a sip of water. "What?"

"They do all that poking around in there and still my pee is normal. I mean, it's great, it's just weird. Fucking doctors. If healthcare is so easy, why is it so expensive?!"

"Yeah, what's up, Dad?"

"I'm cleaning," he says.

"Good for you."

"Want any of this stuff?"

And he succeeds—my smile fades. "What stuff? Mom's stuff? Why? What's going on? What are you doing?"

"I have too much junk in here," he says. "I need space."

"Space? For what? You have a whole house with no one in it!"

"Maybe I'm sick of it! Maybe I won't be living here forever!"

"Can't you start cleaning other parts of the house that don't involve me? Or Mom's stuff? Why throw it out? What's the rush—" I start, but then feel my phone vibrate. I look at the screen. A text from Kathi.

KATHI: Cockring do I need new socks?

"Dad, I think I have to go. Please don't get rid of anything."

"Why would you want any of this junk?" he asks.

"Dad—"

My phone buzzes again and I steal a glance.

KATHI: Can e-cigarettes cause a heart attack?

"Dad—"

And again.

KATHI: Is ecstasy safe? I'm bored.

"Yeah, Dad, I definitely have to go!"

KATHI: When was my last physical?

"Do you want any of this shit or can I put it on the burn pile?!" he yells.

KATHI: Why do I take the pink pill the shape of a testicle?

"Burn pile? I don't know, Dad. I can't right now. I have to go!" I hang up and stand. Kathi's texts continue rapid-fire and wholly out of the blue, like her mind is racing a mile a minute, like she's been buffering her questions for me and is now sending them all at once.

KATHI: Am I friends with Gene Hackman?
KATHI: What's a chode?
KATHI: Do I like cilantro?

They're little interruptions and big reminders I don't quite know her. I don't quite have all the answers. I'm unable to get her exactly what she needs. Shit!

KATHI: Where is that picture of me with Jean Smart at
       Greenblatt's in 2001? Ish. Maybe 2005?
ME: Will try to get answers!
KATHI: I'm home. Where the fuckity r u?

I throw down some cash for uneaten food and jet, no waving to the waiter, no apologies, no time.

ME: Be right there.
KATHI: I have something for you. Where! R! u?!
ME: Lunching.

KATHI: I am a ball of panic that you abandoned me sob-
    bing a fickle flea.

ME: What? Be right there.

KATHI: I need answers cock.

ME: Sorry on my way.

KATHI: We have to talk.

ME: Uh oh. Am I in trouble?

No response.

I dash from the restaurant, jab my key in the ignition, twisting to start the engine, the other keys and Mom's locket spinning with me in a panic.

My phone buzzes again, and I nearly sideswipe a Beverly Hills traffic enforcement Prius as I realize it's not Kathi calling but my dad again. I send the call to voicemail.

I'm thinking, *Fuuuuuck.*

Traffic.

Gate.

COCK.

Park.

Rush up the hill.

Moose.

Fireplace.

Bedroom.

"Hiiiii," I sing as I enter. Kathi doesn't look up at me. The room is full of shopping bags and takeout food containers. This must be *Vegas:* shopping and eating and spending *Nova Quest* residuals. The room is also full of tension.

"Cockring, you didn't respond to my little texts," she says.

"All those questions? Those were real questions?"

"Why wouldn't they be?"

I search for answers like a clown in a courtroom, but none come.

Kathi continues, "I was with a friend and I had medical questions about that pill and stuff. And also, she had some socks she wanted to give me, but I don't know my sock situation."

"I think it's funny you don't know what medications you're on," I say.

"That's why I have an assistant. Don't you think?"

I nod *yes*.

"I mean, you've been here, what, two weeks? What do you do all day?" she asks.

Embarrassment washes over me. I honestly have no idea what I'm supposed to be doing, waiting every day for detailed instructions that never come. Do I tell her that?

Kathi is staring at me, waiting for answers, and my phone buzzes again in my pocket and I slap it through my jeans, clicking the side button to restore the status quo—tension.

"Do you need to get that?" Kathi asks.

"No, no. Sorry."

I'm thinking, *Dad!*

I'm thinking, *Rage!*

I'm thinking, *Someone kill me!*

"So, what do you do all day?" Kathi asks again.

"Waiting—" I start.

"Waiting for what? For me?" Kathi asks, smiling kindly. "I'm not a leader. I'm a follower. It might look like I'm a leader because I'm in movies, but I'm just a follower who's in movies and I happen to have other followers following me but we're just all confused followers following followers following followers and it's a clusterfuck of following. There's a line of people following me and thinking I'm leading them and I'm just, like, trying to find somewhere to take a nap."

"Oh," I offer with hesitation, uncertain if follow-up questions are helpful or if they just contribute to the follower culture she's telling me she wants to cull.

Kathi pulls back the covers beside her and reveals a new gray cardigan with shiny brown buttons—like they've been carved from polished wood. It's folded neatly, like it just came out of a tissue-lined box. "I got you this gift. Feel it. Feeling is critical."

"You got me a gift?" I take the cardigan in my two hands. It's soft. It's cashmere. It's like squeezing a fistful of feathers. "Why?"

"I need you to step it up," she says.

"Step it—"

"Up. I need you to take this job more seriously."

"I thought it wasn't a job, it was a lifestyle," I say, an attempt at humor, unmitigated.

"Okay, I need you to take this lifestyle more seriously," she says, swallowing my joke and taking the life out of it. "I'm a little crazy and there's not a lot of space in my head for things and it would be helpful if you picked up more slack."

"I'm not doing a good job?" I ask, reality feeling less like a punch to my gut and more like disembowelment.

"No."

"Acting?" I ask playfully, tepidly.

"No."

"Oh. Okay, yeah. I'm sorry. What should I be doing?"

"I don't know. I told you I don't like this kind of employee thing. I'm not a manager. I'm busy maintaining my image as a quirky person."

"But I can't help you if I don't know how."

"If you don't know how to help me, Cockring, that's no help to me," she says, peering at me from over her glasses, making sure her point lands, looking at me as if she's delivering this line in a Quentin Tarantino movie before the bloodshed begins.

I'm thinking, *I'm in over my head.*

I'm thinking, *I can't do this.*

I'm thinking, *I can't go back to my old life.*

"Got it," I lie. "Sorry. I'll dig deeper, and I'm looking forward to the chance to really show you how I can be there for you. I want to be an A-plus assistant for you."

"Great," she says.

"What grade would you give me right now if you had to?"

"I guess an F," she says.

"An F!" I shout in horror.

"A D? I don't know."

"I'll do so much better."

"One more thing," she says, pausing, choosing her words carefully. I'm nervous, I'm vulnerable, I'm dreading what might come next.

She says, "I'm going to need you to stop cutting your hair."

Blank stare. "What?" I say, eyebrows raised, my hand reflexively going to my head, pressing at the curl perpetually unruly above my ear.

Kathi looks up at me, pulls the e-cigarette from her mouth, and says, "I'm going to need you to stop cutting your hair. I think this current way you're cutting it isn't doing you any favors."

Cue blushing, cue confusion, cue challenge. Cue . . . comfort? I've always hated my hair. Always. Never is there a day where I look in the mirror and think I'm nailing it. I blame my shit Louisiana genes. I've asked people all my life what to do with it: No one is ever honest. No one ever has ideas. Every barber butchers it, makes it worse. And here, finally, someone has an opinion on it. Someone, finally, sees me, or at least sees my potential.

"You don't necessarily look bad with the haircut you have now," Kathi says, "but I have a plan for you and I need you to trust me and maybe occasionally hold me, and this is now part of your job, if you still want it."

Her plan is to remake me in her image and likeness. In her style, her look, her crazy.

"Deal," I say.

Maybe this is more of just what I need.

Kathi wiggles in the bed, weaving her legs deeper into the covers, takes off her glasses, lies down, her eyes fixed on the ceiling.

"Last night I dreamed I was feeding an eagle and I was a little bit afraid of it, but I kept feeding it anyway. It had very short feathers and was buzzard-like and sassy and reminded me of you in some strange but also beautiful way. It felt real. Was it real?"

My mind is racing, my adrenaline is pumping, or excreting, or whatever it does when I'm teetering on the edge of something important, something that feels important.

"It was absolutely real," I say to her.

She smiles, takes a deep breath, some comfort washing over her. "Enjoy the sweater."

"This seems like more of a bribe."

"Enjoy the bribe," she says, rolling over and back into her amazing mind. "And remember, if you cut your hair you're fired."

Fired. Her reminder that this job is not just a job. Now I have duties and subtext. To show her I'm not a shitbird. That I want this job, this change, this lifestyle. That I don't want to go back to TV news, to nights, to nothing. That I'm at risk of losing this, this weird magical position in this weird magical place, of having to go crawling back to the TV-news world, to see Jackie's smug face, to beg her to put me back on the schedule, put me back in the dark, in the night. If I can even go on living at all.

I leave Kathi's bedroom and sit back down on one of her Chinese Parisian chairs. I can feel my hair growing by the second. By the minute. By the hour. Sitting, hungry, empty, still not knowing exactly what Kathi Kannon, film icon, really expects of me, still not knowing exactly what I need do to make her happy, what I need to do to keep this job, this suddenly fragile new lifestyle.

Hey, Siri, I need help.

I pull out my phone and see my pathetic reflection in the glass. A push of the home button pulls up the colorful apps, and the cheery designs seem to mock me. I look at my voicemails—three new messages from Dad—all surely deletable. His timing has always been perfect. I call him back.

"Just get rid of whatever you want," I say.

"I don't care," I say.

"Nothing matters," I say, my other hand clutching my keys, my thumb rubbing, squeezing, nearly crushing Mom's locket.

6

☆

'm about to lunch with film icon Kathi Kannon and Rita Wesson, a former child actor—Kathi worked with her many times in the early years—now turned go-to crisis publicist for emergency (and celebrity) cases only. She's actually more like the opposite of a publicist: Her job is to keep her clients *out* of the press. That straight heartthrob caught with his gay lover—he paid for Rita's house in Montauk, and you'll never know he's a happy queer. That bleached-blond Disney star photographed smoking a joint while driving down Sunset Boulevard— she paid for Rita's Bentley, and those scandalous pictures will never see the light of day. That beloved Oscar-nominated grandpa accused of embezzling from his charity—he paid for Rita's newest face, and, well, every mysteriously missing dime is now enthusiastically accounted for.

"Please drive faster, Cockring," Kathi says.

"Sure," I say, pushing the gas harder.

Hey, Siri, I want to impress. I want to be the best assistant. I want to rescue my failing grade.

I'm nervous to meet Rita, sure. But I love an outing. I'm grateful for the few moments in this job where I have a clear objective, a clear task to accomplish. Step one: Drive Kathi to our lunch. Easy. I mean, easy enough. I'm still anxious having to drive her Lexus, the first one I've ever been in, much less behind its wheel. I'm careful with her in the car, as I would be if carrying glass, flowers, puppies. I yield to everyone. I let other cars ahead of me at STOP signs. I stop at yellow lights.

"If you stop at one more yellow light, Cockring, you're fired."

"You are precious cargo," I say. "I'm trying to keep you safe and—" I look over and she's glaring at me. "I mean to say . . ." I correct myself, "sure, got it!" I nod to her and to myself, reassuring me that clear instruction is good and helpful and an antidote to my floundering, my wondering what on earth to do, what on earth Kathi Kannon wants from me.

The lunch outing plays out exactly as one would imagine—valet parking, escorting Kathi into Katsuya in Brentwood, eyeballs turning toward us, fans looking at her, looking at me. We pass through the glass doors and there's Rita, in leather pants and hair that only looks so perfect when it's treated to a blowout at least three times a week. That producer accused of peddling child porn—he pays for her hair care.

Kathi and Rita make eye contact and are drawn together like magnets, Rita awkwardly complimenting Kathi's figure and Kathi curiously observing Rita's hair, pinching a clump of it between her fingers and mumbling something through gritted teeth like, *Don't you look pretty.*

I'm waiting for my moment to be introduced to Rita when the Katsuya hostess gets my attention. "May I help you?" she asks kindly, unfazed by the mini-spectacle brought on by our entourage convening before her.

"Table for three, please," I say. The hostess looks down at her iPad and starts tapping away, entering numbers and swiping to reveal a map of tables, the layout of the bar, and, finally, a lower-level area with a few booths.

Kathi reaches out and grabs my forearm, softly squeezing it—squeezing it or wiping her hand on it, who can be sure. "It'll just be a table for two, Cockring," Kathi says to me, her other arm still entwined with the lovely Rita's.

The math is brutal—a subtraction, a cut. And the one severed is mercilessly me.

"Right, of course," I say, blushing, learning my place in a painfully hot instant. I turn back to the hostess, shrugging like it's something that happens all the time, me being surgically excised from a lunch that has been living its life as an elaborate fantasy in my mind over the last twenty-four hours, now dead in a fraction of a second.

The hostess turns to Kathi and Rita; I no longer exist. "This way, ladies," she says pointedly, the air from her movement toward them blowing my hair back like a fart scene in a campy comedy. She leads Kathi and Rita to their subterranean table, this entitled hostess, her perfume mixing with the smell of the sushi and my humiliation. My stomach growls as I look down at the coral-colored valet ticket still in my hand, that ticket to an event that will never come.

PEOPLE WILL ALWAYS DISAPPOINT YOU! I hear my father yelling, the same way he yelled it on the soccer field when I was a kid, not to me but to my teammates, while pointing to me and teaching the other boys that I was their weak link. That I was the person who would always let them down. That I was the reason we lost the game, that I was the disappointment, that they couldn't count on me to move the ball up the field. And yet is he right? Just as I constantly disappointed him and my teammates, do I disappoint Kathi Kannon? Is this our human curse, all of us forced to share a planet and none of us satisfying one another? I wish to prove my father wrong, to prove that there is an order to this chaos. Therapista says I only need to prove it to myself.

I step outside the restaurant and take a seat near the valet stand, on a wood bench that looks as out of place as it is uncomfortable. I imagine some designer architect balking at it, screaming, *What is that doing here outside of my beautiful restaurant?! I don't care if people need a place to sit! Tell them to go eat at Wendy's!*

I make eye contact with a young woman sitting beside me and I force a smile, wondering if she's judging me, if she saw my recent rejection, if she's going to ask me about Kathi and Rita and my new, fancy life.

"You must be Charlie," she says, in her bright-yellow tank top and black leather pants, shockingly similar to the ones Rita is wearing. I give her a look up and down, racking my brain to figure out her identity, when she catches me staring. "Oh . . . yeah, these pants. Such an awkward coincidence. Rita bought two sizes of these and this pair didn't fit her, so she gave them to me. When I showed up to take her to lunch today, she was wearing hers but there was no time for us to change, so we're kinda twins. Sick, right? Hi! I'm Jasmine. I'm Rita's assistant."

"Oh," I say, pulling myself together, wiping oil off my forehead, arching my shoulders so my anxiety back-sweat doesn't wick onto my shirt.

"You and I emailed about setting up this lunch today," Jasmine says, almost mockingly.

"Yeah, of course. Nice to meet you."

"Did you think you were having lunch with the two of them?"

I look at her with intent, irritation that she would bring up my embarrassing moment, a spoil that now makes it impossible to pretend it never happened.

"Just now," Jasmine continues, almost belligerently, "I thought I heard you ask the hostess for a table for three and then Kathi said two—"

"Yeah, yeah," I say, defeated. "You heard correctly. You are accurate. Yeah. I was cut out at the last moment."

"You were always cut out. You just realized it at the last moment," Jasmine says. "I can tell you're new. How's it going?"

"Great. Fine. Yeah," I say, wondering if she can read that lie on my face, too. "It's just, I'm mostly in a stasis of constantly asking, *What's happening?*"

"When I first started, I went to Rita's closet to start cleaning. I was taking initiative, you know? And she had all this shit in there, like dusty old garbage, a disgusting backpack, like homeless-people shit. I started unpacking the backpack and found filthy clothes and candy wrappers and ticket stubs for Burning Man—I figured she must have gone and not wanted to deal with the mess so she just stuffed the dirty bag in her huge closet. So I emptied the bag, sorted it all out, put the junk in a trash bag, and was about to throw it out and wash the clothes when Rita stopped me. The bag belonged to her dead brother. He passed away a few months after he went to Burning Man, and this was the bag he took there. It was like a time capsule of a treasured life and I was about to destroy it! Thank God she stopped me." Jasmine shakes her head, reliving the moment. "It happens. We don't know what to do so we do what we think is best and it's a fatal error. Having initiative can be deadly."

I drop my face into my hands. "Yes! I feel like I'm the boss to my boss and no one is managing me. And then I get a job review and I'm sucking at it, but all the job responsibilities seem written in invisible ink in a notebook that no one can find." I look back up at Jasmine. "I'm like Alice in Blunderland."

Jasmine smiles and shimmies her head so her bangs reset perfectly. "You'll get the hang of it. This job is mostly crushing humiliation and, based on what happened with the hostess back there, it looks like you're able to handle that just fine."

I'm now feeling the sharp edges of the bench cutting into my thigh, marking my skin red with the pattern of my jeans, wishing that the elitist restaurant architect had conceded to putting a designer bench out here, one that's more comfortable than the one I'm resting upon right now.

"The job, I love it. And I hate it," I say, quickly adding, "Sometimes! I only hate it sometimes. And *hate* is the wrong word. I mean, I always love it and sometimes it's . . . tricky. You know?"

Jasmine's eyebrows rise. I can't tell if she's busting me—ready to tell on me, throw me under the bus to advance her own standing with her boss and mine—or if she's just heard me utter some kind of red flag.

"You love it and you hate it?" Jasmine asks.

"Don't you?"

"I think you're ready," she says.

"Ready for what?"

"We all know how you feel," she says.

"We?" I ask, as if interrogating her, as if my worst fears are confirmed and I'm on camera, on a reality show broadcasting my many mistakes to a laughing world audience.

"*We,* as in other assistants," Jasmine says.

"What, is there, like, a celebrity-assistant union or something?"

"No! A union? Don't be ridiculous." She leans in close to me. "It's more like a secret club."

I smile, warmed with a hope that I've found a tribe, a team, a tether to which I can cling and find answers and guidance. I flick the valet ticket between my fingers as if it's a winning card at a casino, like it's an ace and I'm the coolest of guys, about to slap it down on the poker table and clean house.

I say, "Tell me everything."

Mother. Fucking. *Bruce.* I see his perfectly shaped haircut from afar and regretfully recognize it instantly. I'm standing outside a bar on Melrose called the Village Scribe and can see him through the windows—that broad back, that dark hair, that unmistakable fade. First I thought it could be a mirage, someone else, what are the odds he's here? But then, the math. I'm here to meet Jasmine. I'm here to meet her Assistants

Club. And, who could forget, Bruce is an assistant, an executive assistant, to be exact.

Bruce turns to see me enter just as I check my fly to make sure it's zipped up.

"Hey, baby!" he yells. "Your dick okay in there?"

"Thank you, yes."

"So you know Jasmine?"

"Yeah. Are you in—I don't know what you call it? Do you call it an assistants club?"

"I call it the 'network the fuck out of your life day and night so you can get ahead, because it's proven the more you work the net, bro, the more options you have to slip and slide into that big-money office' club."

"God," I say disgustedly, aloud, uncontrollably. "Been promoted yet?"

"Not yet, baby," he says. "I wouldn't be here if I was. Soon, though. Meantime, welcome to work drinks."

"Welcome to what?" I ask.

"Work drinks. It's basically networking and comparing cock sizes, but no one wants to call it that. And it's better than calling it just 'drinks,' because that could imply it's a date, which it's not, although, who are we kidding, we're all young and horny, right?"

"Yes. All of us. Right. Definitely," I say, my body stiffening with anxiety.

"Get you a drink, Frodo?"

"Please call me Charlie."

"Oh, shit. Nicknames not your thing? You might be in the wrong business."

"Where's Jasmine?" I ask.

"They're all in the back," he says. "I'm just getting a drink. What can I get you? Dignity? Integrity? What do you need? Intelligence? Looks like you could use some self-respect?"

"Bruce, screw you, okay—" I start to walk away, and he grabs my shoulder.

"What, what?" he says. "Those are the drink names." He points to a chalkboard of overpriced libations with, sure enough, names like Self-Esteem and Awareness.

"What's your poison?" he asks.

I look up at the options, and say, "Truth." It's a pineapple-and-rum drink with grenadine, a splash of soda water, and a very gay cherry on top. Apropos.

Bruce raises his hand. "Yo!" he yells, the bartender turning to him instantly, smiling and rushing over. Beautiful people have it so easy. "Truth!" he shouts, and the bartender nods and gets to work.

Every time I try to order a drink at a bar, I have to wait at least twenty minutes, sweating it out over whether someone is going to cut in front of me, forcing me to suck it up or, sometimes, to abandon that spot in agonizing defeat and go to another part of the bar and start all over. My greatest fear is I'll stand up for myself and yell, "I'm next!" and then get beaten up. But, *Bruce* thrives with utter ease, endless confidence. I hate him.

Moments later, Truth in hand, I'm heading through a crowd of drunks, Bruce leading the way and turning back to me now and then to fill me in: "The so-called Assistants Club is less a club and more like an endless email chain," Bruce says. "It's basically like thirty or forty email forwards in front of the subject line, because whenever an assistant sends some request, everyone just replies to the same old thread."

"What do you email about?"

"Whatever you need, bro. Like, 'Any recommendations for a high-end stereo-system tech?' Or, 'Who do you guys use for at-home tailoring?' Or, 'Where's the best spot for an abortion?' You get it. The email chain dates back years—a veritable Yelp for the best colonics, caterers, cocaine. Everyone's on it, new assistants, old assistants, dead assistants."

I stumble my way past a table of drunk Hollywood types—a lady wearing sunglasses inside, a man wearing a scarf with a short-sleeve T-shirt.

"Yesterday," Bruce says, "I opened my email to one that read, 'Who wants to have work drinks with Kathi Kannon's new assistant?' I was like, *Yeah, my boy!*"

We pass the kitchen, the bathrooms, and slip into a back room decorated with black fabric walls and polished brass sconces casting a golden glow upon everyone inside. The crowd is waist deep in conversation and neck-high in alcohol.

"Time to revel," Bruce says, putting his arm around me, spilling some of his drink on my pants. "Time to recover from the salacious thing that binds us, the common thread that links all of us together, which is not so much having famous or powerful bosses but being fucked by them every day, amirite?!"

"What?" I ask, wiggling out of his half hug.

"Not literally—" he starts, his face turning sour that I'm not following his every bro-ism.

"Baby!" Jasmine yells, approaching me from behind. "Don't talk to Bruce too long. You know, he's an *executive* assistant, so he thinks he's better than you. Come." She pulls me from him. He waves goodbye easily, knowing I'll be back, that he's curated himself an orbit. Beautiful people, they're never really alone. *Truth.*

"Who needs him anyway," she says, she lies.

"Yeah. Him and his talk about silt and all that, right?"

"What the fuck is silt?" Jasmine asks.

"Oh. Oh, nothing."

Jasmine takes me to the only corner of the room—the other walls are rounded—leaving us at the point of a teardrop. We sit on a crushed-velvet oversized sofa, crushed by what—big Hollywood deals, first loves, breakups? We're shoulder to shoulder as she whispers into my ear all the dirty details of the many members of this secret club, zeroing in on her targets like a sniper and popping off

shots of critical information about each assistant and, more important, about each assistant's employer. Jasmine points brazenly to this
one and that: a guy carrying two drinks, a woman with an Hermès
scarf, a bro in a suit jacket with shorts. She flicks her hands and rolls
her eyes, commenting on each of them while they're just feet away,
though it could be inches—it doesn't matter; they're all in their own
networking universe.

"That's West," Jasmine says, pointing to a dowdy brunette wearing a
man's sport coat and nursing a flute of champagne. Her body is actually
shaped a bit like a W, her torso thick and her arms long and thin. "Her
boss is an iconic singer with an even more famous drinking problem.
And this singer, she actually hired an assistant on each coast, but she
can't remember their names so she just calls them East and West. West
loves being a posh assistant. She only drinks champagne. She's a lifer."

"A lifer?" I ask.

"West will be an assistant forever. It's her calling." Jasmine turns to
another curved section of the room, pointing her chin at a guy wearing all white. "He doesn't want to be a lifer but probably will be. We
call him House. He was hired by a certain divorced Real Housewife,
who really can't afford an assistant. So this so-called Housewife, she
uses her kids' child support to pay his salary." I look at House and his
brand-new white sneakers, which match his white belt and the white
bandanna tied around his neck. "That drink House is drinking is paid
for by money intended for two cute kids' school supplies, sports equip-
ment, class field trips."

Shaking her head, looking at a dimly lit twenty-something across
the room, Jasmine says, "We call him Titanic, that guy over there,
swathed in Gucci and acne. His boss was a big teen heartthrob. Titanic
got hired because, with all that acne, he won't steal women from the
boss, and the Gucci is all from the boss's scraps. Also, Titanic's boss,
he only hires male assistants who are his exact same size. This way, the
assistant can be a perfect stand-in during dreaded wardrobe fittings or

shopping sprees. Titanic also shares the boss's sense of smugness and entitlement, if you ask me."

Turning to the right, Jasmine points fearlessly to a woman in a wheelchair. "She was hired by an aging handsome leading man who is now a leading has-been, a former James Bond type. The rumor is he wanted a physically disabled assistant to soften his celebrity image, to make him look kind, but then he had to hire another assistant to assist the wheelchaired assistant, and now it's a living sudoku of who's carrying the luggage to the car, does the limo have a handicapped lift, who's making sure the red carpet has a ramp?" Jasmine shakes her head. "Both assistants are here tonight, one occasionally rolling the other across the room. It's nuts, but they're nice. We call them Bond 1 and Bond 2."

The crowd of assistants lingers and sways back and forth like seaweed in a current, like a palm tree farm in a strong wind. Besides personal assistants, there are *executive* assistants here, as well, but they don't sway like the others. They're sturdy and grounded, or look that way. "The assholes," Jasmine calls them. "You already know Bruce. The other assholes you can identify by their suits."

Clustered with Bruce are a couple other guys and one lady, all in some version of navy with loud shoes—loud not from color but from the click-clack they make while crossing the bar.

"That guy works for the head of a failing studio," Jasmine explains. "The other guy assists an attorney for famous rapists. And the woman is an assistant to a top agent at you-know-where."

"No," I say, "I really don't."

"Very good," Jasmine says, winking.

"No, no," I say. "I have no idea. I studied journalism in college."

"Guys!" Jasmine yells. "Come meet our new baby!" She stands and motions toward me. I stand, and I brace myself as a sea of greedy faces approach to see what my life may yield for them.

They all come at me at once, these assistants, my new teammates, jutting out their arms for handshakes or fist bumps. I hardly catch any of their real names, not that it matters. All of them go by some twisted version of their employment, all of them strangely, proudly using their nicknames, their Hollywood identities—maybe the only identities that matter—West, Titanic, House, Bond 1, Bond 2.

Others trickle in during the night. Crooner works for a pop star, and you can tell—he's got hot-pink hair extensions and glitter nail polish, like he's ready to be in a music video. Friend is a big older guy who works for a former star of a must-see TV show—Jasmine says he got hired as half assistant and half security. Red works for a fiery comedienne and may as well take the stage herself the way she rants as if she's doing a one-woman show.

"Clean their closets every week," Red spills, whipping her large head back and forth so vehemently in an effort to make her point, I'm scared it will snap off her thin neck. "Take their name-brand shit, the good stuff they don't want anymore, the swag they'll never use, and sell it at recycled-clothing stores, online, on street corners. It's like printing money!"

"Always use your personal credit card to make purchases for them and then get their accountant to reimburse you," Titanic tells me, his sweet face flushing from either the acne or the excitement of talking about low-grade embezzlement. "That way, you get all the credit-card points. Like, I book all of my boss's private planes with my Visa and now I have 976,000 miles racked up. I've also got points for hotels, rental cars, Yogurtland." He holds up his glass of champagne as if saying, *Cheers,* but he's mostly met with blank stares, Titanic not being one of the more popular assistants at our séance, our conjuring of the secrets of the dead-souled living celebrities who help us pay our rent.

"When you order from the personal chef," Friend says, pulling up on the waistband of his size-36 pants, "always order a little more than the family needs, and then there's extra for you to take home and you're eating gourmet cooking for free."

Their advice, they all give it freely, but they also want to take. They want to know not how I got the job with Kathi Kannon, or even why, but what I'm getting out of it: What's the pay, what are the hours, what are the perks? They're like sharks circling my position, as if they think I may not survive, as if they may want a bite if I don't quite cut it in these first weeks. *Hey, Siri, I want them to be wrong.*

No one is interested in the minutiae of Kathi Kannon herself. None of these bleary-eyed modern assistants care about the details of her celebrity. They already know the big picture: mansions, money, mess. They get it. The broad strokes are apparently the same at all these jobs. Instead, they want pity, attention, to make sure the hard edges are just soft enough so they can amuse the world with their stories of martyrdom at the hands of beloved cultural rulers (for better or worse), back-dooring compliments as reminders that they're important, their existence imperative, and they're ostensibly a coveted arm's length from the spot the rest of the world would die for: sitting at the right hand of the Holy Star.

Friend grumbles of his employer, "She once asked me to have a water softener installed in the house. I found the best brand. I spent thirty thousand dollars of her money. The next day she told me, 'Now the water is too soft.'"

West takes another sip of champagne and rats on her boss: "I've never seen her drink a glass of water. Never. She pees straight champagne—and the good stuff, not this crap," she says, with no sense of irony as she guzzles another gulp.

House elbows into the conversation: "I have to go to Whole Foods every day and text my boss pictures of the salad bar so she can pick out exactly which items she wants me to include in her lunch."

Red, not to be outdone, whips out her tale of martyrdom: "Well, I cook chicken and rice for her dogs to eat for breakfast and lunch and dinner. I feed them; I walk them. They're so happy to see me on Monday mornings that it makes me think there's a chance she doesn't feed them at all over the weekend!"

Crooner stops biting his glitter nails for a moment and shouts, "You get weekends off?! I was getting so many text messages from my boss on my days off—'What's the Wi-Fi password?' 'Can you unclog a sink?' 'Where's my hair gel?'—I literally just moved into one of his guest rooms. For real. I gave up my apartment, sold my furniture, and now live in a mostly empty wing of his mansion, and I don't even think he knows I'm there."

These other assistants, they're all sharing their horror stories with a slight smile, these weary travelers, who wink to their knowledge that they're complaining about the weather in paradise, their wallets full and their arms outstretched; I wonder how many of them are like me, wearing bribes from their bosses, little gifts to encourage them to work harder, keep secrets, stay drunk on a gatekeeper's power. All these people complaining, they're also in awe of their own lives beside their golden idols. I'm thinking, *How much am I like them?*

"How do you know what to do all day?" I ask the group.

All these eyes stare at me and all these jaws drop—not with wisdom but with shock.

"No one told you?" West asks.

"Told me what?"

"No one left you an Assistant Bible?" House asks.

"A what?" I wonder aloud, a fool at the bottom of a well.

"An Assistant Bible is a document that tells you everything about your boss," Jasmine says. "It includes their likes, dislikes, passwords, allergies, medications, important phone numbers, airline frequent-flier miles, rules and policies, et cetera, et cetera. Every time an assistant leaves a job, they hand the Bible down to whoever is replacing them. You don't have that?"

"No," I say, playing a victim. "I think I replaced one of her fuck buddies."

"Work on an Assistant Bible right away," Crooner says.

"And the rest should be easy," Red says, bobbing her head so intensely I'm not sure if it's how she likes to make a point or if it's a medical condition.

"Easy? Am I missing something?" I ask. "Once I have a list of her passwords, what am I supposed to do all day?"

"These jobs are not about *doing*," Jasmine says, touching my knee. "That's not the hard part. These jobs are about *being*. Rule number one is simply being there the second they need something. Of course, they want the daily tasks done and whatnot but never at the expense of— nothing is more important than—being there for them."

Smiles break across all of their faces. They all nod. They are living these tales, these unverifiable tidbits of tawdry, these little living anecdotes who ease the pain of their boss's celebrity, who dose their famous employers with the cures of commonality, banality, of the everyday.

"Just be there for her, baby. Cheers," Jasmine says, and this time everyone lifts their drinks.

"Cheers," I say, shoving my drink toward theirs, and among the ringing of cheap barware a bell goes off inside me. I'm thinking, the thing Kathi wanted while I was trying to eat a cheeseburger and fries at Mickey Fine, the thing I failed to give her that upset her, I now get it. She wanted me to be there. I realize that *being*, the thing Therapista says is hardest for me to do, is exactly what's needed at this job. I have to *be*: to accept life as it happens, to be still and rest in knowing the universe is friendly, that good things will come, that good things are already here, that "good things" include tidying her house, getting her car serviced, sorting her pills, surrendering my needs to hers.

My job responsibilities include proving my worth, growing my hair, becoming what she wants of me. I look at Titanic's clothes. I look at Bond 1 in her wheelchair and Bond 2 standing behind her, both of them happily following along the absurd game in which they're immersed. I watch Jasmine relish her moment as the leader of these others, and I'm thinking, *Time to get to work.*

I savor my Truth and close my eyes and see myself in Kathi's bedroom, in Kathi Kannon's life.

I imagine her mess.

I imagine her chaos.

I imagine her crazy.

I'm thinking, *From now on, this is my mess, my chaos, my crazy.*

Hey, Siri, I want to clean it all up.

7

☆

oday is my new first day. My *real* first day. I'm wearing
my bribe—my gray cardigan, this cashmere costume, this
buttoned-up bowing-down to my efforts to improve my failing assistant grade. Kathi Kannon doesn't come with an owner's
manual—yet.

As I prepare to clean up her life, my thoughts naggingly remind
me of my dad cleaning up his. I think about him tidying our old Perris house, making an empty home even more empty, fighting with the
garbageman over just how much of my mother's possessions he can
have hauled away each week. Fighting with nature as he tries to burn
whatever he can; his burn pile is a joke—Louisiana humidity keeps
everything wet, so his trash pile never actually burns, just grows. Dad,
finally trying to clean the house, burn the trash, cut the baggage, it's all
decades too late.

I'm purging, too. Purging the ideas I had about this job with Kathi
Kannon. I'm trashing what I thought I knew about my role and getting ready for a new approach. I'm still mourning the losses no doubt
piled at the front of that red-clay driveway—imagining Mom's clothes

in trash bags, her old melted spatula in a landfill, her memory crushed by garbage-truck hydraulics. But fuck Dad. I was helpless then and I'm helpless now. I have to let Mom go and orient to a new North Star. I have to look forward. I have to believe Mom would want it that way. I have to look to Kathi Kannon.

This is where my writing background comes in handy.

This is where certain policies become clear.

This is where the first of my celebrity-assistant rules are written in a Google doc I dutifully title "Assistant Bible." This mansion has a tennis court and a pool house and groundskeeper's quarters but no human-resources office. I'm going to write my own job description, my own duties, seize control of this operation for real, give this a real shot, no more waiting around. I'm doing . . . *and* being.

Assistant Bible Verse 1: Get information! I find answers to all her questions to date: "Yes, you could use more socks; e-cigarettes are not known to cause heart attacks, but I'll make a cardiologist appointment anyway. Don't do ecstasy. Or any drugs. You're sober, right? I'll schedule you a physical. The testicle-shaped pink pills are hormones for lady functions. A Google Images search shows that you and Gene Hackman met at least once, because you were photographed together at a party in Aspen. A chode is a fat penis. There's cilantro in La Scala salads, which you eat, so I assume you're tolerant. And I'll search for the Jean Smart picture."

Assistant Bible Verse 2: Merge. I add her iCloud account to my phone and input her contacts, calendar, Safari bookmarks. No more scraps of paper with appointments. I need her contacts and bookmarks synced with mine to get my job done, so I can answer Kathi's questions: "What's Dr. Miller's cell number?" "When are we going out of town?" "What's that website with those things I hate in that store I love?" Merging phones, merging lives.

With Kathi's contacts at hand, I'm filled with power. I can reach out to any assortment of famous people—though sometimes, to get to

Kathi, the stars call me. I speak casually with Shirley MacLaine, asking her about the weather, of all things, while stalling so Kathi can finish eating a scoop of Magnolia Bakery banana pudding. I take a call from Sean Hayes and make him hold while I explain to Kathi who he is. Beverly D'Angelo calls me frequently, though there isn't much time to chat; before I say, "Hello," she says, "Where is she?"

Assistant Bible Verse 3: The personal assistant should never give a celebrity drawers, nooks, crannies, crevices, folds. The personal assistant knows the celebrity will stuff everything into anything, and when they ask you for it later, you won't be able to find it.

Tap, tap, tap. Fizz, fizz. Crackle.

Every inch of Kathi Kannon's estate is filled with photos and memorabilia: Stacks of casual snaps from birthdays and literal Hollywood history, with living and dead actors alike captured forever in old Polaroids and black-and-white lithographs. Pictures of the pictures before they're the pictures you see published. The no-makeup, no-wigs, bareboned, and vulnerable snaps any tabloid would pay top dollar for. In one drawer, smashed together black-and-white images of a past generation. In another, crumpled images of another generation. Pictures of parties. Young Penny Marshall sitting on chairs where just hours ago I was sorting Kathi's pills. Fresh-faced Robin Williams wearing a chicken costume in Kathi's kitchen. Ageless Sally Field sitting at Kathi's piano, tickling keys, with some quip that left bystanders laughing. The inventory of her life is staggering.

In her bathroom sit vintage magazines with Miss Gracie Gold on the cover, young and fresh and holding baby Kathi, the two of them posing for the cameras as naturally as the rest of us breathe. There are dozens of these magazines, marking the multitude of moments of attention Kathi and Miss Gracie have received their entire lives. I go on Amazon and order magazine protectors to keep each one preserved, safe, so they don't accidentally get pee on them. I'm certain Miss Gracie would appreciate it more than Kathi, me preserving their picture-perfect legacy of mother-daughter devotion, though the reality is more complicated. Miss Gracie seems less a mother and more of a brand. I have yet to meet her. Kathi is keeping a little distance between us for reasons I have yet to discover. So many mysteries here, including why everyone, even Kathi, refers to her as "Miss Gracie." When Kathi's iPhone rings, the caller ID says "Miss Gracie," because that's how Kathi has entered it. It doesn't say "Mom."

Besides magazines with my boss on the cover, throughout the house are other less sentimental bits of clutter—gifts, swag, cell phones, designer scarves and gloves, dozens of pairs of eyeglasses: Prada, Gucci, Dolce & Gabbana—all unopened. Even the little towelettes for cleaning the lenses are still in their safe plastic packaging. She approves me donating them to Agnes and Benny and Goodwill.

I note Kathi's favorite toiletries. The moisturizer, the makeup, the boring essentials: Q-tips, perfume, hairspray. I clear a cabinet under her bathroom sink of old makeup and unopened hand-soap samples and put labels like a mini-store so when she needs some cream, she can just go grab it, and every week I can check to see what needs to be restocked. She'll never run out of anything again: her lotions from Le Labo; her toothpaste from Aēsop; her Tom Ford Amber Absolute perfume, which is discontinued and has to be purchased in various used quantities from strangers on eBay. If they only knew where their old toiletries were being misted: a Hollywood movie star's neck, wrists, toilet bowl.

When Kathi is ready to go out, she walks into her massive closet—less a closet and more a room for clothing—and sheds whatever she's wearing. She opens all the doors to her cabinets and wardrobes and grabs this or that and heads out into the world. I put a dirty-clothes hamper in the room and take all the cabinet and wardrobe doors off the hinges; this way she never has to close one to open another and the bang, slam, yank, grind of getting dressed is eased, at least a small bit. She can now walk in and see all her options at once, every shoe choice, every legging, every blouse and jacket.

In her closet, she has a shoebox filled with precious metals and gems scattered about, necklaces knotted around diamond rings, brooches pinned through emerald earrings. I clear out a sock drawer and fill it with velvet jewelry holders to sort her bracelets, hold her rings, untangle her chains. Loose diamonds go in one section, crystal earrings go in another.

Kathi yells, "Where's my orange brooch with the doodads and blap?"

I yell, "In your jewelry drawer."

Kathi yells, "I have a jewelry drawer?"

I puff my chest. "You do now."

Under her bedroom is a small basement with an empty four-drawer black file cabinet, so I fill it with contents I find scattered all over the house: family pictures, press photos, headshots, intimate letters from family and friends and exes. Everything gets put in manila folders and filed in alphabetical order.

Kathi wrote all of her books by hand on thousands of pages ripped from yellow legal pads. The looping writing of her thoughts turned to words that stretch for miles across page after page in various color inks and without regard for the silly blue guidelines that came printed on the pages—those lines are for the birds, not for film icon Kathi Kannon, whose writing sometimes appears in circles from the center of the page, twirling prose all the way out to the edges, on the backs of pages, with arrows and lines and new words inserted here and paragraphs scratched out there. All of these pages are sorted and filed. I look forward to helping her write more.

As Agnes naps in the kitchen, I turn to the problems of the pantry, using Post-it notes to mark the designated places to put brown sugar, white sugar, powdered sugar, noodles, tomato sauce, napkins, paper towels. I print the inventory so when Agnes orders groceries, she knows exactly what is needed. I sort kitchen drawers and stick Post-it notes to each. Utensils. Pot holders. Mystery items.

Kathi continues with her life, me in her orbit. Or is she in orbit around me?

Sleep, bake, Vegas, *repeat.*

"Do you want to do any writing today?" I ask, pen and legal pad in hand.

"No, thanks, Cockring. I'm going to *Vegas.*"

"Again? What's left to buy? Your room is full of new stuff from *Vegas* trips this week."

She says, "There's always room for more."

She says, "I'm helping the economy."

She says, "Why drink from a puddle when you can drink from the ocean?"

Kathi walks to the front door and turns. "And by the way, everything is looking good," she says, waving her hand about as she strolls out, leaving the door wide open. I gleefully hop up and close it for her. I get back to work, her life.

Sleep, bake, Vegas, *repeat.*

Unanswered emails get answered.

Her lawyer and agent are loving me as shit gets done, handled. Paperwork gets signed. Kathi starts getting small tasks completed—a favor for this hanger-on, for this magazine, for that producer.

I say, "Hey, Kathi, *People* magazine wants to know how you would describe yourself?"

She says, "I'm sorry."

I repeat it, louder this time. "*People* magazine is asking—"

"No, I heard you," she replies. "I'm answering you. That's one way I'd describe myself. Sorry. I'm also bipolar, manic, OCD. I'm postmenopausal, over the hill, a former drug addict. I'm short, overweight, single, poor-ish. I'm loud, smart, insecure. I'm a pinup and an antique simul-

taneously. I'm bloated and pretentious—those last two go together."
And *slam*. She closes her bedroom door, in for the night at three P.M.,
to be asleep in moments. Easy for me to think it's a waste or a loss. But
in truth, I wish I could take a nap in the middle of the day. Who's to say
it's not a more productive life for her to work when she wants, to create
when she wants; perhaps she needs more rest than other mere mortals,
perhaps her brain works harder, longer, perhaps her heart beats faster,
harder.

Sleep, bake, Vegas, repeat.

I ask, "Am I the best assistant you've ever had?"

"Not yet," she says coyly. "But keep at it."

"What's my latest grade?"

"I guess a D."

"A D!" I yell. "I was a D, like, two weeks ago, and look at all the work
I'm doing!"

"Well, I don't know," Kathi says defensively. "We're still new together. I can't give you an A! I don't even know what time of day you
poop! How about a C minus?"

"WHAT?!" I yell.

"I'm still figuring out if I like what you're doing! I don't know how
I feel about my panties sorted by color!"

Hey, Siri, this is painful but progressive. Therapista says not everything in life has to be tied in a neat bow, that's not how life works—we
have moods, people get diseases, nothing is perfect. Therapista says I
can't let this be a setback, a mudslide into my familiar suicidal thoughts.
Therapista says I must steady this happier, more hopeful course, trust
the process.

Sleep, bake, Vegas, repeat.

I order more pale-blue pill cases so on the first of every month I
can take her new prescriptions, which are hand-delivered to her house
by pharmacy staff, and fill all the cases at once; she will be set for the
month, and I'll know at a glance when it is time to order refills.

"Do you want to write today?" I ask.

"Maybe tomorrow, Cockring."

I cleared seventy-two new and unheard voicemails—some as old as two years—and several from—my heart swells—Miss Gracie:

Beeep: "Hello, dear. It's your mother. I don't expect you check your voicemails and I know it's possible you won't get this message ever, but I wanted you to know we are out of bologna down here, so that should tell you all you need to know about how I'm doing. Goodbye. Thank youuu."

Beeeep: "Hello, dear. Don't sleep in the same room with your cell phone. They can cause cancer. I saw it on the news. Terrible cancers. Maybe that's why you're always so tired. Maybe you're dying. Anyway, good night, sleep well. Thank youuu."

Beeeep: "Hello, dear. I'm ordering a chopped salad from Brighton Catering. Do you want anything? Hello? Well, I'll get one for you and if you don't want it, I'll put it outside for the raccoons. I tried poisoning them, but they survived, so now I'm accepting them. Thank youuu."

Assistant Bible Verse 4: Delete unhelpful messages.

Kathi is constantly misplacing her cell phone, so I drill a tiny hole in her phone case and put it on a lanyard to wear around her neck. She's always losing precious jewelry, so when I see a piece lying around, I pick it up and lock it back in her jewelry drawer. She's always losing her favorite scarves, so I make note of designer and style to easily order replacements.

"How's my assistant grade now?" I ask Kathi as she puts the phone and lanyard around her neck, swinging it around like she's a topless dancer.

"Solid C-plus," she says.

"That's it?"

"It's better than average," Kathi says. I nod, I get it.

She looks at my outfit—the bribe I'm wearing like my new uniform. "Nice cardigan," she says.

Sleep, bake, Vegas, *repeat.*

I give everyone a weekly list of duties set to a schedule, and that gives everyone a bit more structure: me, Agnes, Benny, and, it seems, delightfully, Kathi.

KATHI: What size shoe r u again??

ME: 9.5. Why?

KATHI: Shoe size should be on your resumeeeee. Next to
     age and length of scrotum.

Her *Vegas* shopping sprees are great for Agnes and Benny and me. Kathi buys us hair products, sunglasses, clothes. She comes home armed, charged. "Cockring," she says. "Take off that hideous sweater you're wearing and put this on." She hands me a new one that cost $350 from H. Lorenzo on Sunset Boulevard. "Never wear the other one again."

Sometimes, I listen to her fashion advice. Sometimes, I wear my "unflattering" normal clothes on weekends, when I know I won't be subjected to her judgment. Sometimes I return the one $350 sweater and exchange it for four new shirts, two pairs of pants, and a new pair of shoes from the sale rack. Or I exchange it for cash if possible. What I need more than a $350 sweater is money for rent. Money for food. Money for debt—I'm still paying off student loans; I'm still paying off credit cards from making no money in the news business, from buying things I didn't need in failed attempts to fill dark corners of my vision board.

Kathi Kannon's gifts include a ceramic plate in the shape of an eye, a necktie with little penises, a bag that says HUNG TA (it's in Vietnamese and no one knows what it means—she just likes that it says "hung").

Assistant Bible Verse 5: Check in frequently with their wants and needs.

"Do you want to write today?" I ask.

"No, thank you, Cockring," she says.

Hey, Siri, is it sarcasm, is it annoyance?

I'm wearing new electric-blue loafers Kathi bought me at Opening Ceremony. "Size nine and a half," she says, handing them over like Santa Claus. I would never have bought them for myself, but they look good; they're actually fun. Perhaps she knows me better than I think.

I'm shuffling those shoes, my feet, into her room, tidying up while she bakes cookies in the kitchen. I pull her comforter taut, clear junk from her nightstand, grab that day's pale-blue pill case—and notice that some still remain. I open the case and count.

I'm thinking, *Did I put too many in?*

I'm thinking, *Is this my mistake or hers?*

I'm thinking, *How bad could it be?*

It's not unusual to get text messages from Kathi in the middle of the night. It's almost charming, the idea that I'm on her mind in the wee hours, that I serve some purpose as part of the rumbling of things that go through her mind late at night. But as I wake up on this Tuesday, I'm alarmed not that she texted me but that she texted me so often, and with so much intensity, while I was asleep.

> KATHI: Change the bedding and strip into sheets shitface marble cock!
>
> KATHI: Where do-est thou reside and if thou-ist not alone may you be impaled by the best of all that the planet has to offer and many a time over, spilling out of thee and dripping into the milky way's wondrous wound.
>
> KATHI: Are you getting these? They are brilliant-adjacent. We should make bumper stickers. Or just stickers, sickly sweet globs of printed paper bits of happiness for ur skool locker.

KATHI: I take your non-response as a yes.

KATHI: Have you ever heard of a prolapsed vagina?! Let's panic and puke together, lass.

KATHI: I don't feel well.

KATHI: Nevermind I feel great.

KATHI: Where do we keep the knife sharpener?

KATHI: Are you

KATHI: Cack?

I sit up in my bed, yank the charging cable from my phone, and rush to text her back. She sent the last text hours ago, but I still feel an uneasy urgency.

ME: Hi. What's up?

And almost instantly . . .

KATHI: ME! I haven't slept at any age and Life is a party.

ME: u okay?

KATHI: U Coming to play?

ME: On my way.

That gate.

That code.

That woman!

As the gates swing open, I see Kathi Kannon, film icon, turn and spot me. She's wearing a bright-blue fitted bedsheet with a hole cut out of the middle, like it's a poncho. Because the sheet is fitted, the rest of it bobs around her body like a jellyfish. She's in the driveway and rushes, flailing, toward the open gate, toward me, or my car, or the street behind me—who knows. Her eyes are wild, searching, pained.

Benny stands nearby, hedge trimmers in one hand and his other waving around, urging Kathi away from the open gate. "Come back, come back," he's shouting. His upper torso twists back and forth, like the waist of an old He-Man action figure, with his legs stiff and still, like they're bolted to the ground, like he's just going through the motions, like he's a rerun.

"COCKRING!" Kathi shouts, rushing over to me, twirling, bobbing. "You're a B-plus!" she yells.

I roll my window down; the peeling tint crackles and shrieks. "Hi," I say.

"Ewww," Kathi says. "This is your car? It's so sad."

I say, "Thank you."

"COCKRING! You're a B-plus! Did you hear me?" Holding her arms out like a T, she says, "Hey, look at this dress I made!"

"Is that a fitted sheet you're wearing?"

"YES! You like it? What's wrong?"

"What are you going to sleep on tonight? I'll have to find you a new one."

"Don't live in the future! Don't you think people will like it?" she asks, fluff, fluff, fluffing her dress-creation and turning away from me and toward the traffic rushing by—*puff, puff, puff*—on Beverly Canyon Drive behind me. Kathi takes a few steps toward the current of cars.

I throw my Nissan into park and twist my keys to turn the engine off—those keys growing in number as I accumulate the ones from her estate, twisting them alongside my sweet mother's locket, the long dangling reminder of some miracle that led me here, a reminder that as my hero advances into traffic, this job is what I wanted, this job is an answer to my prayers.

Click. I unlatch my seatbelt, open my car door, and step alongside Kathi, my arm outstretched to guide her home, to turn her around. "This way, please."

She says as we turn from the traffic, "I wanna swim in it."

I say, "I know."

Kathi tries to walk in reverse, toward traffic again. I grab one of her wrists and try to hold her back. That wrist, the same one everyone can see garnished in jewels in *Nova Quest*, that wrist is now in my tight grip, because right now it's the wrist of a follower of some dark, confused instruction.

"No . . . I want to see the people in their cars," she says, trying to get free of me.

"Nope," I'm groaning back at her.

I'm pulling at Kathi.

She's yanking away from me.

Benny points at Kathi. "She's manic," he shouts.

"Very helpful, Benny. Thank you!" I say.

"Yeah! Go to hell, LIAR!" Kathi shouts at Benny, then turns to me and calmly says, "He's right, I'm manic."

"Benny, go get Miss Gracie, please," I say. Benny starts but doesn't get far.

"Stop right there, Benny, or you're fired!" Kathi yells.

Benny stops and instantly returns to tree trimming.

"Thanks a lot!" I yell to him.

"You're welcome," Kathi says to me.

Benny ignores us both.

Kathi reaches her two hands out to mine, an invitation for me to grab on, and I do. "Let me ask you something," she says seductively. "Are you afraid of the human body?"

"Maybe," I say, releasing her hands, putting mine on her back, and gently pushing her past my car, farther from traffic and danger.

"You're so diplomatic, Cock-cack. That's something I like about you. That, and your long neck."

"Thank you." I guide Kathi past Benny.

"You need medicine," he says to her.

"You need it!" Kathi shouts at him.

She shouts, "LIAR!"

She shouts, "You don't know what I need!"

She turns to me and says quietly, "I need medicine. Meet you inside?"

"Yup." I nod, and just like that Kathi twirls up the hill, shouting down to Benny as she goes.

"I love you, Benny," she says. "It's my mental illness that hates you."

Benny turns back to pretending to service an already perfectly manicured bush. He continues with his duties as if this outburst, as if Kathi wanting to play in traffic wearing a bedsheet, is just another ordinary workday.

Chinese emperors.

Mateo the Moose.

Fireplaces.

In Kathi's palatial closet, the fitted sheet is on the floor, and she's now wearing pink leggings and an oversized sweater with plastic eyes stitched all over it.

I ask, "How are you feeling?"

"I feel like all of these eyes should have eyelashes glued on, so I'm going to go to Home Depot to see if they have any."

"Maybe we can take a moment and talk about your health. Did you take your meds this morning?"

"I feel great," Kathi says. "Except for these leggings." She starts tugging at her leggings, struggling to get them off. "Ten seconds ago I wanted them, but now I see that leggings are one of mankind's strange wearable Rubik's Cubes."

I go to her nightstand and look for yesterday's pill case. I give it a shake. Empty. I rustle in the drawer, through papers and pens and books and hair clips, and there on the bottom—the pills, the magic beans, unsowed, and more than there should be for one missed dose. I collect them and bring them to her.

"Kathi, you have to take your medication," I say.

"My medication takes me," she says, having traded the pink leggings for gold.

"No, they don't. Please take them."

"I thought I took all of them."

"These were all at the bottom of your drawer."

"I think those are old," she says. "Did you forget to give them to me maybe?"

I open my mouth to deny it but feel a surge of heat rising in me. Did I forget? Did I fail her? "Shit, Kathi. Maybe I did. Are you sure the ones in the drawer are old?"

"It doesn't matter! I'm flying," she says, raising her arms, keeping eye contact with me. She's intense as ever, playful in a way that's kind of drunk, and determined in a way that's kind of dangerous.

"No, you're not. We need to pin this down."

"I'm not pinning the butterfly to the wall of your collection," she says. "I'm catching fireflies in a jar and lighting your way with them till one or all of us burn out."

"What can we do to avoid us burning out?" I ask.

"Get some milk from the holy cow to put out the fire."

"I can't do dairy," I say, trying to keep us on point.

Kathi laughs, opening her jewelry drawer and putting everything on her body, wherever, however it can be attached: multiple earrings in her ears, rings on every finger. "If you could really understand me, you might say it sounds like a plan. As it is, it just kinda looks like one."

"Okay," I say. "The plan is just to get you level, you know?"

"Maybe you can save me from me, if you're so good at it. Or explain me away. Far away, where there's no reception. Wedding or otherwise. Invitation to a beheading. Bring your children. Show them what not to be."

"Okay. Can I take you to see a doctor so you can get some meds to help you rest?"

"No, thanks. Sweet of you. I'll take some Beethoven to rest," Kathi says, grabbing for her cell phone on the lanyard around her neck. She starts poking at apps.

"This seems like it's going to end badly. Has this happened before? Should I call a doctor?"

Kathi opens her mouth as if to speak, but instead, from her phone she plays Beethoven's Symphony No. 7 in A Major Op. 92-II, Allegretto, the harmony filling the room as if it's coming from inside her.

"What do you think of the music?" she asks.

"It's pretty," I say.

"It's so pretty, Cockring," she says, choking up, her shoulders collapsing, her arms reaching out for support, her hands, they find mine.

"We have to get you on the right medication," I say.

The music is building, building.

"Wait," she says calmly, listening.

"Can I see if Dr. Miller is available?" I ask. "Maybe a phone chat is all we need to get some helpful information."

She looks at me, tears in her eyes, and raises the volume on the Beethoven even higher, pounding in our lives, in our heads, in her closet.

"Or I can call Miss Gracie," I say loudly over the music.

"No, do NOT call her," Kathi snaps. "She's been unwell, and I don't want you to stress her out and kill her." She keeps staring at me, as if in a trance.

I say, "Look, this is not healthy. I care about you."

"Let me have this one manic indulgence, and then when this song is over, I'll take some fucking meds."

"Fine. How long is the song?"

"Could be days," she says. "I have it on repeat."

"Absolutely not."

"Fine, it's just eight more minutes."

"Okay, great," I say. "What meds will you need? Seroquel? I'll get everything ready."

"First step is, you need to dance with me," she says, grabbing my body.

"No," I start as she spins me around.

"There you go! Look at us dancing!"

"This is not dancing. This is technically assault."

She whirls me around again. Again. She laughs. The music is building, building, layers upon layers upon layers of instruments.

"I need you," she says.

I put my hand on her waist, an attempt to wrest control, to slow our spin, to dampen this dance.

"No, no," she says. "I'm the man." She moves my hands from her waist to her shoulders, and with her hands on the sides of my pelvis, she rocks me in a melodic sway and says, "You have women's hips."

"Thank you. How much longer?" I clomp, clomp, clomp my feet beside hers.

"Your dancing is so terrible, Cockring, you're ruining my manic high."

"You're welcome."

Kathi stops suddenly, then reverses our spin in the middle of her closet.

"Wait."

"No. I lead," she insists. "Remember, I'm the man!" Her legs move fast, wide. She steps sideways and my chest follows her, angling as if we're about to coast across a ballroom floor. "Don't fuck this up," she says, dancing me out of the closet and down her hallway, the music growing faint as the orchestra enters a quieter part of the melody, settling, preparing for their next burst from the phone around Kathi's neck.

Step, step, step we go, down the hall, together, chest to chest, heart to heart.

"The gay gene doesn't include dancing, eh?" she asks as my feet clutter around hers.

"I had a bad experience dancing when I was a kid," I say.

We reach the end of the hallway, our feet stomping upon each other's, our arms growing sore from being outstretched. Just outside the red room, Kathi looks at me. "Now we go back," she says, changing our positions and pulling me back toward her closet.

Step, step, step.

We move slower this time, our pace matching the increasingly gentle lulls, the tempo coming to an end. I'm not sure if we're moving slowly to match the pace of the music, for Kathi to stretch out this moment, or maybe both. Maybe we're all, finally, getting in sync.

As we return to her closet, Kathi releases my arms, removes her hands from my waist, and looks me in the eyes. "Thanks, Cock," she says, turning from me and muting her phone, ending the song without regard to its final seconds. She retreats to her bedroom as I head to my stash of her meds in my desk, fishing out some of what's needed.

I bring her a soda and a few Seroquel. She's standing by her bedroom window, looking out at her backyard, shaking her butt, still in dance to the music now only in her head.

"Time for rest," I say, guiding her to bed.

"But . . ."

"No," I say. I hand her the soda and pills, and she grumpily sits on her bed and takes them as promised and then finishes off the soda.

"You're no fun, Cockring," she says.

"I know."

Assistant Bible Verse 6: Never let them get away with murder. Or spit food at you. Or throw things at your face.

"You really are a B-plus assistant." Kathi hands me her now-empty glass of soda. I put it on her nightstand.

"Am I? Are you sure? You seem under duress today."

"True," she says. "We will have to reconsider your grade when my mind is back home with itself."

"I can live with that," I say, making my way across the room to sit in a side chair.

"Thank you for the lovely dance, Cockring."

"You're welcome."

Assistant Bible Verse 7: Always make time to dance.

I look at Kathi, but she looks away.

"You know," she says, "the mania is great. It's the coming down that sucks." And in the quiet moment that follows we're in sync yet again, dancing a careful emotional dance, where she has space to make her moves. And I start to have space to make mine.

And now it's me who looks away. "I'm sorry if the pill mix-up was my fault."

Kathi pulls her blankets tight again, urging them from the tucking between the mattress and box spring, and lies back down on her pillows.

She says, "Don't worry about it."

"How often do you have manic episodes like that?"

She says, "They're very rare."

She says, "They're very fun."

Kathi pulls the bedding up to her chin. She holds her phone over her face so she can continue looking at it—texting, reading news, I have no idea.

I watch her fondly. I'm thinking, *B-plus, I can live with that.*

I put my hand in my pocket, its home base, my left fingers finding my key ring, and I guess where each key fits—her front door, her shed, her pool house. Then my fingers find the locket. I remove the keys from my jeans and take a look. That aging empty locket, the places it has been, the years it has traveled until this very moment, bearing witness to me caring for my beloved Priestess Talara. I slowly unwind it from the key ring, freeing it at last, after its long journey from a Perris basement to this Beverly Hills mansion.

As I hold it up to marvel at its survival over the years, the dangling locket looks awkward without a key ring, naked, precarious—like a dog with no collar.

"Hey," I say, the impulse arising within me and spitting itself out like its own living being, like the thought is an exorcised demon with a great personality. "I have something for you," I say.

Kathi jolts up in bed. "A prostitute?!"

"No." I stand at her bedside and she turns to look at me. It feels like a scene at a hospital bed, that familiar scene in almost every movie where there's even the slightest injury and someone ends up laid out under emergency care. The powerless patient looks up at the adoring visitor, but here, instead of beeping machines and the smell of pee, I'm dazzled by the fog of Beethoven from a cell phone and Tom Ford Amber Absolute.

I open my mother's locket and say a silent goodbye, looking at my reflection in its surface, definitely not the face of young Charlie.

Kathi squints to identify the object in my hand. "What's that?"

"It's yours now," I say. "It's a gift." I dangle the locket in front of her.

"Did you steal it?"

"No!"

"You stole it and now you're planting it on me so I'll go to jail for you?"

"No. It belonged to someone special. And now I'm giving it to someone special." I hold it out to her.

The locket, swaying between my fingers, starts to reflect the colors and lights in Kathi's wizard-ish bedroom, absorbing the enchantment, suddenly and dazzlingly at home in her world, free from the beige of mine. It seems to like her, as if maybe Mom does, too.

"Okay. Give it to me," Kathi says, her hand reaching to receive it.

"No." I pull it back, having second thoughts about putting it in the hands of someone in mental crisis.

"What?! You just gave it to me! It's mine! I want to hold it and see how long I can clutch it before I lose it or break it!"

"Exactly," I say, turning from her.

"Where are you going, Cockring?"

"Bathroom."

"I'm learning your pooping schedule after all," she says.

I grimace at the thought, but kinder feelings flow within me. I walk into Kathi's bathroom and close the door. I walk to her purse, unzipped on the counter. I reach in and take out her key ring—her collection of jagged metal bits that are less functioning keys and more an archive of her past lives, past residences, old cars. Kathi Kannon's purse—like my mother's—is a graveyard.

I see myself smile in the locket's reflection as I let it go, as I start to wind it onto Kathi's key ring. I twist, twist, twist and wiggle the clasp delightfully onto its new home. This locket is a protector, swimming with my mother's magic and miracles, and now I leave it to serve Kathi.

8

☆

Agnes wobbles toward me slowly, bracing herself on the colorful hallway walls. "I have a message from the boss," she says quietly. I watch from the living room as she stops in the doorway to the kitchen, winded, weak. She takes a breath.

"The boss seems fine," I say. "She's asleep."

"Not Kathi. The other boss, the real one. Miss Gracie wants to see you. Right away."

Assistant Bible Verse 8: Everything is an emergency, always.

I bounce up. *Hey, Siri, this is my chance to expand my universe.* If only I had a second locket, to place in the palm of sweet Gracie Gold, to show that I'm here for both her and her daughter, to show how thankful I am that this job is saving my life.

When I finally told my dad I was working with Kathi Kannon, he yelled, "*WHO?!*"

I told him, "Kathi Kannon is Gracie Gold's daughter."

He perked up. "GRACIE GOLD! HOLY SHIT!"

As Kathi is a star to my generation, Gracie Gold is a star to his. I stand a chance of impressing him now, possible redemption as a bump on a branch on Kathi Kannon and Miss Gracie's family tree. My dad hated me being terrible at sports, hated that I idolized strong women, hated that I worked for liberal media. But finally I have a job he might like. Or at least a boss. Or at least a boss's mom.

My job responsibilities include mending my relationship with my father.

"Be careful," Agnes says as I rush away from her. "Miss Gracie thinks she knows everything. She once starred in a movie with a dog, and now she thinks she's an animal expert. One time she played a cheerleader, and now she thinks she's an athlete. Another time she played a nurse, and now she goes around giving medical advice like she's a real doctor." Agnes shakes her head in disapproval.

Hey, Siri, take note: Miss Gracie can perform an emergency tracheotomy, if it ever comes to that.

Agnes says, "Don't let your guard down."

I rush to Miss Gracie's house at the bottom of the hill, in the shadow of Kathi's home. I stop at my Nissan and pull out an emergency sport coat I keep in my trunk for moments like this—interactions with celebrities, royalty.

Miss Gracie is so bold and fearless in her life that she hired one of her most extreme fans—some may even have called him a stalker—to be her assistant. It was certainly convenient. A teenager named Roger would stand outside of the stage door after each of Miss Gracie's performances. He followed her from city to city. Miss Gracie would perform; Roger would be waiting outside, a familiar face among the throngs of her other fans. Eventually he no longer bothered to get her autograph, content to stare at her, make eye contact, and just casually wave as if to say, *See you tomorrow.* And so, as Miss Gracie recounted on an episode of Oprah, her right hand twirling in the air to accentuate her point, as if she were entertaining royalty, "When I needed a new assistant, Roger was around all the time, anyway," Miss Gracie said. "Plus, he already knew everything about me. Why not?"

Agnes also warned me about Roger. He lives in Miss Gracie's home with her and her dog, Uta Hagen. Agnes says Roger is an old-school gay with a delicate mix of sass and class you don't see much anymore: He uses hairspray, he's never worn shorts, he uses a padlock to keep Miss Gracie out of his bedroom. He has a signature fragrance—he either applies some sort of scented talcum powder every day or he's simply pickled from having been inseparable from Miss Gracie and her luxury lotions and oily perfumes for decades. Roger is mysterious to me, a ghost. I rarely see him, adding to the lore that he's a sultry, salty veteran of this lifestyle, someone who knows the politics of what's going on here, someone I can maybe turn to for answers when needed.

Beyond the fluff and fun of Kathi's home is the fake cute of Miss Gracie's world. She lives in what used to be the groundskeeper's house, but after Kathi bought the property, Miss Gracie remodeled the home endlessly. Agnes says she added a huge master bedroom and master bath, which includes a bathtub that's actually a small in-ground—the size of a hot tub—filled with salt water, which stays full constantly, filters always running, water always swirling, in a room just off her bedroom.

All the plants outside of Miss Gracie's cottage are bright and beautiful and fake. Her car is a maroon-colored Lincoln Town Car—old and solid, real steel, not like new cars with their pathetic fiberglass. There's a neon diner sign that says GRACIE'S DRIVE-IN, which should be lit up but is always turned off because, Agnes says, "Miss Gracie hates it." It was a gift from Kathi.

I round the corner, past the Lincoln Town Car and the neon sign, and there's Miss Gracie's back door. Mysteriously ordinary.

I tap on the glass.

"Come in," a man's sweet voice sings. I'm thinking, *Roger.*

I push the door open. Entering Miss Gracie's house feels like a trap. It smells like food and old lady. It smells like history. And it's full of it. The walls are lined with photos of Miss Gracie with celebrities, mostly dead, fixtures of Hollywood's golden age. Miss Gracie with Bette

Davis, Phyllis Diller, a host of men I don't recognize. Some pictures are autographed. Some are just snapshots from this party or that. Her life is framed in black and white all over the walls of her kitchen, her dining room, her laundry room, the guest bath. Her Facebook wall is her actual house. Other than the pictures, it's a normal-looking home.

In the kitchen, there's food cooking on the stove; at the controls is an older man, slightly pudgy, fragile bottled-brown hair coiffed just so, and a tired look in his bright-blue eyes.

Uta Hagen starts barking.

"Shut up! Quiet! Ya turd!" he yells. And the barking stops.

"You must be Roger. I'm Charlie."

"I know who you are."

Uta Hagen approaches me, sniffing me, judging me.

"Git!" Roger yells, and Uta Hagen offers some very skilled side-eye and shuffles down the hall, leading the way for what I suspect is my eventual path to Miss Gracie.

"That smells good," I say, referencing whatever Roger is cooking on the stove. "Making yourself some lunch?"

"Not for me," he says. "Never for me."

"That can't be true," I say sweetly, trying to nourish a bond between us, a real one in lieu of the unavoidable one we both share in our roles as family assistants.

Roger stares down at the stove for a moment, then he looks up and says, "Good luck. She's in there." He nods to a hallway, to my fate deeper in the corridors of this old house. Miss Gracie's voice, now calling out impatiently, "Hellooooo? How much longer am I supposed to wait for you, dear?"

I cross into the dining room. It's dark. There's stuff everywhere. Several dozen dresses hang, crammed onto a wardrobe rack in what used to be a bar. Dishes are packed inside of a china cabinet—an impossible number of gold-plated dinner plates, saucers, teacups—like it's not just one person's china collection but multiple lifetime collections of collections of collections. Side tables are full of candle sconces, like this is a home that only recently got electricity. I can't help but reach out and touch one of them as I pass, trying to lift it slightly, if only to feel the heft in my hand, but it barely budges.

I hear a voice call out, "Richard Burton gave me that candelabra as a thank-you after we made love in July of 1954."

I don't dare turn around. I know it's her.

"I wanted so badly to have his child," she says. "I laid on my back with my feet in the air for hours following our congress, but no luck."

My eyes refocus on the silver. "It's heavy."

"That's because it's *real!*" Miss Gracie shouts. Then, "Please enter, dear. Let's begin this scene."

I turn and head toward the voice, *that* voice, coming from a dimly lit living room carefully protected from sunlight by dark window coverings. There, she waits. With Uta Hagen by her side, Miss Gracie is standing in the center of the room like it's a stage. She's chic and casually stylish for being eighty years old, wearing a peach turban-type wrap on her head and what appears to be a pink silk nightgown over a blue silk nightgown. Silk on silk on silk. She looks like she dressed to match the drapes. It's a room that looks decorated by a movie studio set-design department. The curtains are from the fifties, pastel and faded and velvet. The couch is floral and long and boxy, with cushions so old they're indented with butt impressions—perhaps the asses of Cary Grant or Gene Kelly or Ann Rutherford.

I walk down a step that leads to the living room, careful not to knock over a table filled with headshots—some of her and some of Kathi—each with a Post-it note attached and a name scribbled on it: for Dave, for Michelle, for Tony.

"Those are pictures sent to Kathi and me by our many fans," Miss Gracie says. "They mail us headshots asking for our autographs and I always sign them and send them back. However, Kathi ignores them because she doesn't like to sign free autographs—she prefers to sell her signature at conventions and whatnot, like some kind of pinup girl. But, in my day, you respected your fans, so I hired a handwriting expert to forge her signature, and that takes care of that. Please sit down."

The floors are carpet but also covered in rugs. Carpet on carpet on carpet, so many layers to this universe. I look down and Miss Gracie suspects judgment.

"I once owned numerous homes that were tens of thousands of square feet," Miss Gracie says. "I used to have so much room for all these rugs that I didn't have enough of them. Now that's all changed. Now they're all piled on the floor beneath us. You're standing on history."

I nod politely and walk to the couch, passing an open door to my right. I can't help but look inside.

"My bedroom," Miss Gracie says. "Filled with treasure. Ignore the mess."

There's an unmade bed with a headboard not connected, just propped on the wall behind the mattress. A wig sits on top of a vase. Jewelry is piled in a cardboard box on the floor.

The apple doesn't fall far from the money tree.

Behind me, photos cover a piano that's too big for this house; a huge mirror hangs over the mantel. Miss Gracie's gaze follows my every movement, and like Kathi, she seems to be able to read my thoughts.

"That mirror belonged to Bugsy Siegel, the weary gangster," she says. "He used to keep it at his bar so he could always see who was coming up behind him. No one was ever going to stab *him* in the back. Or me! Right, dear?"

I smile and look to the other side of the room, to a bookshelf packed with biographies and autobiographies of her friends. One shelf doesn't have books. It has—

"Yes, that's the original Rosebud sled," she says. "From the classic film *Citizen Kane*. I find the film's performances to be quite offensive. The sled, however, I always loved and snapped it up at an auction."

The sled's runners look as if they're held to the shelf with a large clump of the cheap white tacky stuff teachers use to hang posters on their classroom walls. A pair of men's black dress shoes are beside it.

"Humphrey Bogart wore those in *Casablanca,* dear," Miss Gracie says. "Don't touch them."

Assistant Bible Verse 9: Don't touch anything.

I turn from the history of the bookshelf adornments to the history of her being, Miss Gracie, living and breathing and before me.

"Hello, dear," Miss Gracie says, waving for me to sit on a wing-back chair. She and Uta Hagen take their places across from me, on the aforementioned worn but wonderful sofa. "I once had a dancer named Charlie—I'm hopeful that it will help me to always remember your little name, even though it's so common."

"Thanks," I say, but then slow down, trying to keep up with Miss Gracie's word games. Did she mean my name is "common" as an insult? There's no time to know. "I love all of your movies," I tell her.

She winces. "I'm not in *movies*," she says. "I'm in *motion pictures*." She shakes her head, then continues. "This is Uta Hagen," Miss Gracie says, motioning to the furry beauty beside her, a white Pomeranian. "I named her after the monster."

"Nice to meet you, Uta Hagen," I say to a blank and disinterested doggie stare.

"I wasn't sure if you would survive Kathi's employ for this long, all these months," Miss Gracie says. "Many secretaries don't."

"Thanks. It's so vintage that you call me a secretary. These days we call ourselves assistants—" But I stop as I notice Miss Gracie's face melt.

"You're a secretary," she says. "Let's not jest ourselves."

"Right. Yes, ma'am."

"Additionally, it's hard for me to invite new people into our lives, our family. At least until I realize they can keep up. You do realize, you're part of our family now, right?"

"Yes, ma'am," I say, a brief bit of my father's life lesson (*BE POLITE!*) making itself present in the room.

"Ma'am? Oh, you're very sweet. Are you Southern?"

"Yes, ma'am, I'm from New Orleans."

"Oh! New Orleans. What a wonderful city. I once shot a film there— well, it was a scene in a film, in a cemetery. In the scene, I cried and held that city's dirt in my hand," Miss Gracie says, standing, making a fist, reliving the moment. "And I cursed the gods for taking my beloved husband and forcing me to visit my lover's rotting corpse in this grue- some grave!" She exhales, sits, speaks normally. "Of course, I was just acting. In real life, I've hated all my husbands."

"Yes, ma'am," I say.

"My daughter is mentally ill. You must make sure she doesn't leave her purse in Nordstrom again. Or her glasses at Mr Chow. Or her car keys at Givenchy. And take all the credit cards out of her wallet. You control them. You're in charge of the money. Do you understand? I will fire you."

"Yes, ma'am." I resist an urge to correct her, an urge to say she can't fire me, that I don't work for her, I work for Kathi. But the power Miss Gracie commands onscreen is the same in real life. Her presence in the room is crushing.

"I heard Kathi had a medical incident," Miss Gracie says. "Roger was cooking and saw the whole thing out of the kitchen window. He saw you with Kathi by the gate. He was narrating it to me moment by moment while our quiche burned. I couldn't go out and help because I had a mud mask on, and Roger couldn't help because he has diabetes. But when he told me that Kathi outstretched her two hands to you, and you outstretched your two hands to her in return, and you held her—"

Miss Gracie stops, breathing heavily.

As if on cue, as if she triggered a silent alarm, Roger dashes in and hands her a handkerchief. She accepts it without looking up, without acknowledging Roger at all, like the handkerchief magically appeared in her hand. Roger exits swiftly, silently, the same way he entered. His movements are precise and perfect; he's done this a million times before. Like Benny and Agnes, everyone here seems to move with a sort of muscle memory—they're in a familiar matrix, they've seen everything, done everything, know every ending of the choose-your-own-adventure that is this lifestyle.

Roger, *a lifer.*

"I was so moved," Miss Gracie whispers, dabbing her eyes. "I thought you could be lovers, but then I learned you were homosexual, and, well, I'm still getting used to it. But it told me you're smart and you're not afraid to connect, and I like it and also I'm watching you."

"Thank you?"

"I'm concerned, however, that the episode may have been your fault. Are you confident you gave Kathi all the proper medications? Did you see her take them? Do you have proof?"

"I'm—no—" I stutter. "I'm not sure. It may have been my fault, and I'm very sorry."

"Watch yourself," she says.

"Yes, ma'am."

"I'm familiar with your types, you know what I mean?"

"Gay people?" I ask.

Miss Gracie reaches down and pulls a bottle of chardonnay from a Brookstone wine cooler on the floor beside her. Like magic, like a second act, Roger appears again, putting a wineglass down on a coaster on the coffee table, and vanishing again. Without breaking eye contact with me, Miss Gracie unscrews the bottle, pours a sip of wine, swirls it, smells it, tastes it, nods approval. "It's fine," she says to herself, then pours more into the glass.

"I've seen many secretaries and helpers and whatnot come and go," she says. "Mostly go. Almost always, they go." Miss Gracie shakes her head, shakes it off. "Well, they don't call it show *business* for nothing. That said, you need to know I like our help loyal. I once had a limo

driver who worked for me for decades—always picked me up, always—
and then one day I call the limo company to schedule him and he's
not there and I ask, 'Where the hell is he?' and they say, 'He retired.'
Retired! Can you believe the nerve?! Why would anyone want to retire?
What are they going to do all day? I'm never retiring. I'm working until
my last breath, believe me. And that's what I expect from the people
around me. You understand?"

"Yes, ma'am. Absolutely." I blush, not because I'm lying but because
I'm embarrassed that I'm telling the truth. Why would anyone ever
want to leave this show, *The Kathi and Miss Gracie Hour*—eight hours,
actually, daily, Monday through Friday—playing on repeat, forever?
Does Miss Gracie judge me for not having a life, for wanting to be a
part of hers? She stares at me a moment, studying the slightest movements of my face, then continues.

"Additionally, you should memorize all important phone numbers.
Our lawyers and agents and whatnot. You can get a complete list from
Roger. He memorized all of them with flash cards. Oh! And in case of
an emergency," she says, closing her eyes and shaking her head, "do
not *ever* call 911. First, call our plastic surgeon, Dr. Felton. He'll know
what to do. Roger has his number, naturally. And if Kathi or I have to
go to the hospital, insist it is Cedars, no matter what, even if you must
wrestle the ambulance steering wheel from beneath the driver's steely
fingers. I give Cedars so much money what else is it good for? You're
getting all this?"

I nod *yes.*

"Is that a yes? I can't hear you, dear. I'm not psychic, though I did
once play an extraordinary supernatural medium on *Murder, She
Wrote* and was nominated for an Emmy, despite Angela being a shrew."

"Yes, ma'am, I understand. Thank you."

"And I suppose you know about vegetables?" Miss Gracie asks, sipping her wine.

"The existence of vegetables? Yes—"

"Don't be smart. I give money to Agnes each week to buy fresh vegetables, and now I'm going to start giving that money to you to buy the vegetables, because Agnes is a crook. I once saw her stealing a television from Kathi's house. Just putting it in the trunk of her car. I could do nothing, because Kathi likes her, says she gave Agnes the TV. Can you imagine? I can't for the life of me get rid of her. I've fired her many times, but Kathi rehires her because Kathi, who is mentally ill, likes her, and so I allow it because I love Kathi unconditionally. You understand?"

Therapista says unconditional love is a condition.

Therapista says judging others is really judging yourself.

Therapista says qualities you see in others are qualities within yourself.

"Yes, ma'am," I say.

Miss Gracie puts her wine down on the coffee table and opens a leather-bound ledger, pulls out a thick envelope, and hands it to me. I reach for it, but—

"Not so fast," she says, pulling the envelope away. "I wasn't born yesterday. Sign here." She pushes the ledger and a pen toward me. On the paper is written, in her scratchy, elderly handwriting, "I acknowledge receipt of two thousand dollars cash for vegetables."

I sign. "Two thousand dollars? That's gonna buy a lot of vegetables."

"Don't worry about it," Miss Gracie says. "It all comes out of Kathi's inheritance." She takes the pen and ledger and theatrically turns page after page after page, revealing a long list of other signatures—Kathi, Agnes, other *secretaries*—all marking other withdrawals from the Miss Gracie Bank and Trust.

"Did I mention Kathi is mentally ill?" Miss Gracie asks.

"Yes, ma'am. A couple times."

"Well, it's important. And you know Kathi is a drug addict, don't you?"

"Well, *former* drug addict," I correct boldly, suddenly seeing the whites of Miss Gracie's eyes as her gaze widens, consumes. "I mean, as in, like, I've heard 'once you're an addict you're always an addict,' you know. I've never seen anything." I fidget.

"She's had overdoses and nearly died many times. Do you think that's funny?"

"No, ma'am. Not at all. I take all that very seriously. And I won't be an enabler, if that's on your mind. It's not me at all. And like I told Kathi, I want to be the best assistant she's ever had, and that means respecting her health and safety."

"Dear, I have some advice," Miss Gracie says, leaning forward only a few centimeters, but she may as well have come nose-to-nose with me, she's that engaging. "You're family now, so I can share this with you. You know the story about the man who wanted to fly, so he made wings out of wax, but he flew too high and the sun melted the wax and he fell back down to earth and landed flat on his ass in front of Jesus? It's in the Bible."

I'm thinking, *That's not the Bible.* I'm thinking, *Do* not *correct her.*

"Yes, ma'am," I say cautiously, worried she may ask follow-up questions I'm not academically qualified to answer.

Assistant Bible Verse 10: Become an emotional ninja. They don't want to see you or hear you. Keep opinions to yourself. Facts don't matter.

"Well, dear," she says, touching my arm, an act of kindness, a sweetness, a chilling and electric signal for me to pay attention. "Don't get too close to the sun."

Hey, Siri, my new family is intense.

"I'm mailing you stuff," Dad says, the sound of cardboard clamoring and duct tape ripping in the background. "I'm at the UPS Store right now. What's your address?"

"Wait. What are you mailing me? What stuff?" I ask, balancing my cell phone to my ear, straightening magazines on one of Kathi's antique side tables, fluffing fresh-cut flowers in a vase given to Kathi by Renée Zellweger after Kathi helped Renée compose a perfect break-up text.

"Stuff from the house. You said not to throw anything away," he says. "So, what's your address?"

"What are you trying to send me exactly?"

"Why are you being so sneaky?" Dad asks.

"I'm not being sneaky. You're being sneaky. Why are you suddenly obsessed with cleaning? What are you trying to send me? Mom's stuff?"

"TELL ME YOUR DAMN ADDRESS!"

The shouting, I'm still shaken by it. I'm sure it's Pavlovian. Therapista says it's common for kids to be stunted by screaming, stunted all the way into adulthood. Screaming is a form of violence and aggression, and children are unable to defend themselves—they're physically weak, and mentally they don't have the words. Therapista says sometimes for adults it's like PTSD. We have to remind ourselves that we are not helpless, that we now have a vocabulary, that we don't have to accept violence.

"Dad. I absolutely do not—"

"WHAT IS IT?!" he yells.

I give Dad my address and hang up. Even at this age, I'm picking my battles.

As I slip my phone back in my pocket, I wonder where I'll put all the shit he's sending me. My kitchen doesn't even have a pantry. My bathroom sink is the size of a spittoon. My closet is packed. No room for new things. In fact, every time Kathi buys me something, I have to throw an older thing away. Like a body sheds cells and is new after a certain amount of time, such is my wardrobe, maybe my life.

Kathi is out of bed, groggy but dressed for the day.

"Did you take your meds today?" I ask, as she ruffles through her purse, walking toward the front door, pulling out her car keys, Mom's locket jingling patiently, unassumingly.

"Yup," she says.

"Want to write today or are you heading out?"

"I'm heading out, darling."

Darling?

That's the first time I've heard her say *darling*. I mean, in the last many months she's called me everything, even names that are not names and words that I'm not sure are words. There's Cockring, Cock, Jimmy, Bubbles, Bubbles-Dundee, Nipples, Nipples-Dundee, and Niblet.

I assume nicknames are easier to remember than *Charlie*. Therapista says a nickname may help her keep me at an emotional distance, help her not see me as a real person. I get it. To really know someone, to really respect a human being with a real name, it's harder to ask them to do things like pick up your hemorrhoid cream or clean your nose-hair trimmer.

There's Tinky, Winkus, Daddy, Assfuzz, Cack, and Rosco.

But never *darling*.

It's so strange and unsettling. *Cockring* at least makes sense, at least fits the picture: a strong woman subjugating me, reminding me who's in charge, who has the power here, a nod to me being gay. But *darling*, it's an endearment, a deferment, a kindness that catches me off guard.

"Miss Gracie gave me this—" I say, holding up a wad of cash as Kathi glides toward me.

"Thanks," she says, snatching the two thousand dollars from my hand.

"That's for vegetables."

"As if I would spend it on anything else," Kathi says.

"But I'm supposed to give it to Agnes for the grocery."

"Don't worry about it."

"Want some company?" I ask.

"Nope," she says, leaving the room. Leaving the porch. Leaving me. *Darling.*

"Am I still a B-plus?" I shout as she walks away, but she doesn't hear, doesn't respond.

I watch her walking to her car, moving her driver's seat forward because I'm the last person who drove it, exiting that gate, nearly getting T-boned by another driver in the busy crook of Beverly Canyon Drive.

Is she safe out there? Can she be alone? Do I want her to be alone? I think of Jasmine and the other assistants, about *being* there for Kathi. I should be with her? I want to be with her. I want to be a helper—the best she's ever had—a protector, apart from the other secretaries who failed and fled and couldn't cut it. But what about moments like this, where she expressly doesn't want me along? Am I *being* if she's not around? Do I exist without her?

I feel the expensive fabric of the shirt she bought me, the soft pants that she said fit me too perfectly for her to pass up, the designer shoes snuggling my feet, which she said would look just right with my growing hair.

I'm wrapped comfortably in the bribe of my gray cashmere sweater.

I'm thinking, *Was the last manic episode really my fault?*

I'm thinking, *Where is Vegas?*

You know Kathi is a drug addict, don't you? I hear Miss Gracie in my head, telling me the not-secret secret the world knows too well.

Standing in Kathi's living room, surrounded by art and wealth, it doesn't feel like the drug den Miss Gracie seems to think lurks under the surface. Sure, Kathi is a mess, she's a project, she's part of a tribe of misfits I've been drawn to my entire life, one of those types who make me feel alive, amused, seen. I can help her. I'm a good influence: I didn't have sex until I was twenty-two. I never even saw cocaine until I was twenty-seven and I refused to partake because I was convinced I'd have a heart attack. Surely I can be a good example for Kathi Kannon.

Assistant Bible Verse 11: You know best. But they can never know that. Since childhood, I've gravitated to those who are different. Marco was the absolute most effeminate kid at St. Peter's Elementary School, and he and I became fast friends. Lonnie was hands-down the most obese kid in all of St. Zachary Parish, and we had sleepovers and joined Cub Scouts together. In junior high, I befriended Luis, who barely spoke English and was the first and last exchange student to ever attend my small, conservative, rural school. There was Clark, with his perfect hair and big gay secret, which we never—to this day—have discussed. Paul and I rode bikes and spent afternoons in capes, running around as superheroes in front of his parents, later revealed to be white-collar felons.

These years later, little has changed. I like wild outliers. My mom used to say I was always drawn to people who need love. My father used to scream, "LEAVE THE FREAKS ALONE! UNLESS YOU ARE ONE?!" I'm thinking, *Maybe.* But mostly I think I'm drawn to differences because I'm bored with everyone else, everyone else with their ordinary, sad, normal lives. Maybe I'm hungry for people who are real and honest, perhaps because for so long, as a gay kid in a strict and rigid household in backwoods Louisiana, I was not. Perhaps I'm drawn to people who are different because I feel different, too. It's not so much that I want to help them as they help me feel less alone. My therapist says helping others is helping yourself.

Bring me your tired, your sick, your mentally ill.

I can feel my hair growing longer by the second, stretching and waiting with me for Kathi to come home, her with my mom's locket in tow, snugly wound onto her key chain, my thumbnail still bruised from the effort, my heart still swollen from our moment up and down the halls of this home, our dance with mania and madness and Mom— with me then, and now with Kathi, my newly knighted Hollywood mother. The locket is well placed: Kathi could use a mom like mine, loving, present, protecting. *Thanks, Mom, please keep her safe.*

I can't wait to see what new item Kathi buys me for my rapidly expanding wardrobe. I look forward to becoming this new person, forged not just by Kathi's purchases and proclamations but by my own will and openness to this experience.

I'm keenly aware of a shift inside me, all around me, as I let go of a past life, past feelings, a voiding of the once always-present aftertaste of hating my existence so much that I considered ending it.

Drugs, lies, warnings, whatever. I can do this. I must.

I read somewhere that travel is a wonderful alternative to suicide. That travel can sometimes siphon you from your stressors, making the world feel bigger and your perceived problems smaller. I rub my palms together like I'm a contestant on *Survivor* trying to start a fire with a twig, like my time lost in a jungle of darkness and disillusionment is over, like a spark of life has set my old self gloriously ablaze, and I'm standing anew in the ashes with great things ahead for me, old troubles abated, my lucky break finally breaking. I'm thinking, tearfully and weightlessly relieved, *Finally, finally.*

Travel is a wonderful alternative to suicide.

Lucky me, because Kathi Kannon is a real trip.

Part Two

☆　　☆　　☆　　☆　　☆　　☆　　☆

BRUSH FIRE
IN THE SPIRIT
WORLD

9

☆

H*ey, Siri,* Kathi Kannon and I are late and I'm in trouble. We're standing in an office-building parking lot, looking at the three-story structure with wraparound balconies on each level, making it appear more like a motel than a professional complex. A meeting with her friend Rick was supposed to start ten minutes ago and she asks me which suite we're supposed to visit.

"I don't know. One second," I say, checking my emails to find the answer, but she doesn't want to wait, so from the parking lot, to my horror, she starts screaming, "RICK! RICK! RICK!"

Slowly, faces start to peek from behind curtains, behind vertical blinds, looking down at us in the parking lot.

"RICK!" she screams.

Doors open and secretaries poke their heads out to get a glimpse of what's happening, to see who's yelling, to see who's screeching like a car alarm.

"RICK! RICK! RIIIIIIIIIIICK!"

Finally, a body emerges from the door of Suite 307. Rick, of course, smiling, waving. "Up here," he says.

"Hi!" she yells, and starts walking to the stairwell.

I follow behind and whisper, "Here it is," holding up my phone with the email and the suite number. "You couldn't wait five seconds?"

"Nope. Thanks anyway, Cockring," she says, grabbing my arm and squeezing, a sort of innocent sign of aggressive affection, her fingers rubbing, rubbing, rubbing my forearm.

"Are your hands clean?" I ask.

With a devilish grin she shakes her head *no*.

SUMMER

Hey, Siri, we're coming in for a landing, a little midweek jaunt home from seeing Kathi's friend Dave Matthews at a charity concert in San Francisco. The seatbelt sign is fully illuminated, flight attendants are buckled in after just making the announcement to stay in our seats, and Kathi says to me, "I have to pee."

Before I can protest, she unclips her seatbelt, stands, marches right past the shocked flight attendants, and goes into the lavatory. The entire plane is watching, people behind us craning their necks in the aisle, popping their heads over the seats in front of them. I'm blushing, unsure how I can help ease the confused fury on the flight attendants' faces. One of them reaches for his seatbelt but stops as we hear a clang in the bathroom. Then a clank. The lock jiggles, going from LOCK to UNLOCK to LOCK to UNLOCK. The red X and the green LAVATORY AVAILABLE lights keep flicking on and off, on and off, further capturing the attention of the jetliner's jetsetters.

The bathroom door opens a crack and then slams shut again. Opens and slams.

We all wait with crushing anticipation.

We hear a flush.

The lock flicks open again.

The door swings ajar.

Kathi Kannon slowly walks back to her seat, flicking her bangs back, oblivious to the theatrical production she just provided free of charge. She nestles in her seat as the plane touches down.

"What?" she says, staring at me staring at her.

"How are you able to break the rules like that with such abandon?"

She says with a shrug, "To the manor born."

FALL

I'm sitting with film icon Kathi Kannon in an otherwise-empty movie theater, eating chocolate chip ice cream and watching some fantasy-type movie because Kathi is friends with Meg Ryan and her son has a small part in it and the two ladies are supposed to see each other soon.

Through the thunderous music, the busy action scenes, the fast and loud dialogue, I hear next to me: *thwp!*

I look over at Kathi, her spoon bobbing in and out of the ice cream container, her eyes glazed and droopy but fixed firmly on the film.

I look back to the screen and then again hear: *thwp!*

I turn back to her. "What are you doing?"

"What?" she asks, seeming annoyed that I'm interrupting the film.

"What's that noise?"

"I know, right? This whole fucking film is noise," she says, shaking her head, bobbing her spoon, slowly loading a blob of ice cream into her mouth, and then—*thwp!*—spitting out a chunk of chocolate.

I look around in a panic, confirming that we are the only ones there, that no one else is seeing what's happening. "What are you doing?" I ask.

"When?"

"Right now? Are you spitting out the chocolate chips?"

"They're too big," she says, her words slightly slurred.

"Too big?!"

"I'm an expert," she says, and turns back to the film.

The spoon.

The bobbing.

The mouth.

Thwp!

Thwp!

Kathi looks over at me looking at her.

"You can't do that," I say.

"What else am I going to do with them? Do you have a tissue?"

"No."

She turns away from me. *Thwp!* "Anyway," she says, "I'm bored."

"Shall we jet?"

"Yup. All this screaming is giving me a headache." She stands and looks down at the darkened floor, trying to navigate her way out. "Try not to step in all this fucking chocolate."

WINTER

Hey, Siri, take note: We're at LAX and paid six hundred dollars for VIP treatment so a handler will escort us to our gate in a golf cart on our way to Utah to a mental-health charity dinner where Kathi is a speaker.

Beep beep beep, make way!

Throngs of people, including the elderly and children carrying their heavy luggage, have to step aside.

Beep beep beep, pardon us!

I turn to her and ask, "Do you think it's weird that we're making all these people move so we can ride to our gate in this cart? Shouldn't we walk? Don't you feel bad?"

She looks up from her phone, turns to me with a wry smile cracking the sides of her mouth. "Not *that* bad."

SPRING

Hey, Siri, we're in Joshua Tree, on an ill-advised adventure shopping for antiques—which don't exist here, not to Kathi's liking anyway. We're both hot and exhausted, and Kathi wants to check into a motel to have a nap to let traffic die down before we drive back to Los Angeles. We stop at a place called Pioneertown and get a room, plus a heaping amount of side-eye from the motel clerk, sizing up Kathi, then me, then her, then me. "You think he's my prostitute?" Kathi asks the sassy teenage attendant.

"That's your business, ma'am," the clerk spits.

Kathi puffs her chest. "Well, he's my . . ." Kathi begins, pausing, considering which phrase will play out the best with a young woman who may be simply a minimum-wage local trying to get by—a sheltered citizen of Pioneertown who doesn't exactly recognize or care she's in the presence of *the* Kathi Kannon. "He's my . . ." Kathi starts again. "He's my . . . stepson," she says, snatching the keys from the clerk. "But if you must know, yes, we are having sex!"

I knew I was family.

"Acting," Kathi whispers to me as she marches us out, off the office's front porch, past the "saloon," past the "bank," and to our bungalow.

"That escalated," I say.

"I couldn't tell that poor woman you're my assistant. How pretentious."

"It hasn't stopped you before."

Kathi smiles. "What are you complaining about? You've now received a promotion to the coveted position of my stepson. And whore."

"I'm honored. Is there a pay raise?" I ask, tugging on my shirt—a bright-orange button-down Kathi bought me at Maxwell's—a smirk on my face, knowing full well that with all the gifts she gives me, I'm wearing my pay raise.

"I pay you in Shine," Kathi says, entering our desert hideaway, dropping her glasses on the floor, tossing her purse on the bed, artfully removing her bra through her shirt sleeve.

"Shine? You mean your cheery disposition?" I ask, picking up behind her—the glasses, the bra, the existentialism.

"No. I mean my famous disposition. That's fame. It's a shine, a glow. And the people around me get addicted to it."

I stand there facing her, still and stoic. "You think I'm addicted to this?" I ask, waving her bra in the air a little.

"You, Cockring? You don't seem addicted to the Shine. Yet. But I've been at this a long time. The glow always rubs off a little. I used to have an entourage, you know. You could tell the ones who loved it, who loved the Shine. You could almost see it smeared on them, like people arrested on *Cops* who deny huffing spray paint but they have a huge circle of silver smeared around their mouths."

Kathi claims the bed closest to the bathroom, and per usual whenever we reach our destination (women's clothing section of Barneys, corner table at La Scala, American Airlines VIP lounge), Kathi immediately empties the contents of her purse, searching for whatever tool she needs in the moment—a hairbrush, a piece of candy, her pill case. Today she's looking for a ring she took off in an antique shop so the owners wouldn't think she had too much money. As her hand shifts and scatters the contents, she finds her ring, slides it onto her finger, and smiles adoringly at it as she puffs on an e-cigarette. She grabs her daily pale-blue pill case and stands to go to the bathroom. The pills rattle inside and stir me like they're an alarm.

"You didn't take your meds today?" I ask.

"Oops. Will remedy that right now."

"Please be on top of that, Stepmom."

"I am on top of it, mostly, Stepson. You haven't seen a manic episode in a while, have you?"

They're very rare.

They're very fun.

I give her a cool thumbs-up as she closes the bathroom door, my cue to put everything back into her purse, including her keys, my mom's locket still suffering on Kathi's key chain, having been tossed and tattered and scratched and stained the last year with her but still here. It's my reminder that I'm committed to Kathi, that we're intertwined in a strange way, and if Mom's spirit could be anywhere, certainly she'd prefer being tossed around in Priestess Talara's purse—beside me—a guardian angel to my Hollywood mother, or I guess now, stepmother.

I'm worrying about Kathi while I'm meeting Superman, or Superman adjacent. He's the latest in new assistants who've entered the fold in the last year. They're all piled in the Village Scribe again, rehydrating with drinks like Power, Superiority, Privilege.

Superman's boss is an actor who's a failed superhero, though his chiseled face still gets him work. I'm watching this new assistant, who's wearing what looks like an outfit from Target—don't worry, he'll get the hang of it—mix and mingle with the other assistants: Jasmine, West, Titanic, Crooner. There are also some new bloodsuckers here to see what they can squeeze from our ranks. Catwoman and Catwoman's second showed up. Speed is here. Sparrow just arrived. *Bruce* is here on a date with, of course, a guy who has the exact same high-fade haircut and perfect cheekbones as Bruce. *Bruce,* ugh, is dating himself.

We're at the bar when Bruce acknowledges me, only for the express purpose of me acknowledging his date.

"Hey, baby. Isn't my date handsome?" Bruce asks me, his arm around his twin.

I look to Bruce's date. "Do you really need me to validate you?" I ask coldly.

"Yes, please," the date says, scoring snickers from Bruce.

"You're both gorgeous."

"Thank you," they say in horrific unison.

"Now, do you have any compliments for me?" I ask.

The two of them are gut-punched silent. I roll my eyes and turn back to Jasmine and West.

West is nursing a second voraciously bubbling champagne and going on about how her boss stacked new responsibilities upon her, forcing her recently to go to the grocery store at nine P.M. "How nice it must be," West says, "to see someone eating sautéed mushroom soufflé in a movie and then call your assistant to call the studio to call the director to call the writer to get the exact recipe from the screenplay and then have me go to the grocery and buy the supplies and then cook it!"

"Wait," Crooner says, flipping his hot-pink hair behind his shoulder. "You cook for your boss?"

"She's a singing icon! What am I supposed to do? She wants soufflé and the chef is off, so guess who's fucking mixing large brown eggs and chopping shiitake mushrooms at ten at night. It's so stressful!" West takes a gulp of champagne from her flute. "Ah, this helps."

"This is our life," Jasmine says, sipping her martini, looking out at the crowd—the assistants we like, those we don't, the ones who are *executive* and the ones who are *personal,* the lifers who will be here for years and the new ones, like Superman, fresh and innocent, like I used to be. "Isn't it amazing?"

I look out, unsure if I'm seeing exactly what she's seeing.

"Look at all these people we know," she says. "If we could harness the full power of all assistants, we could own this town."

"Is that your end game here?" I ask.

"End game? Fuck no. I don't want this to ever end. I'm a lifer! I love being a gatekeeper. It's better than the alternative, a fucking consumer.

Can you imagine watching a movie and not knowing any names in the credits? Hell! Do you know Vanessa Redgrave's mantra before she goes out onstage?"

"No," I say, raising my eyebrows, bracing for a possible taste of genius.

"Her assistant told me that before every show, she closes her eyes, pictures the audience, and says, 'Fuck you, fuck you, fuck you, fuck you.' She says 'Fuck you' to the people paying to see her! It's almost like she'd rather be in an empty theater, like her art is the treasure, she's not doing it for them, she's doing it for her. Isn't that amazing! That's how I feel! I'm an assistant for my own pleasure."

"But you don't make art," I say. "You're an assistant to a publicist."

"A famous celebrity publicist! That's my art, baby!" Jasmine says, putting her martini to her lips and taking the last sip. "Oh, fuck," she says. "There's Poker Face. Do I look cuter than her?" Jasmine turns to me and fluffs her hair as a pop diva's assistant passes us.

"Do you think it's weird that I call you Jasmine and not a nickname?" I ask.

"Jasmine is my nickname," she says.

I nearly drop my drink.

"Oh, careful, baby," she says.

"Who are you guys?" I ask.

"I like the name Jasmine. It was inspired by a bag of jasmine rice, because that's the first thing my boss ever made me buy and I spilled it all over the floor of her Bentley and two years later we still find bits of it stuck in our sandals."

"Don't be shocked," West adds. "None of us have real names, or real lives." She turns to a passing bartender. "I guess I'll have a glass of champagne, please," leaving out that it'll be her third.

"Bruce?" I ask.

"Short for Bruce Wayne," Jasmine says. "His fancy agent boss represents the old Batman."

"Holy shit, what is real? What do you guys call me?"

Jasmine pauses.

Assistant Bible Verse 124: Never ask about your nickname.

"You can tell me," I say.

"Baby," she says.

"Baby!" I shout.

"Yeah," Jasmine says. "Like 'Kathi's baby.'"

"What? Kathi's *baby*?! That's the best you could do? Baby?"

"Well, there was some debate," Jasmine says.

"But we decided it's sort of perfect since you nurse at her tit," West says, her eyebrows cocked.

"Her—what?! I do not!" I yell.

"I can't believe you're so surprised," Jasmine says. "We've been saying it to your face."

"When you've said, 'Hey, baby,' to me, I thought you were just greeting me affectionately!"

"Well, we don't all have great nicknames," Jasmine says. "We're all victims of what others think of us, of our identity based on our employer. It doesn't matter who you really are, it's how you're perceived."

"But I'm not Kathi's baby," I complain. "I'm her equal."

"Oh, sweetie," Jasmine says, putting her hand on my shoulder, giving me a gentle shake. "No, you're not."

"But we've been together a lot, and month and after month we're getting closer. I've been a huge help for her mental illness," I say.

"You're lucky your boss admits she has mental illness. The rest of us mostly have to manage up," West says.

"See what we mean," Jasmine says. "You're like a baby fearing Mommy will be unwell and hold back the milk."

"It's not about the mommy milk." I say, cringing. "It's just: Shouldn't we help?" I ask, wringing my hands, feeling sweat on my forehead and back, the telltale signs my anxiety is piping up. "Shouldn't we do something for them? Find better doctors or something?"

"Just take her money," Jasmine says. "And don't get too involved. Or, in your case, try to get less involved."

"I'll drink to that," West says, her glass reloaded.

"But I'm helping her," I insist. "I'm proud of that. I really do feel like family—not her baby, but her family."

Hey, Siri, I want to be open, to be honest, to get credit. I want my colleagues to give me praise, which doesn't come.

"These people will never be our family," Jasmine says.

"But I'm so close," I say.

"No, you're not," she says.

I smile, my lie, my default emotional setting, better than my default physical one: sweating and clawing at the (now longer) curl on the side of my head. No sense in arguing with Jasmine et al. Maybe they're right. I hear my father screaming inside me: *DO NO HARM!* It's a doctor's oath, but Dad mistakenly thinks it's the Boy Scout motto. He forced me to be a Scout and had fantasies of me going all the way to Eagle, but it was clear early on that I wasn't destined for it. I was more obsessed with which of my handsome scout mates would be sleeping in my tent with me than how to start a fire with lawn clippings. He finally let me quit after I broke a glass in our kitchen. It slipped out of my hand and shattered. He was at work, and I didn't want to get in trouble, so I gathered up all the broken bits, put them in a Ziploc storage bag, and threw them into a briar patch next to our house. When he got home, he happened to find the one tiny millimeter-sized sliver of glass I must have missed. "WHO DID THIS?" he screamed. "WHO BROKE THIS?" I copped to it, shyly, meekly, in a head-down kind of plea for mercy. He wasn't violent with his hands—he never hit me or spanked me—he was violent with his words, which cut me and still labor in my head. "WHERE'S THE REST OF THE GLASS?!"

I told him it was in the briar patch and he exploded.

"WHAT IF A FUCKING RABBIT CUTS ITSELF ON THE GLASS?! DON'T THE SCOUTS SAY, 'DO NO HARM'?! GO FUCKING GET

IT! ALL YOU DO IS HARM EVERYONE AROUND YOU!" I spent hours inching my way into the briars to try to get the little baggie of glass. Fearing snakes and cuts and the sight of my own blood, I finally got one of his ladders from the basement and plopped it on top of the briars, walked across, and retrieved the contraband. No rabbits harmed.

DO NO HARM! His scream still rings inside me, still applies to my life—and now to Kathi's—despite my best efforts to quash his violence. Therapista says a mature mind can decipher which thoughts to keep and which to ignore.

I'm thinking of Kathi as I drink beside these new friends, new colleagues. I'm thinking of how I can help her, free her from harm. The alcohol soothes me, the sharp taste and warmth in my throat remind me of times when my drinking and pot smoking were a regular ritual.

I decline another drink as Jasmine and West order more, apparently making a long night of it. Crooner switches from a vodka soda to a Cosmo, his pink fingernails matching his drink.

"That's colorful," I say.

"Just like your boss," he says.

"Yeah. But I'm working on it."

Do no harm.

"And, anyway," I add, "her colors are a little fun, right?"

"You know what they say about color," Jasmine says. "Put all the colors together and it just turns to black."

10

☆

The boxes arrive en masse, a little more than a year after Dad's threat to send them, his timing always horrendous. They're a collection of the tattered remains of my mother. They're waiting for me on my front porch like bombs—six boxes, twelve by twelve, duct-taped within an inch of their cardboard lives, and the handwriting in Sharpie on each is unmistakably Dad. I taste PTSD, triggered simply by the way he writes, the whirl and edge of his letters like when he would mark up my school book reports and force me to rewrite them from scratch. That same handwriting from childhood cards my mother would force him to sign. That same hand, which hasn't given me a card since the day Mom died those many years ago.

After a long day surviving Kathi—she went on a shopping spree last night and this morning asked me to return everything—plus a long commute home, I'm tired and have to go to the bathroom and just want to rest, and now Dad has sent more work for me to do. I put my bag inside and start hauling the boxes into my tiny apartment.

These boxes: Between my mother and Kathi, now I have two women taking up space in my life.

The boxes still smell like my father's basement, the smell having survived shipping across the country, a no doubt violent packaging and delivery, and worst of all they survived time—these things should have been sorted years ago. I resent him for making me deal with them now because it's a convenient time for him. What about what's convenient for me?

I stack the boxes in front of my small, ratty sofa to use them as a cramped, ugly coffee table of memories of Mom. I have no urge to open them. I'm too busy to dive into Dad's mess. I'm too busy with a new mother figure to deal with my old one.

Kathi's life has been mostly mellow.

Assistant Bible Verse 125: Never let your guard down.

Sleep, bake, Vegas, *repeat.*

The sleep schedule is the same—this is one very tired movie star.

The bake schedule is elevated, with the kitchen of late often filled with cookies, apple pies, three-layer chocolate cakes.

Vegas trips mostly happen when I'm not there—on nights and weekends—or not at all. The bank account has been stable; Kathi's business manager is harassing me less and less about Kathi's spending—which I suppose by their standards has been in check. And I feel like I have her life under control, her details a fixture in my psyche: Her alias at hotels is Aurora Borealis. Her favorite dinner is Magnolia Bakery banana pudding. Her preferred psych ward is Cedars.

I watch Kathi Kannon live her life—have lunch with William Shatner, buy a new giant plastic cow for her front yard, autograph a fan's buttock—and I feel alive, electrified, perhaps by proxy, but no matter. Kathi Kannon has been my antidote.

Hey, Siri, I'm having a blast.

Hey, Siri, I'm part of the family.

Hey, Siri, I want more.

Therapista says greed knows no end.

Why drink from a puddle when you can drink from the ocean.

In the almost two years since Kathi came into my life, or I came into hers, I feel a new surge of aliveness within me. I now crave the things that come with a mindset no longer besieged by depression: I want a home, dog, health, stability, a relationship—all the treasures that feel within my reach having taken this journey so far, treasures at the opposite end of the Kathi Kannon rainbow.

If travel is a wonderful alternative to suicide, so is dating, especially when you work for Kathi Kannon. Dating is not so much an escape from reality as a way to augment it. It's looking at endless other people and seeing them as possibilities in your life, wondering how your world would transform with them in it, how you would look in their social-media feeds, their apartment, sharing their clothes. Dating can make new, brighter things seem possible. Of course, it has the opposite effect if "dating" goes on too long and consistently doesn't end well. But, for now, I'm looking at my options with optimism. I feel worthy of a relationship, maybe for the first time ever. It also feels easier now that I believe I have something to offer, now that I have a secret weapon, an advantage, a confidence. I don't have great beauty—I'm, like, a 6 by Los Angeles standards, surrounded by competition like models and guys wearing designer boots at nine A.M. at Ralphs. I don't have real money or political influence. My superpower is: I work for Priestess Talara.

People in Los Angeles seem to dread the question "What do you do for a living?" Most people here are not doing what they want to do. Their day jobs as waiters and baristas are rebranded as "survival jobs," but it's all the same—something they don't want to define them. But not me. Not anymore. I want to be asked. I wait for it. I bait people into asking the question. They ask me, "What do you do for a living?" And on more than one occasion I point to the T-shirt they're wearing, the T-shirt with *Nova Quest* and Kathi Kannon's iconic image on it, and I say, "I work for her."

I want my job to define me.

I'm updating my OkCupid account with a new picture of myself, with my new, longer hair—now past my chin—and new glasses. Kathi took me to a store on Robertson Boulevard that only sells high-end vintage frames, and she picked out a tortoiseshell number that I'm getting used to, trusting her that they look good. All of the changes she's making in me are requiring cautious adjustment. I'm still not sure whether she's just amusing herself by making me into as much of a clown as possible, but even if she is, I admit, I'm enjoying the attention.

I'm finally filling in my dating profile, answering the dumb questions, taking the steps to finally be someone who's actively dating—not just watching from outside the arena.

My self-summary:

People say I look like Frodo. I want to adopt a dog and name her Whitney Houston. I have an irreverent sense of humor. I might have a therapist. I'm from New Orleans but don't have an accent. I accidentally signed up for a women's gym one time, but they were very nice to me.

Nice to meet you, HipGuy2. He looks a little too much like Mr. Bean.

Nice to meet you, Footballer. He's hot but a little too into feet.

Nice to meet you, Wine&Travel. He's chronically unemployed.

I've been making a mini-career out of OkCupid. I'm messaging dude after dude, waiting for one who writes back, and writes back something interesting, compelling, some proof of my worth of companionship, of having a whole, living, human experience.

What I'm doing with my life:

I'm an assistant to an actress. I used to write TV news. I have a sweet tooth.

I'm meeting men in marathon swaths, sometimes several per week, all dates, no sex.

Nice to meet you, Tye: so boring.

Nice to meet you, Matt: lives with his parents.

Nice to meet you, Tal: not as pictured.

I read their profiles, search for them on Facebook, try my best to screen them, but mostly I find myself putting these guys up against a new standard: Could I ever introduce them to Kathi? It's a new twist on: *Can you bring them home to meet your mother?* My self-esteem isn't quite high enough yet that I would rule all of the duds out if left to my own devices, but I think enough of Kathi that the thought of bringing them to her adds a new hurdle they have to clear, an obstacle course in my mind, where Kathi is taking up residence, holding me to greater goals, becoming my surrogate self-esteem.

I now buy clothes with colors in them. I like that I can tuck my long hair behind my ears. I had my 2002 Nissan Sentra detailed for the first time ever, and as soon as I'm out of debt, I'll get a new car—something that goes well with the new me.

The most private thing I'm willing to admit:
I've never been in a serious relationship. I guess I haven't met the right person. I think I haven't been emotionally available before now. I think I didn't know what I wanted before now. Don't worry, I'm putting together a list. ;)

My Facebook game is also improving. I'm no longer seeing everyone as having a better life than me, because I'm feeling like mine is pretty decent these days. I actually start responding to event invites, liking photos of friends, and forcing myself to be social again—even if my social scene is a little work-related. My friendship circle is a Venn diagram of my Assistants Club and my real life. In the last weeks I've had a cupcake with West. Brunch with Crooner. And coffee with Bruce.

Ugh, *Bruce*. Our hanging out wasn't as formal as it might sound—I ran into him in the pain-relief aisle at Rite Aid and we walked next door for an espresso. His fade is growing out, his fancy shoes clanking a little less loudly these days—he's waiting for the next hot hair-fashion trend, he's waiting for the next move in his executive assistant career, but every path has been dry. I pat him on the back. "Hang in there. Remember silt? You can't have a mountain without a valley every now and then."

He says, "Huh?"

I relish the Shine of Kathi Kannon. I brag to my friends and dates about working for her. I try to drop into conversation as casually as possible, as often as possible, that I work for Priestess Talara, for Kathi Kannon. I show them how her famous iPhone contacts are merged with mine in my phone. I show them how her calendar has pink dots, which are her appointments, merged with blue dots, which are my appointments in my calendar app.

I love telling people I work for Kathi Kannon, film icon. I get mixed but always interesting reactions:

My doctor: "Who's that?"

My landlord: "She's still working?"

The clerk at Rite Aid: "She came in here once and stole something."

These random people, I get some of them autographs for their birthday, as a thank-you gift, as a party favor—like Therapista, who got a framed picture of Kathi as Priestess Talara with an autograph that reads, "I'm blowing you now."

If a celebrity calls my phone looking for Kathi, and I'm with a date, I put the celebrity on speaker and we hold our mouths in hushed awe while I take a message.

I'm showered with celebrity sightings, with gifts, with cash when I do something above and beyond. I google her just to see myself in the background of paparazzi photos, often with my face blurred or my body cut out, disembodied, where my arm is all that remains in the shot, or my foot, wearing a shoe she bought me.

I'm at a friend's house for his birthday party—one of those affairs with a handsome bartender and too many balloons. I'm in the middle of one of my classic Kathi Kannon stories—the one about how we're in some five-star luxury hotel in Spain and I'm trying to scrub a creamy white blob of Baskin Robbins Cookies 'N Cream ice cream out of the blouse she has to wear to Rufus Wainwright's birthday opera in twenty minutes and, as I tell the crowd, "Then Kathi says to me, 'That's not ice cream.'"

Everyone laughs. It's the usual charmer.

But tonight I spot a new face in the crowd.

He says, "Hi. I'm Drew."

I say, "Hi. I'm Charlie."

He says, "Nice to meet you, pal."

"Pal?"

"Yeah, I bet I'm the last guy in the world who still uses that word, and I think it's a shame."

I say, "Alas."

And he smiles.

And he gets it.

And just like that, chemistry, that old but familiar feeling, one I haven't felt in a while. It's old-school style, meeting Drew, meeting this other human face-to-face at a party. No computer between us to hold us back like glass between prisoner and visitor.

Drew is cute in a kind of Scooter-from-the-Muppets sort of way. He's a friend of someone here at this party, someone he quickly ditched so he could hang with me. Drew writes screenplays. He's in a writers' group. He's got a cat named Lucifer.

He says, "So, you work for Kathi Kannon? That's a cool job!"

I say, "Sometimes."

He says, "Tell me everything, pal!"

Pal.

I'm thinking, *What would Kathi Kannon think of him?*

I take Drew back to my place. My apartment isn't the prison it once was; I'm actually starting to be proud of my small, humble home. It no longer needs to be dark and depressing, no longer needs a blackout curtain as mood lighting. Now I dust. I clean. The pay from Kathi is helping me get my head above financial water, so I treated myself to a new small sofa. I added some bookshelves. I bought new sheets and a new comforter for the first time in ten years.

"You moving?" Drew asks, eyeing the boxes Dad sent me.

"No. It's a long story. My mom is in there, basically."

"Oh, okay. That's not weird at all. Let's make out!"

We crash on the sofa and writhe. I consider covering the boxes just in case Mom can see. But who has the time?

I fantasize about Kathi coming to my apartment. Maybe one time when she's in the neighborhood? Maybe one time she needs to stop by to get something—sugar, coffee, validation? I find myself wondering, what will she think of how I live? Will she, like Drew, also judge my mother's unopened boxes in my living room? In my fantasy, I give her the tour of the three hundred square feet: *Here's my kitchen, where I cook. Here's my closet, where I keep the clothes you bought me. Here's my bed, where my dates and I cuddle and I tell stories about you, the fun things, how you're hilarious, how you're kind, how you're my friend.*

Drew and I rush to the bed, our clothes falling on the floor in piles like we're raptured, our bodies sweating and pumping. But this time, I use a condom, because for the first time in a while, I now feel like I have a life worth protecting.

"I miss you when you're not here," Kathi says from the warmth of her bedding as I wake her on a Monday morning. "It's been a long weekend with no Cockring."

Assistant Bible Verse 126: Always keep them wanting more.

Sleep, bake, Vegas—*Cockring—repeat.*

"Did you take your meds today?"

"Yezzzzzzz."

"Want to write today?"

"Noooooooo."

"Everything okay?"

Kathi looks at me. "I'm so tired, Cockring. Tired of thinking all the time. Tired of worrying all the time. Tired of feeling like I'm never good enough. I'm not skinny enough. I'm not in enough movies. I don't have enough money. I'm just so tired. I just want to do nothing. I just wanna think about nothing, but meditation escapes me and I don't look great with a beard."

I pat her on the shoulder. "Acting?" I ask.

Kathi rolls from bed, hair like an anime character. "Hey, I need you to drive me to a friend's house to pick up something. The street is under construction, so it's a bitch to park. That okay?"

"Sure!" I say, excited to do something instead of sitting around. "Want to brush your hair before we go?"

"No, I don't."

She's already mostly dressed, probably in the clothes from yester-day but that's fine. She hands me her keys, Mom's locket shining in the morning sun. I rub it, the warmth entering my thumb and radiating through my body, like I'm hugging an old friend. "I can't believe you haven't lost or broken this yet."

"Broken what? My neck?"

"No, the locket."

"What locket?" she asks.

My hand drops, the keys jingling by my side. "Are you kidding me? Like, ages ago when you were manic I gave you this—my mother's locket."

"A locket? Like from *Annie*?"

"No!" I snap, then, "Well, yeah, kinda. A little."

Kathi approaches and looks at the key ring. "Oh, yeah," she says. "I wondered where that came from."

"You're welcome," I say, shaking my head. "Is nothing sacred?"

"Everything. Which means nothing."

Our ride to West Hollywood leads us through the greens of Beverly Hills to the even more colorful gay bars and sex stores of Santa Monica Boulevard. At a red light, I notice Kathi looking at a store selling bondage gear.

"You need some whips and stuff?" I ask.

"Definitely," she says.

"I knew you were dirty."

She says matter-of-factly, "Yeah. I can't even cum unless I see blood."

As the light turns green and the world outside our car windows becomes a blur again, I exhale and clear my throat. "Speaking of. I met someone."

Kathi slowly looks over at me. "Speaking of cum or blood or both?"

"I met a guy," I say.

"Oh, God."

"What? Are you horrified? Or you can't believe it?"

"No. It's just, relationships are dangerous for assistants," she says.

"You don't want me to get hurt?"

"No, I don't want you to quit working for me!" she yells. "Blythe Danner thought it would be cute to introduce her little assistant to a designer she loved and then the designer and the assistant fell in love and then the assistant quit to go live an exciting gay romantic life in Paris or somewhere greasy and meantime Blythe can't find someone competent to take his place and who's going to help her eat?! It also happened to Mary Steenburgen. And Faye Dunaway, but that's also because she once sprayed her assistant with the hose for asking to come inside to use her restroom."

Assistant Bible Verse 127: It's hard to live your own life and also live theirs. It's hard to service two people at once.

"But I'm happy for you," Kathi says.

"Thanks?"

"Who is he?"

"His name is Drew and he's a writer."

"Ugh," she says.

"What?! His name is dumb?"

"No. Writers."

"Should I avoid dating a writer?"

"What kind of writer?" she asks, fumbling with the AC vent like she needs air urgently.

"Screenwriter."

"*Ugh!* Run!"

"Really?"

"Anything I've seen?" she asks.

"No. He sold a couple scripts to Lifetime, but they haven't been made yet."

"Oh, you're probably fine, then. Try it," Kathi says. "I haven't had much luck with writers in the love department. Of course, I haven't had much luck with anyone. Tell me more about him and we can judge him accordingly."

"Well, he's—"

"Not right now, though, Cockring. Can we do it later?"

"Sure," I say cheerfully, as GPS guides us down a beautiful side street to a bright-orange apartment building. "Where are we?"

Kathi looks ahead with no joy, no focus. "*Vegas.*"

"Vegas?" I ask, confused, trying to understand.

"I'll be right back," Kathi says, getting out of the car and slamming the door.

"*Vegas?*" I yell again to her from inside the car. I'm thinking, *She must be joking.*

As she walks away from me, the sunshine streaming down between tree branches, the light reflecting off car windshields, and Kathi Kannon's body almost illuminated, I think of the Shine. I savor the thought of my life brightened by her. And as she makes her way into someone's apartment, vanishing behind some cheap door in some cheap complex, I feel a sudden disconnect.

Assistant Bible Verse 128: Never leave their side.

I feel a sensation of being out of place—both me and her.

The glow of her is gone, the spell broken. I wonder, *Where are we?* I wonder, *Where is she?*

The Shine, I feel it, I feel it fading.

11

☆

ey, Siri, I'm carrying a purple leather backpack full of cash. I signed Miss Gracie's ledger and she handed me three gallon-sized Ziploc bags full of vegetable money. "This is ten thousand dollars, dear. Don't give it to Kathi or else she'll waste it. And if you steal any of it, I will prosecute and I will seek the death penalty."

Kathi has been restless at home, and Miss Gracie suggested using veggie money to do some traveling and relaxing. Kathi jumped at the idea and sent me down to Miss Gracie with this purple bag to collect the dough. Kathi said she hated the generic backpack I've owned since college. She asked me to use this new purple one for work from now on. It perfectly holds all the money, like it was made not for books or gym clothes, but for cash.

I hate to brag, but it's all I want to do. I want to boast about my new life with Kathi, boast about the money, the celebrities, the upcoming trips: New York, Indonesia, Australia, Japan.

Assistant Bible Verse 129: Pack sunscreen, aspirin, speculum.

Roger gave me specific instructions, showing me exactly how much Miss Gracie expects us to spend on tipping, et cetera. The big expenses—

lodging and airfare—are all covered. The cash is already converted to local currency: rupiahs, Australian dollars, yen. They're already broken into fives and tens and twenties, based on Miss Gracie's estimation of how many cars we will need, how many meals we will eat, how many bellmen we will need to bribe. Miss Gracie has it down to an art.

Booking lodging was simple. Kathi once did some script doctoring for a wealthy woman who owns a timeshare in Bali and paid Kathi with visitation rights in perpetuity. So Kathi is making a trip of it—and while we're over there, Kathi reasoned, let's see Sydney and Tokyo. And on our way out there, we'll stop in New York for good measure.

Pack scarves, Christmas lights, glitter. Kathi likes to bring the party with her and uses scarves over hotel lamps to set a mood, Christmas lights—as many as we can fit in the luggage—for ambiance, and, of course, glitter, always. I stuff everything into her luggage—two big antique red trunks with leather straps; even her suitcases are interesting.

Booking airfare was easy. I called her travel agent, provided the destinations, got flight options. Kathi picked the flights, and the travel agent bought us two first-class seats next to each other. Kathi always buys a first-class seat for me. I'm not sure if it's because she's being kind to me or if she just prefers falling asleep and drooling on me instead of a stranger.

"Are you ready to do some relaxing?" I ask cheerfully as the first leg of our journey begins out of LAX.

"God, Cockring," Kathi says, "bring it down a notch."

"Did you take your meds today?"

"Yup."

Pack Seroquel, Suboxone, Lamictal.

Kathi Kannon stops in New York like normal people stop at a gas station. She's here to refuel, to fully charge, to fill up—just for one night. We leave tomorrow for real adventure, to Bali, but first, Big Apple.

"Checking in," I tell the front desk clerk at the Greenwich Hotel.

"What's the name?" she asks.

I lean in close, raise my eyebrows, and say, "Aurora Borealis."

The clerk smiles faintly, looks down at her computer, then says, "Ah, yes."

Kathi steps up to the front desk. "I just want to confirm that my room is bigger than his, please?"

"Of course," the clerk says, tapping away at her keyboard, and then, "Yes, I can confirm it is." The clerk grins, thrilled to have inserted herself in the little joke. Kathi and I stare at her seriously. The thing about Kathi having a bigger room, it's only barely a joke.

I put Kathi in her room—large, bright, airy, as promised. Kathi gets a deluxe suite with sitting area and bathtub. We drape her scarves over the lamps, turning the room from white to peach and blue and purple. We string Christmas lights from one side of the headboard to the other. The glitter stays in her toiletry bag, for emergencies only.

The hotel is peak luxury. All items in every room are curated, even in my room. The sofa is an antique; you can see the outline of the old springs imprinted in the velvet cushion. Books on the built-in shelves are hardcover literature, frayed edges telling the tales of their storied lives, stories within stories within stories. There's a tiny brass lamp with a crooked little bend that makes it look like a character from a Pixar cartoon; it looks like the little lamp is waving to me, welcoming me. I want to take it home.

Snap: I take a picture to email to Jasmine, Bruce, West. *"Even the lamps in NYC are cool!"*

Snap: I take a picture of Kathi's bathtub to email my dad. *"Mom would have loved this, right?"*

Snap: I take a picture of my king-sized bed to email Drew. *"Wish you were here."*

Hey, Siri, I'm thinking, *everyone's gonna be really impressed now.*

Later, a housekeeper mentions that Bradley Cooper is working out in the hotel gym. Kathi races down in a knit Chanel sweater and Miu

Miu ballerinas and casually hops on a treadmill beside him. I watch from the towel station as she cranes her neck to make eye contact with him. He smiles politely. She makes her move. "What's a guy like you doing in a gal like me?" she says seductively. He grimaces.

"Oh, shit. Did I fuck up the saying?" she asks.

He nods.

"Ah, fuck it," she says, maneuvering off the treadmill, leaving it running empty beside him. He turns to watch her walk away with me rushing behind her.

Like Rite Aid is a vortex of tragedy, the Greenwich Hotel is a vortex of celebrity.

Later that evening, Mel Gibson sidles up beside Kathi while she's ordering a Coke Zero at the hotel bar. "Hey, I know you!" he says.

"You do?" Kathi says coyly. "Are you an actooooor?"

"Sometimes," he says. "Can you tell because you recognize me from some hit motion picture?"

"No," Kathi says, grabbing her Coke Zero and turning to leave. "I can tell by your veneers."

Later, Ewan McGregor walks by and spots Kathi, looks at me with her, and says, "Hello."

I say to him, "Hi. I loved you in *Trainspotting, Velvet Goldmine, Moulin Rouge*! You're such a talent, a genius, a star. Great to meet you!"

Kathi swallows a gulp of Coke Zero and says to him, "I was just looking at your penis on Google."

Seconds of small chat later and Ewan moves on to another group of admirers.

"Feeling relaxed, enchanted, entertained?" I ask Kathi.

"I'm bored," she says.

Film icon Kathi Kannon has it all: fame, money, tooth pain.

Kathi started to complain about *something* being wrong, in steady progression, from the time we left New York, to getting on the plane, to getting off it twenty hours later in Indonesia, of all places to be unwell.

Bali, that elusive paradise I've only seen on the screen saver at my old news job, I'm now seeing with my own eyes, breathing the air, appreciating the ocean view to my right and the homeless child begging for food to my left. Surely there are doctors here.

By now my senses are trained on Kathi Kannon. I see problems before she does. It's in my best interest to stop anything before it advances, progresses, entraps. I hear her sniffle, I buy Claritin. A scratchy sound in her throat, I buy cough drops. Not using a roll of toilet paper fast enough, I buy laxatives.

"Do we have any Tylenol?" Kathi asks. "My tooth is killing me."

Is it? I wonder. I haven't seen the signs. I haven't seen her rubbing her face, flexing her mouth. Is she angling for meds? Is this getting too close to the sun? Is this what Miss Gracie was talking to me about?

Of course I packed Tylenol. I packed Advil. I packed water-purification tablets.

Assistant Bible Verse 130: Being an assistant is tricky at home and even worse on the road.

If you want to really know someone, travel with them.

I reach into the purple backpack. I hand her two Tylenol.

She says, "Four please."

"But your pancreas!"

She says, "I don't think I have one. Wasn't it removed in the nineties?"

"I don't know."

She says, "I hope we survive Bali."

I don't know exactly what she wants to survive or what she fears might not survive: Our relationship? Our lives?

The sweet driver, in broken, shattered English, asks where we're from.

Kathi replies, "Space. But, unfortunately, my home planet was blown up. I'm still upset about it."

The driver nods in polite, confused agreement. Kathi turns to me. "Distract me from the pain of living."

"How?" I ask sincerely.

"Are you having . . ." And she pauses, playfully rolling around in her mind what to say next, considering the many words in her inner thesaurus she wants to use to punctuate her sentence. "Are you having . . . sex?"

"Oh, please," I say.

If you want to really know someone, travel with them.

"Because I'm not. As you probably know," she says. "And at least one of us should. So, how's your lover?"

"Drew? Is he my *lover*? I don't know. I've never been in a serious relationship."

"You've never been in a serious relationship?!" she asks. "Why not? We all deserve to live that fucking nightmare at least once in our lives."

"Haven't found the right person, I guess."

"Who told you there's a right person?"

"Therapista says—"

"Who the fuck is Therapista?" she asks. "What the fuck kind of name is that?"

"Therapista, my therapist—"

"Oh, Jesus," she says. "Never listen to them. Therapy is not about you, it's about them. They're giving advice to themselves. You are your best teacher. Want some advice from a woman old enough to be your sexual abuser?"

I say, "Absolutely."

"Life only exists in your mind. Everything you see, everything you hear, all of it, it goes through your eyes and ears and is processed by your mind, and the mind can lie, can be sick, can get it wrong."

I say, "Wow," and then, "That's so wise," and then, "What does that mean?"

"And do you want to hear my advice about relationships?" Kathi asks.

I nod. I'll take all the advice I can get.

She cups a hand in front of her face as if she's holding something delicate, opens her mouth, and gives an air blowjob to a huge cock, enormous imaginary balls resting in her other palm.

I stare at her a few seconds. She's holding in her laughter.

"Is that the advice?" I ask.

She cracks herself up and nods *yes*.

"How's your tooth?" I ask pointedly.

Still giggling at herself, she says, "It really hurts, Cockring."

"You need a dentist?"

Laughing, she nods *yes*.

Hey, Siri, the timeshare in Bali has it all: private swimming pools, outdoor showers, an on-call dentist.

This is a teaching moment.

Assistant Bible Verse 131: The personal assistant will never let their celebrity consult with a doctor alone. The celebrity will either give too much or get too much.

A chauffeur drives us to a tiny dental office that looks more like a preschool. While the dentist takes some x-rays, I hear him talking to Kathi about things like "problem areas" and "decay" and "prior drug use."

The next time you see a star on the red carpet, remember you never know what's going on inside their mouth.

While Kathi is getting her dental work done, I turn to my own life and start to email Drew. The stakes with him seem higher the farther away I get, perhaps because the more the miles, the more the time zones, the weirder the cell-phone carriers, the less and less control I feel I have—or, rather, the illusion of control. The thought lingers, of course, that if I don't make it happen, it never will. So I carry on.

Hi, Drew. Hope you had a good visit with your family and they loved seeing you in Los Angeles. Maybe it's good I didn't meet them yet—less pressure to introduce you to my insane father. Ha! Xo C

Hey, pal! My parents loved hearing about you and your work stories! Missing your face. And your entire body. I'd love to meet your dad. I can get some tips about unbanking. LOL. Happy travels.—Drew

I feel the opposite of Kathi's tooth pain, my body radiating with excitement, my body heat rising so much, blood pumping with such ferocity that it feels like my heart has new marching orders, to exalt this beat, carry this torch, dance this song forever.

About an hour later, and the dentist rips off his exam gloves and stands over Kathi. She sits up and wiggles her jaw.

"Good as new," he says.

"Not really," Kathi grumbles, spitting.

I pat him on the back and usher him away from Kathi.

"So, she was really hurting?" I ask.

"Oh, yeah," he says. "Damaged filling. No problem now."

I lean forward to hug him with relief, appreciation, but he backs away.

"What pain medications is Kathi allowed to take?" he asks.

My job responsibilities include managing her money, managing her medications, managing her addiction.

"What's the least addictive thing you can give her? She's an addict."

"Recovering!" Kathi yells from across the room; her hearing has never been better. "*Recovering* addict!" She starts to walk over to us.

The dentist asks, "What has she safely taken in the past?"

I say, "Lemme find out." I'm holding her purse, her emergency-contact numbers, my integrity. I open Safari on my phone. The great thing about having a celebrity boss is that almost everything is online. Birth dates, career lows, drug history.

Assistant Bible Verse 132: Get the biggest international data plan possible for your cell phone. You're gonna need it. Consider maps, consider emails, consider pulling up a fifty-eight-year-old's medical history on the Cedars hospital website.

I'm scanning the Web for Kathi's prescription history, but the dentist is ahead of me. He hands me a full bottle of pills to get us through the trip.

"Here," he says. "Just take these as needed."

"What are they?" Kathi asks.

"Tylenol with codeine." He hands them to me.

"Cockring, give me those," Kathi says, wiping her mouth and ripping the paper bib from her chest, approaching me like a star to her mark. "I know what I'm doing. Believe me."

She reaches for the pill bottle, but I resist handing them over. "I'm nervous about this. Considering everything. Miss Gracie says you've overdosed several times."

"No. That's crazy," Kathi says, keeping eye contact, a steady gaze, a movie scene.

The dentist watches like we're a comedy act.

"Why would Miss Gracie lie to me about your drug overdoses?"

"She's not lying. She's joking." Kathi reaches for the pills again. I pull away again.

"She's joking about your drug overdoses?" I ask.

"They were hilarious. You had to be there. And that's all years ago. Way behind me."

"It didn't seem like a joke when she said you nearly died. Repeatedly."

"Miss Gracie is over eighty," Kathi says. "Her memory is severely affected by age. And chardonnay. It never happened like that."

"She said you'd say that. That you'd hardly remember because you were so out of it."

"I'm not dead, am I?" Kathi asks.

"No."

"So I must know what I've been doing these last many decades and counting."

"Well—"

"Darling," Kathi says, trying to soothe me.

Darling. That word again.

"Don't worry," she says, turning to the dentist. "Pills don't make you high if you're in pain. Right, Doctor?"

"I love your movies," he says.

I'm thinking, *Pfft.*

Kathi turns back to me. "See?" she says, taking the pill bottle and slipping out of the dentist's office like a warm knife through a stick of butter, me following behind, like that gross waxy paper that sticks of butter come wrapped in.

Riding back to the timeshare, I stare at Kathi, still looking for signs of a lie, signs that this actress might be acting. But there were x-rays and a doctor. I have no evidence, only bias based on Miss Gracie's paranoia and my desire to keep Kathi alive because I love her, my paycheck, and my newfound panache.

Kathi casually stuffs the pain pills in her purse along with whatever other mess she's collected earlier in the day, the week, the year: loose change, paperclips, oatmeal—all stuff I'll fish out and sort and discard later.

She sees me staring at her. Her eyebrows go up: *What are you looking at?*

I just smile. What do I know for sure?

Bali is a blur outside our car windows.

Snap: The gorgeous white-sand beach.

Snap: A pack of rabid dogs.

Snap: An entire family of five riding on one rickety Vespa.

"These people are us," Kathi says, staring out as Bali spins past.

She taps the pills in her purse and they rattle.

"Cockring," Kathi says, "I give you an A-plus for getting these meds."

My heart explodes. *A-plus.*

I'm thinking, *Dreams come true.*

I'm thinking, *I'm the best.*

I'm thinking, *Did I just sell my soul?*

Kathi looks at me. She says, "I'm bored."

Snap: We fed bananas to monkeys.

Snap: We got mud baths at an ancient bath.

Snap: We met a wise elderly shaman who cleansed my aura but only half of Kathi's, because in the middle of the ceremony his cell phone rang and he had to take the call—his ringtone was "Pour Some Sugar on Me."

After a long day of privileged adventure, there's nothing like the warm lighting, huge bath, and expensive linens of a five-star luxury timeshare in Bali to remind you that you're all alone, no one to kiss in the dim lights, no one to share the tub with you, no one sleeping by your side. In bed, I look out the windows at the lush greenery swaying gently in the soft lighting, framed by the clear black sky. I tug at the covers, trying to bunch them around my body, my nest of pampering and platitude. The moments before I fall asleep are precious seconds for me to gift myself the illusion that I'm being cared for instead of just doing all the caring. Longing for someone to be there for me, I pop open an email to my guy.

Dear Drew, Bali is enchanting. We fed bananas to monkeys. The poor monkeys. Some of them have open sores. Hope I don't have some disease now. Cheers! Leaving here soon. Xo C

Dear Oak, I wanna kiss all over your monkey-diseased body! Hurry home! Have fun! Smoochfest.—Drew

P.S. *I can't believe I wrote "DEAR OAK!" I just noticed my phone autocorrected the word "Pal" to "Oak"! Guess your new nickname is Oak! Thanks, iPhone!—Drew*

Oak. That thick and stately tree, symbolic of both strength and beauty. I feel a certain ownership of the species, having grown up in New Orleans, where great oaks are a sign of wealth, lining St. Charles Avenue, framing the mansions that sit under their great shade. Curly clumps of gray moss dangle from the branches like fresh-permed hair of old witches, adorning the foliage with a magic that's both frightening and hallowed. *Oak.* Better than Frodo, Baby, and Cockring.

Maybe Drew is feeling what I'm feeling, a fragility underscored by the time and space between us. Maybe Drew is signaling his hope for something solid to be ours. Maybe Drew or, at least, maybe his phone.

"I hope we survive Australia," Kathi says playfully, as our plane touches down in Sydney in the middle of the night. We go directly to the Four Seasons. Relaxing is exhausting. Our ride there feels like we could be anywhere, darkness in all directions.

"Reservation for Aurora Borealis," I say to the front-desk clerk.

Keys in hand, I open Kathi's hotel room door and let her go in first. She instantly makes a mess, rummaging through the drink fridge and candy bar, cracking open a can of Coke Zero, and emptying her purse on the floor, looking for her hairbrush or her e-cigarettes. She opens her suitcase and hunts for the scarves to drape over the lamps; the Christmas lights get tossed about.

I look out of the window.

Snap: I take a picture of the Sydney Opera House. I'll email everyone in the morning: "*How cool is this view?*"

I say, "Good night."

She says, "Good night, Cockring."

Before I go to bed each night, I work out a little. I use the hotel gym sometimes, but I also pack an exercise ball, which I inflate with a small battery-powered air-mattress pump. I'm keeping my core tight. I do push-ups and triceps dips on the bed. Fitness has found a place in my life where there was not any before. My diet has gone from fast food to gourmet room service. My hair is getting longer and my waist is getting smaller. I'm decked in winter cashmere or summer couture, depending on our time zone. I look at myself in the hotel bathroom infinity mirror. A million versions of myself, so different from the days of newswriting and no sleep and suicidal confusion. I see a million lives, where it seems a short time ago, there was barely even one.

Dear Drew . . . Sorry to miss your birthday. Things have been hectic but I have so many great stories to share with you. How's your new screenplay coming? How did your meeting with the agent turn out? Wish I was there to hear all this in person. Xo . . . "Oak"

I'm becoming friends with the send button, its crisp blue letters on my iPhone less and less intimidating when I write to *Him*, to Drew. How careful I used to be with my words and punctuation and pronouncements in the early days of our dalliance. And now I'm just getting the message out, trusting the subtext, if any, and counting the moments until he writes back, holding my breath, turning blue in the most marvelous, longing, childlike way.

I'm opening my hotel room door, my purple backpack in hand, the morning's cold soda ready for her, about to deliver it to her room and start a new day, and I smell smoke in the hallway. It's a cigarette in a no-smoking hotel. I have an idea who's breaking the rules.

I rush down the hall, the carpet absorbing my impact; it feels like I'm running with sponges in my shoes, running in quicksand.

"Good morning," I say loudly, smoke twisting in cinematic swirls as I open and close Kathi's door. Her room is a hotbox.

Her television is on, her head slouched to the side—as if asleep— a lit cigarette in her hand. There's a small burn mark on the comforter. All these people in the hotel have no idea how close they are to a film icon who almost killed them. From one degree of separation to 451.

I watch her for a couple beats. Sometimes, before I wake her, I wonder what I'll do if she won't stir. If she's dead. If I'm ever in a real-life nightmare. Isn't this how they—those so-called "assistants"— always find their celebrities? Doesn't TMZ document the demise of whomever—Prince, Elvis, Whitney—with some story about how they were late for lunch or didn't answer a call and the assistant goes to find them and, *bam,* they're found "unresponsive"? Remember the next time someone thinks this job is glamorous, assistants are the ones who have to deal with their boss's dead body.

I reach to take the cigarette from her fingers and she immediately moves, bringing it up to her mouth, taking a breath, as if she was a TV show on pause and I hit the play button. As she exhales, before I can say a word, she doesn't skip a beat: "Cockring, was your stool black this morning?"

I give my usual response: raised eyebrows and leaning my head forward toward her as if to say, *Excuse me,* though I don't say it, not aloud.

"Mine was," she says. "Black. Or a dark gray. A Spalding Gray." She chuckles at her own joke, and I smile, too. There's not another human being on the planet like her, and I'm the luckiest voyeur on earth, unless she kills us all in a five-alarm fire.

"You could have burned the hotel down falling asleep with that cigarette."

"What cigarette?" she says, pulling it to her mouth and taking its last breath. She snuffs it in a hotel glass with other butts soaking in an inch of old, watered-down Coke Zero.

"And where did you get cigarettes?" I ask.

Kathi shrugs.

"How's your tooth?"

"Better," she says.

I begin my usual routine. Tidying the room. Removing the wrappers of candy she's eaten during the night and stuffed in shame between the headboard and the wall. Wiping off the wet rings from her glass of soda, which are slowly staining, ruining the hotel furniture, leaving her mark everywhere she goes, like a child writing in wet cement. On the nightstand, I place her fresh new glass of Coke Zero right beside the pill bottle we got from the dentist. Is it less full? She sees me eyeing it, studying it, calculating its contents.

"Am I still famous?" Kathi asks.

"You're a sensation. Did you take your meds today?"

"Yes, Cockring."

"Would you like to write today?"

"No, Cockring. We're on vacation. Let's go shopping. Where's the cash?"

I turn to my purple leather backpack and rummage through the thousands of dollars of vegetable money Miss Gracie entrusted to my care.

"How much cash do you want today?" I ask.

Kathi holds up her fingers as if she's measuring: two inches, three inches, one inch. "About this much," she says, a wicked smile on her lips.

I'm thinking, *Miss Gracie didn't account for all this.*

Kathi grabs her fresh glass of soda and goes into the bathroom. As the door clicks shut, I notice the bottle of pills is no longer on her nightstand.

If you want to really know someone . . .

Suddenly the bathroom door swings open and she sticks her head out and we stare at each other. "Are you monitoring me?!"

"Yes."

"Here," she says, tossing me the bottle of painkillers. "Then you be in charge. You be my pharmacy. I'm due for my next one in six hours."

She goes back in the bathroom and slams the door. I shake the pill bottle, victorious, proud of her, and put it in my bag.

Dear Drew, hope to be home soon. How are things with you? Haven't heard from you in a while. Have you been getting my pics? Xo—Oak

Spiraling is the wrong word, for I'm not quite spinning hopelessly out of control as much as I'm steadying myself for the folly of thinking something's wrong. Surely there's been a glitch. Surely Drew's emails to me have just gone to a spam folder or have been lost in the ether, the in-between where memories and hopes and forget-me-nots are lost, accidentally misshelved in the library of living. I'll laugh about this with him, this mistake of me not receiving his emails, of me panicked he's no longer interested. He'll tell the story and I'll laugh. And we'll be at brunch holding hands under the table and his friends will drink in his retelling and we'll laugh anew at this hilarious mistake where he didn't write me for weeks and I thought he was ghosting me and the whole time he's wondering why I'm the one not writing him back. Oh, the glee of love, of trying to love. *Love?*

This isn't my first time at the rodeo, or at the mall, which isn't much different. At least a mall in Australia is more exotic than one back home.

Being a celebrity assistant is a lot like raising a child, or a puppy. Assistant Bible Verse 133: It helps to wear them out.

And so here we are, doing laps and walking in and out of stores.

"Relaxed yet?" I ask.

Kathi, looking sad with puppy-dog eyes, shakes her head *no.*

Some people shop by sight—what looks good—but Kathi Kannon shops (and lives) by touch—what feels good. She brushes her hands across a colorful sweater or scarf or sock, and if it's soft, she'll take it. She spends a quarter inch of cash on a snug sweater she may wear once and then gift to Agnes. She spends a half inch of cash on an Australian alpaca trench coat. "This seems pretty. Maybe for Benny," Kathi says.

"I'm sure he has lots of use for it, living in your shed."

"Cockring, what has this Australian alpaca coat ever done to you?" Her speech is slurred. We're both exhausted.

"Time for my next pill?" she asks.

I look at my watch. "Yep. You sure are good at telling time."

I fish the pill bottle from my purple backpack, open it, finger out a pill, and hand it over. She pops it immediately—I don't even see her swallow. She winks.

I ask, "What's next?"

She says, "I'm bored."

"I hope we survive Japan," Kathi says, looking down at Kyoto, its bright lights piercing through the night sky as we come in for a landing.

Snap: The limo that drives us to the hotel.

Snap: The finely groomed white-sand sculptures.

Snap: The boat that takes us to the lobby.

Hey, Siri, our hotel in Kyoto is accessible only by boat. The Hoshinoya is built along a river. It's the kind of place tourists pay money to pass by and take photos. And we're staying here, sharing a villa.

"Reservation for Aurora Borealis," I say at check-in.

"How much to dress him as a geisha?" Kathi asks the front-desk clerk.

"I don't want to," I say.

"He's very officious," Kathi says to the clerk. "But I'm sure there's a wild man in there who comes out at night, his testicles wrapped in a bright-yellow thong, cheeks of his buttocks red from a fresh walloping, right?"

Kathi turns and stares at me, daring me to react. I don't budge. We both turn at the same time to look at the clerk to see if she reacts. She's fucking confused. She doesn't understand the brilliance of that moment, where an icon whips from molecules of space around us a twisted and erotic tale that's so compelling you want to get high off it. I'm drunk with awe of how a human being like her can take the most ordinary of moments—checking in at a hotel—and turn it into an otherworldly memory, a thrill, an essential ingredient in what makes a life feel full.

Worn out from a day of airports, I get Kathi settled in her room and prepare to leave her for the night. I watch her. She tinkers with her phone, fiddles with her e-cigarette. She's in a strange room and is just as comfortable as if in her own home, just as comfortable living her life with me staring at her as with me not staring at her, probably more. Kathi Kannon has never been alone. She's been surrounded her whole existence with help, nannies, assistants, chefs, directors, doctors, enablers. She can sleep soundly with throngs of people around her, impervious to noise. Therapista says learning how to be alone with others is a key part of a healthy relationship.

"Well, good night," I say.

"What is the meaning of it all, Cockring?" she asks.

"Of Japan?"

"Of life." She looks up at me for an answer.

"I don't know."

"Why do you wake up in the morning?"

"I just wake up."

"But what forces you from your slumber, what urge, what drive, compels you from your bed?" she asks.

I think for a minute while Kathi does her movie-star thing, her technique where she stays deadly still, letting the imaginary camera in the room capture the seconds of silence. In a film, this kind of blank space is where the audience can ascribe their own emotions and feelings to the moment. But, alas, this is a moment just between Kathi and me. She is motionless and open, not unlike her quiet poise when I first met her years ago—Kathi Kannon, film icon, waiting for me, loser, to speak up, to tell her why I want to work for her, and for her to pipe down, to listen, to see where her scene partner will take her next. And I've—we've—ended up here, across the world, me assigning to the quiet between us the role of "interest," assigning to Kathi a curiosity about me, assigning to her the role of interviewer, for a change. And in the silence comes truth: I'm not prepared to be like her, to be an interviewee, to grab the microphone and profess some wise insight to the universe. Instead, I'm happy but it feels precarious, like I'm still bumbling around in the dark, taking baby steps to avoid tripping and falling, waving my hands and knocking things over, clumsy and inept, grossly unable to articulate any reason why I might actually have a true, tangible desire to be alive, what I have to live for, truly, besides her. My possible answers are stifled by confusion, dismay, and, I daresay, also a warm and surprising questioning of why she is asking about me at all, why she would even have any interest in lowly me—an assistant—and my egregious humiliation that I have no immediate answer for her, for what does get me out of bed in the morning? Really?

"I don't know," I say. "Is that sad?"

Kathi considers it for a moment. I wonder if she will stretch this time out, too, a great pizza dough spinning in the air until the inertia is too much and it becomes spotted, spoiled, unwhole. But she doesn't. She takes the reins again, steering us, guiding us, though to where, I'm not sure either of us knows.

"It's okay to not know. That's genius mind," she says. "Not knowing is what makes people discover great things, do great things."

"You sound like the message in a fortune cookie. Or like the moral of some kids' cartoon show."

"Well, I am an action figure."

"And so what forces Priestess Talara from her slumber?" I ask.

"Usually you do. Waking me up at all kinds of ungodly hours."

"And when I'm not there?"

She pauses. "I don't know," she says.

Genius mind.

I look at Kathi Kannon with great fondness, my boss, my big, living, human action figure, fierce, strong, a fighter. I try to imagine how she would have fought back against my dad had she been there with me all those years ago, all those many moons ago when he yanked her plastic image and likeness from my hands. What a fitting replacement I've found in her actual presence in my life.

She says, "All I can think about right now is . . ."

And I guess: "Life? Death? Love?"

"A jar of peanut butter in my purse that I shoplifted today."

"WHAT?!"

She stares at me, like she's bracing for admonishment, then sits up straight, a smug look on her face. "Acting."

I breathe a sigh of relief.

"I'm just fucking with you, Cockring. I paid for it."

She looks at me over her glasses, a cue for me to grab the contraband. I fetch the jar of Jif peanut butter from her purse but then walk across the room, away from her.

"Hey!" she yells.

"Calm down!" I say, like a parent to a child, fishing two plastic spoons out of my backpack—this thing has everything. I walk back to her, hand her a spoon. I unscrew the top, peel back the foil, and give her the jar.

Kathi Kannon and I are eating Jif directly from the container and watching the film *Baby Boom* on a small TV tucked into a bamboo armoire. We're catching the movie God knows where—the beginning, the end?—and no attempt is made to change the channel and find something else.

On television, it's the scene where Diane Keaton's character is talking to her doctor about sex and how she doesn't enjoy it, but she's still upset that she's not having it.

Therapista says things missing from your life are not voids but gifts.

I think about Drew. About the happy picket-fenced life that I'm not living. I wonder if Kathi is feeling the same, the void of things in her life she dreamed she'd have at this point—marriage, independence from Miss Gracie, the kind of Teflon fame that transcends tabloid fodder. I'm thinking, *At least we have each other.*

Kathi reaches out to me. She grabs my hand, she turns from Diane Keaton on the television to look at me, staring me in the face, her eyes watering with either gratitude or dryness. Her grip tightens and mine does, too, me clinging to my star, on our cloud of hotel bedding, in our atmosphere of acknowledging each other, finding resolve in the fact that we aren't alone, that we're doing just fine on this journey. Kathi nods her head, purses her lips, and before I have a chance to blurt out my affection for her, she beats me to the podium:

"You must never quit working for me!" she says, an electricity flowing from her to me, and that mysterious energy that forces our hearts to beat is suddenly shared between us. Instantly, two electrical currents are connected, forcing a dollop of grace to pop in her and a lump of love to catch in my throat, my shoulders collapsing beneath the might of the biggest emotional hug I've ever received. "But if you do, you must promise to never leave me for someone like Diane fucking Keaton!"

I deflate but only slightly, wondering how the two of us could be on opposite pages. Me near tears at the promise of our pseudo-ethereal engagement to each other, and she talking about the earthly and disappointing semantics of my potential employment to, I guess, one of her competitors. I'm thinking platonic-relationship commitments, and it seems she's thinking IMDB. But her gaze doesn't leave mine, and her emotional connection to the point seems real, and I can't help but think maybe this is as close as one can get with Kathi Kannon, measured not by our closeness but by my distance from Diane Keaton, and it still leaves me warm.

"I promise," I say, now squeezing her hand.

Kathi smiles and taps her watch. "Time for another dose."

In my room, I tuck myself in. I keep the thermostat set low so I can snuggle in every luxury Japanese sheet and blanket I can find—overdosing on it, since I won't have these sheets or this air-conditioning (or any air-conditioning) when I get back to my apartment in L.A.

I leave my bedside lamp on until the last possible second I'm awake. The shade casts a shadow on the ceiling that looks like the spaceship from *Nova Quest*. How strange that this is my life. In some ways, the reality of my time with old Priestess Talara makes my childhood fantasies of her adventures seem silly. There's a part of me that wishes someone would have pulled me aside and held those little plastic figurines up and told me all of their real names, told me all of their real stories, told me that they live in Los Angeles and have homes and interests and parents and problems. If someone had made it all more tangible, I think

I would have a very different view of all that I'm experiencing around me now. That I'd be more chill and easy and accepting when things look human, flawed. Instead, I'm still looking into shadows, hoping the lights hit just right, that my childhood idolizations are still recognizable all these light-years later.

I check my phone one last time before ending the day, and still nothing from Drew. My mind races to fill in the blanks—he's busy with work, his phone is dead, he's hospitalized in a coma. My mind wants it to be anything but the possible truth: Maybe I'm not good enough for him.

I turn off the lamp.

On my nightstand, illuminated by the red light of the alarm clock, is the bottle of painkillers Kathi gave me to manage for her. It's in the spot some people would put a photo of a loved one, a trophy, a souvenir. It's our pact. It's my proof that we're on an adventure together, through Japan and Australia and Indonesia and through space-time, through addiction. This bottle of pills, it's more and more empty, but it's here.

Hey, Siri, we schlep to Kinkaku-ji—Temple of the Golden Pavilion—in the rain. A taxi drops us off and we carefully share our umbrella and walk the half mile down a muddy gravel road toward the sacred, iconic temple.

"Are you centering the umbrella on me or you?" Kathi asks.

"You."

"Impossible. My ass is getting soaked."

"Sorry," I say, twisting and shoving the umbrella farther in her direction, my shoulder getting wet, our feet still shuffling along in slop, behind other tourists laughing and pretending they're not in hell.

We turn a corner, and there it is. We lay eyes on this historic site, glistening from the glare of the rainy day, tourists all around us taking pictures, marching forward toward the masterpiece.

It's a sweet, magical moment.

Snap: The Golden Temple. "*Look how fucking famous it is!*"

Kathi turns to me, I look at her, bracing for our touching exchange. She says, "Okay, wow, let's go."

She turns and starts to trudge back to the waiting taxi. I lurch behind her, keeping her head safe from the rain.

"Wait. We're not going to go in?"

"Nope," she says, her back to me, her feet shuffling, shuffling toward the taxi.

"But we came all this way. In the rain. Shouldn't we see what the inside looks like?"

"We can google it," she says.

In the cab, she lets out a whoosh of air, an exhale of accomplishment, as if to say, *We saw it, history, architecture, wonder.* And then—

She says, "I'm bored."

She says, "Time for another pill?"

I say, "You're all out."

Kathi locks eyes with me and says, "This changes your grade to a C."

Dinner is a royal and gruesome affair.

Assistant Bible Verse 134: Always carry breath mints, cell-phone charger, puke bags.

Here at the Hoshinoya, the emperor's chef heard that *the* Kathi Kannon wished to dine at the hotel, so he planned a special dinner for us in a private room off an enormous white-sand-and-stone garden raked to perfection. Kathi and I sit at a tiny table as two waitresses prepare the settings in front of us, each of them occasionally stealing a glance at my American celebrity boss and, every now and then, making eye contact with me, smiling as if to say, *You're so lucky to be eating here.*

The waitresses bow and leave the room, and Kathi and I sit, visible boredom rising in her like a tide. "What the fuck is happening?" Kathi asks, brushing her hair out of her eyes. "I'm starving."

Before I can answer, the waitresses return with two plates of lobster sashimi, except these crustaceans, on both Kathi's plate and mine, are still alive, their guts exposed, waving their antennae at us, begging us for mercy. Kathi and I stare with eyes the size of tennis balls.

The waitresses put the plates on the table in front of us and then look at us, awaiting our reaction. The room is immediately and eerily silent, like someone accidentally hit the mute button on a war film.

"Oh, goodie," Kathi says. "I can't wait."

"What?!" I whisper to her.

She leans in to me. "Acting." Kathi looks up from the plate, back to the waitresses. "Wow," she says, bowing. "Arigato gozaimasu."

I follow her lead. I bow. "Arigato gozaimasu," I say as the servers exit.

Kathi and I look at the living sushi, then at each other.

In my mind I hear only the voice of my father, screaming, *EAT IT!* That's what he said when I was a child and I asked for spinach so I could be like Popeye. My sweet mother said I wouldn't like it. She said spinach doesn't taste good directly out of a can, how Popeye eats it. But she humored me, twisting, twisting, twisting the can opener, draining the water, lovingly putting a spoon of the spinach onto a plate. I had a taste; I didn't like it.

"EAT IT!" my father shouted from across the table. "We don't waste food in this family! She opened the can, now you open your mouth!" I grabbed my fork, a child's fork, with a thick plastic casing and dulled prongs. I stabbed the mound of spinach and put a leaf or two in my mouth. "EAT IT!" I threw up on my plate, my insides spilling out, my inner world now bile and rage in a puddle in front of him. This happened again a few years later over Brussels sprouts. And a couple years after that when I opened Oreo cookies, ate the cream filling from most of them, then threw away the chocolate cookie top and bottom. I buried them deep in the trash, but somehow he found them, of course. "DON'T WASTE FOOD!" he yelled, fishing the cookies out, soggy from coffee grounds and eggshells. "EAT IT! TAKE RESPONSIBILITY

FOR YOUR LIFE!" Again, I barfed at our kitchen table. And every time I retched, the reaction was the same: He was disgusted not by the puke but by his son, his son's weak stomach, weak everything. Each time he simply got up and left the table in a huff, leaving me alone to clean the plate full of my mess. I was too young to know that I actually won those three battles. That he retreated and I foiled his attempts to force me into spinach and Brussels sprouts and garbage Oreo cookies. Instead, at the time, I viewed his walking away as my own failure, my own lack of enough charm or appeal or worthiness to keep him at the table, to keep our family whole. And his searing scream still lingers with me.

EAT IT!

The creatures on the plates before us stir; they won't be ignored.

"We have to get rid of them!" Kathi says.

EAT IT!

I'm looking at the lobster's little pained face.

EAT IT!

I'm looking at its splayed intestines.

EAT IT!

I'm looking at its antennae.

EAT IT! EAT IT! EAT IT!

"Maybe we should eat it?" I ask.

"Are you fucking crazy?!"

"My dad always said to eat everything, kids are starving and stuff—"

"Your *dad*?" Kathi spits. "Who the fuck cares what your dad thinks? You're an adult! Fuck him!"

And just like that, my dad's screaming stops for a moment, a reprieve, my overbearing father reduced to breath from the mouth of Kathi Kannon, him suddenly powerless and emasculated, dying in that moment, squirming like our dinner before us.

"Okay," I say. "Fuck him!"

"Quick!" she says, grabbing her Hermès purse and plopping it on the table. She pulls out her wallet, her keys—Mom's locket crashing down on the table. She pulls out a bag of Weight Busters cereal, rips it open, grabs a handful of the lightly frosted whole-wheat O's, and starts stuffing them into her mouth.

"What are you doing?" I ask.

"Eat some, hurry!" she orders, holding the cereal out for me. "We need the bag!"

I grab two handfuls and start chewing. It isn't until she finishes the last of the cereal that I realize what she's doing.

Kathi points to the flailing lobsters. "I'm not eating Laurel and Hardy, are you?"

"No," I say with a mouthful of dry oats.

"Then, quick! Get them in here!"

I grab chopsticks and plop the squirming guys into the empty Weight Busters bag. One critter and then the second.

"I'm so sorry," I whisper, as I lower them down.

Kathi puts the crackling cereal bag in her purse and closes it just moments before the servers arrive with the next course—something liquid, gray, and inelegant, with floating lumps, in two bowls, one for each of us.

"Wow," Kathi says, *acting*. We can hear the prior critters moving around in the cereal bag.

Crackle. Crackle. Crackle.

"Wow, thanks," Kathi says as the bowl is placed in front of her.

"Should we clear some plates?" one of the servers asks, looking around the table, eyebrows furrowed. "Where are the shells?"

"Oh," Kathi says, mild panic in her eyes. "We were *very* hungry."

As the suspicious servers leave, Kathi exhales, then turns to the latest serving. She leans over and sniffs her bowl. "Fuck," she says. "I think it's alcohol." Kathi picks up a chopstick and pokes one of the lumps, and a living shrimp spins around, glares at her, and tries to jump from the bowl. "FUCK! These shrimps are drunk!" she gasps. "They want us to eat these goddamn lit baby shrimps!"

Kathi grabs her purse and we quickly try to pluck each innocent being from their drunk destiny into the Weight Busters bag. We're fast and stealthy but breaking a sweat. She stuffs the cellophane bag back in her purse.

The servers arrive with the next round. As they approach, I keep one eye trained on Kathi's purse, fearing at any moment an innocent little life will come crawling out and drag itself across the floor, to everyone's horror.

"Mmmmm," Kathi says.

I look down at a bowl of live octopi flipping us off with each of their tentacles.

The waitresses leave and Kathi dumps her new plate directly into her purse. "Gimme yours! Quick!"

"Eww. Your purse! Who's gonna clean that?" I ask.

"The cereal bag is full," she grunts. Looking down into her purse, she says to the critters, "Hey, no pushing!"

The waitresses keep coming, the purse keeps getting more and more full with the most exquisite delicacies in all of Japan, raw, squirming critters and beasts and something tarantula-like. I try to gently pluck each of them to safety with the chopsticks, but the servers are impossibly fast.

Kathi looks to the door. "Use your fucking fingers! There's no time!"

I flick a couple of terrified crawfish off the plates, and Kathi whips the purse to her side as the next course arrives, a big smile on the face of the server.

"You sure are fast," Kathi says to them.

"For you, special guest, special dinner," the waitress says, putting down in front of us a plate with a little fish bending back and forth and gasping for air so desperately we can hear it.

"But do you have anything fresh?" Kathi asks, sarcasm as alive in her words as our latest course.

The servers look confused, dejected.

"Just kidding," Kathi says. She points to me and says, "By the way, this is my assistant, not my lover, just in case this is a hidden-camera show."

"Arigato gozaimasu," one of the waitresses replies, bewildered but polite.

My face twists with the awkwardness of it all, my fingers starting to feel numb from the jelly or whatever was on the last delicacy now in Kathi's care.

Another course resembles the lower half of a seahorse. Another, like seaweed, except it keeps trying to stand. Yet another, unrecognizably flayed, its exposed heart still pitter-pattering.

Kathy says suggestively to the servers, "Maybe the next thing out will be Baskin Robbins Cookies 'N Cream ice cream?"

A polite giggle, and the waitress says, "Only five more courses."

"*Only* five more," Kathi says, her purse desperately twitching under her arm.

"Don't you want to snap a picture of this, Cockring?"

"I only brag about the good stuff," I say.

I carry Kathi's purse back to the room.

"I'm not touching it!" she says.

"I don't want to touch it!" I yell back, but I know where I fit on the totem pole.

Once inside, I walk over to the sliding paper partition that separates our villa from the outside, the cool, fresh air hitting me, the sound of the river flowing below filling the room. I toss what has to be thousands of dollars of living, mutilated fish from the purse, out of our hotel room and into the river outside. I look back into her purse and, still clinging to life, clinging to the inside lining of that designer bag, is one of those critters my father's voice was yelling at me to eat. He's breathing heavy, his tentacles waving at me, praying I'm his savior. I also toss him over the rail and watch him splash into the river, not dead, perhaps life inside and ahead for him yet, free from me and my father's barking orders.

I turn to find Kathi behind me.

She says, "I'm giving you the best shit to write about."

She says, "This will all be funny one day."

I'm in a kimono filling out postcards, my body freshly washed and slightly less stressed following the evening's dinner of mutilations. Kathi pokes her head in my room; she's also wearing a kimono, the two of us, trauma twins.

"I'm bored," she says.

"Does your tooth still hurt?"

"My whole being hurts," she says, looking at my postcard spread. "Who are those for?" she asks.

"Various people, friends in L.A."

Kathi flips through the postcards, reading the messages to Drew, Jasmine, Bruce (ugh), and my signatures on each: "Love, Charlie," "Love, Charlie," "Love, Charlie." But she pauses, holding a fourth card, upon which the signature is just "Charlie." Kathi flips the card over to read the address. "Who's this one for, in Perris, Louisiana? The one you don't love."

"It's for my dad," I say.

"Why didn't you write 'Love, Charlie' on your dad's postcard?"

I look up at her. "Dads are complicated."

"Tell me about it," she says. "So are mothers."

"Tell me about it," I say, knowing I've said it in a tone of somber care, the kind of accent that births a beat in the room, one so delicate even Kathi holds for a moment. I continue, with a deep inhale, "My mother dropped dead in front of me when I was twelve."

"Your mom is fucking dead? How am I just hearing about this?!"

"I don't love the subject. Don't be sad—"

"Sad? It's fucking riveting!" she says, plopping down beside me. "Leave out nothing!"

"She collapsed in church."

"She died in a fucking church?!"

"For a long time," I admit, "I thought God struck her down because she wanted to divorce my dad."

Kathi shakes her head. "Religion can be such a bitch."

"I remember this girl in the pew in front of Mom. This girl, she had this crooked ponytail. She was my age, but we didn't know each other. When Mom went down behind her, all these ushers rushed over. This girl, she turned and was watching, watching my mom die, but then an usher and her parents, they grabbed her and pulled her away, shielded her from the sight, protected her from seeing a dead body, my dead mother. They took this girl out of the church, far from the drama. But, protecting her, it only made my view better. Because I was on the altar. I was an altar boy. And that girl, that stranger, she got whisked away, but I'm standing there in my black-and-white robes and I'm frozen, I'm still watching, I'm still in service to the church, the Mass, the priest—though even he left the altar to help. No one rushed to me. No one pulled me away. No one shielded me. And with that girl and her parents gone, I could see my mom lying there. I could see under the empty pews, her arms flopped weirdly under her. I stayed up there, on the altar, so close to God, the closest one to God in the room, up there separated, the best view, like there was some holy boundary no one could cross to come comfort me. My poor mom, her arms, the pink sleeves of her blouse, the ruffles of the cuff, lying flat, lifeless on the church carpet."

Kathi says, "Carpet?! In a church?!"

"Every day I wonder how my life would be different if Dad would have dropped dead instead."

"I'm sorry I didn't know about your mom," Kathi says.

"I don't want to bother you with my silly burdens."

"You think the death of your mother is a silly burden?"

I'm taken aback by her forwardness, and her interest, and my own admission, and Kathi's sharp catch. All these years, Mom's absence has felt like a lack of something, more like a void, until Kathi Kannon's magic brain shared some of its boundless energy and gifted life to a feeling I only in this moment can see is true: Mom's death isn't something that happened back then, my memories of her locked away in the old boxes; it's something present and here and a weight on my shoulders and a buzz in my ears all the time. My mother's death is not a hollow ghost but a solid and constant punch in my gut, even now. I feel the opposite of blushing—I feel pale and cold.

"What was her name?" Kathi asks, sitting beside me.

"Amy. Mom's name was Amy."

I look down at my feet, across at the window, anywhere but at Kathi, while I try to spell out some sentiment that I'm not even sure how to put into words. "She had that locket. The one I gave you. That I put on your key chain. I gave it to Mom when I was in second grade. It was from a school thing—I'm rambling." I take a glimpse at Kathi. She's watching me more than she's listening to me, calmly, coolly, her eyes soft and open—I can't help but debase it by imagining how it's a skill to look at someone that way, how it's an art, how her looking at me would look through the lens of a camera, and why her grip on an audience is so powerful. "Anyway, the locket is . . . I think the locket . . . I'm glad you have it."

I glance up and lock eyes with Kathi, her rare gentle smile now appearing, a smile of kindness not amusement, a smile that with a twist could signal pity, but it doesn't.

"This all sounds so silly," I mutter.

"Your feelings aren't silly, Cockring. Thank you for sharing."

I inhale, my messy signal that there's more for me to share. I wait for her to ask more, to ask more about my childhood and my life, but I close my mouth, I shut it down, I look away, I choose not to burden

Kathi any further about her bearing the torch for my mom, a desire that sounds so cliché, so unreasonable and irrational when spoken aloud, when considered in the sober reality of a cold and quiet hotel room, no matter the country or coast.

"Parents, right?" Kathi says with a huff, breaking the awkward silence and bringing levity and life back into the room. "God, I should send my mother a postcard. Do you have extras?"

"No," I say, "but you can take this one I already wrote on and scribble out the name and write 'Miss Gracie' instead."

Kathi takes the postcard and grabs a pen and starts crossing out the writing on a card I was sending to Bruce. "You sure you don't mind? Is your friend going to mind?"

"He'll love it when I tell him why he didn't get a postcard." Watching Kathi make an utter mess of the postcard, I ask, "Is Miss Gracie going to worry what the fuck is going on out here when she gets that card with all this scribbling on it?"

"Oh, Cockring, no. This will help reassure her that everything is normal."

I watch Kathi remake the postcard, swirls of black ink blotting out "Bruce" and "Charlie" and replacing those with her own name and message. The only sound in the room is the creek outside and her pen mangling the paper.

Kathi brushes her bangs from her eyes. She takes both hands and gently tucks her hair behind her ears. The action makes her look so young, like a schoolgirl, her face exposed in a way I rarely see, so much skin, no makeup, no artifice.

"Me and Miss Gracie," Kathi says, "we're our own universe—a quirky push and pull over money and fame and speed limits for the driveway. Sometimes I think she loves me so much, it's too much. And I love her too much and it's not enough." Kathi drifts a moment, and I wonder what film is playing in her head. Is it actual footage of her actress mother in one of her movies? Or is it the same kind of jerky series of flickering images we all play in our heads, our own selects, our own director's cut of our lives, our parents and how we want to see them, our shitty fathers, our dead mothers.

Kathi looks at the postcard, at the message she's written—a message on a message on a message. An inkblot to be heard round the world, in her mother's town, her mother's home, her mother's grasp.

"What did you write?" I ask her.

Kathi smiles.

"Is it too personal?"

Kathi shrugs and waves the card around to dry the ink, clear the air.

"It must be personal," I say. "Something sweet for Miss Gracie. Sorry I asked."

Kathi looks at the postcard. "It says, 'Not relaxed send help.'"

"Poor Miss Gracie."

"She deserves it!" Kathi yells playfully. "And I think she likes it. She needs a hobby."

"You're a hobby?"

"To my mother and many people the world over. Maybe even you, Cockring."

I don't deny it. I don't do anything. *Being.* I just look at her, her kimono loose and free. I worry that I'll see a breast, but it's not worth interrupting our little moment to express concern.

"And my father," Kathi continues, "he was never there but always there. He was famous, too, but not quite enough, never quite enough of anything, you know?"

"No," I say, smiling. She looks up at me and smiles back.

"You don't love your father?" Kathi asks.

"Do you love yours?"

"Very much. I keep his dentures in a 'World's Best Dad' mug in the guest room refrigerator. You didn't throw out Dad's teeth, did you?"

I say, "Not yet. Should I?"

"Nah. I like him there. It's nice to love someone when they're just dentures, when the rest of them only exists in your mind. You can just curate the parts you like."

She hands me back the postcard she altered, with chunks looking like they've been redacted by the government. She says, "Loving your parents when they're flawed and flesh and blood, that's harder to do."

I say, "I get it."

I'm thinking, *I could never leave all this for Diane Keaton.*

Kathi fishes a lighter and a pack of cigarettes out of her pocket and turns to walk out to our balcony. "Wanna come outside and party?"

Kathi steps out and I follow. She looks at the landscape before us, framed in tall bamboo shoots, little carefully planted flowers and tiny mindfully placed rocks lit by moonlight.

"Am I not justified in detesting my dad?" I ask. "What if he's an asshole? And hates that I'm gay? And thinks I should unbank?"

She drags on her cigarette, blows the smoke into the thin night. "Sounds like that's his business. Where's the problem? My mom is always telling me what to do and all that. I just say, 'Maybe so.' Because, maybe so! Maybe she's right. I don't know. It's better than being at war with her. I follow the weather, Cockring. Know what I mean?"

"I assume I'll always be cold. So I just wear layers," I say.

"No. I mean, I follow the emotional weather. Sun is sun, dark is dark, warm is warm, always a fifty percent chance of rain. It's like 'go with the flow' but the celebrity version. It's how I like to live my life. It's not always how I actually do live my life—I've had plenty of screaming matches and epic fights with my parents—but when my mind is calm, everything can be okay. No war."

Kathi, like a reflex, like an exclamation point, tosses her cigarette over the balcony. It spins in the air, in slow motion. The oxygen causes the butt to glow bright orange, and you can hear the thud it makes in the sand garden. It's a scene right out of a movie.

"JESUS!" I yell. "You're gonna start a fire!"

Kathi cringes, rare self-awareness taking hold of her for a moment, and she throws her legs over the decorative wood fencing and marches out and grabs the butt, leaving her footprints in the raked white sand, turning and knocking driftwood and stacked rocks, breaking thick old bamboo. "Wanna scratch our names in the garden rocks?" she asks.

I'm thinking, *She's going to destroy what's left of an ancient, historic site.* But then instead I wonder: *Can it be both? Can it be vandalism and art? Can we love and hate at the same time?*

Kathi comes back toward the room, leaving a second set of her footprints in the sand, crawling back onto our balcony, hurling her leg over the barrier.

"Look out!" I yell, too late, of course.

Kathi breaks a little pottery vase holding a tiny shoot of bamboo growing in the shape of a heart, a thistle that's perhaps been growing for hundreds of years.

Kathi shrugs it off. As she walks back into the room she says, "I'm bored."

I look back out at the trampled scene outside of our room.

Her life. So much fun. So much destruction.

> ME: Hey! Stopped in NYC. Almost home. Thinking of you.
> DREW: Sorry been out of touch, Oak! When are you home?
> ME: On my way soon. Excited to see you. ;)

No response.

There's pee everywhere.

I'm thinking, *I hope we survive New York.* We're here, back at the

Greenwich Hotel so Kathi can destress from her vacation and return to her hard life in Beverly Hills.

"Isn't he cute," Kathi says from her hotel-suite bed, holding up a brown-fur puppy with a white patch on his chest and two lower fangs awkwardly poking out of his mouth.

"Whose dog is this?"

"He came with the hotel room," Kathi lies. The dog curls farther into Kathi's breasts, glares at me, judging my face, my clothes, my inner worth.

Now the only one stressed is me, seeing this new puppy and calculating the number of tasks I should add to my usual duties: feeding, training, neutering.

The dog looks at me with spite, like he can read my mind.

"Look how his teeth extend out like weapons," Kathi says, touching the dog's two white projectiles.

"What's wrong with him?" I ask.

"Nothing. This is how he was made. He's a chug."

"A what?"

"A chihuahua-pug mix. His name is Roy. Roy, meet Cockring."

Assistant Bible Verse 135: Pack pee pads, chew toys, dog food.

"Are we keeping him?" I ask.

"Yup," she says.

"Ugh," I say, turning to leave the room, worried that my job just got a lot busier. "I'll go to the pet store and get supplies."

"He doesn't need much, Cockring."

"I'll start with food. He's probably starving."

"No, we just ate," Kathi says, motioning into the room. I step farther into her suite and see a room-service table with nothing on it. I walk around her bed and find all the plates on the floor, a mess of food chewed and licked over and left discarded for housekeeping—or me—to handle.

Kathi lowers Roy to the floor and he rushes up to me. He looks up and stares—God, he's so judgmental. Then he pokes me with his underbite. Dammit; I'm enraged, and in love.

"How are we going to get him home?" I ask.

Snap: Now I have a second soul to brag about.

Snap: Now I have a second soul to keep alive.

12

☆

A Google Alert can change your life. Several Google Alerts can be catastrophic.

I jump from Kathi's dining table—my phone is buzzing! A series of emails have come through.

My phone is dutifully set up to get alerts anytime Kathi Kannon is mentioned on the Internet. Most of the time, the alerts are absurd.

The headline says: KATHI KANNON SEX ORGY.

The headline says: KATHI KANNON NUDES FOR SALE.

The headline says: KATHI KANNON BANKRUPT.

We've had false alarms, false Google Alerts, like the headline that read KATHI KANNON ATTENDS LAKERS GAME LOOKING ROUGH. I knew the night before she was supposed to hang with a friend with Lakers connections, and I thought, *Oh, no.* Almost as the alert arrived, TMZ called the house and I answered, coy and cool. I said I couldn't help; "I don't know anything, Kathi isn't here," I said—with Kathi sleeping soundly a few feet away. I pull up the article on my phone. It wasn't Kathi in the picture. It was just some unfortunate woman who now has to live the rest of her days knowing she looks like what people think is a trashed, tragic, worst version of Kathi Kannon.

But this newest Google Alert, this is not a mistake.

My job responsibilities include: organize her life, dispense her meds, break bad news. It's time to get her up anyway.

"Good morning," I say calmly but sternly to Kathi, still snug in last night's nest, Roy asleep beside her, both with no knowledge of what the day holds.

Kathi doesn't move. "I have to tell you something unpleasant," I add.

"What?" she says, alive, awake.

"It's a Google Alert."

"Who's that?" she asks.

"No, it's not a person. It's an email I get whenever you're mentioned on the Internet. And you got several mentions this morning."

"Oh, no," she says, bracing, sitting up in bed.

"A tabloid posted a picture of you—"

"Oh, no—"

"And there's an unflattering story attached to it—"

"OH, NO—"

"And it mentions me!" I yell. "What is everyone going to say about me? My father? My fellow assistants? Everyone's going to think I'm not taking good care of you!"

"Who gives a fuck about you?" Kathi says. "Give me the phone. What about me?"

She reaches, but I turn away from her and read the headline: "It says: 'Is Kathi Kannon Back on Drugs?'" I look up at her, glaring.

"WHAT?!" she screams. "Give it!" she yells, ripping the covers off her body and hurling herself out of bed. Roy perks up but doesn't follow—he knows when to hang back.

Kathi tries to wrestle my phone away, but I block her as I read, "'Kathi Kannon has been spotted suspiciously coming and going from a strange apartment in West Hollywood for at least a week, maybe longer. She always emerges a few minutes later, frazzled, jumpy, erratic. Sometimes she arrives driving herself,'" I continue, now getting louder, "'AND SOMETIMES SHE'S DRIVEN THERE BY A YOUNG MAN!'" I face her and I gasp accusingly, "ME! And there's a photo of me! Outside of that orange building I took you to in West Hollywood! Holy shit! Is that *Vegas*?! Is *Vegas* drugs?! I look like an enabler! Am I an enabler?"

Kathi rips the phone from my hand and looks at the article, the photos of her, ragged, dazed, unflattering, framed indeed by that orange West Hollywood apartment complex we visited before our recent trip. "Oh my GOD!" she screams, pacing the bedroom, kicking a pile of dirty clothes. "All these pictures must be photoshopped!"

"I don't think so."

My job responsibilities include: Tell her the truth.

"That's what you wore," I say. "That's what I wore. That's how you did—or didn't do—your hair. And there are other photos, from other days, when I wasn't with you."

Kathi continues her nonstop movement through the room, a tour of shame in laps around her bed. "I mean, you could make anyone look like a drug addict if you take enough pictures of them at the wrong angle, with terrible light, with wind and whatnot, or, like this one, while I'm fucking blinking!"

"What about that picture of me in your car?"

"What do you care?" she asks. "Isn't that your favorite part?"

"No!" I yell. "They're basically saying I'm a fucking accomplice to you doing drugs!"

Snap: Look how cool I am now. Look at me, the fool, exposed.

"Am I?" I ask. "Am I an accomplice? Are you doing drugs? Were you doing drug deals?"

"Barely," Kathi says.

"BARELY!"

"Please," she says. "You feed me drugs every day in those pill cases."

"I don't feed you illegal ones! And I don't put photos of it in magazines for everyone who knows us to see!"

"Has Miss Gracie seen this?" Kathi asks.

"I don't know."

"I'm innocent!" Kathi proclaims. "I was just visiting my friend from AA! So what if I didn't brush my fucking hair for several days in a row!"

"What about me?" I yell. "I'm an enabler! What do I tell people? I've been bragging that I'm your stepson!"

"This is not about you!" Kathi yells, throwing my phone back at me, dashing from her bedroom, through the red room and the living room, out the front door, running down the hill screaming, "Mommy!"

Roy and I follow, sprinting behind Kathi to Miss Gracie's house, passing her garage, noticing the Lincoln parked, the driver's door open, and Miss Gracie sitting inside.

We all stop in our tracks.

"That's an angel, that's a sweet girl . . ." Miss Gracie is saying, apparently to no one.

"What are you doing in there?" Kathi asks, both of us wondering if it's a stroke.

Miss Gracie looks up, revealing the spoiled four-legged bundle of fur in her lap. "Having a talk with Uta Hagen." She notices the frenzy in Kathi's eyes. "Oh, no, now what?"

"Mommy," Kathi whines.

"But I'm so much more than that!" Miss Gracie says. "An accomplished actress—"

"A tabloid says I'm ugly and on drugs again!"

"Are you?" Miss Gracie asks coldly.

"Am I ugly?"

"No, are you on drugs again?"

"Of course not," Kathi says. "Please help me!"

Miss Gracie turns to me and says, "This is why she needs her mother, dear. Never forget that."

"Yes, ma'am," I say.

Miss Gracie, her gaze still locked with mine, her hands now tightly gripping the steering wheel, asks me, "Is she on drugs, dear?"

When Miss Gracie looks at you—a gaze perfected by a lifetime in front of cameras of all shapes and sizes—it's stunning. Not in a good way. I am actually stunned. Like someone is using a Taser on me. So I say nothing. This is a trap for sure. Miss Gracie continues staring. Kathi, not used to being out of the center of attention, is quiet, looking back and forth from me to Miss Gracie, wondering how this will play out.

I stand with my mouth open, blushing, still praying Miss Gracie will move on, as she says, "This is a question, dear. I'm asking you a question."

Instead of sweating, I have simply "sweat," with all my body's moisture dumped out of me at once through my forehead, upper lip, neck. Armpits, too, but they're not visible as I have my arms clenched tightly to my sides, as if I'm a Transformer action-figure version of a celebrity assistant, trying to convert back into an ink pen or notepad, trying to squeeze my arms into my body so the rest can fold up and disappear. The sweat causes my glasses to start sliding off my face.

"We're innocent victims," Kathi interjects, in my defense.

"I warned you," Miss Gracie says to me, pointing her finger.

"It's all lies!" Kathi says.

"Well," Miss Gracie says, turning to Kathi. "You know what is true? I'm old and sick and have nearly died many times."

"No, you have not," Kathi says.

"I'm tired and fragile! And somehow you're spending all of your inheritance on I-don't know-what and being written up in these horrid tabloids and I don't have enough time or enough heart medication to deal with this right now. I have broken ribs—"

"No, you don't!" Kathi yells.

"I've had broken ribs since I was forced by the studio in the 1950s to wear a corset and dance for days on end with no rest!"

"That never happened!" Kathi shouts.

"I'm self-diagnosed!" Miss Gracie yells.

"You're not a real doctor!" Kathi yells.

"I played one on *M*A*S*H* and was nominated for an Emmy!"

Kathi storms away and Roy rushes beside her, following her, until she stops abruptly, her back to us, just in the doorway of the garage.

I freeze again, like I'm watching a familiar song-and-dance to which only Kathi and Miss Gracie know the choreography, both of them used to performing it over and over through the years. After a few tense moments, Miss Gracie starts—

"Do you need rehab again?"

"Mommy, you're missing the point!"

"You want me to call my publicist and attorney and have them exonerate you?" Miss Gracie asks.

"Yes, please," Kathi says sweetly. She turns to Miss Gracie. "Thank you, Mommy." She marches away, Roy beside her.

Then, to my horror, Miss Gracie turns back to me, looks me up and down. She says calmly, "You look guilty."

Another trap. I should have run out of the garage with Kathi and Roy, and now I'm stuck. Miss Gracie stares at me, awaiting my response, my reaction. "I'll never understand what it was in her life that forced her to turn to drugs. We talked about all this, dear, remember?"

I nod, defeated.

"Drugs," Miss Gracie continues, like she's doing a monologue. "That's the real issue here. Tabloid aside, all her money, my money, goes to—where else?"

"I don't know, uh . . ."

"You've seen her use drugs?"

"No. Never," I say.

"Never?" Miss Gracie asks, with a face that looks genetically sweet, but she's got a firm, knowing tone.

"I've never seen Kathi do drugs. Sometimes it seems she's . . . like, her medication is off. Like, when she got manic before. That was unusual, right? She's tired a lot. But aren't we all? I wish I could nap all day every day."

Miss Gracie is still staring at me. She's not satisfied.

I gather courage. I raise my eyebrows, stiffen my spine. I say, "I know she doesn't eat vegetables."

"Oh, please!" Miss Gracie says. "Are you accusing me of financing her drug problem with vegetable money?"

I study Miss Gracie a moment, the many lifetimes she's still living in her tired eyes, the things she's seen, done, and tried to do—for herself, for her daughter. I think about my time with Kathi as an adult and can't help but wonder about Miss Gracie's time with Kathi in the decades before me. Before Priestess Talara, before addictions and boyfriends and overdoses. Before she was a film icon, when Kathi Kannon was just a baby, a toddler, a little girl, a teenager, a young talent.

"You should know," Miss Gracie says, "that a parent will do anything for her child. I've done everything for Kathi. I sold my antiques. I moved onto her property. I've saved her life many times. But still, this monster persists." Miss Gracie catches her breath, her lower lip trembling slightly, feelings forcing themselves to the surface as she continues, "I push too hard and it ends badly. I don't push hard enough and it ends badly. I just try to do the best I can. And can't a mother simply encourage her daughter to eat her vegetables, like I've done since she was a little girl? 'Eat your vegetables!' Right? Do you understand? That's what mothers say, right?"

With Miss Gracie's celebrated voice cracking, my heart softens, my spine sags. I think of my own mother, delicate and loving, trying her best to save us and herself from our version of a monster—my father.

"I've seen little things," I say. "Sleepiness, frazzled—"

"Ahh. You've seen little things," Miss Gracie repeats, amused. "Well, dear. What did you think the *things* would look like?" Miss Gracie looks away. "They're all little things until one of them kills you."

She lets go of the steering wheel, her hands falling gently into her lap, perhaps the first time I've ever seen her really relax. "I've talked to so many psychologists and experts, and they all say the same thing. Normal people have a thing they call 'bottoming out,' the worst thing that happens to them to scare them sober. Kathi will never bottom out. She has too much support around her. She'll never be homeless, she'll never be alone, not really—people always want to be around her. I can fire them, and she hires them back. I can forbid her from seeing them, but she's a grown woman. She'll never get cut off completely. She can sell her house and have unlimited money and then what? Then how many *little things* can she buy? How many *little things* will you see? I've been down these roads, and it's—there's no peace down any of them. I just know we can't afford all of this forever, not our wallets, not our bodies."

I say, "Why don't you threaten to cut off all the cash?"

She says, "Why don't you threaten to quit?"

The garage is alive, electrified, Beverly Hills birds chirping— gossiping about us, as if they're calling this moment like sports commentators. Miss Gracie turns to me so forcefully, the keys in the Lincoln ignition start swinging slightly, jingling, suddenly so loud. I break from Miss Gracie's gaze, staring at the junk piled around the car: more candelabras, a big vase on a pedestal, a gold-plated (never used) shovel for the fireplace—everything looks so unwieldy.

"Come here and help me out of this damn car," Miss Gracie says.

Uta Hagen hops out first, and I extend my arm for Miss Gracie to grab. She holds my hand and pulls herself out of the car.

"You can go now," Miss Gracie says solemnly.

Assistant Bible Verse 136: Accept defeat with grace.

I smile at my much more skilled sparring partner, turn, and start to walk away.

"Tell Kathi," Miss Gracie shouts to me, as if an afterthought, the carefully scripted button on a classic film scene, her hand extending delicately into the air as if to pull focus, "that I still love her very much, despite her many flaws."

As I leave Miss Gracie and walk up to Kathi's home, the messages begin. Friends who've seen the tabloid start sending their worried texts, Facebook messages. I have emails from Jasmine, West, Crooner, *Bruce*—and all these personalities, all these perspectives, and all the same general message: "WTF?!"

> JASMINE: No, no, no! Bad assistant!
> WEST: OMG call if you need anything.
> CROONER: Get out, bud.
> BRUCE: We need to talk.

I'm sure Bruce wants to share the horror from Kathi's agent, but I have my own fallout to process, my part in Kathi's decline locked in pixels online, archived forever as my failing, failing to see, to act, to protect.

I get a voicemail from my father: "YOU NEED A NEW JOB!"

"It's all going to be okay," I tell everyone.

"I'm fine," I say.

"Kathi is fine," I say.

"These are lies," I say.

It seems the only person I don't hear from is Drew.

I feel the encumbrance of gravity of this world—not the Kathi Kannon world but my world, the real world, with its judgments and consequences and disapproving looks. I feel a backslide into my depression, of a dark void welling within me, of untenable and unsavory solutions to this mess—I don't want distance, I don't want to quit, I don't want to leave her.

"Mommy will fix it. Problem solved!" Kathi shouts as I enter her bedroom. She's getting dressed to go out.

"Not really," I say. "What kind of drugs are we talking about here, Kathi? What's happening?"

"It's like nothing," Kathi says, growing impatient. "Jesus, it's not crack or something. It's just medications. I'm just supplementing."

"Supplementing? Supplementing what? A doctor should make adjustments to your meds if that's what you need."

"Who needs doctors? I once played one on TV," she says, mocking her mother, making knowing eye contact with me, a star's attempt to reassure me, her audience, though it's not working, not this time.

"I'm going to *Veg*—" she says, pausing and restarting. "I'm going out." She storms into her bathroom and slams the door behind her.

"No, you're not! We have to have a big fight about this!" I yell to the bathroom door.

Roy hops off her bed and sits by the bathroom door, angry he's been shut out. He's glaring at me, willing me to open the door for him, begging me to help him. I say quietly to Roy, "I can't save you."

Suddenly, Kathi opens the bathroom door and looks at me, mistaking my comment to Roy as a comment to her. She says to me, "I don't need you to save me!"

Roy trots inside, and Kathi closes the door again, safe and sealed off from the rest of the wild world, with its silly standards of health and wellness and responsibility.

I don't need you to save me.

I'm thinking, *Maybe you do.*

I'm thinking, *What are people going to think of her?*

I'm thinking, *What are people going to think of me?*

Date night should be a grand distraction from the fits and starts of life with Kathi Kannon, but I can't get in touch with Drew. Texts have gone unanswered for a couple of days. I'm sure he's busy. I'm sure life is hectic. I don't want to be a pest.

I decide to reach out in a different way.

I stop at the grocery to buy him a little oak tree in a cute, industrial-styled vase that'll be a perfect match to the décor in his loft. I'm pretty sure this "tree" is just a trash plant, but it's the closest thing I could get to an oak sapling, a nice way (I hope) to show my affection, and a bribe to fill in the space between us when I'm out of town and unavailable because of my job. It's also a way to soften what might be a weird day, seeing the guy you're dating photographed in a tabloid beside an accused drug addict/film icon.

Hey, Siri, I want this to work out.

I park outside of his apartment building and make the journey up. I approach his door and wonder if I should knock. I lean forward and listen to see if I hear anything inside, but there's only the same thing I've heard from him of late: silence.

I put the oak tree on his door's welcome mat, along with a little note I scribbled: "Thinking of you. Hope all is well. All good with me. Miss ya. xo Oak."

Back at home, I'm starting to feel crowded by my own filth. I'm still not caught up with laundry and housekeeping after all my travel with Kathi. My luggage is still on the floor, plus all of the boxes Dad sent—I legit look like a hoarder.

Despite Dad's protests, I have yet to open Mom's boxes. It's my small victory over him, my baby step in usurping his authority, his demands.

Fuck him.

I wonder what Mom would think, me using her stuff as a coffee table, eating my TV dinners on her old boxes of—what? I assume old clothes and books and kitchen utensils. I can't help but also wonder what else I'm avoiding, what else I'm not unpacking.

I fall in and out of sleep on my sofa, me with my phone in hand, no response all night from Drew, and my last text to Kathi, also unanswered:

ME: You okay?

13

☆

A scrappy firing squad is assembled, waiting for our target: Kathi Kannon, film icon. She's expected at any moment from a jaunt out to run "errands." Of course, Kathi Kannon doesn't run any real errands on her own. *Errands* might be the new code for *Vegas*.

Seated in the circle of imported leather emperors, animated by the twirling bits of sunlight reflected from the dangling disco ball, is the team of assassins: me, Miss Gracie, Roger, Agnes, and Benny.

"How much longer?" Miss Gracie yells. "All this waiting is giving me arthritis." Roger immediately takes her hand from her lap and starts to massage it.

"She's on her way," I say.

"This is important," I say.

"This is for the best," I say.

Hey, Siri, I want Kathi Kannon to live a long, happy life. Or at least long.

The front door swings open, and Kathi Kannon is there, backlit by

Beverly Hills. She's not the least bit startled or worried to see everyone encircled in front of her, silent and waiting in her living room.

"Oh, God," she says wryly. "You guys need to get out more."

"Kathi," I say. "We need to talk to you. This is an intervention."

"An intervention?!" Miss Gracie pipes up. "No. I'm not dressed for that." She stands and motions for Roger to help her exit. Roger jumps up and Miss Gracie admonishes him, "You told me Kathi had an announcement."

"That's what he told me," Roger says, pointing to me.

Glaring at me, Miss Gracie shouts, "Him! He can't be trusted!"

I catch a glimpse of enjoyment on Kathi's face, a reveling in the discord.

"Okay, okay," I say. "Calm down. Please stay. I really want to have an honest and helpful chat about recent issues."

"There's nothing to discuss," Kathi says. "That tabloid story was nothing, not true."

"That's not what you told me in private." I turn to my tepid teammates. "She said she was using but barely."

I'm surprised by the faces absorbing this news: Agnes looks at me with almost a cringe, pity, sorrow, like I'm the one getting bad news; Benny is detached; Roger is focused on Miss Gracie, who is exasperated; and Kathi is stoic, practically daring me to continue. "I think we should discuss whether Kathi's prior manic episodes were from doctor meds or *Vegas* meds."

"Cockring, I'm telling you, that's all over, okay?" Kathi says, looking around the room. "Are we done now? I feel good about this."

"Sounds good to me, boss," Agnes says, waving goodbye.

"Me, too," Benny says.

"Call me later, dear," Miss Gracie says, now arm in arm with Roger and heading to the front door.

"No, no, no," I say. "This is an opportunity to effect real change and start exploring root causes of . . . things. And to set boundaries and expectations and hope and all that, right?"

"I'm too old for hope," Miss Gracie says, clinging to Roger and walking out the front door. Agnes is gone, too. So is Benny. Even little Roy, his butt shaking with the excitement of the moment, dashes away toward Kathi's bedroom, no doubt to snuggle in bed, leaving the room empty except for Kathi and me.

Kathi approaches me slowly, skillfully, fiery determination in her eyes. I feel flames of hell at my feet, rising as she approaches, heat from my toes to my knees—she's getting closer—fire burning my stomach, my chest, my face, as Kathi stops in her tracks in front of me and says calmly, flippantly, "This was the worst intervention I've ever seen."

"Thanks," I say, my arms waving up and flopping back to my sides.

"I mean, this was *the worst,* and I've been in, like, a thousand of them."

"I'm trying because I love you," I say.

"I love you, too, Cockring. But you have to stop with this."

Standing in that empty living room, I'm thinking, *I'm alone here.*

I'm thinking, *Her sobriety is up to me.*

I'm thinking, *Better luck next time.*

Exasperated, I ask, "So, like, do you have any tips for the next intervention? In case I have to ever do this again?"

"First, I've noticed snacks always help," she says, turning her back on me and walking to the bar in the red room. I follow.

"Okay, so catering. What else?"

Kathi fixes herself a Coke Zero. She doesn't offer me one. "Sometimes people write letters ahead of time and read those, so that's really fun and painful. Mostly I would say get more people in here and make it more dramatic, but the truth is, these haven't really worked well for me. I prefer rehab or psychiatric lockdown."

Hey, Siri, make a note of these preferences.

Kathi turns and heads to her bedroom. "Or a sober coach."

"What's that? Is that what I think it is?"

"Yeah. Someone who comes here and lives here with me and stays with me twenty-four/seven, even in the bathroom, to make sure I don't . . . stray."

I trot behind her, just like Roy. Just like a follower. Just like I nurse at her tit, just like my fellow assistants accused. But I push the thought aside. "Great," I say. "Do you have someone you'd like to work with again?"

"There was a guy once named like Rick Sommers or something, and he was so helpful and he had the biggest cock—"

"Okay. Very funny."

"It's not a joke! We made so much love I didn't need drugs. Then we both relapsed and I gained a ton of weight and he's brain-dead in a nursing home in Dayton."

Therapista says you can't help someone unless they want to help themselves.

Kathi enters her room and walks into her bathroom and closes the door.

"I just want to know how I can help you, Kathi," I shout through the door.

"I don't need your help, Nesbit Twelp."

I look at Roy on Kathi's bed, sleeping soundly, not a care in the world, reveling in the unknown of what's going to happen next, faithful that whatever it is will be a gift from a kind universe. If only we all lived with such optimism.

I sit on the bed beside Roy, my back against Kathi's headboard, my feet stretched in front of me. I'm looking at her bedroom door. I'm looking out into that hallway where it seems like just a sunrise ago I was younger and more innocent, standing there, about to enter her life for the first time, my first morning as her assistant. Everything was so new and interesting and shocking—*I'm here with a childhood icon! There's her bathroom, her clothes, her bad habits!* I'm thinking maybe if

I called Diane Keaton, maybe if she was hiring, I could have that rush of feelings again.

Kathi walks out of the bathroom, Tom Ford Amber Absolute electrifying the air behind her, fresh glitter sparkling on her eyelids, an e-cigarette in her mouth. She paces, typing on her phone.

"I'll never drive you there again," I say.

"Where?" Kathi says.

"To *Vegas*."

"Oh, God, of course not," Kathi says, taking a deep breath, too deep. "You can't anyway. If we went there again, it would look really bad."

I throw my hands up. "Not the point."

"Look," Kathi says, her steely exterior starting to crack. "Do you really think I enjoy going to fucking *Vegas*? That I enjoy all this?!" She takes the e-cigarette out of her mouth. She lets her hands drop to her sides, her cell phone falling until the lanyard catches it, the lanyard breaking the fall, the lanyard I made her, to prevent the phone, at least, from bottoming out.

Kathi's head drops; she sits. She starts to cry, where tears just fall off of your face, where you gasp for breath and don't even care that you can't breathe through the heaving, don't even care that you can't see through the tears. "I'm trying, okay? I just don't want you . . . I don't want anyone to think badly of me."

Kathi Kannon doesn't always look like her action figure. In certain light, I see the star, I see the priestess, I see her royalty in both this world and the imaginary one. But here, now, in the dim light of her bedroom, I just see a woman struggling, crushed under the weight of her body, her age, her feeling that options are limited, fearing that her fantastic life is suddenly a fraudulent one. She's tired. I'm tired. Maybe I've been struggling under the weight of her, too.

A million griefs bubble up in the room, in her, in me. My feelings want to spill out of me like the bleeding red clay of my dad's driveway in Perris, helpless in my father's house, helpless in Kathi Kannon's.

EVERYONE WILL DISAPPOINT YOU! I fear Dad may be right. What have I gotten myself into? Have I put my friend, my movie star, my action figure, in danger? Have I contributed to the unspeakable?

I take a deep breath, trying to keep it together.

Assistant Bible Verse 137: Maintain a professional demeanor at all times.

I suck it up, like tugging at my sweatpants to hide my pink socks.

Therapista says everything comes to light eventually.

Therapista says all things have ups and, most notably, all things have downs.

Therapista says the moment you attach to something or someone outside of yourself is the moment suffering begins.

"I don't think badly of you," I say, my voice quivering.

Kathi looks up at me slowly, notices my emotion, and almost angrily asks, "Now why are *you* crying?"

"Are you getting too close to the sun?" I ask, my own sobbing beginning.

"What?"

I take deep breaths. I'm thinking, *This is just a job.* I'm thinking, *This is not my life on the line here.* I'm thinking, *Why do I care so much?*

I say, "Miss Gracie told me this thing about a guy with wax feet or something and he flew too close to the sun and his feet melted or something and he crashed."

"That's one of her Bible stories," Kathi says.

"It's not from the Bible."

"From wherever!" Kathi yells.

"Maybe from her life. Her story, from her experience. From her experience of you. From my experience of you."

"What the fuck are you rambling about?"

"You know addiction is an incurable disease—"

"*Ugh.* Don't worry about it, Cockring."

"You have to quit. This can't last forever," I say.

"I know that! It's not like it consumes me. You never even brought it up until the damn tabloid."

The comment pierces my heart, the truth hurting. "I don't know what I'm doing, okay?"

Agnes pops in, notices the drama, the tears. Her eyes widen. Kathi and I both feel her in the room—our senses at peak levels, reading every atom and molecule of the air carrying our words, our wishes, our jabs. Agnes observes the scene for only a beat, the quiet, the tension, and immediately and without comment turns and exits.

Kathi continues, "What do you want me to tell you? Do you want me to tell you it's not what you think?"

I nod. *Yes.* I'm thinking, *That's exactly what I want.* I'm thinking, *And I want it to be true.*

Kathi Kannon, film icon, smiles sweetly, stands, walks up to my side of her bed, touches my arm. "Darling," she says, warm kindness radiating from her body to mine and a rote sincerity in her voice. "It's not what you think."

Kathi takes her hand away and brushes her bangs out of her face, offering that rare glimpse of a human being underneath all the Beverly Hills highlights and lowlights and makeup and glitter and fame and wealth and their disgusting, addicting draw.

"There's nothing further for us to discuss. I'll prove it to you, okay? You're an A-plus-plus assistant. Or at the very least a B-plus."

"I'm going to start grading you on your sobriety," I say.

"You have no idea about my sobriety," she snaps.

"Then I'll just guess!" I yell.

"Fine. I'll start," she shouts. "I'll grade myself! Right now, I'm probably a D, okay?"

"Not okay. I don't want you to die!"

Kathi doesn't respond. She walks out to the back patio, alone, with only her phone and the mysteries of whoever she's texting.

My head heavy, my shoulders slumped, I walk to the kitchen to get a drink.

"What was that all about?" Agnes asks from her station at the breakfast nook. "Back in the bedroom?"

"I was out of bounds, I think. I shouldn't have said all that."

"I thought you were reading a script for a movie. It felt so . . . I don't know. Intense."

"I feel bad."

"Don't. Someone had to say it to her. Someone should have said it to her a long time ago."

I take a deep breath and hold in a guffaw, one of those awkward laugh-turns-to-tears moments, where breath and life want to punch out of your guts like the creature in *Alien*. I suck in the outburst and will the tears away. I don't blink. I hold my breath. I smile slowly so Agnes can't see any quiver in my lip, any clue that I just hosted what feels like a test and I failed. I didn't move any goalpost; I didn't crack any hard outer shell; I haven't changed a thing; I'm not a good example. At what point does fault break the bow of intent, of character, of principle—or a lack of it?

"Agnes, do you know where Kathi keeps her drugs?"

Agnes pauses, averts eye contact; several painful moments pass. Then, slow and unsteady, wobbly in her baby-blue-colored socks on the slippery, shiny hardwood floors, or maybe wobbly from the uncertainty of the upcoming betrayal of her longtime employer, Agnes leads me through the mansion. We walk past the French doors looking out into the backyard. We see Kathi out there pacing, smoking an e-cigarette like it's her last, texting someone, some figure in a secret life.

We glide into Kathi's room, then into Kathi's bathroom. Agnes steps to the vanity, where Kathi's purse is open, contents spilling out like a Thanksgiving cornucopia, Mom's locket right there in the thick of the crime scene, now tarnished with a new scar—my mother's spirit, like me, bearing witness, aiding and abetting.

I'm thinking, *Mom, what have I gotten you into?* I'm thinking, *Mom, save us.*

Agnes reaches into the purse, unzips an inside pocket, and pulls out one of the pale-blue pill cases I give Kathi each day. She shakes it and the meds inside rattle. Agnes holds it out for me to take from her.

"You didn't find these from me," she says.

But I don't accept them. "No, no," I say. "False alarm. These are the pills I give her every day."

Agnes pulls her arm back, brings the pillbox close to her chest. She looks down at it and, almost as if confused how to open it, her elderly, fragile fingers search for grooves, and she pops the container open. She extends her arm again. I reach out my cupped hand. Agnes pours out the contents of the pill case. Tiny white circular pills I don't recognize drop onto my palm.

"What are they?" I ask.

Agnes takes a breath, considers her words carefully. "Not vegetables," she says.

I say to myself, "Fuck."

Agnes puts the empty pill case on the vanity. She looks down at the floor and slowly walks away. She says quietly as she passes me, "She keeps two. The pill case you give her every day and this one she has in her purse. I suppose she thinks your pill case is the one spot you won't think to look."

Agnes leaves me and I stand alone, feeling like a clown who has been played, angry at a reveal of corruption levied upon my innocent system of giving Kathi her daily meds. Indeed, I've seen a stray pill case around the house, in her nightstand, in her purse. And Agnes is right, and Kathi is right: I don't give them much thought; I never open them to check exactly what's inside, to see if there is competition.

I feel a sizzling inside me, a rage and profound disappointment. When my mother died, I wanted to scorch the earth. Now that same feeling is back. I want to throw the pills across the bathroom, to see them smash on the wall and scatter on the floor, these bits of poison and waste. Therapista says I have a problem accessing my anger. Therapista says holding in feelings is only a temporary fix. Therapista says all that fury has to come out eventually.

I walk to the toilet. I dump the pills into the water. The sound is pretty, a couple dozen little splashes that sound like a second's worth of the life of Kathi's fountain outside, the one she made from smashed plates and garbage. So pretty, that sound, these pills, so innocent, so dangerous.

I flush and watch a smattering of problems go away.

"What are you doing, Cockring?" Kathi asks, now behind me, surprised to find me in her bathroom.

"I'm watching you," I say.

Kathi walks close to me. "I'm a movie star, darling. Who isn't?"

I take a shower and try to wash the unsuccesses of the day off of my skin, to let the hot water spray my shoulders, warming the muscles tense and taut from facing Kathi, and to watch it all go down the drain, no longer my problem—not tonight, anyway.

DREW: What's up? Sorry out of touch. I'll explain. Hang?

Finally! At least I have Drew. He's on his way over for a long-overdue date and catch-up. And I'm looking forward to downloading about Kathi Kannon.

I defrost some salmon fillets. I cut some green beans. I prepare for our date, just a quiet night taking up some space in my apartment, pillows and blankets on the floor, Netflix streaming on the TV. I cover Mom's boxes with a sheet, because class and decor.

I'm having a good hair day for a change. I brush my teeth. I change my sheets.

Drew is parking, my handsome guy.

Drew is arriving, my pal.

Drew is crying, my pain.

Drew, standing in my apartment, is holding the plant I left on his doorstep, in its cute and perfect little pot. He's handing it back to me. And I take it.

"It's not you it's me and blah blah blah," Drew says. He actually says the "blah blah blah" part. "I'm just not ready to be in a relationship," he says. "I'm sorry, pal. I'm sorry."

I look down at the little tree, my new memento of failure and rejection.

I'm angry but disarmed by his emotion. Am I supposed to plead with him? To negotiate this thing back into being? Sadly, I used up all my tears with Kathi.

"Is my job the problem?" I ask.

"No, no. It's not something I can explain. I'm sorry."

I can feel myself closing some doors, shutting down some feelings about relationships and partners and dumb fucking nicknames.

And as Drew leaves, I close the door, lock it, walk to the kitchen, and I throw our little sapling in the trash. I sense the beginning of resentment toward Kathi, a job—a lifestyle—that surely made it harder to maintain my thing with Drew. As the baby tree hits the bottom of the trash can, I hear the vase crack.

I delete my upcoming dates with Drew from my calendar. More blue dots gone.

Therapista says I should stay friends with Drew.

Therapista says I need to have a life outside of Kathi Kannon.

Therapista can go fuck herself.

Hey, Siri, my friend Jesse is throwing a Christmas party. Behind his back we call him Lenny from *Of Mice and Men,* because Jesse is very rough and handsy. He loves to get loud and narrate the slightest party happening, introduce this guy to that one, and announce arrivals. "This is Charlie," Jesse says, grabbing my wrist. I'm arriving single, but I'm not really solo. *She* is always with me, more or less.

"Charlie works for Kathi Kannon."

I've heard him do this before; I've heard others do it. It works. Everyone turns. I feel important. One minute I'm smelling the armpit of Kathi Kannon's blouse to see if it's dirty and the next I'm the hottest guy in the room.

The rest of the night, I try to mix and mingle, looking for my next so-called boyfriend. Everyone I meet asks the same question:

"How's Kathi Kannon?"

"How's Kathi Kannon?"

"How's Kathi Kannon?"

I get that question a lot, all the time, everywhere, from everyone. And as I stand there, chatting, sharing my usual stories, I'm thinking: *How's Kathi Kannon?* I'm thinking, *Interesting that no one asks me, "How are you?"* I'm thinking, *No one ever asks about me.*

But I switch into autopilot, mentally donning the familiar costume of humble assistant, wearing the fabric and illusion of my restless, fabulous life. I stand at the table of Jesse's homemade Christmas-tree cookies and mistletoe punch and force a smile and share. "Kathi Kannon is great," I tell this guy and that. "Sure, I work for her, it's cool." I tell them that I have Bette Midler's cell-phone number, that I have a screenshot of a text message from Helena Bonham Carter that says "have her call me pimple. I mean please." I show my—I mean, *our*—calendar.

"The blue dots are *my* appointments," I say, "and the pink dots are *her* appointments." It rolls out of my mouth like an actor with lines. I've said it a thousand times to a thousand different people, bragging, preening. I know the desired effect like a stand-up comedian knows which jokes kill. But this time—

"Wait," Jesse says. "There are no blue dots."

I grab my phone back and look.

Assistant Bible Verse 138: It takes a special person to be a personal assistant. It takes a person willing to yield. To pause their own life. To make their life secondary. To miss dates and special occasions because your boss at the last minute wants you to pick up dinner, or travel with them to Bhutan.

My phone in hand, I'm looking at the day, the week, the month, the year—and the years—ahead. There are no blue dots. There is no me. There is only her.

So much destruction.

14

☆

J asmine is hosting a round of work drinks that's way more drinks than work. Her dad is in town, an oncologist from Minnesota who's pounding draft beers and leaning forward to show how much he cares, how much he's really listening to our celebrity stories. Jasmine jumps up and rushes over when she sees me enter.

"Hi, enabler," Jasmine says jokingly, handing me my drink, Truth, cold and colorful and, tonight, bitter.

"Not funny," I say.

"Bruce can't make it," she says. "He's working late to get his promotion."

"Our loss," I say as I take a big gulp of the booze. Jasmine puts her arm around me and guides me to her father. "Please tell my dad all the best stories."

As we approach, Titanic is already in the midst of an epic tale. "My boss's gate wouldn't open, because he hit it with his Porsche," he says, detailing his household's emergency last night. "It was two in the morning and I had to rush over, find an emergency number for the gate repairman, and he couldn't come until the next day, so I had to then wait outside the house all night to make sure no one snuck onto the unsecured property."

"You had to wait out there all night? What's on that property that's so valuable?" Jasmine's father asks.

"A big ego," Titanic says, to great laughter from Jasmine's father, the innocent Minnesotan, and polite laughter from the rest of us—it's not funny when you know it could happen to you.

I take another healthy dose of Truth. I'm thinking, sitting here with these guys, at this late hour, our entertaining a man who could—in some flip universe—be my own father leaves me fucking parched. I signal for a second drink.

"The gate repairman didn't get there until ten A.M.," Titanic says, "and I'm still in my pajamas and then I had to go do the grocery shopping."

"Wait," Jasmine's father says, "you couldn't even go home to change?"

"No," Titanic says. With his back to the sconce, his face is in shadow, hiding his blemishes, and he looks handsome, fragile. "I mean, I could, but here's the thing: I could have hired a security guard to come stand out there all night instead of me, but how long would that take? An hour to find a security company, a couple hours to connect the company with the business manager to arrange payment, a few hours waiting for the poor security sap to arrive at the house, have him sign an NDA, and on and on. And then I can't skip the grocery because it's a Tuesday and the chef comes on Tuesday, and if I don't go to the grocery, there won't be any fresh lettuce for him to make salads."

"He can't pick up some lettuce on his way?" her father asks, kindly, ignorantly.

"Negative," Titanic says. "Don't be silly. My boss only eats the organic living butter lettuce from Lassens, and the chef only shops at Whole Foods."

"Assisting is the worst," West says drunkenly.

"The worst," Crooner confirms.

I rattle the ice cubes in my little glass and signal the bartender for a third drink as the mostly familiar faces at the table all turn and look at me, cueing me to add my nugget to their storied heap. I'm quiet for a beat too long.

"Who do you work for?" Jasmine's dad asks me, leaning forward again, into my space, seemingly eager to hear what I have to say, a gentle smile on his lips, a living cliché of a warm father engaging with his daughter's friends.

The bartender arrives in a blink and I take a sip. I eye the faces ready to swallow some of my usual stories, but the easy crowd-pleasers don't pop to mind; nothing pops to mind.

I open my mouth to speak to Jasmine's dad, and I'm feeling like a child again, some kind of young student facing a favorite teacher, desperate to impress him. In a strange way he does remind me of my own father—his advancing age, his cellular vulnerability—but he's a shadow of my father, a faulty copy, for the qualities defining this guy—kindness, curiosity—are absent from mine. My dad would never, and has never, traveled from Perris, Louisiana, to see me in Los Angeles. The suggestion he would ever want to meet or engage with my friends is laughable—even more absurd that he would want to entertain someone I'm dating, or was dating, like sweet Drew. My father would never listen to me and my stories about work with curiosity and care. He'd never reserve judgment or opinion. His reactions would be swift and brutal. His disgust would be immediate and pervasive, starting first in his eyes and spreading to his forehead, the squinting, the peering down and into me. Then his cheeks rise and his mouth grimaces; he turns away from me—he degrades me as not even worthy of his countenance. His mouth opens and he spits some rash opinion or worse—

DON'T YOU DARE! I hear my father screaming at me, so vividly, as if it was yesterday. *DON'T YOU EVER TALK ABOUT WHAT GOES ON IN THIS FAMILY!*

Or, in *that* family, the Kathi Kannon family?

I'm thinking, *Maybe don't talk about Kathi Kannon anymore.*

I take another sip of my drink. Another. Another. I smile coyly at Jasmine's father.

DON'T YOU DARE!

I think of how to rid myself of Dad's curse, the aftertaste of my childhood, Dad's monologues not so easily dismissed.

As my fellow assistants spill the beans on their employers' lives, alcohol swirling in my mind, I hear my father screaming at me not to speak out, not to share secrets, not to trust these people with Kathi's life. My dad's voice in me: Who is Jasmine? Do I even know any of these people? Who is her father? Who is this guy asking me these questions? Do I know him? Do I know any of them well enough to trust them with stories harvested from my livelihood?

"Well?" Jasmine's dad asks, turning back to me, leaning closer to me.

DON'T YOU DARE! surges the shout of my father, some revulsion reaction inside me, making me distrust—no, hate—this man in front of me, the things I want to tell him, the things I want to tell my real father.

And I drink.

The first time my father yelled "DON'T YOU DARE!" to me, Mom was still alive, sitting quietly with me in the living room while he railed, angry that I had mentioned to a neighbor that we couldn't afford a family vacation. "WHAT HAPPENS IN THIS FAMILY STAYS IN THIS FAMILY! MY BUSINESS IS NO ONE ELSE'S BUSINESS!"

I get it now, looking back at that one moment of many, realizing his humiliation, his reaction. But I now also understand this is the language of an abuser, someone who fears truth, someone who harbors shame. And at what cost? Rage because of economics and employment and assemblage of coin that's more or less out of his control? Therapista says boundaries are an act of selfishness, that the fewer our boundaries, the more honest we are, the more we all see one another, the more

united we become, that sharing our secrets is true intimacy. But I wonder if my father could convince her otherwise—his powerful voice and
throbbing jugular make very convincing arguments. His point lives
inside me, seared there, following me and defining and occupying the
voices, the home of my childhood, of my adult apartments, of my current employment.

"Charlie must be feeling shy," Jasmine says, shooing away my
silence.

"No," I say, shaking my head, scrunching my toes inside my shoes,
shoving my glasses back on my face, clenching my stomach tight, dart-
ing my eyes to the bartender, waving to get his attention, and shouting
to him, "Could I get another drink over here, please?"

"Slow down, turbo," West jokes. I laugh along with her, painfully
fake and slow.

I turn to Jasmine's dad. "I work for Kathi Kannon," I say. "Star of
stage and screen and *People* magazine's Worst Dressed list," I mutter,
my familiar quip, always popular at parties, first dates, jury duty. I add,
"I help her. I love her."

"I love her mom," Jasmine's dad says. "Have you met Gracie Gold?"

"It's '*Miss* Gracie,'" I correct him as the bartender brings over my
fourth drink. I want to grab it out of reflex, like the cool guy in a movie,
like some basic popcorn flick set on a college campus where I'm wearing a tweed sport coat and we're all chatting about something—maybe
poetry—and the bartender brings me more Truth and I'm in the middle of a punch line and just before I deliver it, I swoop to the bar and
grab my new glass and take a sip and then, *boom!* Punch line! Laughter! Praise!

But I snap out of my daydream and look down at the full drink
already in my hand, to the new one now on the counter across from
me, a reminder that I'm moving too fast, acting too thirsty, getting a
tad drunk.

"Kathi's been in the news lately, no?" Jasmine asks, prompts.

"None of that's true. They're gonna publish a retraction. Honestly, Kathi is great," I say, eyeing my drink, putting it down on the bar, retreating from it. "Kathi and Miss Gracie are really great. I have no complaints."

"Oh, please," Crooner says.

"When we first met Charlie," Jasmine says, "he was a bit of a chicken with his head cut off. But he's getting the hang of it all now. He even dresses better." She nods to my body and my Kathi Kannon cardigan, shirt, pants, belt, shoes.

"I'm wearing clothes that Kathi bought for me," I say, adding playfully, "She's remaking me in her image and likeness."

"Yikes, be careful," Jasmine's dad says.

My head cocks, some instant and immediate reflex that surprises me, though nothing has ever felt more natural than to defend Kathi. "What is that supposed to mean?"

"Oh, nothing," he says. "You know, just, she is an admitted drug addict, right?"

My eyes open wide and I take stock of the room. Jasmine avoids eye contact, and the silence reminds me I'm alone; I'm as alone as Kathi Kannon. "She is not a drug addict. How dare you?"

"She has said publicly over and over she's a drug addict," he says.

"Dad—" Jasmine says, trying to stop the train.

"She's not a fucking drug addict now!" I yell. I stand. "She's trying so, so hard, okay? You don't know her! You don't know how hard it is!"

"Baby," Jasmine says kindly. "Calm down. Have a seat."

But I continue, leaning toward Jasmine's dad. "Kathi Kannon is a fucking human being! Your life is so perfect? Fuck you and fuck you twice again."

"Charlie!" Jasmine says.

"Sorry, man," Jasmine's dad says. "I'm just saying be careful when someone wants to change you. What if you don't want to change?"

I step slightly toward him. I glance at my two drinks sweating on the bar together, both of them looking so delicious and so detrimental, both of their fates already imagined inside me, both of them going to waste, me calling my own limit, making a sober choice—as sober as possible—to shut up and keep Kathi's business Kathi's business.

I'm thinking, *Fuck my dad.*

But I'm also thinking, *Fuck this guy, Jasmine's dad.*

I tuck my long, growing hair behind my ears—making a note to myself that even my hair is a gift from her, something I owe her. "It's okay if Kathi Kannon is changing me," I say. "Because I'm changing her."

Sitting in my car, alcohol and angst pumping through me, I'm feeling spent and dissected and unable to drive. Just sitting feels good, still and quiet and cool in the California night with the support of the seat of my trusty Nissan Sentra. I run my hand across the dash like it's a hot guy's leg. I use my finger to wipe some dust from the radio buttons. I look down at the mats on the floor, covered with dirt.

I'm thinking, *I need to vacuum this car.* I reach down and try to scoop up some of the mess and leaves, but most of the bits are impossibly tiny.

I scroll through mixed and merged contacts in my phone—there's the number for Ben Affleck, for Cher, for Toni Collette—and past all those options, all those celebrities I could theoretically call and bullshit with, I land at the most infamous character in my life: Dad.

It's two A.M. in L.A., so it's four A.M. in Louisiana.

I'm thinking, *DON'T YOU DARE!*

I push the call button and close my eyes, imagining the signal bouncing from my phone to some tower to outer space to some satellite, back down and to my father's phone on his stupid nightstand in his stupid bedroom in Perris.

Ring.

I'm thinking about being naked in that room, forced to wear my dead mother's panties.

Ring.

I'm thinking of all the creative dreams that died that day, in that room.

Ring.

I'm thinking of all the things that died in my childhood, not the least of which—my mother.

Ring.

"Charlie?" Dad says, answering his phone, groggy and alarmed. "Everything okay?"

"I'm wondering about you," I say, trying to project an air of adulthood.

"Are you drunk?" Dad asks. "What's wrong?"

"My therapist says that when you talk to others, you are talking to yourself. So when you said way back, like, when I was a kid and you made me eat Oreos out of the trash and you said, 'Take responsibility for your life,' were you really talking to yourself?"

"What Oreos?" Dad asks, growing frustrated. "What are you talking about? Why the fuck are you calling me at four in the morning?"

"Because I think when you said 'take responsibility for your actions' to me—you were actually talking about yourself, right? You were saying I should take the blame for wasting those cookies, but that means you believe you should take all the blame for your own flaws in your life, and maybe you think you're to blame for your bad marriage and your unfinished house and your sad family and your not having money and stuff. I think that you think that it was all your fault, right?"

Dad is quiet on the other end of the line. I wait for his response, watching passersby on the sidewalk, barflies ejected at the two A.M. last call, lonely and horny and still on their hunt for more. Dad never responds.

"I mean, some of it was your fault, but I don't think it's all your fault," I stammer. "I don't think it's true that everything was your fault. I think some things happened that were not in your control. Or my control. Your problems were relative? Right? Some things just get dirty. Anyway, this just occurred to me because my car needs to be vacuumed."

"I'm going back to bed, Charlie."

"Of course you are," I say. "It's four in the morning there? Yeah. You should go back to bed. And sleep soundly, you know. Now that you have this new information."

"Are you home?"

"Nope."

I shake my head; I sway to the music of the traffic outside, the booze inside.

Dad asks, "Can you get home safely?"

I say, "Of course, *darling.*"

I hang up and feel my heart pumping inside me. I open my phone again. I text Jasmine.

ME: Sorry.

15

☆

That old pill bottle Kathi gave me back in Sydney, it's still on my nightstand in my apartment. A reminder: I can trust her, sometimes, at least. It's a symbol, though an empty one.

Hey, Siri, I want to trust her.

Also on my nightstand, a brass lamp. It's the same brand of lamp that was in my room next to Kathi's at the Greenwich Hotel in New York, its crooked neck and arching shade still looking like a cartoon character, still giving me a little wave: *Welcome home.* I wanted a piece of NYC, a reminder of this great life, at arm's reach. I looked under the lamp at the hotel and found the manufacturer website and ordered one—my own treasure, my own bit of luxury, a little out of place in my dumpy dwelling but still proudly lighting my way through the small corners of this apartment, of my life.

They both sit there, the pill bottle and the lamp, both gathering dust, lonely and sad, just like me, my empty bed, my empty calendar.

I turn to my trusty vice: OkCupid.

It's time to get back in the game. To recharge my relationship batteries. To see what's out there, who's out there, who can save me.

Nice to meet you, LA2LA94. He's too religious.

Nice to meet you, HPOTTERFAN. He's a Hufflepuff.

Nice to meet you, NYC1980. He hated *Nova Quest.*

I email CALI-DREAMING, even though I only gave him one star out of five because I didn't like his clothes in his pictures, including one where he was in a caftan. Not that I have a problem with caftans—I love them—it's just the pattern was all wrong for his body type. Alas, sitting alone in my apartment I'm thinking, *Maybe I shouldn't be too picky.* My email to him was mostly cut-and-pasted from the many others I had sent to potentials. But he wrote back: "Hi, I'm Ben."

Ben is tall and so much better-looking than his profile picture, handsome but accessible, quirky but not awkward. This moment with him feels new, and it feels authentic. And I want more, more, more.

We meet at Intelligentsia Coffee in Silver Lake and are having iced coffees together when a film crew walks up to us. They're doing a survey for a local election and we oblige with our opinions, and the leader gives me her card and they take our picture and they're gone.

"Was that weird?" I ask him. "That was so random."

"Nah," Ben says. "I've never been on a date in L.A. that didn't involve media somehow."

We laugh and I think how much I liked his answers to the interview questions about school choice and speed humps and clean-air initiatives. We seem to be on similar pages, and we "cheers" our iced coffees. "To clean air," Ben says.

When I get home, I have a good feeling about our first date, so I email the crew and ask for a copy of the picture. If Ben and I work out, it will be so special to have a photo of our first meeting.

I'm thinking, *Blue dots at last.*

Hey, Siri, the show must go on. We're in Seattle. Kathi agreed to shoot a TV show that we've never heard of, never seen. She's agreed to play a character whose name she can't remember, from a script she hasn't read. But money is money, and working occasionally looks good and appeases her agents and her mother.

In our hotel lobby, we spot k.d. lang. Does she know who we are? Does she want to meet Kathi Kannon? Does she think I'm Kathi's lover or son? Does she want to ask me to hook her up with an autograph, a meet and greet? Does she think I'm important, too? I'm back to feeding my addiction. With k.d. is a young companion, male, stylishly dressed, possibly an assistant. He looks over at me. He smiles and nods—to our being gay, to our being assistants? I'm not sure. I'm thinking, *Maybe there are too many assistants in the world, too many gatekeepers for too many gates.*

Kathi and I are wearing weird hats she bought at the airport—her in moose antlers and me, reluctantly, in a woolly Russian-lumberjack-style getup. Roy in tow, we turn from k.d. and her companion and get in the elevator. A drunk guy enters behind us as the doors close. We all stare at one another for a moment. I wonder if he recognizes Kathi, whether I'm going to have to fight with him, or more probable, lose a fight with him. And as we start to ascend, the guy mumbles at us, "Weirdos."

I'm trying to assess the degree to which we are maybe in danger. Kathi is still. Roy is still. I look over at Kathi, her makeup smeared, glitter in her eyelashes, her wacky hat askew. I look at Roy, tired, hair matted from his nap in the limo. I imagine my face, exhaustion, my eyelids droopy, a nasal drip starting in the back of my throat. We are a mess. Maybe we *are* weirdos.

The elevator dings and Kathi and I exit, not murdered after all. I safely take her to her room, with a promise I'll see her in a few moments to say good night. I go to my room and start to unpack and prepare for the next day.

As I'm about to leave my room to go back to Kathi, I hear the drunk guy yelling in the hall. He must have followed us or remembered our floor. Is he looking for us? Is he lost, confused, dangerous? I watch through the peephole. There's a threat between me and Kathi Kannon—I'm thinking, *Not the first time.*

A short time later, the man's friend collects him, tells him to be quiet or they'll get kicked out of the hotel.

I stand at my hotel door for several minutes, my face squished against the peephole, looking for any signs the threat is still lingering. I hear nothing, see nothing.

Therapista says some threats are silent.

I slip out and go to Kathi's room.

Kathi is snuggled in bed, Roy snoring beside her. She's watching TV, clicking channels.

Click, click, click.

I sit next to her, that awkward moment where I wait to be dismissed, wondering if she really wants me to leave or really wants me to stay, to be with her, to share some common thread, some companionship.

Click, click, click.

And on the television, suddenly, it's *her*! Her movie. *The* movie! *Nova Quest.* The film that truly birthed her celebrity. I gasp. Everything stops. She freezes. I freeze. The AC in the room shuts down, every molecule turns to see what happens. Kathi watches herself as Priestess Talara onscreen for a few moments. Her young face, her young body, her young hand—all while her current hand, her real hand, clutches mine.

It's a dramatic moment in *Nova Quest:* One of her co-stars is dying, worrying he failed in his mission to save the planet. Priestess Talara holds him tight and whispers her iconic line, the one that has lived on, survived these decades on T-shirts and posters and coffee mugs. She says the line that defined part of my childhood and brought me comfort in the dark days of my young life. Priestess Talara says, "It's all the All."

Awesome! In awe, I look at Kathi. Her lips part. I stop breathing. She's deciding what to say. The quiet wakes Roy and he perks up like the rest of us.

Hey, Siri, I want her to become my hero, Priestess Talara, to show me she still has it, to show me she gets it, the lore and the magic. I want her to validate my childhood and my jagged journey to being in the room with her. I want her to leap from the film to the screen to this hotel room and make me a part of this iconic moment, even if it's just by proximity to her talent. I want to stand, I want to lock eyes with her, I want to be a part of this insane scene both in the room and on the television, in this tall order that lies before us. I hold my breath.

Kathi shakes her head and says, "Asinine," lets go of my hand, and changes the channel.

Click, click, click.

I'm thinking, *A million infomercials seem more interesting to her than her history, her life.*

"Did you take your meds?" I ask.

"Yes," she says.

"Want to write?"

"No."

"Want to go over your lines for tomorrow?"

"Definitely not," she says.

I bid her farewell.

Asinine.

I'm naked and I call Ben.

The usual exchanges about our day only get us so far, and we both turn to what we really want. We start masturbating on the phone together.

My eyes closed, my hand rubbing myself, my mind in a room, in a bed, intimate with Ben, I say, "I wanna feel you inside me."

"I wanna feel you inside me," he repeats.

I open my eyes, wondering if he'll say more, but he doesn't. "Is that it?" I ask.

"Is what it?"

"I just said, 'I wanna feel you inside me,' and then you repeated it."

"Right," he says.

"No, no. That's not dirty talk. You have to say something fresh. Not just repeat me. Or you can repeat it, but you have to, like, add to it, move the scene forward, you know?"

"Oh, right, right, yeah," he says. "Um, I'm gonna get inside you tonight."

Perhaps Therapista is right that relationships are an ever-shifting pie chart, with some slices big—like Ben's everyday good looks and kindness—and some slices smaller—like his ability to talk filthy. But right now a small slice of talking filthy is just fine. I'm more nourished on this night by the slice of Ben's pie that seems biggest and warmest: He's here for me, at least on the phone.

We laugh, we talk, we orgasm. As I end the call, I'm thinking, *This would have been so much more fun if I wasn't so many miles away.*

It's five A.M. and I have no idea where I am.

The digital clock on my nightstand displays the time in a glowing orange oval with black numbers, giving the hotel room the feel of a spaceship.

Time to wake up.

I grab my phone and scroll through my emails. Sweet nothings from Ben. Credit-card payment is due—I'm almost out of debt. Spam offering me hot Asian women.

I roll out of bed.

Time to make the Kathi donuts.

I knock assertively on her door before inserting the key card. I walk inside her room. There's trash on the floor. The TV is on. The bathroom lights are on. Something feels off. How can she live like this? Is this living? Is she living?

I look at Kathi Kannon, film icon. I've seen this before. She looks just like she has in my imagination, just as I've seen in my nightmares, the kind where you wake yourself up by the sound of your own gasping for air—because in these dreams, she looks dead.

But this is no dream.

My movie-star boss is looking blue, maybe dying from a drug overdose.

Roy stirs and the movement startles me. He jumps down from the bed and comes to me—begging? For what? For help?

Assistant Bible Verse 139: Always assume the worst.

I rush to Kathi's side. "Kathi!" I shout. Her famous breasts are flopped to and fro, the nipples pointing in opposite directions under her thin nightgown.

Roy presses against my calves, wiggling nervously, like he knows something I don't. Or perhaps my fear is now contagious, Roy taking a defensive position behind me, bracing himself, abandoning me on the front line.

"Kathi," I repeat, my voice pocked with worry, wondering if she'll stir and her blue skin will flush pink as she takes a deep, dry breath.

"Kathi," I say a little louder.

"KATHI!" I shout.

Roy looks back and forth, from me to her, me to her, willing me to *do something*.

I hope we survive Seattle.

I'm blushing. I'm sweating. I'm thinking, *Fuck*.

Assistant Bible Verse 140: Be prepared for last-minute auditions, paparazzi in the azaleas, mouth-to-mouth resuscitations.

I touch her shoulder. Cold. I put my fingers on her neck. Cold. I put my hand over her heart. Cold. I push, and her body heaves, bounces on the bed. I push again. I put my other hand on top of the first and push down again.

"Kathi? No!" I yell. "I need you! Please don't leave me!" I push, push, push.

One, one thousand. Two, one thousand. Three, one thousand.

Pump, pump, pump.

The bed bouncing, bouncing, bouncing.

"HELP!" I yell, turning to the nightstand, to the phone. With one hand I grab the receiver, and I take my other hand off her cold chest to dial.

"Cockring?!" she gasps.

I stop, turn, stare at this miracle.

Assistant Bible Verse 141: The job never ends.

Roy hops back up on the bed, licks her face once, and then circles and circles until he plops down in a perfect little ball of comfort. He's thinking, *Naptime*. He's thinking, *This is just another morning*.

I hang up the phone.

Kathi says without moving, "What time is it? Were you just screaming?"

I exhale, not just my breath, but I release every cell, every muscle, every thought. My mind goes blank, my body limp, standing, swaying slightly before her. I think of Kathi as my mother for a brief moment— flashing back to Mom's death, watching her collapse in church and seeing her lifeless body, remembering my deepest prayer that she would just stand up, be reanimated, alive again. I remember wanting to run up to her, to grab her, to shake her awake. I wish she would have snapped to attention all those years ago, just like Kathi Kannon did a few moments ago. I wish I could distribute miracles equally among the women in my life.

"My throat hurts," Kathi says. "And my back is killing me."

"Time to go to work," I say, worried I'm talking to a ghost.

She tries to sit up in bed but struggles. As she moves the comforter away from her, I think I see vomit in the bed, or maybe it's just some other kind of mess in our lives. She pulls the comforter back again to hide it.

She looks up at me. "What's wrong?"

"Nothing," I say, and in a fever begin to tidy up, walking to a lamp to turn it on.

"Wait. Were you just touching my breast?" she asks, waking, awareness starting to pump through her veins.

"No, I was giving you CPR."

"That's not how you do CPR, Cockring," she says. "It's okay. You don't have to deny your sexual feelings for me."

"I thought you were fucking dead."

"Dead? That would have been a travesty of a travesty of a blap."

"I'm not kidding."

"I'm not dead, I'm jet-lagged."

"This seems like more than jet lag."

"It's rich-people jet lag. It's worse for us."

"I give you an F," I say.

"For what?"

"You know what!"

"Then I give you a C for giving me an F!" she yells.

"That's fine, because I already know I'm an A and the C is just because you're mad at me!"

"I'm not mad, I'm sleepy!" Kathi tries to sit up again, but she's wobbly. She coughs. She tries to move the covers off her legs, but her movements look mired in molasses. She hovers on the edge of the bed. She steadies herself on the nightstand.

"I don't think I can film the show today," she says.

"They'll be pissed."

Kathi glares at me, our nonverbal communication. I concede. "What do you want me to tell them?"

"I'm sick. I'll do it tomorrow," she says. "Or this afternoon maybe."

"I'm not sure that's how it works."

"Then fucking cancel it, Cockring. Get us a flight home. Fuck it."

I nod *okay* but don't move, my feet locking my body in a stare-off with her.

"What now?" Kathi asks, noticing my gawking.

"What if you had been dead? In this shitty hotel room, at this shitty hour, far from home, on a stupid weekday morning, about to shoot a stupid TV show. Is this really where and how you want your life to end? You want this on your IMDB page? Am I supposed to update all this on your Wikipedia?"

Kathi sits still for a moment. Then, "What's a Wikipedia?"

"You can't die this way."

"Why not?" she asks.

"Because you're too interesting and special. You need a quirky death when you're, like, a hundred. And don't do it in a way where I'll be blamed."

"You'll be with me when I'm one hundred?" she asks.

"Maybe."

"You'll be my Roger?"

"Roger? Jeez," I say.

"What's wrong with Roger?"

"Nothing. He just seems, I don't know, defeated. He's lost in Miss Gracie's life. Why do I have to be him? Can't I just stay Cockring?"

"Maybe."

"The point is, you have to die alone somehow, in some capacity in which I could not save you or have even known you were in danger— like you choke on your Weight Busters alone in your room at three in the morning. Or you fall asleep with a cigarette and burn to death."

"Jesus Christ, Cockring," she says.

"You know what I mean. Sorry. This was a scary start to our morning."

Weirdos.

We sit quietly in that room for a few minutes. The moment has transformed the space from a generic place to sleep to a tomb, a hallowed place, the place where perhaps she could have died. I know in my bones, to my core, that this room is not worthy of her death—it's barely worthy of her life.

"God," Kathi says, hauling herself out of bed, steadying herself against the sick-colored wall, then staggering into the bathroom. Roy perks his head up and then plops it back down for critical continued rest, unfazed by this monotony of human minutiae.

Kathi Kannon. A moment ago she seemed dead, and now she walks around in a nightgown, nearly lifeless and completely exhausted. I wonder if I would be this comfortable around someone else. Comfortable enough to wear my pajamas, to be seen so vulnerable. Kathi seems resigned to it, accepting of it. Perhaps it's show business. Performers change clothes in front of one another. Performers share bathrooms and have diarrhea before shows. Maybe this is all a show. Her show. I'm in the cast. Do I get a credit at the end? Is there an end? For her? For me? How long is this episode? Will it end one day with me finding her dead for real?

Hey, Siri, I hope I survive her.

Hey, Siri, am I her Roger?

As Kathi closes the bathroom door, she turns back to me. "Cockring," she says. "Maybe it's time for me to get a little help."

"Okay," I say.

Immediately, while she's in the bathroom, I start my search for a sober coach for Kathi Kannon, film icon. Google turns up some random results, but I'm looking for the real thing. My next step is to search Google News, to see if "sober coach" or "sobriety coaches" turns up anything recent—maybe some other celebrity used someone, or a news station interviewed some expert, someone vetted and verified. No luck.

I turn to my trusty Assistants Club. I find our last email, reply all, and put out the call. These guys know the best bars, the best yacht captains, the best place for anal bleaching. Surely they can refer me to a sober coach. West comes through for me, sending me referrals for not one or two sober coaches but a list of seventeen.

> Hi! We've met with and hired all of them at one point or another. But Orion Towers (he's Greek!) has been the best for us. Kind, firm, doesn't mind watching the client pee.
>
> —Good luck,
> "West"

I email Orion Towers about his availability.

16

☆

ednesdays are the worst, less like a midweek hump and
more a hand grenade—problems always popping up at
the halfway mark and threatening to ruin the rest of it.
Not to mention, today is a travel Wednesday.

We left Seattle in a daze, landed in Los Angeles, and are now riding
home in a limo. Kathi wants a cola with ice, but the cup of ice in the
car's bar has melted a little. So she picks it up, pours the melted water
onto the floor of the limo, and then pours her soda onto the remaining ice.

She notices me staring at her in disbelief, as the puddle on the car-
peted floor of the car starts to grow, grow, grow.

"How can you do that?" I ask.

"I was raised by wolves!" she yells.

When we arrive home, lined up in Kathi's driveway is a row of
people, greeters, like we're at the front door of Downton Abbey. Roy
whimpers with excitement at the sight of it—he's the only one in the
car who appreciates a receiving line.

"Oh, for fuck's sake," Kathi says.

It's Agnes, Benny, Roger, Miss Gracie with Uta Hagen in her arms, and Orion Towers, even more handsome than the headshot on his website or the selfies on his Instagram. He's got midnight-black hair, bright blue eyes, and tan skin that has clearly known luxury lifestyles poolside, oceanfront, and sun-kissed. He's dressed modestly, his muscles only slightly visible under his loose clothing. He has a tight chest and thick arms that have experienced the pleasures of personal trainers, nutritionists, cosmetologists. I'm thinking, *Is he gay?* I'm thinking, *I hope he's gay.*

The car stops and Kathi opens her door. Roy leaps out and begins a happy jog around the friends, family, employees there to welcome us. Kathi gets out next, hugs her mother.

"Welcome home, dear," Miss Gracie says. "This is him. He's costing me a lot of money." She points to Orion and gestures to his physique. "And this is his body."

Orion says through a chuckle, shaking Kathi's hand, "Nice to meet you."

"We'll see about that," Kathi says. "You already know Cockring, I guess?"

I walk up to Orion carrying Kathi's suitcase. "We emailed some," I say, shaking his hand. I blush at the sight of him; his grip is warm and firm and swallows mine. He's got charming eyes, which dart briefly to my open shirt collar, and I'm thinking, *Yup, he's gay.*

"Shall we?" Kathi asks, and she and Orion walk up to the house together, to the backyard, to chat about goals and plans and sobriety. Benny helps Agnes back up to the house, and Miss Gracie leads Uta Hagen down to their home. Roger follows, offering me a wave goodbye.

I unpack Kathi and check that her bedroom is in order. In the room is a rollaway cot Agnes and Benny put together with crisp white sheets. It's the same cot they've used during past attempts at Kathi's sobriety, one perpetually packed in the basement, kept on hand, just in case it didn't stick back then, or then, or then.

Soon, Orion Towers will take up residence on that trusty old cot, beginning his 24/7 time with Kathi, for as long as necessary. For the coming weeks I'll cancel her appointments, intercept her calls, try to keep her life as peaceful as possible. I'm not going to be out of touch, but I'll be coming here less, taking a little time off for myself while Kathi gets herself sorted.

I see them chatting in the backyard, Kathi and Orion. I'm thrilled to see her smiling and laughing with him, the two of them looking like they're shooting a movie scene together, yard ornaments twirling around them, the garbage fountain reflecting sunlight in its droplets, a small plastic cow on a hill presiding over the whole proceeding, this occasion, this mastering of desires, this tempering of tenets of her addiction. I'm thinking, *I'm leaving her in good hands.* I'm thinking, *I'm leaving her in good, hot hands.*

I walk down Kathi's brick walkway to my car, parked dutifully outside of her garage, and I see Roger milling around inside, looking at the books.

"Hiding?" I ask.

"You betcha," Roger says. "Actually, Miss Gracie asks me to step outside whenever she goes to the bathroom, so . . . "

"Hope she's quick."

"Tell me about it."

"I've been thinking of you. Kathi is calling me 'her Roger.'"

"Yikes, sorry."

"I should be so lucky to be considered as loyal and efficient as you are."

Roger sits on an old tattered bench tucked away to be repainted, recirculated, used up. "Wanna join?" he asks.

"Maybe," I say playfully.

Roger scoots over at great cost—risking snagging his lovely Ralph

Lauren cardigan, perhaps another of the many bribes from this family—and I sit beside him.

"How's it hanging?" Roger asks.

"Drama," I say.

Roger laughs, a chuckle with a hint of sadness, regret. He looks down at the ground. "Their drama reminds me of my youth."

"Were your parents a lot like them when you were a kid?" I ask.

"Oh, no," he says. "Kathi and Miss Gracie don't remind me of my childhood. They remind me of my youth. My fucking youth: my twenties, when I first started this job for them. They've been dramatic, fighting, at odds with each other like this since I've been here. It always upsets Miss Gracie. I tell her, don't think of it as a fight or as hate, think of it as passion, which is love. I don't know if it helps her feel better. It certainly hasn't helped reduce the fighting. But there's love behind it. I know it."

"What a way to spend your youth," I say.

"What a way to spend yours."

"Did you ever think about leaving?"

"Nah," Roger says. "What am I gonna do? Work at Walmart? Drive an Uber for drunk kids? No, thank you. I'll never find another job with all this fame and wealth and comfort. Plus, I do kinda really love Miss Gracie. Always have. I just think it's hard to change, and it's easy to stay. The problem is, like Kathi, I never bottomed out, never had a glaring reason to quit all this, and so my addiction lives—addiction to them, I guess. And how could I leave all this?" He motions toward Miss Gracie's house, the property, the three-car-garage library, the yard of oak trees and ornaments, the city of Beverly Hills, the universe, *his* universe. He says, "What else is there?"

"There's having it all."

"All?"

"Can't you do this job and also have a rich personal life?"

"No," he says.

I say, "I think maybe I can."

"Pfft. There is no way to have both, my sweet friend. Being a celebrity assistant is like working for the Hollywood mob. No one comes before the family, there is only the family, you can't leave the family. If you do, the townies will kill you—not with bullets, you'll just die of longing."

We sit for a moment, the hum of Miss Gracie's bathtub filter system drowning out any sounds of nature. But that's not why we're out here. We're escaping other forces of nature. I stand. "See you later?" I ask.

"Unfortunately," he says. "Same time, same channel."

"Bye, Roger."

"Bye, *Roger*," he says.

I lay blankets on my apartment floor for Ben and me to fool around and watch Netflix.

I shamefully move some of Mom's unopened boxes into my laundry hamper and stuff a few behind the sofa. I'm ashamed of all this mess and clutter, untouched and unexamined for all this time. Perhaps regretfully, I am my father's son.

I have ice cream ready in the freezer. And I have a gift for him: the photo taken of us by the political-survey people outside of Intelligentsia Coffee. Our first meeting—captured forever—framed and wrapped in blue paper with a gold bow, hidden under a throw pillow. When we have our fifty-year wedding anniversary, it'll be fun to have this souvenir.

Ben is on his way. He's bringing wine, he's bringing snacks, he's bringing bad news.

Ben shows up for our date wearing jeans and flannel and puffy eyes.

"I'm so sorry . . ." he says, starting to crack. I'm lying naked and ready for him, tucked in the nest of blankets I made for us, and he's standing in the doorway, his coat still on, his guard still up. I know what's coming.

"Don't worry about it," I say.

I die inside, but I smile sweetly to calm him, to be kind, to service his emotions. I'm good at service.

Assistant Bible Verse 142: Your needs must wait.

"My dad has been sick," he says, "and it's so hard to deal with that plus my job and the travel for my job and travel for your job, and you're amazing, but I'm just not in a place right now for this."

I must still have my assistant hat on, because despite my anger and hurt and nakedness, I turn to comfort, to calm, to de-escalation. My insides are burning, but my face stays stoic; my mind says not to make a scene. "It's okay, I understand," I say, the words coming out robotically.

I feel frustrated that he didn't break up with me sooner, differently. I'd prefer to know immediately when things aren't working out. In fact, I'd prefer these guys not *tell* me at all! I'd prefer they text. Or at least call, instead of a face-to-face humiliation, awkward hugs, boner killers. But Ben is sweet, he's got integrity. He does it in person. He leaves me, and then he leaves me, walking out of my apartment, taking all the slices of our relationship pie with him, none left for me.

I take the photo of us I had framed, still in its blue paper, still in its gold bow, and throw it in the trash. I hear the glass crack. Another waste.

I'm thinking, *There go more blue dots from my calendar,* and I want to throw my fucking phone across the room, have a fit of fury and rage. But I remain still, keeping the war inside, my phone tight in my grip. I'm realizing it's not Ben I want to hurt; it's the phone, it's the job, it's the inevitable loss of me in my life. As I open the calendar app and start deleting my future plans with Ben—the dinners, the movie nights—the blue dots vanish, prompting the pink dots to spread like a virus, filling in all the gaps. It's not their fault. They're just a program. They're my newest teacher: This life is my program. I'm deleting myself.

I walk around the corner to a little café to sit at the bar alone and order a glass of wine while I log in to OkCupid to look for the next one.

I'm thinking, *Ben. Ben. Ben.*

The wine arrives, the glass of liquid gold swishing, sashaying before me. I'm scrolling through dating profiles, annoyed with everyone, including myself, that I'm back on the hunt. Scrolling, scrolling, drinking. And the first glass is gone. I tip it back, try to get every last drop out, and I'm hyperaware that I want another, another pour, more wine, more medicine. I hunger, like Kathi hungers for more out of her life. I want more, more, more, like the primal beast in me that Therapista called passively suicidal.

Greed knows no end.

The bartender asks if I want another.

I'm thinking, *Yes.*

But I say, "No, thanks."

I'm the new me in this moment. I'm feeling like nothing, but now I have a scale to measure it by, because unlike my childhood, when I only knew one feeling—submission—or my twenties, when I only knew one feeling—depression—now having met and experienced Kathi Kannon, I have a reference for how it feels to be alive, to feel like I have a life worth living. I do a reality check. I'm making money. I'm banking self-esteem. I don't need Ben. I want him, but I don't need him. I can find someone else. And anyway, in the meantime I have her, and as long as I have her, I'll find another boyfriend, because Kathi Kannon, no matter her complications, makes me a catch.

Hello, HotJock.

Hello, PalmSpringsWeekend.

Hello, WendellAcrobat.

17

☆

With my boss tucked away in the care of Orion Towers, I'm thinking, *This seems like a good time to replace Ben.* I have to branch out and I have the time. I've handled the short list of people who had to be notified that Kathi is taking a mental health break: agent, attorney, accountant. I notice that Kathi's circle of close contacts is small, just like mine. The absence of blue dots on my calendar is alarming, sad. Am I as isolated as she is? Am I Roger?

I log in to OkCupid to see how many dates I can get before work beckons again.

This guy: smoker.

That guy: long fingernails.

There's the guy who's a devout Satanist, the guy who's a misogynist, the guy who's a nudist "on nights and weekends." The guy who has five foster dogs seems entertaining, and although I'm not really interested, we meet. I can tell he's also not that interested in me by how he's eating a salad so comfortably in front of me. He has the confidence I have when I don't care if there's kale in my teeth because I know there won't be a good-night kiss.

These dates, they always ask the same questions I do; all of these inquiries are gentle ways to skirt asking what we do for a living. "What keeps you busy?" I ask. Sometimes they answer, "You mean what do I do for work?" And I play coy: "Sure." Ultimately, I just want them to ask about me, so I can talk about Kathi, my superhero superpower.

Nice to meet you, Juan: so boring.

Nice to meet you, Tommy: racist.

Nice to meet you, Erik: smug.

Holding fast to the theory that dating and love is a numbers game, I click onward, to this profile and that, just working to get my numbers up.

And then, Reid1976.

Reid—I say his name with a swoon in the middle: "Reeeeeid." His profile caught my attention not with its fireworks but its lack of them. Answering those dreaded OkCupid questions, his brevity betrayed an alluring charm and wit, practicality projecting a steadiness, confidence:

My Self-Summary:
Attorney. ACLU. Fighting for criminal justice and equal rights. On weekends I volunteer for dog-adoption groups and help feed the homeless. Nice guy but in bed I'll slap your ass and call you bitch.

No need for me to read any further. I message him right away. A nice guy who loves animals and homeless people and spanking? A kind man who's a monster in the sack? Here's my phone number, here's my Social Security card, here's the key to my apartment.

Reid isn't like the rest of them, with their endless back-and-forth email banter on OkCupid. I sent him one message, a compliment about one of his profile pictures—him with his strong features and scruffy beard and shaved head and pink sweater that appears to be hiding a muscular body and toned arms holding a cute three-legged terrier. I boiled all of my testosterone-fueled analysis down to: "Hey, Reid, I like your sweater. I'm Charlie." He wrote back immediately: "Thanks. Like your profile. Wanna play mini-golf Saturday at one P.M.?"

I jump from the computer, pacing around my apartment in tight circles like an armadillo in a headlight, wondering how to respond. He's direct and no-nonsense. He's offering an instant opportunity to meet face-to-face, no playing games, and it's a daylight adventure where complications of sex and drinking are virtually nil. Of course, I have concerns: No one wants to go on real dates anymore; who is this guy? He's a few years older, so perhaps his maturity leads him down this path. Or maybe he's a psycho and I'll be murdered. Or maybe he's just out of a relationship and overanxious to get into a new one. Or, or, or—I could go on for days with the potential downsides. Much easier would be to simply say yes.

Mini-golf is a nightmare, confirming that I am terrible at every conceivable sport. Reid is handsome and towering at six foot two. He's kind and gentle and casually uses legal jargon like "tort" and "mens rea," as if I know what they mean, though it doesn't stop me from pretending.

"Why don't you take two turns," Reid offers, after I miss my shot at the windmill, the ball gently edging near the cup but, as if God's cruel joke, not falling in.

"But that's not fair to you," I say, leaning on my putter like guys used to do with umbrellas or walking sticks in the fifties. I'm feeling happy and giddy, and it takes all my might not to kick up the bottom of the club and twirl it around like I'm in a film with Dick Van Dyke.

"I'm so far ahead of you," he says, "I'm still going to win."

"Fine." I carefully tap the ball toward the cup, and it again doesn't go in. "Motherfuck!" I yell, pointing down at the injustice. Reid smiles.

"Fuck it," he says, "let's keep going."

As we weave our way through the faded Astroturf of a mostly

forgotten and shockingly still-open-for-business mini-golf course in Sherman Oaks, we share some details of our lives, our education, our past relationships. Reid's three-legged terrier from his profile picture recently died. He gets emotional talking about it, and I'm smitten to recognize in someone an ability to be passionate about connection with another living being.

Therapista says healthy relationships are about trust and mutual respect.

I'm patiently waiting for my opportunity to name-drop Kathi Kannon, to start whirling and whipping up my standard stories to get predictable laughs and elicit standard follow-up questions about my days, years, time with her. Reid asks about my family, my mother, Dad, growing up in New Orleans, my years working in the news business.

"So, Charlie, what's your passion?" Reid asks, as he gently taps a ball into its vessel just beneath a giant apple with a smiling green worm on top.

"I work for Kathi Kannon," I say, holding up my golf ball and dramatically bending over and placing it in the starting position, aiming for that apple and worm.

"Who?" Reid asks.

My tap of the ball turns to a wallop following his question—one I rarely get. Who doesn't know Kathi Kannon?!

"From *Nova Quest*," I say. "From *Jaws 3*. From *Mork and Mindy*?"

"The actress? You work for her? What do you do?"

"I'm her assistant," I say. "We travel together. We're friends, too."

"Cool," he says.

"Yeah."

"But I asked you, 'What's your passion?' You know, what lights your soul on fire? What makes time stop? What brings you peace?"

I pause a moment. I'm thinking, *What is my passion?* I'm thinking, *Is Kathi Kannon my passion?*

Reid casually taps his ball into the next cup, at station number 12, with its resident garden gnome.

What's my passion?

I relax my shoulders, I drop my guard, and I say for the first time out loud, "I'm not sure."

My mini-golf outing with Reid has none of the usual markers to help guide me into whether it's a successful date or not. There's no ordering more drinks as a signal we're staying longer. There's no watching the clock and rushing to bed because we have to get up early the next day. I'm confused by the lack of a hard-and-fast rule about making out in the daytime—is it even allowed?

As Reid and I putt through the final bits of the course, I start to feel the sunlight exposing me even more, no dim lighting to soften my acne scars. My cute clothes are getting sticky with sweat. The heat is forcing my long hair to curl and protest exposure to the outdoors.

"How do you like *your* job?" I ask him.

"Well," he says, landing another putt in the hole, "it's cool." He walks over to the cup and picks up the ball, tossing it in the air and, on his attempt to catch it, fumbling. It falls back to the ground and rolls a few steps away. He doesn't go after it. He watches it roll. He turns to me. "I used to work for a big fancy firm, and I was so stressed and I hated it. Eventually I got laid off and was devastated. Then I started working for the ACLU, and it's less money but a meaningful use of time and I love it. I think about how upset I was with being laid off and I missed the big picture. I regret I had to be laid off and didn't own my life enough to be proactive and quit on my own."

I'm speechless and find myself staring at him, his long legs covered with bushy blond hair so easily maneuvering through the course.

"Do you think the universe is friendly?" he asks.

"Ugh, you sound like my therapist."

"Oh, no. Do I?"

"Yes. But to answer your question: The universe feels friendly right now," I say, locking eyes.

Reid smiles. "I agree," he says. He stares at me, making a point, I think. "The universe was friendly to release me from a job I hated, friendly to help me find a new one, and friendly to teach me the lesson that I don't ever again want to stay in a situation that doesn't bring me joy."

"Friendly to invite me here today." I smile back, giving him a little nod.

"Are you done with mini-golf?" he asks.

I consider. We have only a few more putts to go, but I'm just standing there, holding my ball and putter like a dope, like a drunk smitten by the grace and beauty of another human being, by a sweet moment shared between two people—even if nothing more ever comes of it. Perhaps this date has been the universe's friendly learning experience for me.

"Yeah. I feel done," I say. "Any chance you want to grab lunch? Maybe a salad or something?"

"How about we have some happiness?"

"What's that?" I ask.

"Pizza," he says, reaching out his hand. I grab it, and we walk in lockstep to his lovely little Volkswagen Beetle, continuing our afternoon and eventually sharing a sweet kiss, tasting in each other the cheese and tomato sauce and longing that made the entire afternoon and evening so delicious.

That night, my level of job satisfaction aside, I text Kathi, "I think I met my husband."

Kathi texts back, "Orion just watched me puke."

I'm not exactly on vacation. Kathi still has her cell phone. So while she's getting well, I'm getting called, and called frequently.

I bring her various treats, mostly banana pudding from Magnolia Bakery on West Third Street.

Kathi and I eat together, providing Orion an opportunity to shower and take a few moments to himself.

"How's it going?" I ask.

"Fine," Kathi says. "He's not ugly."

"As long as it helps. Is he gay?"

"I think he's multi-sexual," she says. "He'll probably fuck anything. Roger starts foaming at the mouth every time he sees him. Poor Roger. So depressed. Glad Orion is helping him feel alive again."

"You think Roger is depressed?"

"Wouldn't you be?" she says. "Working for my mother all day, every day, forever."

And I wonder, *Am I depressed?* And I wonder, *Am I not a facsimile of Roger to Kathi, as actual Roger is to Miss Gracie?* I recall Reid's question about my job: How do I like it? Is Kathi Kannon my passion?

I'm at The Farm of Beverly Hills getting dinner for Kathi because "someone" left the refrigerator door open overnight and all her food spoiled. I'm at Target getting bath towels because "someone" spilled nail polish on the entire stack of old ones. I'm rushing to the bank to get cash before they close because Kathi's credit card is frozen because "someone" bought a life-sized neon palm tree from China and the bank thought it was fraud.

And now I'm rushing home.

Reid and I are supposed to go to dinner and watch some Netflix, but I'm exhausted from a long day running errands for Kathi—she also needed a bicycle, baking supplies, a dildo to send Tom Cruise for his birthday even though I think he has a restraining order against her. I think it's going to take the whole night to wash the day off. And I'm hungry in the kind of way that can only be quenched by having ice cream for dinner, like a ravenous animal—something I do occasionally but only alone; no one should have to witness that.

I don't know what to do—calling Reid and canceling at the last minute is a dick move. The alternative is taking care of myself and my needs, but isn't that a slippery slope toward being alone the rest of my life, a perpetual state of self-care, a perpetual state of aloneness?

I draft a text but delete it.

I draft another and delete it.

Therapista says the only way through the fire is through the fire.

I pull Reid's number up on my phone.

I take a deep breath, searching inside for some guidance, for some signal of what I should do. But it's hard to compete with a quiet, solitary night of rest and an ice-cream-induced coma. I call him, trying to sound weary and worn. "I'm kinda stressed," I say, "because I could use a night in and I'm not sure I'm up for hanging out but I feel bad canceling on you."

As soon as the words tumble out of my mouth, I'm still and quiet and regretful. I'm bracing for his reply, his reaction of inconvenience after this, the first real reveal to him that a good partner I might not make.

"Who cares?" Reid says. "Let's cancel. It's okay. I'm here to make your life better, not more stressful."

I'm silent on the phone for a moment, not exactly stunned as much as turned on—what a perfect response, a blend of caring and concern.

"So, wait?" I ask. "You don't mind if we cancel?"

"Not at all. Let's skip tonight and you can stay in and recharge your batteries. I'll watch TV and get some rest, too."

The pressure is immediately off. What a wonderful way to look at dating: someone who wants to make my life better, not more stressful. Maybe that's something I can apply to every relationship. Do the other people in my life make it better or make it more stressful?

I say, "Never mind. That was a test. Please come over immediately."

"Okay. On my way. Mind if I bring some happiness?"

"Pizza?" I ask.

He says, "Tonight I'm thinking happiness is ice cream."

My early weeks of dating Reid are punctuated by the milestones of Kathi Kannon's recovery.

Our first two dates are during Kathi's first week of her self-imposed home-institutionalization, check-in, and observation with Orion.

Our third date is Kathi's second week, while she's subjected to evaluation and stabilization and Orion's insistence on healthy lifestyle choices—eating healthier, taking long walks, going to psychiatrist appointments, AA meetings, bathing regularly.

Then there's the week Reid and I have dinner at the Magic Castle, around the time Kathi is feeling her best, wondering aloud and negotiating with Orion just how many more weeks he'll be with her.

There's the week Reid and I take early-morning walks together while Kathi relapses a bit, which Orion says is normal. The week Kathi refuses to do family therapy with Miss Gracie gifts Reid and me with time to cook each other our favorite dinners—I make us nachos, burritos, veggie burgers. Reid makes us salmon with ginger reduction, roasted chicken and potatoes, rosemary-and-feta-stuffed turkey breasts. The week Reid and I do a push-up challenge is the week Kathi calls Orion a "cunt fester" and he threatens to quit, until Miss Gracie and I calm him down, me with compliments and Miss Gracie with cash.

In between, I visit Kathi and nap with Roy. I make sure the mansion doesn't burn down with Agnes inside. I thank Benny for pretending to prune the rosebushes. I bring Kathi her favorite foods, her e-cigarettes, her laptop.

"How are you?" I ask.

"I don't know," she says.

"Are you still ready to get rid of Orion?"

"Yes and no."

I tidy her nightstand. "Cool."

"You seem distracted," she says.

I sit on her bed and blurt, "There's this guy."

"Ugh. Tell Orion I'm gonna need to relapse to hear this."

Reid and I use a Groupon to join an Australian circuit-training class called Training Mate, where hot Australians scream at us to work harder, move faster, lift heavier. They give us nicknames, "Reidy" and "Char-o." I mean, my nickname is not as adorable as Reid's, but I'm grateful to be identified with a moniker that's not Cockring. Reidy and I work out, we walk to breakfast, we go back to his place.

Reid owns a home near Larchmont Village, a cute little boutique shopping area not far from my shitty apartment. His home is small but lovely, decorated sensibly, a couple of bowls still sit on the kitchen floor for his late doggie.

I'm looking around. "You're like a real adult," I say.

"Come here," Reid says, walking down a hallway decorated with pictures of his family, his friends. We enter his bedroom, decorated in shades of white, with views of his green back lawn framed in every window. Reid sits on his bed and pulls me close to him.

"May I look at you naked?" he asks.

"What?" I say, looking around, all the lights on, the curtains open, sunshine pouring in.

"You can trust me."

"May I look at *you* naked?"

"Yup. But I asked first."

Reid makes me smile. I'm flattered, amused, aroused.

I slowly reach up and take off my shirt, which messes up my hair. I start to fix it.

"No," Reid says. "Don't touch it. You're perfect." He nods: *Keep going.*

I can feel my bangs dangling in front of my eyes, my tousled locks long and growing, just brushing my bare shoulders. I unbuckle my belt. I let my jeans fall. I hook my thumbs into my underwear and pull them down. I step out of them. I study Reid's sweet, handsome face. I feel safe and alive and a strange ownership of my body, my life, though still, some insecurity lingers. I'm exposed and hyperaware of all the little things I wish I could change.

"I love your hair," Reid says, examining but not touching. "I love your ears. I love your nose. I love your skin—the little scars on your face from some hard days as a teenager. I love the little bit of fat on your stomach, the proof that you enjoy life, that you live for life, not for pictures on Facebook or something."

I'm getting hard, relishing that Reid seems to love all the things about me that I don't love about myself.

Keep going.

"I love your humor, your work ethic, your nature as a caretaker. Turn around," he says.

And I turn, feeling hotter and hotter knowing Reid is bearing down, assessing.

"I love your ass. I love your thighs. I love your back."

I hear him stand. I feel him walk toward me, push his clothed body against my nude one.

"I love this bit here," he says, pinching my stomach.

"I love this bit here," he says running his hand along my jaw.

He takes a step back, slaps me on the ass.

"I love this bit here," he says.

We laugh and I look over my shoulder at his fresh red handprint on my right butt cheek. I reach to touch it.

"No, no," he says, guiding my hand back to my side, guiding my head upright, positioning me to look into a mirror across the room. I watch us. I see him kissing my neck, putting his hands on my shoulders, moving them down, wrapping them around my waist, his big forearms hard and cold against me.

I see in my reflection a warm and happy face, and I feel new. I see that my body is actually getting lean, fat starting to melt away. I see that Reid has been good for my body, mind, heart.

Reid asks, "What's your passion, Charlie?"

I blurt, "You."

Reid smiles, pulls me back close to him, and we fall backward onto his bed.

Everything is dark. I'm sleeping. I'm dreaming of a different life.

"Hey," Reid says, groggy, freshly awakened, prodding me. "Your phone."

I sit up, notice my phone is lit, and reach for it on Reid's nightstand.

> KATHI: WEATHER ALERT! Let's book flights! Northern lights are on fire tomorrow night. Let's go see them! Let's go to Canada!
>
> ME: Canada? Book flights? How does this work? Is Orion coming?
>
> KATHI: Orion left. I'm all cured. I got an A plus.

"Babe," I say softly to Reid. "I think I have to go to work."

18

☆

"A re you sure you want to do this?" I ask Kathi, packing her
suitcases, loading the usual Ziploc baggies of toiletries, underwear, Christmas lights. My eyes are heavy from no sleep,
from leaving Reid at four A.M., from forcing myself awake to call Kathi's
travel agent.

Kathi got an alert from the National Weather Service a few hours
ago that conditions were perfect for a spectacular display of the aurora
borealis.

"Yes, we must go," she says. "I've wanted to see the northern lights
my whole life, and this showing is supposed to be historic."

Some people get weather alerts as a means to save their lives—
tornado warnings, or to save their livelihoods where rain may ruin
crops. Kathi Kannon gets weather alerts for vacation planning.

"I don't understand how we can be leaving," I say. "What happened
with Orion?"

"Don't worry about it. I've had a billion sober coaches. He was the
best one. He said I passed with flying colors."

"Passed? You got a grade or what—"

"Yeah. Don't forget to pack gloves," she says, looking at her phone. "Oh, the time! We have to go!"

Don't swim after you eat. Don't fly if you're too pregnant. But there are no rules for travel upon termination of your sobriety coach. And so it is, potential relapse be damned, that Kathi and I are on our way to LAX to catch a ride to see in real life her beloved hotel-room check-in namesake: aurora borealis.

I resume my questioning in earnest: What happened with Orion? Why did he leave? What's the next step?

"The next step is I quit self-medicating," Kathi says. "One day at a time, you know?"

"And he just left? Is this normal? I want your sobriety to be permanent."

"Nothing is permanent," Kathi says.

"Maybe I'll call Orion."

"No," Kathi says. "Call Miss Gracie if you must. She'll tell you. It's all good. You did good hiring him. You get an A-plus for that."

"Well, I want your sobriety to be as permanent as possible. I want you to stay healthy and happy and for us to continue on our fun journey and whatnot—"

"Orion met with me and Miss Gracie last night. We talked through some of our problems. I feel very steady, very centered, Cockring. And why waste money on him when I can take this trip?"

"It just seems like he left kind of abruptly," I say.

"Abruptly? I was with him for six fucking weeks," Kathi says. "And, anyway, like he says, 'Change comes from within.' So there's really not much else he could do. I want change. That's a win for all of us, no? And I have you."

"I guess."

"Don't worry. I'll prove it to you," she says, tapping my arm, adjusting her hair, turning back to her phone.

"Did you have sex with him?" I ask.

"Almost," she says, baiting me, daring me to ask more questions.

"Good talk," I say.

During the preflight announcements, Kathi opens her purse and pulls out little vials. One is her travel perfume. One is nail-polish remover. She pulls out cotton balls. She pulls out glitter nail polish.

"Are you seriously going to paint your nails?" I ask. "I don't think you can do that on the plane."

"No one cares, Cockring." Kathi opens the vial. "Oops, wrong one," she says, putting down the perfume and grabbing the remover. She opens it. The smell is strong and pervasive. She dabs the remover onto a cotton ball.

"That really stinks," I say.

"Does it?"

"We're in an enclosed space."

"Is it?" she asks.

Flight attendants start to scramble, no doubt looking for the source of the noxious fumes.

Kathi turns and her elbow knocks over the open vial of perfume.

"Oops," she says. "Well, that'll take care of the nail-polish-remover smell."

"I hope we survive Canada," Kathi says as we land in the town of Yellowknife. In baggage claim, I haul Kathi's luggage to a quiet corner and she and Roy watch as I plunder it, plucking out her thick winter coat, her knit cap, her wool scarf, her leather gloves.

I close her suitcases and look over at Kathi, now thick with layers, already sweating, ready for snow and ice.

"What are you wearing, Cockring?"

I look down at my outfit—sensible shoes and jeans and a peacoat from H&M. I shrug and say, "This."

Kathi shakes her head. "Jesus Christ. You don't have winter clothes?"

"This is winter in California," I say, motioning to my outfit.

"*This* is winter," Kathi says, pointing outside to a blizzard. "Let's go shopping so you don't get hypothermia. If you die, how will I ever get home?"

Instead of going to the hotel, we first stop at a mall. Kathi walks over to a computer kiosk with all the stores listed. She moves her finger up and down until something catches her eye. "Fourth floor!" she says, jetting to an escalator with me and Roy in her wake.

Kathi leads us to a furrier tucked in a dark corner, with its pretentious façade and caramel lighting and dark-wood accents.

"I'm not wearing a fur coat," I tell her.

"Who says it's for you?" she says, opening the door and dashing inside.

The clerk, a thin older woman with her hair in a tight bun, looks Kathi up and down like she's a swamp creature. "Can I help youuuuuuu?"

"Hiiii," Kathi says, Roy jerking his leash to and fro as he tries to get a sniff of the pelts. "Do you have any coats in dog sizes?"

I roll my eyes. Of course she's trying to buy a fur to keep Roy warm and cozy and chic.

The snobby woman who works there laughs. "Um. No. We don't have 'dog' sizes."

Kathi's face shifts slightly. She smells an attitude, a fight. She smiles and says, "In that case . . ." And Kathi, not breaking eye contact with the clerk, reaches her hand to the right and grabs the first coat she comes into contact with. "I'll take this one," she says.

Kathi slaps it on the counter, a brown number with black lines—this must have once been a beautiful beast. "Cockring," Kathi says.

I step forward and proudly hand the clerk Kathi's credit card, and we relish the beeping and the clanking of the register as the clerk lets out a huff. As she starts to wrap Kathi's new coat with crisp, fancy tissue paper, Kathi speaks up, "Oh. No. I don't need it wrapped. Do you have scissors?"

And while the clerk stares in disbelief, Kathi Kannon, film icon, grabs the coat, sits on the floor, and slices up the garment, tiny bits of fur flying everywhere, until what was once a woman's luxury coat is now, indeed, dog-sized. As Kathi stands and exits, it's up to me to provide *the look*, and I fix my gaze on the clerk and raise my eyebrows to say, *Don't fuck with her.*

Roy's new fur only stays secured on his wobbly body for a few moments, but the experience warmed him, and us.

Moments later, in a proper retailer for people like middle-class me, Kathi buys me my first real winter coat, a thick scarf, and stylish black gloves. She pulls the coat's hood over my head and tugs the drawstrings tight. "You can't look like an amateur out there with the northern lights," she says. "This trip could be the one that changes your life forever."

"How? By getting frostbite and having all my toes cut off?"

"God, I hope so," she says.

I'm thinking, *I hope we survive Canada.*

Kathi selected our hotel not based on our usual standards of luxury, size of bathtub, or breadth of room-service dessert menu. No, Kathi chose our hotel on this occasion based on convenience—what's closest to the show, the new epicenter of our lives, the aurora borealis.

Our adjoining rooms are perfunctory. Bed, check. Toilet, check. TV, check. But no pay-per-view, no porn titles to peruse, only a few cable channels aptly described as basic.

"We're fucked!" I say, flipping the channels, unable to find anything compelling at eight in the evening in Yellowknife, Canada. "Sorry there's nothing on TV tonight."

"TV?!" Kathi yells from her bathroom. "We need sleep, Cockring. We have a big day tomorrow before we see the lights."

"Oh, no. What are we doing before the lights?"

Kathi emerges from her tiny bathroom and in the doorway strikes a sexy pose befitting Marilyn Monroe. "We're going dogsledding."

"Ohhh. Please no," I say, fearing what could be ahead—namely, Kathi and I, one or both of us, in the hospital with broken bones, dog bites, regret, all under a cloud of what might be her fragile sobriety.

Assistant Bible Verse 143: Pack tourniquets, iodine wipes, cyanide pills.

At a crisp and bright ten in the morning, we leave Roy asleep in bed and hop in a ride sent by the hotel concierge—some guy in a Ford Explorer—and sit side by side in the back, both of us shivering, me from the cold, and Kathi from the shock of being awake, out and about, and fully lucid at this hour of the day. The driver is polite but disinterested, wearing only a cardigan and stealing glances in the rearview mirror of us wrapped up to the size of sumo wrestlers.

"Do we look like locals?" Kathi asks him.

"Yeah," he says, as sarcastic as possible for a Canadian.

"I'm here for the full experience," she says. "Almost the full experience. I won't drink the tap water, because I don't need dysentery. You?"

"Huh?" the driver asks.

"We're good," I interject. "Thank you!"

"I aim to make love to that man," Kathi whispers.

"No, you don't," I whisper back. "You're busy." I point out the window to the landscape.

Kathi turns to the sight of the snowy hills, smiling, beaming. She's so wrapped in furs and down, I'm doubtful anyone will recognize her, and out here in brilliant sunshine, pure white snow all around us, fresh air and uncertainty ahead, I'm not even sure I recognize us. We're in a strange and rare black hole of anonymity and raw living. There are no agendas here, no publicists trying to shuffle us around, no agents or attorneys telling us what to do, where to go. Even me—with my rigidity and reluctance—I'm at Kathi's mercy, following her lead. And Kathi, a woman who has traveled the world already—more than once—who's practically seen it all, is finally going to be able to say she's indeed seen everything, *the* thing, in fact. That she's finally seen the aurora borealis with her own eyes. She's finally able to be a random citizen of planet earth and enjoy a simple pleasure, the not-so-little act of crossing a big goal off of her bucket list. She looks at her watch, seconds moving slower than ever in their march to dark skies and those beautiful lights.

"When we arrive," Kathi says to the driver, "don't stop. Just slow down and we'll throw our bodies out of the car."

I say, "No, sir. Please come to a complete stop."

"I'm so excited!" Kathi yells. "Cockring, we must be present."

"I can be present and also not dive out of a moving vehicle."

"Where are your battle scars?" she asks.

"Where are yours?" I argue back.

"Mine are internal," Kathi says, raising her eyebrows, challenging me to a duel.

"You win," I say, gloved hands up.

She grabs my hand and we look ahead as we arrive at our destination.

As the SUV leaves, having properly deposited us at the unmarked gates to a dogsledding adventure land, we're able to hear the dogs— barking, yelping, anxious. We can see them in their kennels, pacing, mirroring the disquietude inside Kathi Kannon, who's itching to do anything to distract herself from the slow passage of time and the bane of her existence: waiting.

There's a buzzer at the gate and Kathi pushes it once, twice, three times.

"Give 'em a second," I say.

Kathi grips the vertical beams of the gate, holding them and thrashing back and forth. "HELLO!" she screams. "I WANT THE DOGS!"

"When has your screaming ever worked?" I ask.

And then, *click*, the gates start to swing open, Kathi marching inside, not even bothering to turn to me as she says, "Screaming works nearly every time, actually."

A handsome man, tall and bearded, is approaching us, and even through his thick coat and gloves you can see he's pure muscle.

"Hi and welcome," he says. "I'm Matt."

"I'm deeply in love with you and your body, Matt. I'm Kathi and this is my stepson, not my lover. I have no lover. I'm single. Available, some might say. Some might also say I'm deft, open, supple."

Matt looks at us a moment, then raises his eyebrows and nods. "Alrighty, then. Let's get you geared up."

The dogs get a little quieter one by one as Matt walks past their kennels. It's clear they know he's the leader, each of them trained on him, waiting for him to give a command, to say something they'll recognize, to call them out and signal that their time has come to run, run, run.

The dogs are gorgeous, mostly white fur, a few of them with dazzling blue eyes. They're tall and muscular and focused.

"I have a dog named Roy," Kathi says to Matt, motioning to his animals. "Roy is back at our hotel. He wouldn't leave without a proper coat, which is impossible to find. Want to come back and meet him?"

"I've kinda got a full day," Matt says politely.

"Roy is very similar to your dogs in terms of, sort of, having dog qualities."

"You have an Alaskan husky?"

"Well," Kathi says, "he's definitely husky." Kathi looks to me to help, but I shake my head *no*.

Ahead of us is a sled, the sled, our sled. It's steel and shiny, unpainted, with clearly visible seams where it's been welded together as if from scraps. It's a simple frame, like a go-cart with no wheels. There's no floor, only a spot for one person to sit and prop their legs up, and a spot on the back where someone stands and holds on to a little safety bar, or, in this case, what appears to be the suggestion of a safety bar.

"How did you find these people?" I ask.

"Concierge," she says.

"What's their Yelp rating?" I ask.

"What's Yelp?" Kathi looks at the sled suspiciously and turns to Matt. "Do you offer a model with a seat warmer?"

"Or one with a steering wheel?" I add.

Matt laughs. "It's easy to handle. These dogs know the path. Just let them lead you along. There are no reins to pull or jiggle to make them go faster or slower; these guys only know one speed: *run*. The only control you need is the brake."

Matt stands on the back of the sled and pushes his foot down on a sliver of metal that looks like an afterthought, a leftover hunk of steel, something stuck on by mistake. His foot pushes it into the snow. "If there's an emergency and you need to stop, just step down on this. Step hard, so it goes into the snowpack. Sometimes, if you're lucky, the dogs will stop."

"Wait," I say as Matt walks away. "You're not riding with us?"

As Matt starts to explain, Kathi grabs my shoulders. "We don't need him! We can do this! You can do this!" She releases me and turns to Matt. Pointing to me, she says, "This ride is part of a trust exercise his psychiatrist says will help make him more comfortable coming out of the closet. You know what I mean?"

Matt nods politely. "I'll be right back. I'll go get you some dogs," he shouts as he walks away. I turn to Kathi.

Looking at the sled, still unsure how to board it, I ask, "Who's driving?"

Kathi says, "I am."

I playfully bow and extend my arm toward her chariot. Kathi climbs on back, gives the brake a little tap with her foot. "Get in, Cockring. Let's risk our lives!"

With uncertainty, I squeeze onto the sled, my legs resting on a couple of wayward steel bars so they're off the ground, my body snug in the seat. I'm forced to look straight ahead, at miles and miles of frozen white pasture, framed by tall and stately evergreen trees and powder-blue skies—even the heavens look frozen.

Waiting for Matt to bring the dogs, I realize that for the first time since we landed in Yellowknife, I'm sitting still. I feel the icy breeze on my face. And as I lay my hands in my lap and wait for this to get going, I feel the strangest sensation of being present, of being in the moment, not hours or days ahead with dreams of Reid or nightmares of tomorrow, not months or years in the past with regrets about my parents or my news career. I'm here. And I'm with my hero, her snow boots snug against my ass.

"Your stepmom looks ready to go," Matt shouts as he returns with a couple dogs.

"Let's fucking get on with it, Jesus Christ," Kathi says.

The dogs, the beasts, they know what's happening, they know what's next, howling and yapping, begging for a mission, a purpose. Matt guides them on long connected leashes and starts strapping them to the sled like Santa's reindeer.

Matt whistles one of those wild shrieks you see on TV but think no human can actually make in real life. A couple of handlers walk over with more dogs, all of them manic, wild, excited to run. They're all barking or whining, wondering why they're being held back, all of them ready to be let loose and pull us into the bright yonder.

"Apply the brake," Matt yells.

CRUNCH!

Kathi jams her boot down hard onto the metal sliver, and it cracks into the icy ground.

Matt and the handlers finish connecting the twelve huskies to the sled, and the steel beams holding me in place suddenly feel electrified. The sled shimmies, shakes with anticipation, the dogs now going insane, barking, growling, ready.

The handlers step away.

Matt steps back and yells, "Whenever you're ready."

I look up, up, up, my head craning back, away from our path ahead, over the treetops, across the blue sky, until I'm looking upside down, seeing Kathi's face, smiling, fierce, determined, the cold breeze forcing her to squint slightly, the glitter on her eyelashes alive and dancing in the sunlight, as if when she looks out at the world all she sees is a rave, a party. She looks down at me and yells over the barking, "Ready, Cockring?!"

I yell back, "Ready, *Mom!*"

She laughs, looks down at her boot on the brake. She takes one more glance at Matt. "If I'm thrown off this thing and become unconscious, will you be the one to do mouth-to-mouth?"

Matt grins and nods *yes* as Kathi smiles and lifts her foot off the brake.

We're transported. The dogs are instantly silent, at peace, quietly fulfilling their life's mission, doing their jobs—running. The only sound we can hear now is wind, cold and yet comforting—slightly reminiscent of the ocean back home in California, of being a small part of something big.

We're racing across the earth, over little mounds of snow, breaking through clumps of ice. We could be on a lake, we could be on a pasture, we could be on another planet altogether, honestly. We have no idea what's beneath us, or ahead of us, for that matter. We have to trust. Our faith now rests in nature, in twelve furry tour guides ahead of us delivering us wherever they want, connected and at one with us through leather straps and clumsy angles of welded metal.

"It's perfect!" Kathi yells.

I look over the side of the sled as we race along: All the snow is just a blur, like we're on miles and miles of white paper, like swaths of blank 8.5-by-11 pages begging to be filled with adventure, art, Kathi Kannon's writings of love and loss and living. We're here, penning our own journey on these snowy pages, forging yet another new bond, more miles under our belts, just like the dogs. I touch her feet on either side of me, an act of connection, of affection—the best I can manage in the circumstances.

"You okay?" she asks.

Sitting here, a passenger, an observer on this jaunt of my lifetime—both with these dogs in Yellowknife and with Kathi Kannon, film icon—I'm thinking: *Yes, it's perfect.* I give her a thumbs-up. She gives me a thumbs-up in return.

The dogs, our partners in this passage of time to the aurora borealis, race effortlessly into the future with us, past an old shack, alongside fallen and frozen trees, their rot on hold, in suspense and on ice until warmer weather, this season, their sweet reprieve. Our dogs run past a frozen pond, up a little embankment, and around a rusty red tractor, circling back, seeming to mark our halfway spot, signaling our return to Matt and the schedule we so gratefully forgot as our minds melded into the snow and spectacular all around us.

Kathi's feet wiggle in her boots beside me, and I look up to see what's going on. She's taking off her hood, her gloves, her knit cap—stuffing them in her pockets. She's loosening her scarf, her hair now free and flowing wildly behind and atop her. She leans her whole body forward, her waist touching the so-called safety bar. She closes her eyes, she raises her hands, extends her arms like she's on a roller coaster.

"Jesus! What are you doing?"

"I want to feel it!"

I look ahead at the whites and the blues and the greens of the earth. I'm thinking, *Fuck it.*

I pull my hood back, rip off my gloves and knit cap, and close my eyes. Now Kathi and I are hearing the same sounds of metal on ice, of paws on snow, of panting and delight; we're both breathing the cold air, the same as the dogs, everyone connected and speeding through shared atoms and quarks and doing exactly what we're meant to do in

this moment: the dogs running, Kathi Kannon being, and me learning
to let go.

Kathi reaches down and squeezes my shoulder; I reach up and
touch her hand. Both of us icy to the touch and yet warm and safe, one
with nature, all of us—dogs, trees, sunshine—together.

We fly past saplings and weathered fence posts, dead leaves and
fallen branches, whipping along like the tick, tick, tick of a clock, our
countdown to this being over, to this ending with real life. Kathi's hand
leaves my shoulder.

The dogs continue our whirl back to the starting point, with Matt
coming into view, the handlers ready to corral the pups.

"I don't want to stop," Kathi says.

"Me, either," I say fondly, the dogs still clipping at full pace.

"No, I mean, I don't want to stop," Kathi says.

"Um, Kathi," I warn, the kennel rapidly coming more and more into
view, Matt waving his hands: *Slow down, slow down.*

"Why does it have to be over?" Kathi asks.

Matt is growing frantic, looking around, crouching like a football
player in formation, bending over as if ready to make a quick maneuver
out of our path if it comes to that. His handlers are pulling other dogs
to the side.

"Kathi, please!" I yell.

Kathi places her boot on the brake and, after a couple seconds,
pushes down. Ice cracks and crunches under us and the dogs take their
cue from the friction, finally starting to slow us down, down, down.

The two in the lead ease forward to Matt and his now-outstretched
hands, which they nuzzle into lovingly, gratefully, quietly—no more
barking; they're content for now. They had their fun; time to rest and
recharge until the next tourists come running, come paying. They'll go
off to their cages, until their work calls again, and I relate. I feel a little
bad for the dogs. They seem to enjoy it so much; do they know they're

trapped? I start to feel a little bad for myself; I wonder: Am I trapped? Am I just pulling Kathi's sled?

Matt turns to us. "What happened?"

Kathi shrugs. "Sorry. Just couldn't figure out the brake."

I look behind us and see where the brake dragged us to this moment, the stretch of earth sliced open as if with a scalpel.

Matt says, "How was it?"

"Fucking freezing," Kathi says, rebundling herself.

"That was fun," I say, putting my scarf back on, my knit cap, then turning to Kathi. "Do we still need to see the aurora or does this count?"

"Don't be ridiculous," Kathi says, then, turning to Matt, "I'll pay you a million dollars for a cup of hot chocolate."

As night begins to fall, we meet outside of our hotel with Josef, allegedly the best aurora tour guide in this little town. Kathi found him via a flyer on a bulletin board in our hotel lobby. He also comes with a strong recommendation from the hotel. He's about the same size and stature as Kathi but drives a giant SUV outfitted with fancy wheels that make it ride high and make passengers like us—and even him—grovel and moan as we hoist ourselves up and inside. The windows are tinted and it's hard to see anything outside, not that there's much to see until our magic moment.

"We gotta get way outta town to see the lights," Josef says. "I got a great place. Nice and private."

"Sounds like the perfect place for a murder," Kathi says as Josef locks the doors.

Josef is silent in an unsettling way. Kathi looks at me and cringes.

I lean my head back and turn to look out the window at the wilderness as we start to drive. I see a slight reflection of myself in the window—it looks like the trees outside are smacking me in the face. I also see Kathi's reflection. She's getting more and more bouncy, more and more excited, looking from her window to mine, to the windshield and the view ahead, not wanting to miss anything.

I turn to Kathi. "I'm proud of you," I say.

She faces me. "For being an internationally famous actoooor?"

"For Orion. I'm glad you did that. I know it's not easy."

"Please don't let me die," she says. "From now on, I'm an A all the time."

"Great," I say.

"Or at least a B-minus sometimes—"

"Wrong answer!"

Kathi smiles, putting her hand on mine, safe, touching a friend, as she looks back out at the world. I stare at her a moment, happy, and I look out of my window again, too. Both of us seeing different universes, both of us on the same route.

Josef turns onto a gravel road. Now, with nightfall, the only thing visible out here is whatever his headlights happen to scan. Out of his windshield, through the tips of the treetops, I can barely see a green haze.

"Is that it?" I ask.

Kathi grabs my arm, throws herself onto the middle console, and looks up.

"Holy fuck!" she yells. She lifts her iPhone and tries to capture the moment forever, snapping picture after picture.

"Don't hurt yourself," Josef says. "You're gonna get a clear view for pictures in just a sec."

Kathi takes another picture then sits back. Perhaps she's living in the moment here, too, just like I was on the dogsled, present, not caught up in her past or future but living in the now and capturing the great northern lights as they are to her in this second, in this second, in this second, in this SUV. Therapista says we only have this moment, and everything outside of that is past and future and a lie, unprovable, an illusion. But every human sometimes suffers the same sick doubt: What if the *right now* doesn't get better? And so we are all Kathi Kannon, grabbing our phones and snapping our pictures and sending those texts and emails as we try to expand our reach and prove we meant something to the world. If Kathi Kannon has no future, no past, she is rightfully only what's caught in her phone—the faint image of the aurora, through the lens of her camera, through Josef's windshield. And if I have no future, no past, I am only what's happening now, sitting beside Kathi, watching her delight.

Josef hits the brakes and Kathi flies forward.

"Dick!" she yells.

"Sorry," he says.

Kathi leans back in her seat.

Josef gets out of the vehicle first, and as his open-door light dims and turns off, I turn to Kathi Kannon, film icon, and I ask, "Are you ready?"

"Now or never," she says.

I open my door and get out of the SUV, and Kathi shuffles over to my side, to follow me.

Followers following followers following followers.

I hold her hand, help her out, and we both check our balance on the slippery ground beneath us.

"Frozen lake," Josef says. "In the daytime you can look down and see fish looking up at you."

"Gross," I say.

"Cockring, be nice!" Kathi admonishes.

"What? You called him a dick a minute ago."

"That was a compliment—"

"There it is," Josef interrupts, pointing.

Kathi and I turn, and over the roof of his SUV we can see them, the lights, her lights. We see greens and purples and pinks slicing across the sky like they were painted there just a few fresh moments ago, a spill of neon and vibrancy.

Kathi takes several steps around Josef, the treetops retreating the farther onto the lake she gets.

I worry for a moment whether it's safe, if she could fall through. I look over at Josef, who's done this a million times before, and he recognizes the worry on my face, and he puts his hands out to signal, *It's okay, it's okay.* I turn back to Kathi, who has her face, her eyes, locked on the sky, with its sweeping flow of colors. She pulls off her hood, she tugs off her knit cap, she loosens her scarf. I'm thinking, *She wants to feel this, too.*

She turns and looks at me. We smile at each other and I move carefully to meet her. We look up, and here we are, in this moment, the only one that matters. We hold hands. We stare at the great northern lights together.

"Old timers say it looks like a brushfire in the spirit world," Kathi says. "I like to think it's more like they're on some really great acid in heaven."

There's a strange thing about the northern lights. In person, they don't exactly look like they do in photos. Those dreaded screen savers will have you believe the lights are always crystal clear and sharp, making a smooth zigzag across the sky in green and yellow and blue and purple. But in real life, it's different. It's a little more like a haze or a fog. You need the right perspective—through a camera, usually—for it to make sense, for it to fit into the image we're fed in *National Geographic,* on the screen saver of my old computer back at my news job.

"What color are you, Cockring?" Kathi asks, her eyes singularly focused on the sky.

"I'll be pink," I say.

"And I'll be green," she says.

Green. Appropriate and perfect. That's the dominant color up there, the lead dog, the main show. The smears of electric neon green make this sight a force—without the green, we have just a few luminescent hues in the dark, unconnected and unbridled.

And Kathi Kannon is the green. She is the engine in my life and many others—her fans, Miss Gracie, Roy. She is the smear of light that connects so many of us. She is the Shine. These mysterious lights, with their various viewpoints, are not unlike human beings, so many different colors and shades of living, all demanding perspective and focus to understand the difference between fog and show, between a movie priestess and a complex woman, what a father is supposed to be versus what a father is, what a life could be versus the life I'm living, the life she's living.

Snap: "Look at us, friends!"

Kathi is beaming, her chest collapsing a little as if a lifetime of wanting is finally fulfilled. She looks over at me, shakes her head with a sort of disbelief in her eyes.

I smile. "How are you?" I ask.

She says, "Not bored."

She looks back up. She steps forward. She inhales the moment.

She says, "I want to be this forever."

Hey, Siri, I'm thinking of Kathi and happiness and adventure and health and long lives together.

I say, "I want to be this forever, too."

Part Three

☆   ☆   ☆   ☆   ☆   ☆   ☆

PEQUOD

19

☆

'm leaving Reid.

Sweaty and handsome, he sits across from me at our post-workout breakfast spot, Simple Things, famous for ultra-healthy dishes served with slices of pie.

"I'm going to miss you," I say. Reid nods, *I know*.

Kathi and I are leaving soon to go on a gay cruise. She's the secret special guest, capitalizing on her iconic status with the gay community. This insane excursion pays well, of course—gays with their economic clout. She's getting tens of thousands of dollars to perform a show, talking about her life and maybe answering questions. Reid and I are having our final bite together before Kathi and I set sail.

"I got you something," Reid says. He reaches into the pocket of his hoodie and pulls out a small gift, wrapped in mini-golf-themed wrapping paper with a little blue bow.

"I can't marry you! It's too soon!" I say playfully, taking the beautifully presented gift and wondering what's going on. Reid smiles at my genuine surprise. I'm usually the gift giver; I'm usually the thoughtful one in the room. How strange it feels to have the tables turned, with so many tables seemingly turning—delightfully—these days.

I open the gift carefully, untying the bow and letting it fall to the floor. Plucking the tape from the folded sides. Pulling the paper apart to reveal what's inside. There, in my hands, is a toy, *the* toy, the one I was not allowed to play with all those years ago. It's her, the action figure of Priestess Talara, with her white gown and laser gun and eerily familiar face. I stare into her eyes. I'm thinking, *Hello, friend.*

"I thought it would be nice," Reid says, "for you to finally have it, to finally have her back. I mean, this isn't the actual one your dad took from you. I got this one on eBay."

I look from Priestess Talara, from young Kathi Kannon, to Reid, and I realize my mouth is hanging open. This little heroine, the so-called danger my father tried to protect me from all those years ago, the plastic toy that I longed for all my childhood, now seeming fragile, smaller than I remember, resting lifeless in the palm of my hand, accessible, whole. Here in my grasp, she looks so contained and manageable and feels like a part of me, an extension of my life, and as my eyes water and my mind races, my heart is full for both Priestess Talara of my childhood and Kathi Kannon of my every day.

I look at Reid. I say, "Thank you."

I say, "I love it."

I say, "I love you."

"We have to leave in fifteen minutes," I remind Kathi, again. Me, travel-nervous as usual, sweating as I double-check her antique trunk suitcases. Scarves, Christmas lights, inflatable life jackets—check, check, check.

Hey, Siri, I hope we survive Orlando.

Kathi is pacing, weary and unsure, Roy by her side as always.

"Cockring, did you call me last night and warn me about going on this gay cruise? That it's going to be dangerous? Not to go? And then I said I had to go anyway because I want the money and relevance?"

"No, that didn't happen," I say. "Are you okay? What are you talking about?"

She says, "Nothing."

Pardon us at LAX!

Make way at ORD!

We arrive just in time to pose for a picture with Roy under a sign for an antidepressant, which says: HAPPINESS IS A JOURNEY THAT STARTS WHEN YOU'RE A BABY.

"Asinine," Kathi says.

We haul ourselves and her luggage onto the boat. I've got her bag, I've got Roy's bag, I've got my bag. All that, this trip, it's all starting to feel very heavy.

The ship sets sail, undocked, unmoored. We wander; we shop. The boat has everything: a jewelry store, a bakery, a Rite Aid. Kathi attends an AA meeting (they have *everything*).

I've never seen water so blue, beaches so white, and penises so aplenty. Dicks are flopping in every direction the entire trip—men wearing mesh shorts, see-through Speedos, sunbathing nude on their balconies, in hallways, in cafés. Every morning at ten A.M., the intercoms in the rooms and hallways announce the day's activities and a reminder not to have sex in the steam room.

We have a day until Kathi's show and we kill the time the best we know how—lying around. It's a lazy four in the afternoon and Kathi is painting her fingernails on a lounge chair when her phone starts to vibrate, startling her. "Fuck!" she yells, flinching and causing a little streak of blue glitter nail polish to smear across her finger and onto a fine white linen throw pillow on the chair. "Oh, shit! I just ruined the fucking pillow, Cockring!"

A few hot gays look over at us, but we're far from the pool, just on the deck getting some fresh air—or it was fresh before Kathi started painting her nails.

She tries to steal a glance at the phone screen but can't make it out. "Who's calling us, Cockring?"

I stand and crane over and read the phone. "Studio Assistant."

"WHAT?!" Kathi yells. "FUCK SHIT COCK!" She flips her hands over and wipes all the polish off of her fingers onto the pillow.

"What? What? Who is Studio Assistant?" I ask.

"My fucking life!" she yells, jumping up and grabbing the phone. Wide-eyed, she answers. "Hello," she says calmly. "Yes. Yes. Yes. Fine. Thank you."

She takes a step away from me, and I follow her. I'm studying her, wondering what the hell is going on.

"Okay, love," she says. "I'll be waiting. Bye." Kathi hands me her phone.

"What?! What?! Good news?!" I ask, checking that the call is ended.

Kathi looks around to make sure none of the other cruise-goers are nearby. She grabs my shoulders, pulling me toward her so she can whisper in my ear, "I can't say a word about it."

She lets go of my shoulders and I stand up straight. I'm about to say I understand, but then she pulls me right back down again.

"They're fucking doing a new *Nova Quest* film and we're gonna be a fucking star again!" she says, jumping up and down. I mirror her motion, feel her excitement and my own for the continuation of this saga, a literal dream come true for me and other fans—and, apparently, Kathi Kannon—not to mention I get to witness it: the filming, the creating, having a tiny stake in a cultural landmark.

"Really? Who was that on the phone? Who is Studio Assistant?" I ask.

"The head of Sony or one of them—I can't keep up. They called years ago and I guess someone saved the number. I don't know, maybe I saved it, who am I? I don't know. Oh, my God! They're doing it!"

The original *Nova Quest* ends with Priestess Talara sitting quietly and alone in a large war room. Hologram monitors blink and swirl around her, showing maps and strategy and bright lights marking locations where individual battles were won. Priestess Talara sobs on her throne, overlooking the empty space, haloed by the massive window behind her. Her chair spins around and she looks out at her planet, green trees and blue lagoons visible under plumes of smoke left over after the war's end. Lives were lost, scars need time to heal, but the film's final shot is of Priestess Talara looking out at her world, her life, and her face is still for a few moments, international audiences wondering what's next, and she smiles. Cut to the theme music blaring and the credits rolling and everyone watching feeling a surge of hope for whatever may come next in her life, their life, the life of the world. That moment was first gifted in theaters three decades ago. In all that time since, fans have had to wonder what came next. And now, it appears, we'll finally find out.

Kathi yells, pacing, almost dancing, "More motherfucking *Nova Quest*! Me and the whole original cast and we're donning our famous outfits again, dressing to impress, to headline the new film. They want to revive the franchise, bring the story to new generations and old fans alike."

"Holy shit! Congrats!"

"I didn't want to get too excited, you know," Kathi says. "There were rumors for years, but everyone in Hollywood is a monster and it takes so many steps to get there, but this is a big step, Cockring. This is our big step."

"Yeah!"

"Let's get the fuck out of here," Kathi says, grabbing her nail polish and flinging a towel around her shoulders. We gather our things and head back to her stateroom. She spills all the beans:

Reviving the franchise.

Stardom again.

More money.

Shooting in London.

More travel.

I'm thinking, *Cool!*

I'm thinking, *Oh, wait. We're moving to London?*

I'm thinking, *Reid?*

"Bring him," Kathi shouts, winks, smiles, and then fills her lungs with e-cigarette vapor. "We're going to have the best time! The time of our lives! We'll rent a big house in London. Have friends over all the time. I'll make sure you get paid a big per diem from the studio. I'll make sure your name is in the credits."

I die. "My name will be in the fucking credits of a *Nova Quest* film? Onscreen? On IMDB?"

"It'll say 'Cockring: Assistant to Kathi Kannon,'" she says.

Breathless, I float as I follow Kathi up and down the hallways to her room.

A cruise ship is a strange place. It's billed as relaxing but you're never still, the boat always in motion. It's never quiet. You're never alone. The halls all look the same, patterned carpet to hide stains. Fake-wood doors to keep weight down. Twists and turns, like snakes eating snakes. Railing along the wall to help you keep your balance or cling to life during a capsize.

Walking behind Kathi, I'm thinking, *I'll follow her anywhere.* And now, this *Nova Quest* news at hand, I'll follow her to my dreams coming true.

I wake up early the next morning to a text message:

> KATHI: Take the morning off, Cockring. Our lives are changing. I'm going to rest and celebrate in slumber and whatnot. You should celebrate by sucking some of the Moby Dicks on this boat. Meet me later before I have to do my stage show and tell.

Kathi's kindness isn't always what it looks like. Being set free from her sometimes feels like the toddler telling the parent, "Go, go, I'll be fine." Only for the grown-up to return home hours later and find the fridge door open and all the condiments spread on the walls. Sometimes when an assistant is away, it'll mean even more work later.

I make the best of it, grab some breakfast and wander the deck. It's me, overdressed in my modest bathing suit, passing every shape and size gay guy in what seems to be tinier and tinier Speedos. No one makes eye contact; we're all just looking at crotches, as if we've beautifully perverted that old saying into "My eyes are down here."

Tempting as it may be, my heart is with Reid, and I swat away the lure. I sit by the pool, scroll through my phone, peruse the shops, eat lunch, do another few laps on the deck, then head back to my room and plop in bed. As the afternoon sun turns orange and friendly, I take it as a good sign that I haven't heard from Kathi all day. But Kathi resting all this time means she'll be up all night and I may as well prepare for that with a nap. I close my curtains, turn up the AC, kick off my shoes, and put my phone on vibrate. The ocean lulls me kindly back and forth and my eyes grow heavy. With all cylinders always firing, a brief nap can be a welcome and powerful drug.

Hours later, closing in on six P.M., I wake from a deep dream that I'm baking to death in a desert, the sound of water all around me but I can't find it. I gasp for air as I grab for my phone: *Where am I? What time is it? What's happening?*

I have a barrage of text messages:

> KATHI: It's getting late, my glory whole, and I can't snooze booze the bombay in the tinkus any longer. There's a weird smell and smelt in this room and no vacuums within reach to live within my pale sad space of quiet teardrop lemmings and leggings and luxury all a lie

in the face of cracked skin and crumpled hearts you know?????

I hurl myself out of bed. As I put on the clothes closest to me and see my frantic, crazed reflection in the mirror, with the window showing the gorgeous ocean behind me, the contrast is real.

I rush to Kathi's room. The door is open. I dash in and find it trashed, a housekeeper trying to tidy up but not knowing where to even start. There's glitter everywhere, sheets are off the bed, pillows are on the lamps, clothing hangs from art on the walls, there's writing in lipstick and eye-liner on the floor and mirror:

Recognition becomes ordinary after its turn. If they believe my truth or let. It does and doesn't matter that everything has meaning whatever lasting. There really is meaning in everything. If they love me, they believe me. Look for the dreams in things.

Housekeeping asks me if it's okay to clean the mirror, to erase the lines in makeup that may or may not be brilliant. "Where is she?" I ask them, to no resolution.

I run around this floating paradise looking for Kathi Kannon, film icon.

The Rite Aid.

The bar.

The restaurant.

There!

Kathi and Roy are in the dessert section, having a buffet-style feast surrounded by a stark mix of gay dudes—both the kind who are older and well dressed and "supper" together each evening, and the glittery kind who grind their perfect teeth and keep mini packets of lube on their person at all times. These are all the kind of strangers I try to protect Kathi from, people who could coax embarrassing comments

or steal her jewelry or phone or prompt some embarrassing action or
feed Roy grapes.

Kathi spots me.

"Cockring!" she shouts. "Can you believe they have every kind of
dessert! I got you a donut shaped like your anus!"

"Hiii, good evening," I say, wondering what secrets have been betrayed, wondering what photos or videos have been taken, wondering
if these guys think I'm cool because I know Kathi Kannon.

My responsibilities include protect her, protect her, protect her.

I shake some hands.

Kathi bolts up from the table, she visits with other diners, she gets
another plate of food, she leaves her phone at the prime rib station. I'm
rushing around behind her, collecting her.

I pull her aside. "Kathi, we have to go to your room please."

Roy, still licking Kathi's saucy fingers, sort of flips me the bird with
his eyes.

"What's going on?" I ask her.

"Everything and nothing."

"Are you, you know, altered?" I ask.

"How dare you, Cockring? I love you," she says, truth behind her
eyes mismatched with her chemically dilated pupils.

"You're getting an F!" I yell. "And you have to perform soon!"

"We're gonna be rich and famous again, darling. Let's party."

I wrestle Kathi from the buffet and guide her back to her room as
she's tapping at her phone, texting, shopping, searching for pictures of
paradise when there's one right outside her balcony.

Hey, Siri, I just want her to get through this.

Housekeeping is gone, the room has been cleaned as much as possible, and I close Kathi's cabin door like it's a vault. "What is happening?" I ask.

"Cockring," she says, "while you were away today, I wrote!"

"You did? That's great. Now, what is going on—"

"Will you read it and type it up for me?" she asks, handing me a yellow notepad as she settles herself and Roy in bed, the two of them yanking to ruffle the sheets so they can cozy up on the tightly made bed. "I'll rest right now if you read it. Deal?"

"Fine," I say. "Is this the start of your new book?"

"Perhaps," she says, plopping down onto the pillows.

"Don't get too comfy," I say. "We have the show soon. What are you wearing?"

"Oh, who cares," she says.

I look at Kathi's notepad, pride spinning inside me.

But this writing, this notepad she filled with thoughts while she was out of it, it's mostly ramblings, written in circles and squares around the page, with arrows and dotted lines and "See page 6" and "See page 2" and cross-outs and underlines and circles around random words: "truth," "sheets," "fuck."

I turn the page, I'm thinking, *Nonsense.*

I turn the page, I'm thinking, *Not good.*

I turn the page, I'm thinking, *Something's wrong.*

"What do you think?" she asks.

"It's . . . it's . . ." I struggle with the word. "Kathi, I'm worried about you."

"Why? Do you love it? Tell me. I'm a big girl. Even obese by some measures."

"It's . . . not great," I say gently.

Kathi shivers. "How could you say that to me?" Her fist pounds the comforter, Roy sits up to see what's happening. "How could you give me doubt in myself? Even more than I already have, that I was born with? My legacy of doubt, thoughts, prayers, teachings bubbling up from my deep, unruly waters."

I look at Kathi, a whirlwind of energy. "This is not about writing. Something is definitely wrong. I don't think you can go onstage. We have to get you real help. This is not sustainable."

"Not sustainable?" she asks. "Don't you think I know that? I mean, at least give me some credit, which you do a lot, but not in this case, my stepson, stepbrother, step on this. From cute to profound, the full purple range of enigma."

I shake my head, frustrated and sad, crestfallen. I turn back to the notepad she wants me to transcribe. I flip the pages until I get to the cardboard backing. She's written on that, too. She has the strength and stamina of ten thousand manic monsters. Not an inch left uncovered. And on the back of the cardboard, at the bottom, scribbled in big letters over tiny letters and words and thoughts and feelings of the last hours: "Ticker tape parade don't let these be my last words."

I call Miss Gracie. "There's a problem," I say. "Kathi is unwell," I say. "Talk some sense into her," I say.

"Put her on the line, dear," Miss Gracie tells me. I hand my phone to Kathi.

"Hi, Mommy! Yes. Yes. Yes. Okay. Love you." And Kathi hangs up and hands the phone back to me. "She says I'm fine and I'm an adult and she trusts me because she has no choice because she's low on her blood-pressure medication."

"WHAT?"

Kathi hoists herself from her bed and starts taking her clothes off. I turn from her. "I'll be in the bath if you need me," she says to my back, and slams the bathroom door.

Roy hops off the bed and goes to the bathroom. Kathi opens the door until he's inside with her, then she slams it again.

I ask, "What's going on?"

She yells, "I'm celebrating!"

"Oh, my God. Celebrating what?"

"*Nova Quest!*" She yells back.

I call Dr. Miller. "I don't know what to do," I say. "She won't tell me if she's, you know, taken anything," I say. "She seems manic," I say.

"I'm happy!" Kathi yells from the bathroom. "Why won't you let me be happy?!"

Dr. Miller instructs me to give her 800 mg of Seroquel. I'm shocked. "We don't have that much," I tell him. "We usually only give thirty milligrams a day. We don't have enough."

"This will all make a good anecdote," Kathi yells from the bathroom. "That's the nature of it. It's a quarry. A mine. The days, the weeks, the years—they can't all be gems, right?"

I tell Dr. Miller, "We have a show soon." I'm thinking, *Kathi Kannon is manic and on a boat and about to be on a stage in the middle of nowhere, in the middle of a manic episode.*

KNOCK, KNOCK, KNOCK on the cabin door.

"Stage manager," someone calls from the other side. "Here to escort you to the theater."

I hear Kathi get out of the tub, the water dripping from her body, dripping back into the tub, onto the floor, puddling in the doorway.

"Two seconds," Kathi yells.

Dr. Miller tells me to call the boat doctor. I open the cabin door. "Can you get the boat doctor for us please?" I ask. One of the escorts nods and starts to walk off. "Please hurry," I yell after him.

"Everything okay?" the other escort asks.

The bathroom door opens and Kathi emerges, dressed like she's going to Burger King, in old leggings and a black tank top with a small blanket from her bed as a shawl.

"Ready!" she shouts, her hair still dripping wet.

"Kathi, you can't go onstage in front of thousands of people dressed like that and pretty much out of your mind."

"Excuse me," she says. "First, I'm in show business. Second, the show must go on. And third, I can't think of a third one. Let's go."

"Kathi, please," I beg.

She says, "Grab my purse."

I say, "You need to at least put on a bra."

While Kathi "dresses," I go into the bathroom and it's a familiar scene, her purse nearly empty, the contents spread out like a twisted cornucopia—that cornucopia, I know the one, just like from the day Agnes took me into Kathi's bathroom. I put my hand in Kathi's purse, I unzip a little side pocket, I pull out a pale-blue pill container, I open it up, and I pour a thimble's worth of little white pills into my palm.

I'm thinking, *You broke your promise.*

"What are these?" I ask her as she tries on sunglasses, looking at herself in a mirror.

She turns to me matter-of-factly. "Vitamins."

"Really?" I ask. "Then maybe I'll take one."

"I wouldn't," she says. "We can't have two of us estranged from ourselves." Kathi yanks the sunglasses off and throws a scarf over her shoulders, adjusting it just so.

"So if they're not vitamins, what are they?"

"Oh. If they're not vitamins they're morphine."

"Morphine? They make morphine pills?"

"Miracle of modern science," she says, walking to her makeup bag and pulling out a tube of silver lipstick.

"These are morphine? Like from a hospital?"

"I don't know where they get them exactly."

I ball the pills into my fist. "Kathi, what the fuck? Are you kidding me?"

"I tried to get them in, like, a nicotine patch, but it's more complicated." Kathi walks to the cabin door.

"Does this affect your bipolar medication?"

"Oh, I don't ever do both," she says. "No fun."

My body numbs with the thought of the manic episode she had in her driveway, and even the one here on the boat, and my fear that these were my fault, my guilt, when the problem is actually: She's using again, or using still.

"It's their drugs or mine," she says. "And it's my body."

"Please don't do this," I say, hanging on to hope. "They can cancel the show. No one will care. We'll say it's a medical emergency."

"There's no emergency, Cockring. You can come or not," she says firmly. She opens her cabin door and joins her escort to the theater. I lock up and chase after them.

"I'm going to open tonight with the song 'Crazy,'" Kathi says as we rush down the hall.

"What?" I ask. "How? We didn't give them the music. Do you even know the lyrics?"

She says, "I *am* the lyrics."

"No, do you know the words so you can sing it onstage?"

"Fine," Kathi says. "Forget the song. I won't sing it."

Hey, Siri, we're walking to the auditorium.

Hey, Siri, Kathi is ecstatic. I'm nervous. Roy is carefree, per usual.

Hey, Siri, have I done enough? Or will she do like she's done countless times before and brilliantly rise to the challenge? Certainly this isn't the first time she's been un-sober for some dreadful thing she doesn't want to do.

The escort says into a walkie-talkie, "We're here."

"Where's the doctor?" I ask. The escort shrugs and points Kathi to a stage door.

"Showtime," she says, and goes inside.

I'm escorted to a glass-fronted control room on the other side of the auditorium, behind and above the audience with the spotlights and the crew, where I can watch the stage, help with cues, and address any technical problems. As I enter, the lights in the theater dim.

The host welcomes everyone.

Kathi Kannon, Roy in tow, walks onstage to thunderous applause. She looks out, squinting her eyes, cupping her hand over her face to block the bright lights to try to see out.

"Cockring," she says into the mic. "Cockring? Where are you?"

The audience giggles and stirs, expecting a surprise, but the lights don't change, nothing happens, the silence is deafening.

"Cockring!" she shouts. "Cockring, play 'Crazy.' I want to sing! I want to sing 'Crazy,' Cockring!" The mic starts to pitch feedback like we're in a bad movie.

My forehead is pooling sweat. It's not possible to play her music. She said she wouldn't sing it, so the music isn't cued, the iPod not even hooked up to the huge electrical board. And I'm not mic'd. I have no way to talk back to her.

I'm watching, lethargic and paralyzed, as Kathi Kannon fumbles through stories she's told a thousand times, starting and stopping and forgetting the endings, no punch lines, only setups and setups that never pay off.

"My mommy," Kathi says, "was once on the TV show *M*A*S*H*. But then. I'm hungry. Who's hungry? Are you hungry, sir? You look hungry, ma'am. I'm a Virgo, anyway."

I feel far from my responsibilities of protecting her as she stands exposed, blathering, no one to guide her away, no protection from the room which is less and less full of people who want to see her and more and more full of people who want to see her fail, for the spectacle, for the sport of telling their friends about it.

Kathi flings the mic down and starts talking to the crowd, but no one can hear. People are shouting, "What?" People are shouting, "Use the mic!"

Kathi flips them off. She starts to walk offstage to shake hands and mingle. No one knows what's going on. Roy pees on the stage. And then poops.

People start leaving, laughing, pointing, recording.

I turn to the lady running the spotlight. "Is this funny or bad?"

It's an honest question. Maybe I can't tell anymore. Maybe I'm too close to the Shine, too close to the sun. Kathi Kannon has been crazy before and they still loved her. She's been boring before and they still loved her. She's never been this raw before, and I have no idea how this ends.

"Bad," she says.

"Sing it with me," Kathi shouts, again starting the lyrics to "Crazy," but she's unable to carry the thread, unable to find words beyond the first few lines.

"Crazy . . ." Kathi sings. "Ba da ba ba ba da ba whateverrrrr."

She's lost her way, and her audience.

I start to rush down to her, but the cruise director storms in. "I'm not happy!" he yells. "What's going on?"

"I don't know. She's ill, I think. That's why I asked for a doctor."

"How are we going to fix this?" he asks.

"I don't . . . I'm sorry. I'm not her agent or attorney," I say. "I'm just her assistant." The statement sits in the air a moment, swirls and washes over me; the statement drowns me, grounds me, returns me to the helpless altar boy of my youth watching his mother die.

I look out at Kathi Kannon, wondering how this is the place where it unravels, wondering how this is the moment a miracle has finally evaded her, this of all times, with great news about *Nova Quest* in the wings, and her self-destruction in the face of it, on stage of all places.

Kathi is in the middle of a half-told story of her meeting George Clooney at Cannes when she stops, her gaze going soft, her focus lost. The auditorium, full of jeering and laughter, goes instantly silent, creating a pregnant pause that consumes the theater, the boat, the Atlantic.

Suddenly, her stature gives way and Kathi Kannon, film icon, collapses. Her legs fold under her and her body plops on top of them, her head falling back, stopped from smacking the stage by the sofa behind her. The microphone she's holding slams loudly to the floor, and the amplified crash causes people to grab their ears and flinch, as if the world is crashing down upon us all.

The control-room director shouts, "Cut mics! Lights up! Security?!"

The rattle of the sound system turns to screeching and then cuts out completely, yielding to the audible gasps and "holy shits" from the remaining audience.

I shove past the cruise director and dash toward Kathi. I lose sight of her as crew members and a security guard rush to her and circle around. I'm trying to push through audience members who are now standing—some trying to get a better view and others trying to leave and salvage their night of frolic and fucks. I'm moving sideways through the oncoming traffic. I'm ducking under men holding hands and trying to make their way out.

I race toward the stage, winding around corners and weaving through exiting crowds of people gossiping about Kathi.

"What a disaster," they say.

"What a waste," they say.

"Fucking train wreck," they say.

I'm thinking, *Please don't die, please don't die, please don't die.*

Music starts playing—like we're on the sinking *Titanic:* I'm unsure if the music is to distract us or calm us as it all goes down.

The stage is getting more and more crowded as I approach, with cruise-goers jumping up and moving closer to Kathi, taking pictures, video, bystanders capturing I don't know what: Kathi incapacitated? Kathi dead?

"Security!" I start yelling. "Pardon me, security. Medic! Move!" I'm breathing heavy, just trying to get to her, feeling small and forsaken, until at last I'm at the stage and start pulling myself up onto it.

An announcement begins to play over the intercom about the next event, a karaoke night at a bar on the other side of the ship. Already, a collapsed film icon is old news.

No one stops me from approaching Kathi. A security guard on his walkie-talkie is barking at someone on the other end, "She's breathing, she's responsive . . . kinda."

"I'm her assistant! What's happening?!" I yell. "I'm her assistant!" I hover over Kathi and drop to my knees. I touch her shoulder and her eyes roll forward, and for a moment, I think, they lock with mine. "Hi. Kathi. You okay? What's happening?"

She doesn't answer. I look up, hoping for a savior. I see a stranger holding Roy, a wiggly and scared Roy. "Put him down, please," I yell. The stranger puts Roy on the ground, and he bounces over to us and smashes his nose into Kathi's face, his indelicacy startling her conscious again.

"Roy," she says. "Hi, Roy. I love your teeth."

"Kathi?" I ask, touching her face, wiping her hair out of her eyes. She looks at me. "Cockring," she says. "I'm . . . I'm . . ."

"You're bored?" I ask kindly, presumptuously, heartfully.

"I'm scared," she says.

"Want to go to your room?"

Kathi nods *yes*.

I turn to the crowd encircling us. "Move back please!" I yell. "Time to go!" I hook my hands under Kathi's arms. "Can you stand?"

Kathi starts to lift herself up.

The security guard protests, "A doctor is on the way."

"Then either clear this room so she can have privacy or help us get out of here," I say.

The guard looks around, seeing the hundred or so spectators still drinking in their nightly entertainment, seeing the impossible task of peeling them away. He looks at Kathi; she nods to me.

"Cockring," she says. "I want to go home."

The elusive doctor meets us at her cabin and says Kathi will be fine. "A little medication mix-up," he says, showing himself out as Roy and I stare at our master as she sleeps it off.

Assistant Bible Verse 144: It's always the meds.

I try to imagine her feelings on this night—defeat, shame, exhaustion. I can't help but think of my mother and her lonely public death, wondering if Kathi Kannon just barely escaped that fate. I look around for Kathi's purse, to fish out Mom's locket, to see if it's still with us, to beckon its magic and healing, to help us get through this night. But it's across the room, the room swaying back and forth in the choppy waters, and I don't have the balance or leverage left in me to make the journey.

Roy hops off the bed with Kathi and comes to sit beside me on the couch, his body curling into a ball and just barely touching mine, the slightest contact, not enough to infringe on his autonomy or mine but enough to wake him if I move. No one wants to be stranded alone on a cruise ship. I wonder about Kathi, isolated comfortably in her bed. I wonder why Roy chooses to sit with me and not Kathi. Rarely does he choose safety over fun.

I worry about leaving her alone for the night, so I lie down on the sofa, still wearing the same clothes I wore to Kathi's show. And I doze in her room, safely in her orbit, pushing into slumber past my guilt for napping on the job and not having maybe prevented all this.

I call Miss Gracie, tell her there could be photos, videos.

She says, "Never get old, dear."

She says, "Don't live past eighty, dear."

She says, "I'm only living for Kathi, dear."

Miss Gracie charters us a private plane home from the next port.

Snap: My first private plane—I'm living the dream, right? I take in every moment, every detail—the wood-grain accents, white leather chairs, crystal champagne flutes. The bathroom is a bucket under a seat cushion just behind the pilot. The only privacy while using it is a shower curtain you pull around yourself. What a metaphor for this trip I'm on; I always thought a private plane was so glamorous, but it's really just a flying toilet.

I'm putting Kathi Kannon in other hands now, health-care profession-als at Cedars. They take her away in a wheelchair—standard procedure. She's been quiet since the cruise, depressed, distant, lost. Kathi watches me not follow her, like a rejected puppy forgotten by a child who has a shinier toy to play with.

They're asking me about her medications.

They're asking me about her diet.

They're asking me if I know anything about drugs.

I want to scream, *You don't know her life!*

I want to scream, *You can't do for her what I do for her!*

I want to scream, *You don't know the way she likes her soda!*

I'm a kid again, my father snatching her action figure from me. Inside, once again I'm screaming, *Don't take her from me!*

They're sweet to me, these nurses, these doctors, but I know their intentions, their judgments. I know that Kathi Kannon isn't special to them, that she's just a number, a client, another spoiled celebrity. They don't know she's my whole world.

I ask, "Can I see her?"

They say, "Sorry, you're not family."

20

☆

y world is shaking.

Los Angeles is having a small earthquake. Reid is sleeping beside me at my place and it wakes us. I jolt up, my back straight as a board, looking down at Reid, who opens his eyes kindly, calmly, a message to me: *nothing to fear.*

Until, BAM! SMASH!

As the tremor stops, I turn on my small brass lamp, Kathi's old pill bottle from Bali still safe and sound beside it.

On the floor, beside my bed, is a smashed piece of art that was propped on a bookshelf. It's a cheap reprint of *The Lady of Shalott,* the 1888 John William Waterhouse painting based on the poem of the same name. The painting's namesake is a stunning woman, cursed, pensive, alone in her lovely white robe, drifting in a river, in a small boat, en route to her death, two of the three candles on her boat already blown out, the third a mere breath, a mere breeze away from being extinguished. The comforts with her—her blankets, her lantern, her crucifix—none of them can save her; she won't take any of them with her in the end. Even smashed on the floor, she's beautiful.

I've had her with me since college, my one consistent prized possession. The Lady of Shalott has such a sad look on her face, she seems cold and irritated, and I think that during much of my life in depression, I probably looked just like her—unsure, pained.

Now she's on the floor, face up, surrounded by glass, by more danger. A shard has cut a small corner of the reprint. Her visage is intact, but her world is broken, damaged, and yet she still stares into the future, that sweet but fated expression, all of it not unlike the uncertainty I'm feeling tonight as I think about my hospitalized heroine.

"You okay?" Reid asks, now leaning up on an elbow, watching as I get out of bed, tiptoe around Shalott's shards.

"Scary," I say, picking up the painting, careful to keep the broken glass contained. I put it on Mom's boxes, which I'm still using as a coffee table. I'm thankful that the Lady of Shalott is frozen like this, on the brink, locked forever in danger in color and oil, this exquisite young woman who will never see her future, never see what really becomes of her. I wish time could stand this still for all of us in our moments of doubt and fear, give us whatever time we need to feel confident about moving forward. I wish we had a pause button we could press until we figure things out, perfectly know what's ahead, and move forward with clarity, with ease. But if we had that, would we ever un-pause? Would we ever move forward? If we could do everything with boldness, where's the room for genius mind?

"Is this about Kathi, babe?" Reid asks.

I nod, unwittingly emotional, surprisingly raw.

"She's an adult, Charlie. And she's getting the care she needs."

"She'll be fine, right?" I ask with a big exhale.

"Right," Reid says.

"Yeah. She's finally getting great care and will be okay, and I'm sure after a couple weeks she'll be good as new."

"Better than new," Reid says.

"Hopefully!" I shout, and crawl back into bed, lying beside him, his warmth filling me with love. "And before you know it, we will be in London shooting the film and having a blast."

"Totally."

"Will *we* be okay?" I ask.

"While you're in London? Of course. I'll come visit a bunch," Reid says. "You can come back home sometimes. It's not a big deal."

"Right," I say, falling into him, my head on his chest. "I've just never done a long-distance thing—or even a short-distance thing. Are you sure you're okay with it? What if we're apart for a longer stretch than we plan? With filming, anything can happen."

"I'm invested in us if you are," he says, holding up his hand like a mime trying to escape a glass box. I hold up my hand and touch his, our fingers then falling in between each other's knuckles, intertwined, locked, and I lean in and kiss him.

I'm on the list and I'm on my way, heading to visit Kathi Kannon at the hospital, past the valet parking, past the security guard standing watch like a bouncer at a dead nightclub at eight A.M., past the security doors buzzing with electricity and magnetism that hold the locks tight, hold the many personalities inside.

I'm waiting to see her, to embrace her, to squeeze her shoulders and tell her to hang in there. *Hey, Siri,* I'm also thinking about how much I hate this, how much I hate addiction and its demons, how much I long to get her back to her A-plus sobriety with her A-plus assistant.

The waiting room sits off a busy hallway, and it's more of a waiting area than a room—there's no doorway, just an open space where I can see machinations of mental health care. The hallway is lined with empty beds, the same generic kind they use throughout the hospital, with buttons and levers to make the mattresses go up and down, bending half this way and half that, covered in a bright-blue plastic. Nurses rush back and forth, shaking their heads, annoyed and underappreciated, no doubt wondering what the hell happened that they ended up in this job. I'm thinking, *Sometimes, I understand.*

I look out of a window, but all the windows up here are frosted so the people institutionalized can't see outside to the world, to the life they're missing. I see only the vague shapes of life—blurs of cars driving by, other buildings, small and distorted shapes of people walking. It's strange watching a hazy reflection of life before your eyes, forcing guesses and assumptions about what's really happening all around you.

"Are you Charlie?" a nurse says, rushing into the waiting area, no frills, no time to dally.

I stand. "Yup. Here to see Aurora Borealis," I say playfully. I gather my jacket and purple leather backpack, cheerfully ready to start the workday.

"She's not here," the nurse says, turning immediately to leave.

"What? Where is she?" I ask, stepping forward, closer to the hallway, closer to the nurse, my arms falling uselessly to my sides, my backpack and jacket now touching the dirty floor.

"She checked out this morning," the nurse says, studying her clipboard.

"What? This morning? She checked out? How can she check out if she's in a mental hospital?"

The nurse glances up at me. "I'm sorry, I can't say any more. Have a good day," she says, looking me over once, trying to check the size, to figure out exactly what's happening here, namely, who am I, and who am I to Aurora Borealis?

"Wait, wait," I plead. "Who checked her out, where did she go?"

"Sir—"

"We're talking about Kathi, right? I'm her assistant. She isn't supposed to leave." I'm pacing, my feet out of sync with my body; I'm shifting at the waist and turning back and forth. "She's not well. She needs help. She's not here? Are you sure?"

The nurse stares at me with her first hint of kindness, and under the screams and laughter of the other patients, she whispers, solemnity in her eyes, "Hon, she's not here."

That gate.

That mansion.

That bedroom.

And that's where I find Kathi Kannon, comfortably snuggled with a delightfully snoring Roy, in her own bed, in her own space, inoculated from the real world, real consequences—no nurses, no rules, no frosted glass to separate her from reality. No bottoming out.

I'm barely through the door to her bedroom when I start in on her, air rushing past my ears I'm moving so fast. "Hey!"

"Good morning, Cockring," she says groggily, Roy perking up beside her, stretching his head into the air.

I half-plop my body at her feet at the end of her bed, one of my legs folded under me, the other dangling off, like someone ready to make a run for it if things go south.

"Kathi, I just came from the hospital."

"Oh, no," she says. "Are you hurt?"

"No," I answer out of reflex, dismissing her joke and pressing on with pressing matters. "Why aren't you there?"

"I hated that place and I hated all those people and Mommy let me check out," Kathi says, taking a casual drag from her e-cigarette, but when she exhales, nothing comes out, no vapor, no substance. She shakes the cartridge, the battery—empty, or dead.

"What about your health?" I ask.

"I feel great," she says, tossing the covers off her body, rolling out of bed, and walking to the desk where she keeps her e-cigarette chargers. Roy watches her go, his ears jutting back and forth as he calculates whether to unbundle from his blankets and go with her, but he then shrugs and nuzzles back into the comforter, even Roy unwilling to commit to this conversation.

"But you don't feel great," I argue, swinging my other leg off the bed, both feet now dangling, comfort escaping me, escaping the room.

"You don't know how I feel, darling," she says, her back to me as she fumbles with the e-cigarettes.

Darling.

"I know enough," I say, now standing. "You need to go back."

"I'm not going back there. Those people are idiots," she says, as she clips and twists and struggles to electrify her vice.

"Idiots? For what? For wanting you to be healthy?"

"Cockring, please," she says, clanking around, intensely fumbling with power cords and outlets. "Don't do this."

"Was Orion an idiot, too?"

"Sadly, yes," Kathi says, now turning to face me, to engage. Her face looks softer, less certain than usual.

"And the sober coaches before him? Idiots? And your mother, try-ing to get you help before that? Idiot? And me, who wants you to live a long life, I'm an idiot, too?"

"Ugh, you're doing this all wrong," Kathi says. "It has to be my choice."

"I don't trust your choices."

"I'm not going back, Cockring," Kathi says. "We'll be fine."

"We? What about you?" I ask. "Let's be really, really real here. What if this happens in London?"

"Well," she thinks aloud, "I guess I'm gonna need you to research the best psych wards in England, please." Kathi turns away again, to replace cartridges, replace dead batteries with live ones.

"No."

No.

This is the first time I've ever really said no to Kathi Kannon, with my eyes, my soul, my adult voice. The word feels searing.

Kathi looks at me over her shoulder and over her glasses—double the intensity—staring for a few seconds too long, then resuming her fidgeting with her devices while saying it again, colder, harder, "Cockring, I'm gonna need you to research the best psych wards in England, please."

"I won't do it," I say. "I can't."

"Sure you can. It's not rocket science," Kathi says. "Just google 'best psych wards London.' I did it a couple years ago and found two that have horseback riding. That'll be fun, no?"

"No! Not fun. And not a solution. I won't keep checking you into facilities and handing you off to strangers and worrying you're still going to overdose the next morning or the next week or the next month. How many scares do we have to have? Hospitalization isn't like taking your car to the shop," I tell her, my voice shaky and colored with a false confidence she can smell like a shark to blood.

Kathi pauses, slaps the e-cigs and the cartridges and the batteries down, smooshed under her hands, and she stands tall and turns to fully face me. We lock eyes.

"Please don't overstep," she says firmly, walking back to the bed. "I don't need that hospital. I'm really fine. Let's focus on London, on shooting the new films. It'll be great for our life."

"*Our* life? What about *your* life?" I ask. "What about *my* life?" The question draws Kathi's eye, and I immediately realize my irreversible sin. I've pulled back the curtain too far. I've separated us, punctured the veil of non-separation, revealed "our life" as two. Perhaps Roger was right: I can't have it both ways. Perhaps I'm either all in or not at all; we're either united or nothing. Perhaps if I'm not one life with her, I'm one life against her.

Kathi gets up from the bed again, increasingly restless, turning back to her e-cigarettes, her hands moving quickly, frantically, screwing one into the charger, then another, then another. "These batteries are all dead!" she yells, red lights blinking, seemingly faster and faster, seemingly punctuating our growing problem.

"I'm trying to help you. Not just with travel and chores and whatever but to really help you."

"I've been doing this a long time," Kathi says. "It hasn't killed me yet."

"Yet!" I yell, now my eyes heating, burning, red. I feel the welling, I try to stifle it. "That's the part I'm worried about."

"I'm not going back to the hospital," Kathi says slowly, like she's speaking a regretful truth. She turns to face me. "And, I guess, if you don't like it, there's the door."

There's the door.

Like a fool showing my hand, I look over at the door to her bedroom, that familiar wood grain I've befriended in the years of walking in here to wake her up, finding her in all stages of undress and duress, and in the happier recesses of my memory, finding her healthy, joyous, engaged, ready for an adventure somewhere other than so-called *Vegas*. I look at the stained-glass panel in the door, the glass I've studied nearly every day before entering her room with my ear turned slightly toward the threshold, listening for her breath, for whether she's asleep or awake; that door, the silly barrier between our worlds, it suddenly seems my enemy.

There's the door.

Kathi watches me as I nod my head, thinking of the similar comment my father used to make to my mother—*If you don't like it, there's the door*—forcing Mom's hand and all but ushering her out of their relationship. Mom bravely accepted the challenge, taking it as far as she could. And now I find myself facing both of my mother figures: Kathi Kannon, entwined in my emotions, and my real mother, entombed in a locket just a short distance from us in Kathi's purse, both of these ladies calling on me to make a choice, between the two mothers—one who gave me birth and one who gave me rebirth, one calling on me to shutter my courage and the other reminding me to embrace it.

There's the door.

I'm thinking, *She can't be serious.*

I'm thinking, *This is not how I want this to end.*

I'm thinking, *Maybe there's a lot I don't want.*

I can hear the bedside lamp buzzing; I can hear the fountain outside on the back patio; I can hear the second hand of the wall clock moving, the gears turning; I can hear Kathi breathing heavier and heavier; I can feel Roy's now-tense gaze. I can smell the stink of the position I'm in, having to navigate these waters, having to convince a certain someone to take care of herself, that her life matters.

"I won't be an enabler," I say, with a hint of overdone pride. "I won't be, like, your baby, nursing at the Shine."

"But, darling, you already are."

I stand and begin to protest. "No—"

"Oh, don't pretend," Kathi says. "You've known what I buy with vegetable money. You've known *Vegas* wasn't just me going to buy you a new sweater. You've been by my side on airplanes and in hotel rooms, and what lie are you telling yourself? Do you think I tried to run into traffic because of a vitamin C deficiency? Do you think I sleep all day because my blood sugar is low? What lies do you tell yourself so you can keep bragging to your friends that you work for old, cranky, crazy Priestess Talara?"

"That's not how I see it," I say meekly, now tugging at my sweater, now weighted down by it, by some truth in her words.

"You said it," Kathi says, shrugging. "Let's be really, really real here. Fine. We make a good team, Cockring. Some things come with the territory. Calm down. Before you know it, your name will be in the credits of a *Nova Quest* film, darling."

I stop breathing. Now my hands are those of a nervous soldier, flexing in and out of fists.

I say, "No, Kathi . . ."

Hey, Siri, I'm seeing her manic in the driveway and trying to swim into traffic.

I say, "I won't calm down . . ."

Hey, Siri, I'm seeing her secret stashes of pills tucked in purses and pockets.

I say, "I'm frustrated and scared . . ."

Hey, Siri, I'm seeing her body looking cold and lifeless in Seattle.

I say, "I'm overwhelmed and lost . . ."

Hey, Siri, I'm seeing her collapse into a heap onstage in front of an audience of iPhones and ill wishes in waters off Bermuda.

I say, "I'm bored."

And it's like a bomb drops.

I say it quickly, flatly, bluntly, louder than I expected. Even Roy looks up at me. My eyes on Kathi are hard with truth and disappointment and realization.

A sadness rinses my veins, stronger and stronger, just like the silence in the room. I watch the blinking red lights of her cigarette chargers, blood rushing to my head, my limbs growing cold and numb. I feel the unthinkable revelation. I'm suddenly raw and spinning. I'm longing for the hospital for myself, for the frosted glass and electric locks keeping truth and reality at bay. I don't want to see this job for what it is, and I don't want to see this job for what it could be forever—her in constant danger, and me believing I can help her, and I can't.

Kathi sucks on an e-cigarette, inhaling and inhaling, then blowing out, and again, her breath is invisible, no electronic vapor in her lungs, no charge held from the cartridge. "NOTHING WORKS ANYMORE!!!" Kathi screams, now her tears beginning as she pulls it from her mouth and jams it into a charger in an unholy fit. She measures her temper, tempers her feelings—whatever they are: Anger? Hurt? Love? She pulls a new e-cigarette from its charger and pops it into her mouth.

She sucks on the device, long and hard, and finally, her eyes closed, she exhales vapor, filling the room like it's on fire, like it's all burning down.

I say to Kathi Kannon, film icon, "If you don't go back to the hospital, I'm going to leave."

As I look at Kathi, dressed in her tattered black T-shirt and long cardigan, similar to what she was wearing at my job interview all those years ago, my life—my lifestyle—flashes before my eyes: me wide-eyed and eagerly parked outside her front gate for the first time, my hopeful walk up to her front door, our optimistic interview, meeting Mateo the Moose, the passion in these wild fireplaces, the living leather royalty of Emperor Yi, the trips, the great aurora, the cursed cruise, the perfection that is Roy—who's in this strained moment staring up at me with his unending unconditional love, questioning, no doubt, where all this is going, where I'm maybe going, whether I'm indeed going. It seems Kathi is considering, too.

Kathi takes a deep breath, the kind in movies when the hero is wounded. It's the awkward moment in film when the music stops and we hear the slow ringing in the ears. It's the moment when all seems lost. And the audience gets it. And the hero gets it. And right now, Kathi Kannon gets it.

"I thought we were friends," Kathi says, crying softly.

"This is what a friend should have done a long time ago."

Kathi and I stand in limbo for a while, time seeming so silly, words seeming so pointless.

I close my eyes tightly, so tight I feel muscles I never knew existed, and I step forward in her bedroom to a familiar imaginary mark, and in an instant I see myself holding an imaginary award, blinded by imaginary lights and cameras. I'm emotional—not from victory but something else. I say into the imaginary microphone, to the imaginary auditorium, "Is this thing on?"

Kathi turns from me, dissolving into the ocean of imaginary people, the same imaginary audience from when I first met her so many moons ago, back when I was a different person. I wonder if they recognize me? I wonder if they've seen me grow and change and arrive at this very moment.

I take a deep breath; the same oxygen-rich blood vessels gush inside me as if from the first day I saw Kathi Kannon give her imaginary awards speech. God, it's so real. The metal award, though only in my mind, still feels very solid, very cold in my hands. "I don't deserve an award," I say.

I hear Kathi putting down her cigarettes, her feet shuffling. I feel her face me.

And in my mind, I think I spot her in the dark, imaginary theater, behind the lights and cameras and faceless people, and I crane my neck to see her, to speak to her. "If I'm getting an award, it's only because of one person, a woman who gave me life, who gifted me light from darkness, who helped me see a living world behind black corners. I'd like to thank Kathi Kannon for loving me."

I feel a tear drop from my eye, moisture clearing my vision, transporting me back to her bedroom, back to standing alone with her and Roy. I stare at her, moved and moving, slowly, her hands twitching slightly.

And here we are, separated now by more than words and more than space and time. Here we stand, finally, in the home where we birthed our awards-acceptance speeches, where we now concede defeat and disconnection.

Kathi's shoulders slump forward, impossibly low, the crown of her head dipping and dipping and the arch of her back now heaving, dreariness upon her as upon me, the two of us, standing a few feet apart and not touching at all, sipping our sovereignty, trying it on, the itchy loneliness of it, for perhaps the first time since we met.

I don't turn away from her. She turns away from me, back to her e-cigarettes, her friends, a world that's all vapor.

I reach over to her bed and gently touch Roy on the head. His ears collapse faithfully under my hand and I rub the loose skin that sits over his adoring brain. I whisper to him, "I'm sorry, buddy." Another traitorous tear slips from my eye, betraying my attempt to show strength, courage, professionalism—perhaps it's too late for any of that.

I pull my hand from a grateful Roy, turn from him and Kathi, my blood swirling inside my body from the rush of the motion, the rush of the moment. I feel my heart beating in my chest, I can hear the thumping in my ears, I can see it—the pulsing of little halos in my vision, slowly trying to close in on me, like the onset of a migraine or a heart attack or a heartbreak.

I feel every muscle in my body moving as I start to leave her. I feel her turn, I feel her eyes following my every independent motion, seeing me maybe for the first time as an autonomous being, some creature who crawled into her open door at night and now crawls away at first light. I take a step, and another, and another out of that bedroom, so eerily aware of every centimeter of my being, so self-conscious I feel like I'm watching myself from out of body. From above, I see myself leaving, and as I approach the bedroom door, I see myself pause, wondering if she will come after me. But Priestess Talara, now older and rattled, now revealed as Kathi Kannon, mortal human being, doesn't come after me.

I don't feel my legs as I glide out of Kathi Kannon's bedroom. My body moves me clinically, cold and steady, my neck not bending, my head not leaning down at the floor but straight ahead, with purpose, seemingly, for the first time, surprisingly without regard for what's behind me, my boss, my friend. Is she watching me go? Is she in need of comfort? Am I the thing they talk about—the interventionist, the one finally drawing a line in the sand? Am I the sad, good example? Or am I just sad?

Therapista says another word for sadness is love.

I was once with Kathi, shopping for clothing at some store on Third

Street, and as we checked out, the clerk looked at me and said, "Happy Friday!" And I sighed and threw my head back and said, "Happy Friday!"—me expressing joy that it was the weekend, expressing joy that I was about to have two days away from Kathi Kannon—and I wondered, did she know what we were saying? Did she take insult at the *Happy Friday* of it all? I remember looking over at her. She was still shopping, still touching sweaters and jeans, feeling them for softness, for potential. Did she know that Fridays were happy because they meant a respite from my time with her, from her as my job? Is all of this coming into view for her? Because it's coming into view for me.

As I walk down her hall, I exhale a few years' worth of stress, my legs shaking, my body suddenly coming into itself—jarring my heart. What have I done? What am I doing? I remember that young and stressed kid with his short hair and tepid expression, now older, hair longer, eyes heavier. I exit Kathi Kannon's wing, exit her orbit, despite the gravity, her gravity, her glorious pull—that mansion peppered thick with feelings and subtext. Outside of her room, through that old hallway with its art and sass, past the bar where she first served me a Coke Zero and shared a drag of her e-cigarette. This walk, it's so different from the fun, colorful life we've lived up to now, such a contrast, such a journey, for both of us. I finally breathe my own breath, I finally cry, for I'm leaving it behind, I've left her behind, and I know I won't go back—not like the Charlie I was before this moment. I know I can't be that guy again. And I don't want to be.

And in the red room, surrounded by her pillow cushions and boats—too many on the mantel, always so close to collapse—I hear her call out.

"Cockring," she yells. I cover my mouth to keep from responding, to stifle a sob.

"Cockring!" she calls louder.

Every hair, every cell of my body turns toward her, urges me, longs for me to go to her, to run to her. *MEET HER NEEDS! HEAL HER*

PAIN! DO NO HARM! It's all in my mind. But in the end, in that moment, it's not my mind but my heart that turns away, my heart that turns to something that's even bigger than the celebrated Kathi Kannon, something even bigger than the iconic Priestess Talara. It's my heart that turns to love, not for her or Reid or my dad or anyone else, but for myself, something that feels, finally, a little bigger than her.

"Cockring!" she yells a third time.

Against all my primal desires, I keep walking to her front door.

Then, "Charlie!" she shouts, her final gasp.

Through my wet, blurry vision and held breath, I'm thinking, *Goddammit, she does know my real name.*

21

☆

n these final hours of my employment by Kathi Kannon, film icon, the house at 1245 Beverly Canyon Drive is empty and lifeless. Kathi left to run errands, leaving word with Agnes she'll be back soon. Kathi wasn't in her bed when I arrived to give her breakfast this morning. Her soda and cereal and meds sit warming and wasting on her bedside. There will be no special *last morning* moment.

In the two weeks since our pained conversation, neither Kathi nor I have brought up the issue, both of us steely in our positions, truth and honesty a salve that stains. How I longed to walk into her home in these last days and find her gone—bags packed and a note saying she's back in the hospital or rehab or some variation signaling a change. But, alas, we're both playing chicken, or, perhaps, we're both emboldened to endure this heavy break.

Kathi's business manager has sent some new assistant candidates for her to interview, but she wants no part of it. His office will do the hiring for her. They'll play it by ear. They'll just see how it works out. The show will go on. The roller coaster will continue without me.

It's all come to this.

I'm alone with myself. If Therapista is right, I'm projecting my sadness onto every wall, projecting my uncertainty into every corner. I spend some of my final moments doing nothing—sitting, thinking, trying to remember the good times. This is the day I've been dreading for a while, maybe longer subconsciously. I've had many ideas about what it would be like, my departure. Would there be a party, would we have a fight, would something special mark the moment: Cake? Champagne? Crying? But it's none of those things. So far, it's the absolute absence of those things; it's worse: nothing, quiet, for hours, my last moments simply hushed, in such contrast to the past few loud years. They ring in my ears, a temptation to sentimentality and paralysis that I now have no choice but to resist.

I'm thinking, my dad's voice in my head, *NEVER LEAVE A JOB UNLESS YOU HAVE ANOTHER ONE.* But I have nothing lined up. No idea what's next for me. I'm overwhelmed, sure. I'm tired and hungry and yet have no appetite, scared I'm doing the wrong thing. I'm worried I'm making a mistake, abandoning her, leaving this opportunity of a lifetime. Maybe I'm not so changed by Kathi Kannon after all. Maybe under this fancy sweater she bought me, I'm the same weak loser I was when this all started.

I'm sitting at my usual spot in the living room, leather and Mateo the Moose and me, where I've—*tap, tap, tap*—sorted hundreds, probably thousands of Kathi's medications, though there's no more work to be done here. The *tap, tap, tap* replaced by the *tick, tick, tick* of the clock, the countdown to my exit, quickly approaching.

Now, here, on my last day, no recusals or pardons or reprieves in our path, I kill time by looking out of Kathi Kannon's living room window, at the estate and the life I'm leaving behind. I look at the tennis court and the avocado tree. I look at Kathi's gate, remembering the feeling of being outside of it three years ago, all those memories ago, so desperately wanting to be inside, hungering for this new life that I now have, this skin that I'm now shedding.

And in my view of Kathi's front yard, I see movement. I see Miss Gracie, alone, still in a robe, a scarf around her head, not dressed for public, not dressed to be out of her house, ambling up Kathi's colorful brick path.

Miss Gracie moves slowly, with measured purpose. She's solo; for what she has on her mind, for the strong will in her bones, for what she's about to do, she doesn't need Roger's assistance.

I want to run. I want to lock the doors. This fragile old woman, how I still fear her.

I step back and Miss Gracie is out of my sight now, she's on the porch; I can feel her moving closer to me, to the front door, until she's standing there, like a heavenly being, a harbinger of joys, or sorrows, framed by her daughter's address, lawn, life, forever following, cleaning up the mess, now here to fix the latest transition, if it is one.

Miss Gracie steps into the living room, into the circle of emperors, and I know what's next. She doesn't need to say anything. I walk to meet her, to meet this, my fate. She sits and I sit across from her, our dueling positions the same as when I first sat with her in her home down the hill.

She says, "I can't believe you're doing this to us, dear."

I say, "I'm sorry."

"I'm here in a last effort to dissuade you from leaving."

I don't respond. There's nothing more to say.

Miss Gracie is doing the math, sizing me up, readying herself for a scene. "Do you know why women have their period, dear?" Miss Gracie asks.

I manage a suspicious "No, ma'am."

Miss Gracie says, "It's because God wanted us to suffer for our children. I'll take any suffering for my child—I have for years, and I don't love her any less for it. I love her more for it, more than anything. What can I give you to stay? Money? Fame? Want to make movies with me? What? Anything. Kathi's life is my life."

But there is no stopping this bullet train, no sense telling Miss Gracie what she already knows.

I say, "I'm sorry, Miss Gracie."

She nods rare defeat. It doesn't suit her; she's miscast in this role. But Miss Gracie acts as if she's seen this all before, like she already knows the ending. Sometimes I forget there were other assistants— other secretaries—before me.

"Can I help you walk back down?" I ask.

"No, dear," Miss Gracie says. "As you know, downhill is the easy part." She stands slowly, and I rise in tandem with her. Miss Gracie doesn't look at me again as she turns and begins her journey farther and farther away from me.

I watch Miss Gracie slowly walk away, out of the house and out of my life. I rub my hand across the front of my gray cardigan, my uniform gifted to me in the first days, now slightly weathered, slightly sun-faded from all the action, retiring with me.

I sit back down under the sparkle and glory of the great room in Kathi Kannon's mansion.

I watch the sun begin to set, and that's when Kathi comes home, maybe from *Vegas*, shopping bags in hand and soon out of hand—dumped on the floor, trinkets and jewelry and clothing spilling out—things for no one in particular, and yet things, eventually, for everyone, anyone.

"Want to write today?" I ask her, a final jest.

"Not today, Cockring. Maybe tomorrow," she says. Is it a jab? Indeed, perhaps tomorrow she will begin her writing, finally putting pen to paper, finally helping me do my job, when it's no longer my job.

I do my time, 10:30 A.M. until 6:01 P.M.

Our world is still warmed by fading Beverly Hills daylight when I go to find Kathi, to bid an awkward, feeble farewell.

She's on the back porch, spraying vanilla perfume all over Roy. "Stand still!" she's shouting, as Roy bucks and twirls, desperate to escape. Kathi doesn't look up at me as I approach.

I say, "Well, it's time."

Roy spins and jumps under her arms.

She says, "Okay."

I say, "Goodbye, Kathi."

Kathi stops, turns from Roy to me, and stands. Roy stops his jittering and he watches, too. Kathi takes a couple steps over to me and we hug. And she says softly to me, muffled by my grasp but loud and clearly enough, "Goodbye, darling."

Darling. Could it be any worse?

"I'm not good at this kind of thing," she says.

"It doesn't have to be a thing. We can just make it a *see you later*."

She breaks from our hug but still holds my shoulders, looking me in the eyes.

"See you later, Cockring," she says.

"See you later," I say into those familiar eyes, those famous eyes, the gaze decades old, the one I've treasured since I was a boy, my idol, my living action figure.

With that, Kathi Kannon, film icon, lets go, turns, and walks away from me and back into her home. And dutifully following her into their unknown, Roy, trotting behind her loyally and rightfully through that doorframe, now a portal out of my universe. Their exit stirs the Beverly Hills air, the smell of vanilla pooling around me as I stand utterly alone on the back porch of the home of a hero, my heroine, the nearby water fountain made of her broken plates flowing beside me, draining, leaking, emptying—even the fountain reminding me nothing lasts forever.

Assistant Bible Verse 145: You can't win. If you leave, you've left them. If you stay, you become them. No goodbye is ever good, or good enough.

On my way out, I sit at my desk for the last time. I open my laptop and pull up the sacred document, the one that took what feels like lifetimes to compose—my life, Kathi's, Roy's; I print the Assistant Bible for the new guy, whoever her business manager eventually decides to hire, whoever Kathi finally decides to approve and amuse and bless and beguile.

The pages of memories print beside me—so coldly and emotionless those pages tumble upon each other out of the printer, a collated collection of Kathi's likes and dislikes and preferences and peculiarities: Don't wake her before ten; she prefers the tall glasses in the bar; never leave any pale-blue pill cases lying around. As if those delicate details can be captured in black and white. I pull the pages into my hands and tap them on the desk to make a neat stack, a final effort to leave something tidy, some mark of order. I stack the Assistant Bible on the desk. After Kathi and Roy, it's perhaps the hardest thing to leave behind. So many lessons, so much truth, such a big part of my life, now useless to me.

I twist her keys off my key ring—her shed, her pool house, her front door.

I hang the empty purple leather backpack on the chair.

I log out of Kathi Kannon's iCloud, her contacts, her calendar.

And in an instant, at last, painfully, no more pink dots.

22

☆

'm standing alone at the same bar where it started a few years ago, the Village Scribe. I'm looking at their drinks menu—Truth, Self-Esteem, Inspiration—and wondering, *Where's mine: Where's Lost? Where's Worried? Where's Insecure?*

I do a lap, walking around and remembering when it was all new, the smell of the alcohol, the shape of the teardrop room in the back corner. *Bruce* led me here, guiding me, goading me with his high fade haircut and low-level anxiety.

My feet are planted in the same place I stood when I met West and Crooner and Titanic and the lot. Jasmine stood right here with me back then, toasting my life, my newfound power nestled in the heart of a complicated, beautiful film icon. Not far from this spot, she introduced me to her father. He tried to warn me.

I'm here to meet them all for drinks, for our last work drinks, but no one is here.

I sent the email invite a week ago, my last "fwd" in their long line of "fwds." No one wrote back. I followed up again a couple days ago. Only

Jasmine responded: "Sorry, Baby. Can't make it. Good luck. Maybe next time."

But I know there won't be a next time—they have no time for a mere mortal. I get it. I'm no longer Kathi's Baby. I've quit her, and they've quit me. For them to come now would be a violation of sorts, an affront to the purpose of this entanglement at its core. For them to come now would mean it isn't work drinks, it's just social drinks. No one has time for that. And I accept it. I left their world. I left that prima prison, where assistants are shadows, puppets, pawns, cogs in the wheel, known without autonomy and known only by the name of their employer. Who are they to come meet me now, in my own skin, my own clothes, a stranger before them, independent and powerless? And who am I to blame them, these souls who were my support for a time, these great people, unthanked, unappreciated, absurd pseudo-soldiers who give their lives—their time, their youth—to the lives of others who are wealthier, more connected, more famous? These assistants, who put up with abuse and long hours and screaming and harassment and heartless wages and whose names will be forgotten once they're out of the Shine; these assistants, whose real names I don't even know.

23

☆

SPRING

'm at the gate.

The gate, but not *that* gate.

I'm parked outside a new gate now, at my new job at a film studio, wearing the same clothes I wore to the job interview, because that's how much I care.

I lie and tell my friends I'm loving it.

I answer the stray calls on my cell from people looking for Kathi. I tell them I've moved on. They don't ask where.

Kathi's first text to me since my departure came many weeks after I left, filled with everything I could have wanted from her, a whisper that she's well, that she's still sassy, that I'm not an enemy.

> KATHI: Is your hair still growing? Is your heart full? Are
> your fingernails long enough to scratch an attacker
> so the sweet little piggies can bring swift justice?
> Smooches but only on inappropriate places from Roy
> and me, well-bell-do-tell, I'm kissing you on the taint.

Other texts come randomly, very occasionally. Our years of travel-ing the globe and surviving the dramas on the home front together, of bonding and living intertwined lives, sharing sky and earth, all now stripped down to text messages sent rarely, sent in the middle of the night, when there's little chance I'll be awake to respond. Does she not want me to?

I see the texts early in the morning; though they're few, they're a reason I get up every day—I finally found something that gets me out of bed, I guess. I blush, that familiar feeling, that heightened heat ris-ing from my feet to my face, that old insecurity reminding me how far I've come. Strange, my body still having an actual reaction as if she's in the room with me. As if I can actually see her tapping at her phone, typing out the message, smiling at herself, amusing herself with her wit and charm and filthy turn of phrase. I never respond to her texts immediately. I never respond with some flippant whip or whim. That's her, but that's not me. I want to craft a response that's worthy of her, clever and charming, conveying my longing for the good times. My earnest texts—sometimes I think that's not what she wants, sometimes I worry they're boring.

What's Kathi Kannon doing right now?

I still see her all the time, though we haven't been in the same room together for all these weeks. But I see her in the woman in front of me at the grocery store, with her hair in a clip just like Kathi. I see her in la-dies wearing gold leggings and smelling of some variation of Tom Ford. I see her in the haze and smoke of people enjoying their e-cigarettes, everywhere these days. I'm convinced she's the reason they make a special announcement about not vaping on airplanes. And I see her in fan T-shirts. I see her in movie posters. I see her on book covers. I'm thinking, *I used to know her.*

SUMMER

Kathi was with me and Reid as we traveled to Paris, my first trip out of the country with him, and my first trip out of the country without her. But she was there in spirit. She helped my relationship with Reid grow stronger with lessons—*If you want to really know someone, travel with them.* Reid is the one I now sit beside on planes. But the seat he occupies will always be hers, really. She literally paid for it. I used all the airline miles I racked up with her to buy the tickets.

Reid and I moved in together. It was the easiest decision ever and logistically even easier. First, I never wanted to sleep without him again, and packing night bags was growing so tiresome. Second, my entire apartment could have fit in his living room. I actually didn't move a lot with me. I downsized, selling my cheap bed, selling my little sofa. I have my lamp to remind me of the Greenwich Hotel. I have my newly reframed Lady of Shalott. And I have my one real albatross: Mom's boxes, still unopened, stacked neatly in Reid's garage.

FALL

My dad is losing it. He mailed me a Ziploc bag of white goo. I'm holding it up to the light streaming in from Reid's (and my!) kitchen window, squinting, wondering.

"Dad, what is this?" I ask into the phone, having caught him, apparently, in the middle of some construction project.

"You can't tell?" he asks, the sound of hammers banging behind him.

"No. Did you send me something that melted?"

"Maybe," he says. "Taste it."

I look at the glob. "Are you crazy? No. I'm not tasting it."

I hear him breathing heavily—it's a new thing with him, the breathing heavily. It's replacing the yelling. He started this a few months ago without prompt from me. I'm dying to ask about it, about what led to this change, but why mess with what's working? Why start trying to tinker with his settings so late in the game for both of us?

"It's Oreo fillings," he says.

"Oreo, like the cookie?" I ask, pulling the bag closer to my face, as if proximity will now render the contents decipherable.

"Yeah," Dad says. "I know how you like the fillings."

I squeeze the Ziploc and examine, now recognizing some of the patterns left over from the wafers, now placing the sweet smell. "Dad, did you buy a pack of Oreo cookies and scrape off the center icing and put them in a bag and mail them to me?"

"Yup," he says, his voice choking. "I know you like the filling."

"Is this because when I was a kid, I ate the fillings and threw away the rest of the cookie?" *DON'T WASTE FOOD,* I can still hear him yelling. I don't mention the part about how he made me eat the discarded cookie parts from the trash. Maybe we don't always have to say everything.

"Yup," he says again.

I put the bag of Oreo filling down on the counter and brace myself on the edge. I shake my head and smile. I'm so moved, I'm surprised Dad doesn't hear it through the phone.

"You there?" he asks.

"Yeah, yeah. Thank you, Dad."

"I hope that between the cookies and the stuff I mailed you, you know I'm proud of you and all that."

"Thank you," I say, with the sounds of banging and shouting picking up in the background on his side of the phone.

"SHUT THE FUCK UP!" Dad yells to the people around him. "I'm talking to my son in California!" Of him yelling again, I'm thinking, *Well, nothing's perfect.*

"Dad, what is going on over there?"

"Construction," he says. "I'm gonna finish this damn house before I die, even if it kills me."

"Kills you? Nah. You're a survivor. You'll be around for decades to come. I'm convinced nothing can kill you," I say, shaking my head. That old house, no matter the work he does, it'll never be a cheerful home, not after all we've been through in it.

"This house is the one thing I can leave you when I'm gone. And I want there to be at least one nice thing I gave you, one nice thing I did for you," he says.

The thought surprises me, paralyzes me for a moment. I'm thinking, *I don't want a house.* I'm thinking, *All I've ever wanted from you was kindness.* I'm thinking, *You don't always get what you want.*

A deep sniffle and a moment later Dad adds, "Yeah, I better go. Talk to you later, son. Love you."

"Love you, too," I say, and hang up the call. I pick up the bag of filling and I open the trash can, about to toss it in—Oreos are not my thing anymore; we all change—but I note something else is different, too: my father. Perhaps we all grow from age, weathering of time. The father I remember from childhood seems gone. No more fights, angst, screaming—or less of it, anyway. It makes me wonder about the yelling that still goes on in my head every now and then. I attribute it to my dad, this man now frail and tired, but maybe, like the broken, backward horn in my Nissan, I'm only yelling at myself.

I close the trash can. I decide to keep the bag of goop, at least for a day or so. And I wonder about what other things Dad is quietly doing to mend our past. I wonder what other things Dad has maybe quietly already done.

I walk out to Reid's garage, to Mom's boxes stacked in the corner. By now the duct tape holding the contents together is older and dry. I tug at the strips until one box opens, bits of dust flying about like when you pull a tab to open a FedEx envelope. I look inside. Then I rip open another. I look inside. I rip open another, another, another. And these are not Mom's things in these boxes—these are mine, my things. My notebooks from high school that I thought were long lost. My book reports Dad tore up and made me rewrite, now taped back together, the ink old and drifting. There are childhood clothes, pictures from my teenage years, newspaper clippings from being listed on the honor roll—these are things from after my mother died, things he kept for me. There's the Priestess Talara action figure, stuffed unceremoniously at the bottom, her cape creased and wrinkled, her face the same as I remember it from way back then as a kid and from way back months ago, from the real woman. We're reunited at last—and now I have two, the one from Reid and the one from my childhood; like both sides of the coin, a woman I find amazing and frustrating; Kathi Kannon, you can't escape her.

Also, in the last box, there are my cassette tapes, in their tattered jukebox casing, including the tape with the song "Mother-in-Law," my *Star Search* audition number. I open the case and a black mist falls— the decayed magnetic strip that stored the music, like the rest of us, it's older now, worn and more and more fragile by the day. I pull out my phone, I open iTunes, I buy the ditty for 99 cents, and I dance in the garage, alone and silly and exquisite, at last surrounded by my favorite toy and favorite song, surrounded in so many ways by the childhood I always wanted.

WINTER

There's death to deal with. Agnes, finally succumbing to the tumor she nursed while working in Kathi Kannon's kitchen for forty-nine years, much of which featured Judge Judy blaring by her side.

> ME: I'm so sorry about Agnes.
> KATHI: So crushing, life ever the fickle bitch; but from you I
> love the love. I Missus you. Everyone is a ding-a-ling . . .
> and here I sit, missing my ole Cockring.

SPRING

I'm parked and panicked outside the estate of Hollywood royalty Kathi Kannon, star of stage and screen and *People* magazine's Best Comeback list. She invited me to a birthday party she's throwing for herself here at her mansion, my old stomping ground.

I'm nervous, I'm self-conscious, dressed in my fanciest outfit with my favorite accessory, Reid, by my side, chill and confident, not worried at all that I'm finally, after a year away from her, about to introduce him to *the* Kathi Kannon. Him, dapper and poised. Me, sweating and flinching.

"What's wrong?" Reid asks.

"I don't know," I say, clenching my teeth, squeezing my hands into fists in my coat pocket. It feels just like the first day I was outside these gates.

"Remember, I'm here to make your life better," he says gently. I warm to the reference, the kindness, the moment from way back in our early days that helped facilitate bittersweet changes, new chapters in my life. But it doesn't ease my tension, my distrust of whether Kathi has really forgiven me for ending my time with her. It doesn't ease my curiosity about why she invited Reid to come here with me, accepting him, welcoming him into her home, her life—what used to be *our* life, as she put it. There was a time I'd wonder if she was inviting him into my life with her, instead of Reid and me welcoming her into my life with him. Had I stayed working for her, would Reid be the third wheel or would Kathi? It doesn't matter now.

Kathi considered having birthday parties during the years I worked for her but always said she didn't have the money to do them right. Now her resources have increased. Priestess Talara is back. The film is a huge hit, a franchise alive. I was thrilled to see it, but had to watch it multiple times before Priestess Talara became the character versus me just seeing my old friend Kathi Kannon up there on the screen. Suspension of disbelief is harder when you know what someone's thinking, when you know someone's deep, dark tells. I see Priestess Talara's right shoulder move forward and I know Kathi's costume is too tight. I see Priestess Talara blink slightly off rhythm and I know Kathi is too warm. I can see from her face whether she's hungry or thirsty. I can see from her smile if she's tired. That Assistant Bible is still in me; I wrote the book on Kathi Kannon.

I arrived at her mansion driving my new little Fiat, Reid squeezed in the passenger seat, a ride far from the old Nissan that first entered these gates those many years ago—a different car, and me, its very different driver.

TV cameras are across the street from her gate. Paparazzi are clicking away. When I worked here, no one cared who lived up that hill. Now celebrity tour buses are stopping out front and playing Priestess Talara theme music and movie clips, and those tourists are just like me: outsiders.

There, on the wrong side of the gate, before the same smoking Santa painting, the same CLOTHING OPTIONAL banner, I'm thinking, *I want to be back inside.* I'm thinking, *All that time I spent with Kathi Kannon and there's still so much unsaid between us, so much I want to tell her at this party.*

First, I want to tell her I'm sorry. I never thought she was telling me the truth. About my appearance: I thought she was making fun of me. About my abilities: I thought I was inherently inadequate. Introducing me as part of her family: I thought it was a contrived convenience. Calling me her friend as I told her I was leaving her: I thought that was a delusion. And now, looking back, I'm so fucking ashamed. I feel so stupid. I was so trapped in my own inner drama that I couldn't see she genuinely cared. And in the end, I treated her like some random employer. In the end, I'm the one who put the space between us.

I want to tell her that I wish I would have done it differently. That sometimes—often, in fact—I regret leaving her at all. That she's someone who raised me from the dead, who helped me see my reflection in the mirror again, who showed me that everything—just checking in to a hotel—could be an adventure, that humor was everywhere, even in airplane bathrooms, mental hospitals.

I want to tell her how much I miss getting those nonsensical text messages every day. I miss her nicknames for me, words made up from thin air, words that now carry me as I remember the room, I remember her tone, I remember what she was wearing every time I heard a new one: Niblet, Jimmy, Cockring, even *darling*.

I want to tell her she's with me in my friendships, acquaintances, moments of mingling at parties where people are no longer bound by asking, "How's Kathi Kannon," but instead ask about me, how I'm doing, about Reid, about my actual life, not just the sitcom version of it. I talk about my moments with her as fond memories, not fodder, not my life's only value. And the same with my new friends I picked up along the way, like Drew and Ben, who both kindly wished to stay in touch. And like Melody—who also goes by the nickname Jasmine— whose friendship I pursued and nurtured mostly because she was with me during the best times, at the beginning, my equal in the shadow of celebrity, and because she's the only assistant who ever emails me back. As for Bruce, all of his haircuts and fancy shoes couldn't keep him in Los Angeles. He never did get the promotion he desperately wanted. He's back home in Iowa, working for his father, his Facebook now dark, his life now a secret; I'd look him up if I knew his real name. Turns out, both of us are silt.

I want to tell Kathi that I hear her in my head, the things she taught me. Life is meant to be lived. It's not meant for the safe choice all the time. It's not meant to be stubbornly shielded. Not meant to be like the magazines in her bathroom, with their Amazon protective covers.

I want to tell her—confess to her—that sometimes I google her name to see paparazzi photos of us, she and I forever online, some of the images painful, regretful (did I let her wear that?). I examine her clothes in the pictures to trigger memories of the things she loved or lost. To try to place a date: Are those glasses from our years together? Is that the jacket I had repaired for her? Is that the brooch I said looked like a uterus?

I want to tell her I've signed up for weather alerts. I get notified of each aurora borealis, each alert like a little "hello" from my famous friend. The aurora borealis will always remind me of her, will always be her. The messy, beautiful colors take me to her side, become her, the way the lights look foggy in real life but complete perfection in photos, the way their electrons and neutrons and chaos swirl around to make something pointed, marking some memory, something you can only really appreciate while standing on a frozen lake in Yellowknife, with the warm body of a friend at your side, in a coat she bought for you, in a world she illuminated.

I want to tell her I'm still looking for my passion. And maybe that's my passion. Thinking, seeking. Seeking teachers, seeking answers, seeking people who need help, seeking my tribe. But what if it's just a tribe of seekers? Dogs chasing our tails. Followers following followers following followers. Therapista says seeking actually takes you away from what you're looking for, which is peace, peace in the right now. I haven't found peace yet. I hope Kathi has. Kathi and I, both extremes in our own way.

I want to tell her thank you for being a mother figure. I have two now. One I hardly remember, and one I'll never forget.

In front of 1245 Beverly Canyon Drive for the first time since I left more than a year ago, and it's all so different. Everything has changed.

The code to her front gate has changed—I have to use the buzzer again, push that difficult little call button, give my name, get approval from icy security guards.

"Are you family?" they ask.

"No," I say. I'm thinking, *Not really. Not anymore, if ever.*

They ask my name; they ask for my ID. Don't they know I used to be her right hand?

Past security and the valet, Reid and I are holding hands as we wander up that magical hill—the dangling porpoise, the hologram hand flipping me the bird, the colorful bricks. The landscaping is new, fresh, more flowers, more color—as if that's even possible.

We walk through the front door with the ball-sac door knocker. The light switches I had installed. The picture that hangs beside the piano to hide the stain on the Sheetrock where I had an old thermostat removed. Walls now have fresh paint; there are new holograms and works of art everywhere—all signs of her new money, her new life, the one without me.

The crowd here to celebrate her birthday is strange, a group of people who seem out of place standing on her brick porch, on her endangered floors, in my old office. I recognize some of the faces from television and movies, smiling and laughing, drunk on her magical ambiance. There's a joyousness to the event, a fog of celebration wafting around in the air-conditioning from the living room to the red room to her bedroom. I slip into some old thought patterns—noting drinks without coasters sweating on the furniture, noticing trash cans that are too full, noticing pictures hung askew, knickknacks not in their exact places. And then the other thought pattern, the new one, the reminder to myself: *I don't work here anymore.* And as a sentimental longing fights for voice, Reid squeezes my hand. I'm not here alone.

I almost turn and leave Kathi Kannon's party right away, fleeing the people who think they know her. I feel confused, angry. In my time with Kathi, I never saw them in her life. I have to remind myself that I was only with her for part of her life. I'm doing the math in my head in her crowded living room, standing beneath Mateo the Moose. I'm calculating: How many hours were all these people with her? Is it possible that in my three years, eight hours a day, I was actually with her longer, with her more, that I have more claim to her than they? So selfish of me, and yet I humor the ill thoughts. I never heard her talk about some of these people. Some of them, I know she doesn't even like. I want to run out of there. I want to never come back. I want to only remember this place the way it was. The way it was when I was alone in this giant living room—*tap, tap, tap*—loading pills into her containers. The way it was while she was sleeping—still and dreamy, a beautiful lump in the covers. The way it was when she was awake, the smell of her baking cookies in the kitchen. Just her and me watching deer in her backyard, eating peanut butter from the jar.

"Where do you think she is?" Reid asks, snapping me out of my trance.

"I know where she is," I say.

The party is filled with people in every room, every square foot occupied. With Reid at my side, I walk past Mateo. I walk through the red room—fireplace still raging the same flames from my last day, even more boats now piled, teetering on that mantel; it's going to be a spectacular crash one day. I walk past the bar and the bathroom and through the second living room and down a hallway back to her bedroom, my feet retracing the same steps we once took while dancing down this corridor. Sure enough, in her room, in a ball gown, lying in her bed, Roy appropriately at her side, is Kathi Kannon, film icon. At a party filled with Hollywood elites, Kathi Kannon sits isolated from the crowd, surrounded by people I don't recognize, protected in her cocoon of quiet and not quiet.

Kathi and I spot each other at the same time, like a strange sort of telepathy. She stops mid-conversation with John Mayer and hops out of bed and marches directly toward me.

"Cockring, your hair looks so great," she says, reaching up and feeling it.

"So good to see you, Stepmom," I say.

"Is that him beside you?" Kathi asks, not breaking eye contact with me. "Is that the boyfriend? I'm ignoring him intentionally for a moment until I can gather my sense of humor."

"That's him," I say.

Kathi Kannon turns and looks at Reid. She grabs both of his hands. "Jesus," she says, "you're taller than I imagined. Your dick must be huge."

Reid leans toward her. "Massive," he says, not missing a beat, maybe, at last, an equal sparring partner for Kathi Kannon, wordsmith, conversationalist, auteur.

"Now it all makes sense," she says kindly, sweetly, her hands touching his, a sign that she means it. The jewelry on her fingers, the bracelet around her wrist, the earrings dangling under her hair, I recognize all of them, the various items she would forget on airplane seats and under hotel beds and in restaurant parking lots, the items I used to follow behind her and collect, locking them in the jewelry drawer in her closet, until I realized, *What good is protecting all of her favorite things if she never gets to use them?* Her fine jewelry, like her life, like my life, should be worn, used, lived. I wonder how much I held back her spirit versus maybe how much I held back her demons.

Reid nods, now up to speed. A devilish grin appears on his face. He blushes, putting his hands in front of his face as if he's holding a bowl, opens his mouth, and gives an air blowjob to a huge imaginary dick, enormous imaginary balls resting in his cupped hands, a perfect mirror to Kathi's earlier advice to me about relationships.

"Cockring," she says, smiling, half-hugging me. "You're telling him all my secrets."

"Almost all of them," I say.

Kathi turns back to Reid. "Want a Coke Zero? They ran out at the bar, but I've hidden several in the bushes around the pool."

"Maybe later," Reid says, a thrill in his eyes—the same thrill I've witnessed billions of times before in the countless strangers smitten by meeting this wonderful woman, delighted through and through that she's offered a simple soda.

"Nice to finally meet you," Kathi says.

"Likewise," Reid says, this easy exchange, a solace.

Kathi then tugs on Reid's arms, pulling him down to her. She whispers something in his ear. It's strange watching them together, touching, Kathi Kannon and my Reid, the two most favored people in my life, the two most relevant entities in both my inner and outer worlds.

Reid smiles at whatever she's saying to him. She's smiling, too, holding his hands a bit longer than what's natural, a bit sweeter than the mark of some casual moment. And, to my delight, I notice I'm smiling, too, faithful that what's happening here is something special. This feels like the moment of endorsement. Like Kathi Kannon telling me it's okay to keep Reid around, that it's all okay that it ended up here, with the three of us together, our long and storied journey to this point.

While Kathi and Reid have their moment, I scan the room and lock eyes with Roy. He bounces up off the bed, dashes through the crowd over to me, and throws himself at me, adorable lower front fangs first. I squat down and rub his butt the way he likes, him spinning and spinning, happy and safe, seemingly ecstatic to see me—like a dog reuniting with a veteran. "I love you, buddy," I whisper to him, scratching that special spot behind his ear. I'm thinking of Roy nearly every day, these days. We've been through a lot together, we've been through *her* together—us, war buddies, brothers, sharing an experience no one else will ever know. And I think about those dreams Roy used to have at night, where his feet would kick and kick and he was running and running and running—I've always been certain he's running to her. I'm certain because I have those dreams, too.

"Oh!" Kathi shouts. "I have something to show you, Cockring." She turns to me. I stand as she starts to unbutton the top of her gown.

"I've already seen them," I say.

She reaches into her dress and pulls out a gold chain, and on the end of it, an oval-shaped gold locket, *the* gold locket.

I purse my lips. I slow my breathing. I feel my heart beating in my temples. I don't want to cry.

"I had this made for you," Kathi says. "Well, I had it put on a chain for you. But then I liked it too much and said, 'Fuck him, I'm keeping it.' I hope that's okay?"

Through a smile, I nod and say, "It's perfect."

With Roy now nipping at her knees, Kathi turns to Reid. "Okay, you guys, be on the lookout for Courtney Love," she says. "She's coming tonight and owes me seven thousand dollars. Bring her to me as soon as you see her!" Kathi shifts her foot, not much, less than half an inch toward the bed, but I've seen it before. I know she's done.

"Will do," I say, and as I pivot politely away from her, I turn right back. "Wait," I say.

Kathi faces me. That face, so open and powerful and almost begging for attention—I'm reminded, that's the face of a movie star.

"I have so much I want to tell you," I say.

"I already know, Cockring," she says. And with that, and our absurd grins, Kathi Kannon turns, Roy beside her, and the little ocean of people around her parts, allowing the two of them back to their place in bed, swallowing them up again, with me and Reid standing there, not part of it, outside of it, and literally being sent away, sent on a task, to find her obsessive thought and handle it. I'm thinking, with fondness, *Just like old times.*

I'm also thinking, *Greed knows no end.* Not her greed but mine, for wanting, wanting, wanting more from that moment with her, from our time together. Part of me still wants back in the cocoon I left, back in time to appreciate her more, appreciate all this more. I look around this new room, see these new faces, new clothes, new clutter on her nightstand, and I realize how much I miss it. How much I miss her. It reminds me of the old part of me, the loser part, my sad former self. I can see him clearly now because I'm changed. I see my past through the eyes of my present. The hard truth is I know my life is better because of what we went through, but I don't want to go back, however tempting the illusion looks.

Like when a drug company finds a cure, and puts themselves out of business, Kathi Kannon taught me to love, helped me get out of debt, showed me how to live a fuller life, even if it turned out to be one without much of her actually in it. It was generous of her, a rare kindness in Hollywood. Kinder still was that she gifted me power, for having known her, and for having left her.

I turn to Reid and notice he's also looking in the spot where she was standing before us just moments ago, into that slice of space that she once occupied, similarly entranced by her coming and going.

I ask, "What did she say to you?"

He says, "She told me, 'If you hurt him, I'll kill you.'"

Parties seem absurd when you're not there to party. With too much on my mind and shock at all this revelry surrounding my pensive heart, I nudge Reid. *Time to go.*

On our way out, I drag Reid around the house. I look for signs that I made a difference. The labels are still on the shelves in her bathroom. The basement is still full of the memorabilia I organized in plastic storage bins. The file cabinets full of her writing are standing guard, ever ready for more, ready for all the great books and films she has yet to pen.

I say polite goodbyes to the few people I know I won't see again anytime soon, other cast members of Kathi Kannon's life. Benny is still pretending to work. He will outlive us all. Miss Gracie is near the piano, smiling and regaling and making sure no one steals anything. Roger is busy, making sure the catering is in place, the forks and knives in their proper containers. Roger, his life lived for someone else, someone he worships, and I'm thinking, *It's so fucking sad.* I'm thinking, *It's so fucking beautiful.*

For a moment I watch Kathi's newest assistant, obvious in the crowd, the groovy young gay guy holding a yellow notepad, wearing what's clearly a brand-new gray cardigan, with that goddamned purple leather backpack dutifully attached to his shoulders, no doubt full of cash. After I left Kathi, Bruce said, she immediately hired and fired a new assistant. Then another. Then another. Then another. None of them were right. What exactly she was looking for, I can't say for sure. But in my moments of ego and vanity and sadness and doubt and regret, I wonder if she was looking for me.

God, to think I ever said it: *I'm bored.*

Therapista says it's impossible to be bored in this world with all its stimulus and opportunities. She says boredom isn't actually a feeling at all, but the suppression of a feeling—like anger or shame or loneliness. I wish I would have known sooner. I wonder what feelings I suppress. And Kathi? Therapista says a wonderful, healthy life doesn't include a requirement to be constantly entertained. She says what we really want is peace of mind, peace in being. Maybe another word for boredom is peace.

This will all be funny one day.

I walk out the front door, past the message painted above the frame that greeted me all those years ago: KNOCK, KNOCK, KNOCKING ON HEAVEN'S DOOR. I'm thinking, *Yeah, it was kinda like that.*

And I find myself leaving, again. Though it's no easier this time. Something still feels tense. And as Reid and I walk down to my car, something catches inside me. I stop on the path, my feet feel numb, my heart panics, like I'm making another mistake. Tears are being pushed out from the inside. I fear I was too flippant, like I'm at fault for not grabbing Kathi Kannon by the shoulders and forcing her to hear how much I love her. My mind races with thoughts—not of moments or adventures with her—but of looks: The way she looked at me when I made her laugh; the way she looked at me when we both hated our limo driver; the look that meant *save me* from autograph hounds, or from doing a speech, or from a salesman at Bloomingdale's; the look and smile she gave when she wanted to hold my hand as a plane landed or when she said *"thank you"* while literally stuffing my pants with cash for helping her at an autograph show. The look when I told her I was leaving her. The look when she wanted me to stay. The look when I told her no.

Reid pulls me close to him. "I'll drive?" he asks. And as I nod *yes* . . .

"HEY, COCKRING!" I hear her shout. *Her,* the voice unmistakable.

I turn to face Kathi Kannon, star, Shine, mother figure. I suck in my sobs. I want to be dignified for this dance. Perhaps I can be the man this time. She trots toward me, stops a few feet away, that face again, framed in lights and laughter of the celebration—of her—that's going on far behind her.

"I was never bored with you," I blurt.

Kathi Kannon laughs, that infectious laugh, and instantly I'm with her again, instantly transported to our sweetest moments, alone in that sprawling mansion, or in the Greenwich Hotel, or on that white frozen lake, the aurora borealis scorching overhead, Roy's nub of a tail wagging ferociously, all of us there with each other in my inner world, warm, happy, together, forever, in my mind at least.

"I hope we survive Los Angeles," she says, my mother's locket now dangling freely outside of her ball gown.

"Me, too," I say.

Maybe we don't always have to say everything.

And Kathi Kannon, film icon, smiles and waves goodbye. And Reid squeezes my hand. And Kathi turns and walks back up her enchanting hill. And Reid and I turn and walk down her magical brick walkway, all of us on our way home.

Acknowledgments

A galaxy of thank-yous to the transcendent Carrie Fisher, as I was lucky enough to be her personal assistant for a few extraordinary years. This book is fiction. It's not about Carrie. As her loved ones say, if you really want to know Carrie, read her books. But she is one of the greatest forces of inspiration I've ever known, having spent much of her brilliance, charm, and generosity teaching me about writing, life, and friendship. I think of her constantly; I miss her profoundly, and I know I'm not alone. I hope the ice cream up there is perfect, and infinite.

Thank you to my agent, Deborah Schneider, for believing in me, believing in this story, and keeping my heart full. I cried when you said "yes." And to all my friends at Gelfman/Schneider, including Penelope Burns and Cathy Gleason (thanks for my pin!). Much gratitude to the charming Josie Freedman, Sarah Wax, and all my pals at ICM. Also the international team at Curtis Brown with Sophie Baker and Felicity Blunt.

James Melia! James Melia! James Melia! That's what everyone said to me when the manuscript started going around. And how lucky am I that this story found you and you agreed to be its champion and editor. You're a joy and a friend. Thank you. And to all the greats at Henry Holt, including the inspiring Amy Einhorn and her wonderful teammates Maggie Richards, Marian Brown, and Caitlin O'Shaughnessy. Thank you Kathy Lord for your keen eye and great advice—sorry about the speculum thing. Thank you to the audiobook team: Robert Allen,

Mary Beth Roche, Alyssa Keyne, Dakota Cohen, Matie Argiropoulos, and Samantha Edelson.

Thank you to my fairy godmother Elissa Dauria Smith and the freelance editors who helped get the material in shape in the early stages: Molly Lindley Pisani and Bethany Strout. A special thanks to extraordinary freelance editor Iva Turner—I wish everyone could be so lucky to have you review their work, and luckier still to be able to call you a friend. Rob Weisbach, thanks for your very generous support and wisdom. Thanks, Ron Levin, for your guidance. Thanks to all my friends at Sparkpoint Studio especially Crystal Patriarche, Paige Herbert, and Keely Platte. Thank you to graphic designer genius Kyle Cummings for some cover design inspiration.

Much love to the best of friends who helped so much, in so many ways, along the way: Erin Rodman (my official cult leader), Stacy Saxton (SFB—love you!), Tom Lenk, Tom DeTrinis, Jayne Entwistle, Mark Jude Sullivan, Nicola Bailey-James, Tim McKernan, Claire Mouledoux, Rachel Sciacca, Glenn Millican, Cindy Cesare, Brian Larson, Esteban Rey, John McCoy, John Baumgartner, Michael Crowley, Heath Daniels, Beth Grant, Michael Chieffo, Betsy Burnham Stern, Alisha Brophy, Matt Murphy, Michael Peters, Tobias Trost, Zac Hug, Barry Babok, and the magical Jonathan Van Ness. Thanks, Angela Hill for being my anchor and Rachel Bartur for being my parachute. And thank you Genevieve Ramos Matthews—this is all kinda your fault haha.

Thank you Mom, Dad, Tiffany, Scott, Laurel, Ava, Emmy, Grant, "Miss Patri," Ashley, Byron, Aubrey, Buddy, Edy, Robert, Na-Nan, Uncle Noel, and my entire family. I love you all!

Hey, fellow assistants! I see you! Thanks for sharing the tribe. I'll buy us a round at the next meeting.

And thank you to Steven Rowley, my morning light, my nighttime star, and all the magical blue skies in between. I have so much to thank you for: reading endless drafts of this book, helping me live some whisper of what's in these pages, and lovingly building an exciting and crazy life with Tilda and me. I love us. I love you. Will you marry me?

About the Author

Byron Lane is a playwright and screenwriter. He's also worked as a journalist and as a personal assistant to celebrities, including Carrie Fisher. He's originally from New Orleans and lives in Los Angeles with his boyfriend and their rescue dog. This is his first novel.